WINDFALLING

PAUL J. NYERICK

outskirtspress
DENVER, COLORADO

Windfalling
All Rights Reserved.
Copyright © 2015 Paul J. Nyerick
v1.0

Outskirts Press, Inc.
http://www.outskirtspress.com

ISBN: 978-1-4787-5061-1

Library of Congress Control Number: 2015902423

Outskirts Press and the "OP" logo are trademarks belonging to Outskirts Press, Inc.

PRINTED IN THE UNITED STATES OF AMERICA

Windfalling:
A series of unexpected significant emotional events,
in a constant state of flux.

"After all these years, *semper fi* still has meaning."

1

A storm was brewing on the horizon, but it was calm up here on top. The sweet smell of pine and incense cedar flowed on gentle breezes with a ripple. I breathed pure air and exhaled away all of my troubles. Birds sang happy tunes with rhythms that quickened my pulse to the synchronicity of nature. My mind felt at ease. Life was good.

As I enjoyed the sights and smells of the mountains, the valley below did not look good. Dark clouds blocked the healing rays of sunshine as lightning bolted haphazardly across the heavens. Thunder rolled a deafening curse to my serenity. An impending doom loomed over the land. Was the deluge moving in my direction, or would I escape its wrath? I was at the mercy of that evil wind.

From one of those dark clouds sped an aircraft headed straight for my grand perch. It looked like it was in distress, with smoke billowing from one engine. That crippled bird started losing altitude when a lightning flash struck the other engine, and it fell like a rock. A single parachute billowed above the falling wreck. Prevailing winds blew the chute closer to my vantage point. Meanwhile, what was left of the plane exploded into an adjacent mountainside, creating an enormous bright green fireball! The heat from the crash ignited a wildland fire that consumed everything in its path.

The survivor landed just down the canyon from my lookout. I nervously scrambled down the ravine to see if I could help. I knew that this country was dangerous enough on land, never mind tumbling from the sky. Arriving at the fluttering silk, I noticed a body lying unconscious between two boulders. To my surprise it was a woman. Sun glistened on her long red hair as it waved in the breeze and created an angelic illusion. I watched one violet eye open and then the next. A single tear streamed down flawless skin as if to exclaim the anguish of the situation. As I came into view our eyes met and she softly whispered, "We must find the box."

Was this the ranting of a head injury, or an involvement that would change my life? I ignored the initial shock of her statement and concentrated on cutting her loose from the now billowing parachute. The silk took off into the wind like an out-of-control Macy's Thanksgiving Parade balloon. The woman dangled close to the edge of a cliff 1,000 feet above the valley floor. I had seconds to act or she would make another jump, this time with deadly consequences. I dove for the release buckle and freed her from the restraints that kept her prisoner. I watched the chute fly over the edge. Within seconds it vanished.

While the tangled nylon lines and silk floated harmlessly away, I landed right on the woman between those two boulders, my chest on top of hers. A warm feeling enveloped my whole body. She wrapped her arms around my shoulders and kissed me on the cheek in gratitude.

I gasped for air when she said, "Thank you very much for saving my life. I apologize for kissing you without even an introduction. I am so, so grateful. My name is E.D., E.D. Struction."

"Mine's Jerry, Jerry Johnson."

Wow, an angel fell from the sky and thanked me with a kiss! No apology was necessary. I had to get to know this stunning creature, but we had worse trouble with the wildland fire that raced up the canyon. I could feel searing warmth on my cheek. The vegetation around us was beginning to preheat. We needed a plan, and a good one now. As a retired firefighter I knew that fire always burns up canyon during the day and down canyon at night. It was just about the crack of noon, and the fire would be licking our exposed bodies in no time.

I grabbed the fallen angel, E.D., and asked her if she could run up the hill to an outcropping of boulders 200 yards away. She sprang into action like a frightened gazelle, running far ahead of me.

In full stride she stopped and shouted, "My GPS. I need it to find the box!"

As she approached me running down the hill, I grabbed her arm and said, "The fire is down there." Breaking free of my grasp, she sped toward the landing site and retrieved a backpack. It was beginning to smoke as she placed the straps over her shoulders. Then she kicked it into high gear and raced past me once again.

She beat me to the rocks. I finally arrived winded and sore. The smoke choked my lungs enough that I had to hit the ground so I could breathe fresh air once again. There was a deserted gold mine shaft that I had explored a few years ago just below where we stood. With burning lungs I motioned toward the opening of the mine. There was a sign at the entrance, "Keep out, unstable timbers." I decided it would be better to be buried in a mine collapse than burned alive.

We crawled low, below the smoke, and sank deep into the shaft to avoid the oncoming choking, noxious cloud. With the absence of light, I used my hands to feel where the shaft led. I had to be careful because there was a vertical vent shaft somewhere below. I felt old rail tracks to keep my bearing. This tactic seemed to work until I heard the unwanted chatter of a Mojave green rattler in the distance. This was a bad scene, because the deadly bite of a green is both a hemo- and a neurotoxin. Not many people survive this deadliest of reptiles.

In the darkness I could feel the closeness of the snake when a flash and loud noise filled my eyes and ears. Splattered snake flesh painted the mine walls with a Jackson Pollock splash. The cave became bright with the glow of a chemical light stick. A smoking small Browning automatic was in E.D.'s hand and the green light in the other. "What the...?" I stammered as I wiped snake scales from my face.

E.D. looked at me sheepishly and said, "I needed to act fast or that snake would have given you a present. I forgot I had the Browning in my backpack. Besides, I needed to pay you back for saving my life on the cliff."

"What else do you have in that pack?"

"Just a few things I thought I'd need on my flight, a thousand feet of kernmantle rope, beaners, maps, of course my trusty compass and GPS, and a few odds and ends. Oh yeah, a couple pounds of C-4 with the blasting caps and hell box. You never know when you'll need to blast a hole in something." Then she threw me a granola bar. "Are you hungry? I have a little water to wash the snake slime from your face." Reluctantly, I took the canteen and washed my face, but there were still snake entrails plastered to my hair. Yuck. Maybe it was an ancient remedy for hair restoration. Always look on the bright side of any situation, that's my motto.

Who was this woman, and what other surprises did she have in store for me? My solitary lifestyle had lacked excitement of late. I craved the adrenaline rush from my days as a firefighter and Marine. Oh yeah, I was a combat veteran in Vietnam, but that was a long, long time ago. What little hair I had left was all gray and wispy. My back was shot, but I still could hump these mountains with only a couple days' rest.

I lived alone in the mountains, on a full-time quest for beauty. Retired, I taught a couple of classes at the local community college. It was summer, so I was free to do whatever tickled my fancy. Right now I was stuck in an old gold mine with a mysterious woman with a pack filled with C-4, and a wildland fire burning over the top of us. Too much fun!

Getting free from this crumbly coffin became paramount. The fire had burned the ancient timbers from the mine entrance and made the whole superstructure unstable. As the fire burned away anything holding up the mountain, tiny rocks hit us with frequency. This mountain of decomposed granite, where the tiniest of pebbles were dagger sharp. I knew that after the small stuff dislodged, the big stuff couldn't be far behind.

I remembered that there was an airshaft down a side tunnel just a few yards from the main shaft. I saw it there some years ago, but remembered that the hole was blocked by a fallen boulder on top. E.D. sensed my concern and asked, "What's the matter?" I relayed our crushing dilemma to her. I knew the fire had passed by our location, but we would be entombed in the void of a mine collapse and starve to death, unless E.D. had a few hundred more granola bars. No one would find us. Furthermore, cell phone reception sucks when you're encased in three hundred feet of DG—decomposing granite.

E.D. peered up the airshaft, then sprang into action. She pulled a headlamp from the pack. That light illuminated the entire space with an eerie glow. Smoke filtered pure light, as if we were in Dracula's lair. I could not dwell on these mysteries because E.D. handed me the length of rope and told me to uncoil it. I rock climbed a bit when my back had strength, so I knew what to do.

She pounded pitons into cracks in the rock and clipped a carabineer through each hole. She snatched the rope and shouted, "Put me on belay," and scurried up the wall with the agility of a spider monkey. I could barely see the light when I dared to look, because she dislodged debris that was aimed straight for my bald head. Hammering reverberated throughout our enclosure and scrambled my brain. It rattled from one side of my skull to the other.

Just when I couldn't stand the pain, a voice screamed, "Off belay," and E.D. rappelled down the shaft in less than ten seconds. Dusting herself off, she took the C-4 from the pack and fondled it like Play-Doh. "I'm making a shaped charge to blow that cap rock off the hole." I looked at her in amazement as she crimped the blasting cap with her teeth. She handed me the hell box and said in no uncertain terms, "Don't squeeze the hell box detonation lever, or you will be cleaning up more than snake guts."

I said, "Okay" as she sped back up the chute.

As I looked at the hell box, all I could think of was the devastating destruction of a Claymore mine. We used them in Vietnam to repel the enemy. We also took them apart to cook our food, burning the C-4, but throwing away the ball bearings. There was always an alternative.

Enough about ancient history; we had more pressing problems to solve.

E.D. snaked down the rope and grabbed the hell box and yelled, "Fire in the hole!" I most definitely knew what that meant, and hid behind an old rail cart. E.D. joined me and whispered, "Hope this works," then shouted, "Fire in the hole!" once again. She clutched my arm while depressing the hell box lever.

The mine ceiling rumbled as an ocean of dust and debris gushed through the shaft. Dust choked me through the bandana I had placed over my nose and face. I looked like a bank robber from a bad movie, a comedy. I wished I had a mirror to see how stupid I looked. As I pondered my fate, the dust cleared. Sunlight glistened through a newly created opening in the mountain. I could see daylight once again.

An escape route stood before us, but there was no time to lose. The entire mine was becoming unstable with every breath. I said, "Have you had enough fun? Let's get out of here before we become a new kind of pancake."

E.D. agreed and motioned she would go first. "I know where all the hand- and footholds are, and I can guide you up, up, and away." I did not argue, because this woman exuded confidence, the kind that could lead to victory.

I stumbled up the precipice guided by precise directions from a woman I had only just met. We climbed steadily up the shaft. As I looked into the opening, a blinding reflection made me squint. There was a reflection from a shiny object on the wall. As I neared the object, I almost lost my balance. There it was, shining like a star from the heavens: a nugget of pure gold, the size of my fist, nestled inside a crack in the rock. I picked it up and placed it in the pocket of my cargo shorts. Its weight lay heavily on my thigh like the radio battery

I carried in that long forgotten war. There was more gold that would have to wait for another time. The explosion exposed an undetected vein that the sourdoughs must have missed. They were so close to the mother lode, but missed it by a few feet. They gave up before their dreams came true.

Things were literally looking up for me when I reached the top of the opening. The explosion blew the fire out, and we were in an island of unburned mountain splendor. As I reflected on my recent good luck, I forgot about E.D. There was tremendous shaking from below as the entire mine caved in on itself. Wind rushed into the hole as a puff of dust escaped like a smoke ring. E.D. emerged from the middle of the ring, like a seal through a hoop. "Sorry I'm late, but I had to go back for the GPS. We still have to find the box."

2

I couldn't believe we had escaped the fire and near disaster in the mine. I still had a five-pound solid gold nugget in my pocket, the rest of the strike, buried in the still smoking rubble. What karma! I almost died twice and then ended up with the potential for all my dreams to come true. Oh yeah, E.D. fell from the sky into my life. I guess I wouldn't be bored for a while. She became the daughter I never had, and that felt great.

I was dead tired and needed a good long soak in my hot tub. I noticed E.D. pulling a strange-looking device from her pack. It was square with a small antenna sticking out from the side. The strange little contraption started to beep. I asked, "What is that thing?"

"Oh, just a tracker with a GPS inside. I need to activate its honing capabilities so I can retrieve the box. We have to hurry before the Diamond Corporation thugs get it first. Can we please get moving?"

"Wait a minute. Why do we need to hurry and who is the Diamond Corporation? Did I hear correctly, thugs, what thugs?"

E.D. started sprinting down the mountain and only said, "I'll explain later." I was bone tired, but had to find out what came next. I stashed the gold behind a single unburned manzanita bush and tried to maintain the pace.

We followed a series of flashing LCD arrows while E.D. listened to intermittent pings emanating from the tracker. Curious, all I could do was keep up with her blistering pace toward the crash site. I tried to get my questions answered, but E.D. just kept truckin' on an even faster pace. My sixty-something body couldn't take this pounding for much longer. I needed rest. "You go on. I'll catch up as soon as I can feel my legs, and my heart rate falls below 150."

She stopped in her tracks and said, "I'm sorry for moving out so fast. I guess I owe you an explanation. I could use a breather myself. First of all, I need that box because it contains a formula my dad created to extract hydrogen cheaply from seawater using a solar energy process that renews itself with little or no expense. He was a physicist for the Diamond Oil Company out of Houston, Texas. When he got close to a discovery, Harlan Diamond, president of Diamond Oil, threatened to put a stop to Dad's research because Diamond Oil just acquired oil leases from the Alaska tundra. Harlan paid a small fortune to pay off administration officials to get those leases. He's willing to destroy the last wilderness left in the United States, and will lose billions if he doesn't pump every drop of crude from that eco-fragile landscape. He couldn't care less about a few hundred thousand caribou, or that the pollution from burning all that fossil fuel would give global warming an unwanted boost. He put Dad's research on hold for at least twenty years."

"What about the thugs?"

"Oh, my dad got pissed at Diamond and quit the corporation. Dad has the patent on the process, and as long as he stays alive, Diamond can't get his grubby little hands on the prize. Dad set off on his own with financing from a consortium of environmental groups. They gave him the latitude to conduct his research in complete secrecy far from the reach of that unscrupulous fiend. Diamond got wind of what he was doing and sent some ex-KGB agents to shut him up for good. Wasilla Dragaminov and his band of ruthless cutthroats have no regard for human life and will do anything to make a buck, and Diamond will do anything to get the patent. What a pair to draw to, Diamond and Dragaminov. I can't stand either of them."

"Where do you fit into the picture?"

"My mom and dad split up when I was little. She kept me away from him for years. She recently died in a car wreck and I needed to reconnect. After the funeral her attorney gave me a letter she wrote.

She said that she still loved him but couldn't live with his Vietnam War baggage. He's a Vietnam vet with PTSD, and I guess she never could understand. I got in touch with him and he laid out the entire scenario. I'm an oceanographer and security expert for Earthhelp and had knowledge that could help his cause. He always knew where I was and anonymously sent me money from time to time. I thought one of my mother's relatives sent those checks. All my financial needs were taken care of by my dad. He's a great guy. I only wish I could have grown up with him."

This cloudy, bizarre picture started to clear when I wondered if there were others on the plane. E.D. nonchalantly added that she was the only soul on board when the plane took a direct hit from a Soviet SAM from a nearby ridgeline. My heart sank deep into my chest with that exclamation. "A Soviet SAM? These guys must be playing for keeps." That bolt of lightning I saw was man-made. I am opposed to violence and haven't even fired a weapon since leaving the Marine Corps. What strangeness had I gotten into this time?

E.D. said, "We've rested long enough. Let's get cracking before Dragaminov gets there first!" A plane crash, wildland fire, mine collapse, now ex-KGB thugs with automatic weapons, and oh yeah, the Mojave green. This tranquil day started with peaceful joy and turned into a full-blown whirlwind adventure. Definitely in over my head, but I didn't have plans beyond this morning anyway. "Let's go."

We traveled down the canyon into the burn, the landscape void of any vegetation. Everything was burned to mineral soil. The fire had burned so hot that it spalled granite. Granite explodes at 1,200 degrees. That's hot! I noticed the remnants of a tire with only the steel belts lying in a spiral pattern waving in the breeze, like some metallic anemone in a sea of dust. I wished for a camera.

Eerie silence was interrupted by an occasional gust of hot wind. An eagle surveyed the carnage from above. I could only wonder if he recognized this moonscape as his home. No food for him here, he tipped a wing as he flew on, saying good-bye to his beloved canyon home. Would he ever return?

We followed the pings over another ridgeline, and I could see the remnants of E.D.'s plane. It was strewn over about a mile in diameter, yet we persevered. The pings grew louder when I noticed a soot-covered shiny object lying on a rock in the middle of a river that flowed between two mountains. The current was swift because of all the melting snow and fire runoff. There was the box, but how could we retrieve it from that raging torrent?

E.D. took a length of kernmantle from her pack and tied a makeshift grappling hook to one end and threw it on a rock some fifteen feet from the box. She tied off the other end on an Arizona cypress tree that survived the blaze half in the water, one side charred. The tree seemed strong enough to hold her weight. She traversed the line like a shot and made it to the rock in about thirty seconds. She unhooked the rope and jumped to another rock just ten feet from the prize, but it could have been in another state. The current was too dangerous to reach.

The line was tight as a bowstring with no room to maneuver. She told me to untie the rope and head downstream and wait for the box. "If this works, the box will float into your arms." I didn't doubt her reasoning because of the dangers we'd escaped thanks to her many talents. I couldn't help feeling a little concerned because just below where I stood was a fifty-foot waterfall.

I could see the determination in her flashing eyes. She deftly tossed the hook through a handle on the side of the box, like a carnie demonstrating a nearly impossible midway game. She then carefully pulled the box from its perch and slid it into the awaiting churning cauldron cartographers call a river. I stepped into that freezing water and my feet instantly numbed. The lack of feeling gave way to the anticipation of retrieving what E.D. had risked our lives to possess. She swung the rope in a circular windmill motion and threw it as close to the bank as she could, feathering the box with the agility of a fly fisherman.

The box cascaded downstream, like a cork shot from a water cannon. When it was a few feet above my position, E.D. threw the other end of the rope toward shore and shouted, "Grab the rope, Jerry!" It splashed just below my freezing toes. In awe, I clung to the rope with all my might, knowing at times I was a klutz. If I dared to drop that rope, E.D. would probably sign me up for a yoga class.

I reeled in the rope with the accuracy of a winch. I could see a yellow glint just below the froth when it surfaced. One of the hooks got caught on a rock just out of my reach. I eased myself into the liquid ice up to my chest. I finally grabbed the hook that held the box and freed it from the crag. I couldn't feel my fingers, and my chest started to heave from the cold, but I had the box in my tired, freezing hands. I just hoped all of this trouble was worth my discomfort.

I stumbled to the shore, clutching the heavy box. That was when I got my first look at the object that would change my life forever. There it was, an ordinary box shape that wasn't unusual except for the adornments. It was very old, with a yellow lacquer finish: jade, turquoise, mother-of-pearl, and abalone inlays circling every edge. On top there were two carvings: obsidian Quetzalcoatl, the winged serpent god of the Aztecs, and an emerald Tacadama, the fabled bird god of pre-Colombian civilization. Coca leaves spread between both figures. A band of titanium surrounded the middle of the box, making it impossible to open unless you knew its secret. I would bet what little hair I had left that E.D. knew how to unravel its mystery. Besides, the thing must be priceless.

I couldn't stop looking at the figures on the lid. Both seemed to be smiling at each other. I had studied anthropology in college, but had no idea that these ancient civilizations knew about each other. An artifact with Anasazi, Aztec, pre-Colombian, and Inca symbols on the same object? I needed to know more.

As I admired the craftsmanship, the sound of automatic gunfire disturbed my peacefulness. E.D. was a sitting duck on that rock in the middle of the river. She tried to hide under the rock for cover, but it was too late. A lone hang glider, wielding a Scorpion lightweight Soviet automatic weapon, bore down on her. Unknown others fired from the ridgeline above my location. They could not see me, but E.D. remained in plain view.

As the glider got closer, E.D. shouted, "The Browning, get the Browning from my pack!" Without hesitation I grabbed the pistol and put two rounds into the assailant's forehead. Crimson fluid splashed from the back of his head and turned the sky instantly red. Without warning he plummeted to the river like a high-tech Icarus, minus the feathers. I was in awe that I had just killed a man without hesitation. I hadn't fired a weapon since Vietnam.

After the war I vowed never to shoot any type of firearm under any circumstance. I became a full-blown pacifist. I don't even eat red meat, because the flesh of all mammals looks very similar. I guess instinct and military training took over. My mind was a jumble of thoughts about morality versus survival. I would have to sort out these feelings later because E.D. was still in harm's way, big time.

I looked toward the rock to see if E.D. was okay. She vanished from her perch, and a hail of bullets sprayed the perimeter surrounding the river, bank to bank. I searched for a trace of her when out of nowhere her head popped up from the freezing torrent. She shouted, "Jerry, save the box! Meet me at the bottom of the falls. If I don't make it, bring the box to the address in the notebook in the outside pocket of my pack!"

I tried to tell her to be careful, but she disappeared over the cascading waterfall like a torpedo. Just like that, she was gone. I started shaking from the cold water and my emotional state, when I realized that I'd better get out of Dodge, see if E.D. made it over the falls, and keep this box from the clutches of Harlan Diamond, whoever he was.

Looking into the side pocket of E.D.'s pack, I found the address she was referring to as she fell over the falls. There were a couple more surprises in the pack. I noticed a wad of hundred-dollar bills and a plastic-covered envelope filled with a stack of bearer bonds. There must have been a few hundred thousand dollars' worth of cash and negotiable securities in my hands. Why would E.D. carry such a large stash of green, never mind a couple of blocks of C-4 and a handgun? If E.D. survived the falls, she had a whole lot of explaining to do.

I wrapped the box in a plastic bag, shouldered the pack, and headed down the trail alongside the falls. I picked up the dead Russian's rifle and headed downward. I knew a path around the falls that was totally invisible from the marauding horde on our trail.

I took my cell phone from my pocket and dialed an old friend who lived up the canyon. My friend Jake, a marijuana farmer, grew some of the tastiest buds in all of southern California. He was a fellow Nam vet who didn't care much for the deal society dealt him after the war. He chose to become an outlaw rather than conform to what was expected of everyone else. I got along with him because we both had that war in common. We helped each other out from time to time.

"Hey Jake, Jerry here. I'm in a bit of a pickle down by Pinon Falls. I rescued a gal from a burning plane crash, and a bunch of Russians are chasing us down the canyon."

"Wait a minute. Have you been smoking all those buds I gave you at once?" Jake asked.

"I can't go into detail now, but can you help me out?" There were a few seconds of silence, when Jake answered; "Sure, Jake Junior is home from college and hiking by the falls right now. I'll give him a call and see what he can do."

Junior was a college student, but also served in Afghanistan as a Marine sniper. He got out of the service and went back to school at the Scripps Institute in La Jolla to study oceanography. "Wow, what a stroke of luck. Jake, I'll be out of range for a while, so let me call you back when I get a signal. Oh yeah, there may be a girl in a silver flight suit floating beneath the falls."

3

Harlan Diamond sat alone in his penthouse office on the thirtieth floor of the Diamond Oil building in the middle of Houston's financial district. He was a tall, powerful man, standing six feet three inches and weighing 250 pounds. His square chin and crisp features made him look like he was posing for a coin. Boots made of some exotic endangered species sprawled on an immense teak desk. He liked the enormity of such a barrier because he did not want to get too close to most people. His huge eyes pondered the skyline.

"Miss Green, get me e vice president Haney on the horn," Diamond demanded. "I need to talk to him now. Tell him it's important." Diamond was the kind of man who expected immediate results and loved it when people groveled at the tips of his three-thousand-dollar boots.

"Okay, Mr. Diamond, but he's not the vice president anymore. I haven't been able to reach him all day."

"That pencil-neck geek better get off his dead ass and get those drilling schedules to me before those pantywaist liberals block all drilling in my Alaska field. Who do I have to kill to get just one drop of my oil from the ground? I singlehandedly got that bastard re-elected! What an ungrateful son of a bitch."

Harlan Diamond was the kind of man who didn't have to wait for results. He got them by using any and all means necessary. He didn't become the fourth richest man in the world from just talking. He had a small army of lawyers, judges, government officials, and ex-KGB mercenaries with a private air force on the payroll. As long as profits kept flowing from the ground and everyone was getting rich, Diamond was happy. Diamond's net worth was topping fifty-six billion and he expected to squeeze another twelve billion from the last unspoiled wilderness left in America. Greed drove Diamond to the brink of insanity. He lived by his own golden rule: "The one with the most gold rules."

Diamond opened his desk drawer and took out an encrypted satellite phone and shouted, "Dragaminov, where the hell are you? Did you get me that box? I expected you'd have it by now. I hope you took care of Struction and his pain-in-the-ass daughter."

Dragaminov answered reluctantly with a report that made Diamond furious. "We had some problems retrieving the box, Mr. Diamond. After we shot down the girl's plane, a stranger appeared from the mountaintop and helped her temporarily escape my comrades. He killed one of my men, but we are right on their trail. Those frightened rabbits are no matches for the Russian bear."

Diamond screamed, "I can't believe you couldn't get me that box and take care of a little girl! Get me the box! If for some reason she slips away from you commie bad-asses, go to Malibu and beat the information out of Struction. I refuse to let him foil my plans to become the richest and most powerful oilman since John D. Rockefeller!"

"Okay, Mr. Diamond, we will not fail."

"You better not. In my mind there is no such thing as failure, only results. Call me back when you get me the box. Oh yeah, Dragaminov, wipe away all the blood." Diamond turned to Miss Green:

"Get me Haney now, or I'll fly to Washington myself and shove a tumbleweed so far up that pasty bureaucrat's ass he'll taste Texas for a month! Get my jet ready to fly to D.C. now. I'll be at the airport in thirty minutes. Have my chopper fired up so I can beat the gridlock to the airport. I just love gridlock. Look at all that gas being wasted. It just keeps making me richer."

"Okay, Mr. Diamond." Miss Green shuddered. She had worked for Diamond for twenty-six years and knew what a tyrant he could be, but the $250,000 salary and stock options she was paid kept her on her toes. That was the only way Diamond received any loyalty; he paid through the nose for it.

Diamond left his office and headed for the roof, where his executive Kaman helicopter waited with both main rotors whirling at a high pitch. The massive flying machine swept the dust from the roof and deposited it on unsuspecting pedestrians unlucky enough to be walking in front of Diamond's fortress of a headquarters. Diamond couldn't care less about dusting a few unfortunate souls unlucky enough to get in his path. The FAA had tried to force him to stop flying such a big machine within the city limits, but a mere government agency was no match for the army of lawyers employed by the fourth richest man in the world. Those lawsuits would be in litigation for decades.

It took a mere fifteen minutes to fly to Diamond's private airport on his expansive 3,000-acre ranch, where his custom Boeing 747 waited to fly him to the seat of government. "Time's a wastin'. I need to kick some Beltway ass. Break the sound barrier if you have to; I can smell my tundra oil just waiting to be transformed into gold, my gold. I need it now!"

4

I took my time traversing the steep canyon switchbacks. Mist from the waterfall coated my body with refreshing coolness. Rainbows dashed in front of me, creating archways into a dream world I had no time to enjoy. Maidenhair ferns clung to the rocks around the waterfall, giving the landscape a tropical look. No, I wasn't in Hawaii, but running for my life down a slick mountain trail with a band of cutthroats hot on my trail. These guys had no respect for human, or any other, life. I needed to find E.D. and give her the box.

The trail passed through a lava tube two hundred feet straight down. A large anchor chain was bolted into the rock, and foot holes were carved into the face. Railroad spikes were driven into the opposite side to act as handholds. Normally easy, but I toted a large backpack and an automatic weapon. I had to navigate the slippery rocks with precision or I would end up in a heap at the bottom. Each step had to be carefully planned. I almost fell twice. I slid hand over hand on the chain and used the spikes when the tube curved. I jammed my hand into one of the railroad spikes and dislocated my right forefinger. After that hair-raising experience, I finally made it to the bottom.

My finger throbbed, but the rest of me felt whole. My back stiffened and I yearned for a good soak in my hot tub and a nice hot rock massage. I scoured both banks for E.D. but I saw no sign of her anywhere. I noticed Jake Junior's Malamute Nakai scampering up the trail. He was a huge animal with a gentle disposition unless someone tried to harm people he liked. That 150-pound musclebound dog could tear a man in half if he needed to protect his master. He ran up to me, put his paws on my shoulders, and licked my face. "Glad to see you, boy; now go find Junior."

Nakai turned and bolted down the trail. As I rounded the bend, I noticed two figures in a clearing under an enormous Ponderosa pine tree. The two people were E.D. and Jake Junior. I rushed over to them, took off my pack, and collapsed onto the waiting bed of pine needles. With vise-like grip, Junior stood me up and greeted me with a hug. "Hello, Jerry. I'm happy to see you made it down the falls trail intact."

"So am I."

Junior was a handsome kid with a toned body to match. He stood a good six feet two inches tall. Girls melted at his long blond hair and flashing smile, including E.D. She couldn't keep her eyes away from his. I felt an instant connection between them and I was reassured to have someone young and strong to help us on our unbelievable journey. Junior handed me a bottle of water and a Guru Chew. He said that E.D. had told him everything and he was more than happy to help his new friend.

My finger throbbed with pain the dislocation inflicted. I asked Junior if he would pull on it to realign the joints. Without hesitation E.D. sprang to her feet and yanked my finger until a relieving pop instantly stopped the throbbing, and she kissed it like a mother comforting her child. She said, "I hope you feel better. I had to do the pulling fast so you wouldn't flinch and stiffen."

Junior looked at the scene with amazement. He was starting to study this dynamo of a woman.

E.D. asked, "Did you save the box?"

I said, "Yes," but I needed to know more about what mysteries it held. E.D. promised that when we got away from Dragaminov, she would tell me everything. She grasped the box and clutched it tightly and said, "Let's get out of here." Junior strapped some of the supplies on Nakai's backpack to lighten our load. I handed him the Skorpion, telling him that he was a better shot than me. I gave E.D. her Browning back and we headed down the trail to Junior's vehicle, a new Toyota FJ Cruiser.

We had a good five miles to the parking area. Nakai, loaded to the max with gear, led the way. All that weight just made him stronger. That dog loved the outdoors. I was relieved to have him walk point. E.D. went second, Junior followed close behind, and I dragged my tired bones behind everyone else, unarmed. Nakai set a blistering pace that E.D. and Junior did not mind at all, but I repeatedly fell behind.

As we crested the hill, I could see the parking area. My three cohorts were already at the car. I could see Nakai in the backseat and E.D. and Junior in a warm embrace. Oh, to be young again. When I finally reached the car, Junior fired it up and shouted, "Hey, old man, do we need to medevac your sorry ass or what?" I just smiled and stumbled into the front seat.

As we left the parking area, I noticed a black Suburban with tinted windows and Texas plates. E.D. noticed it too and asked Junior to stop. Before he could come to a complete stop, E.D. jumped from the vehicle, slashed all four tires, and put three rounds from her Browning through the radiator. She shattered the back window and removed what looked like a SAM case. Fluid dripped from the crippled engine as she jumped back into the Cruiser and shouted, "We might need this! That should slow Dragaminov down a little. I recognized that car as one of Diamond's. We just have to worry about his helicopter. It must be searching on another ridgeline." She settled in and played with Nakai like he was her dog.

"Helicopter, what helicopter?" I said. "Who does this guy Diamond think he is anyway, the Great Khan?"

Everyone became silent.

Relieved to head up the fire road toward home and my hot tub, I sat for a moment and reflected on the events of this day. I just hoped that this was the last we would see of Dragaminov, but wait; there were still four hours of daylight left. I figured I'd better get some rest while I had the opportunity.

My mind drifted back to the jungle, where adrenaline was the drug of choice. As I remember adrenaline hit fast, and when you crashed, it happened suddenly. That being the case, I immediately fell asleep. E.D. and Nakai were both asleep in the backseat while Junior drove on. The fire roads in the backcountry were rough, but the all-wheel drive of the yellow and white Cruiser flattened out the bumps and made sleeping a relaxing joy.

It took about twenty minutes to reach my cabin. Boy, was I glad to be home. I exited the Cruiser and started salivating as I heard the hot tub heater fire up. I rushed into the house, cracked a frosty Anchor Steam, stripped naked, and jumped into that redwood cauldron. As an old hippie, I had no problem with nudity. Furthermore, I was in no mood for false modesty. E.D., Junior, and Nakai hauled in the equipment in. To my chagrin, both E.D. and Junior stripped to their birthday suits and joined me while Nakai lounged on the deck. E.D. brought the backpack, box, and SAM with her.

"This really feels good," she exclaimed as she put her arms around Junior and kissed him deeply. My heart felt joy to see those two lovebirds enjoy a cosmic interlude that I had a hand in making happen. I couldn't and wouldn't make a move on someone young enough to be my daughter. Love has a mysterious way of finding those perfect rendezvous that end in magic. My turn to make that connection may or may not come to fruition, but I remained open to the adventure.

I started to get overheated. I needed to let the young folks burn off some of those sexual energies dictated by their raging hormones, so I excused myself and took Nakai into the house to fix a light snack for everyone. I put Santana's "Abraxis" on the stereo and piped it to the outdoor speakers. For me Santana was the perfect mood music for making love. I cracked another Steam and daydreamed of my youth and the feelings that came along with the music. Higher vibrations filled the house with an energy that resurfaced every time that music filled my brain. Life was still good.

I slapped together a fast mushroom, shallot, and tomato quiche. I popped it into the oven, and the smells permeated over the mountain. While the quiche baked, I made a salad of spinach, tomato, and roasted red peppers. I added a squeeze of anchovy paste and some fresh tarragon to give it some body. I then made a bowl of fresh guacamole. The meal complete, I set the table and opened a 1986 Beringer cabernet I'd saved for a special occasion. Finding a five-pound gold nugget was special enough for me.

As the wine breathed, I sat back and watched the Pinnacles, spires of rocks separating the high desert from the mountain ecosystem, listened to Santana, and inhaled the cool mountain breezes. Unbelievably, I got my second wind and was ready to find out about the box. I slipped an ice pack on my still-throbbing finger while heavy breathing and E.D. screaming in sheer bliss seeped through the walls. They had such a good time that I forgot my aches and pains. After about fifteen minutes they both came in with contentment on their faces. They had ear-to-ear grins without any thoughts of plane crashes, wildland fires, waterfall plunges, or even Dragaminov.

I beckoned them to the table and motioned that the food was ready. Without a word, both lovers sat at the table, anticipating the feast that would be the finishing touch of an eventful day.

E.D. came running toward me with a picture taken from a dusty photo album that leaned on a shelf near the fireplace. "This picture is of my dad, Diamond, and you." It was a picture from Vietnam I had long forgotten.

"Let me see that please, E.D.," I said. "Wow, your dad is Strutch and Big D is Diamond! He was our company commander, but no one liked him. It still amazes me that his own men did not kill him. You look exactly like your dad. I haven't thought about those dudes in over thirty years. Your dad saved my life and Big D, Diamond, almost got the whole company killed. Back then he was our company skipper, a flaming egomaniac. I can believe that he's the fourth richest person in the world because he always had cash and was from old Texas oil money. No one respected him there, and I bet nothing's changed."

E.D. came up, threw her arms around me, and squeezed me tightly. Tears flowed down her rosy cheeks. Sobbing, she said, "What karma! My dad saved your life, and you saved mine. Wow! Please give me a glass of wine, Jerry. I need to digest what just happened. My dad, you, and Diamond were all together in Vietnam. I was born while all of you were over there, and fate has brought us all together."

Handing E.D. a glass, I looked her straight in the eye and reassured her that I would do what I could do to help Strutch and his daughter bring down Big Dork—that's what we called him in the Nam. I never liked the dude anyway. He screwed me out of $1,200, and if I saw him, he needed to pay me back with compound interest. Junior also wanted to help, for two reasons. He craved the action, and he was falling for E.D. in a big way.

We sat down and ate every morsel of food and then some. Boy, could that Junior pack it away. By that time we had polished off two more bottles of wine. This time we drank an even older vintage. Junior and E.D. looked like they needed a room, so I suggested they go upstairs and relax. E.D. agreed but not until after she cleared the table and put the dishes in the dishwasher. While she and Junior cleaned up the kitchen, I twisted a fatty, some of Junior's dad's finest buds. A few hits would top off this strangest of days. I'd ask the kids if they wanted to join me, but I knew Junior disapproved of his dad's vocation, and it was too complicated to ask E.D. if she wanted to partake in the sacrament of the sacred weed. Furthermore, they had other things on their minds.

After the kids went upstairs, Nakai and I went out to the deck and sat beneath a billion twinkling stars. A nearly full moon sped over the neighboring canyon, creating enchanted vistas of light and shadow. Jupiter and Mars peeked down from the heavens with the ferocity of muted stadium lights. The night was so quiet the crickets forgot to chirp.

I sparked that fat chronic and watched the sweet, healing smoke swirl to the heavens, as if it were a sacrifice to the god of instant karma. As smoke traveled from my lungs to my brain, every cell forgot the events of the day, and it soothed the magnitude of aches and pains I'd managed to pick up on our unbelievable escape. With a smile on his face Nakai yawned and rolled over, dreaming of a pool filled with rump roasts. He seemed as contented as I did. Life was still good.

5

My mind drifted to the horror that I had killed another human being today, even though it was to protect the life of another. I hadn't fired a weapon in thirty-seven years, and the fact that it felt so natural freaked me out. The act was as normal as brushing teeth. I guess there are skills I would never forget. I prided myself on the fact that though I was once a warrior, I became a man of peace. This dilemma would haunt me to my last breath.

I've always believed in the power of karma. I saved the life of the daughter of the man who once saved my life. She reciprocated by saving my life. She was now making a connection with the son of another friend. This was too much to comprehend. What was next? I had better get some much-needed rest. Something told me that I would need all the downtime I could get because the karmic connection between all of these characters would only get stranger.

My mind wandered with memories of a series of events that changed how I looked at the world forever. The brief encounter I had with a gentle soul gave me a perspective on life that never left me. I could smell, taste, and feel the jungles of Vietnam. The hairs on my arms stiffened as all my senses brought me back to that unbelievable time. I could recall every detail of that eventful day with a crystal clarity that seared into my psyche. Just like that, I was there.

In the jungle, 130-degree heat with 90 percent humidity can weaken a mind. Humping in that furnace heated my brain to a slow boil. Hell would've been a relief. I never knew his full name, nor will I ever forget what we experienced together. He will never leave me.

I was the company forward observer and had to navigate for our haggard band of Marines using an antiquated French map that was off by as much as a click, one thousand meters, and had a blank spot in the middle. We were headed right for that void.

The Republic of South Vietnam can nurture torrid conditions contradicted by stunning beauty. In a labyrinth of burned-out rice paddies rose a manicured landscape that rivaled any palace in Europe. Topiary, mazes of hedgerows, exotic flowers, palms, and fruit trees sprouted from manicured lawns. A grove of teak sentinels guarded this Shangri La.

In the center rose a golden pagoda. Off to the side a statue loomed over the entire setting. It was a simple obelisk with a single human finger carved on the top, adorned with garlands of flowers and burning Jos sticks. I felt peace at that moment unlike any other in my life. I needed to find the source of the statue's power. My mind was blown by the unexpected strangeness from this land of ultimate strange.

Saffron-robed monks shuffled peacefully amongst the hedgerows with a rhythmic synergy that rivaled a beating heart. Young apprentice monks scurried behind their masters, devouring every bit of knowledge.

Like a punch in the stomach, our skipper, Big D, barked orders to dig in on the lawn behind the teak barriers. When the gash of the E-tool pierced their sacred ground, the monks freaked. They wept, while we transformed their sanctuary into a pockmarked wasteland. I felt the pain in the older monk's eyes, but it had no effect on Big D. I couldn't believe this irreverent asshole was our leader.

The whine of a Huey overhead stopped me in my tracks. From the bowels of that flying beast leapt an ARVIN interpreter and a shiny lieutenant. As they came into view, Big D nonchalantly informed me that we had a new F.O. trainee and by the way, I was supposed to brief him on the intricacies of the bush according to Lima Company. His name was Steve and his dad was an actor. No way!

After we plotted our targets, I reiterated that the map was not accurate and we had to adjust our fire carefully so we could remain intact. He said, "Cool," but we would have to adjust the fire later because Stars and Stripes needed to interview him now.

I shuffled off to the C.P. in a daze when I noticed the interpreter sitting in the lotus position in meditation. The look on his face sent shivers down my spine. He said, "Do you know where we are and what happened here?" With a half grin I shrugged my shoulders and said, "No." He bowed his head and explained that we were in the exact birthplace of a great Bodhisattva, the Chinese Buddha, and inside the statue was the finger of Buddha himself; this was a monastery that protected one of the most sacred places on the planet. I had no idea that Buddha was born in Vietnam and that I was actually walking on the exact spot, while we, the United States Marine Corps, Uncle Sam's Misguided Children, trashed the place. I envisioned the NVA blowing up the Holy Sepulcher in Jerusalem. We had reached the realm of beyond strange.

I saw impending doom in the interpreter's eyes. Clarity flashed through my thoughts. From that contact we became one. His name was Tam. In the short time I knew him, he taught me the wisdom of his proud people. Through kindness he gave a face to the soul of these gentle people, some our enemy. We talked about life and the hope for a lasting peace. We were both sick of this useless war.

My face went ashen when I heard the roar of an incoming one-o-five round. It found its mark fifty meters from our perimeter. "Who the fuck was stupid enough to call a fire mission on our own position?" Another roar trembled the sky, and without warning my new friend Tam threw me in a hole with three other Marines. We were stacked in that tiny cubicle like pancakes. The round splashed just in front of our hiding place. The concussion rattled my fillings and struck a rim shot on my eardrum. Two others hit directly inside the perimeter.

Dead silence.

After an initial gasp and hearing the screams of the dying, I thought about Shakespeare. If he were here he would write, "Hell hath no fury like a one-o-five howitzer." All I could think of was Instant Karma.

When I slithered from that hole, I found my new friend Tam lying lifeless in the exact spot where I had just stood. Tam's leg was ripped off from the hip and drained of blood from a severed femoral artery. His crimson life fluid became a shroud. Words would never be enough to show my gratitude for his sacrifice in saving my life. I wished I could cry and grieve his loss, but the tears were cemented to my eyes.

One of those stately teak trees deflected the blast and saved Big D's sorry ass. Unfortunately, he survived and to this day, I wonder if he ever realized the karmic consequences of the events he placed in motion. As it turns out Stars and Stripes wanted pictures of Steve calling in an actual fire mission with Big D's blessing, using that antiquated map. They sent Steve back to the rear with the wounded and body bags, including Tam, my friend.

As I surveyed this unnecessary damage, the scourges of war were everywhere, except for the pagoda and statue. They were both unscathed. Somehow I knew they would survive.

I prepared for the retaliation that I knew would come after twilight, the loneliest time of all. As a matter of pride, our enemy would have to inflict payback for the deeds of this strangest of days. I noticed a solitary hand bathing in a shaft of sunlight. It was frozen with the middle digit pointing directly at our position. It was Buddha's finger.

Wow, what a mind trip! I was dripping with sweat that was evaporating in the cool mountain air. I felt a chill that permeated my bones. Shivering, I went into the house to get warm. I needed to remind myself to stop smoking that stuff. Nakai looked so contented lying on his back with all four feet sticking straight into the air. Did he get a contact high from that healing vapor? I just let him sleep in peace on the redwood deck under the stars. I stumbled up the stairs and drifted off with the cool mountain air caressing my aging body. I slept like a corpse for the rest of the night without as much as a stir. My body recharged itself with needed rest.

6

Smells of cooking pancakes filled my nostrils and reminded me that I needed coffee. Bright sunlight blasted my face with natural warmth that invited me to get up and see what this day would bring. I sure hoped the day would be a little calmer than the day before. Another day like yesterday would put me over the edge of physical endurance. Getting out of bed was harder than normal because my back refused to relinquish its restful state, but the rest of my body craved a big cup of that caffeinated brew.

I stumbled down the stairs to a kitchen bustling with activity that rivaled any gourmet restaurant on the planet. E.D. was at the stove flipping pancakes, and Junior stood at the counter squeezing fresh orange juice. Jake Sr., his dad, sat at the table drinking coffee. He jumped up from his chair and gave me a bear hug that expelled the air from my lungs. I immediately retreated and refilled those collapsed lungs so oxygenated blood could be pumped to my heart.

Jake was a large, powerful man with a crushing grip, that could squeeze the air from any man. Living in the forest, isolated from civilization, had eroded what social skills he may have had before he became a pot farmer. He could never get it together after Vietnam to live among regular people. I was one of the only people who understood his idiosyncrasies. I helped him out from time to time with situations that could get him into trouble. He had no respect for authority and couldn't care less about society's rules.

Jake bellowed, "Hey, Jerry, what's shakin', devil dog? I'm glad that you could join us this afternoon."

I looked at the wall clock; Felix had just struck the crack of noon. "Wow, I must have needed my beauty sleep!" Without hesitation I snatched a fresh cup of coffee from the pot on the counter. The aromas from that organic Guatemalan concoction made me salivate. I breathed in a good whiff and sipped from my cup so that I wouldn't burn my lips and tongue. Life was still good.

Nakai sniffed around the deck. He disturbed a sunning lizard that jumped into the brush. He tried in vain to snap at the escaping tail. I noticed a shadow on the other side of the canyon. It looked like one of the Texas SUVs. No, it couldn't, because E.D. shot it full of holes. It must be just a mountain mirage, or so I thought when the whine of helicopter blades made me stiffen with fear.

E.D. heard the same whine, grabbed the box and the SAM, and went out onto the deck. The roar got louder when small-arms fire began to pepper the deck. Rounds pierced the hot tub and turned the redwood into Swiss cheese. Water came streaming out, irrigating the front yard. Junior jumped up and returned fire with one of the Skorpions we had liberated from the Russians. Jake covered himself from the hail of bullets by hiding behind a small river rock pony wall that shielded a wood stove. He emptied a twelve-gauge street sweeper shotgun at the assault. The Russian thugs took cover behind rocks across the canyon. We were in a full-fledged firefight and I was unarmed. Great! Life wasn't so good right now.

From behind a rock in my front yard, one of the thugs jumped in front of Junior and pointed the muzzle of his assault rifle between his shoulder blades. He had the drop on him and was ready to blast him into his next life when out of nowhere Nakai squeezed between the muzzle and his master. This startled the assailant, and a shot rang out of the weapon and struck Nakai in the left hip. The wounded dog yelped, and with blood streaming down his leg, he went right for the Russian's throat. With his last bit of strength, Nakai clamped his powerful jaws around the assassin's neck. The thug's rifle dropped as he fell to the ground while he bled out from a ripped jugular vein. His lifeless body draped across Nakai's bleeding, broken hip.

Junior rushed to his dog's aid. Using his shirt, Junior placed direct pressure on the wound. The poor dog had lost a great deal of blood and shattered his hip. He needed a vet pronto. Junior looked around to see if there were any more bad guys in the immediate area and scooped up the dying canine and placed him in the back of the FJ Cruiser.

"I need to get poor Nakai to the vet now. I'll catch up to all of you later at Dad's place if you make it out of here alive." He left in such a hurry that E.D. only had time to blow him a kiss. As he turned onto the road, the roar of Diamond's chopper grew louder.

Within a blink of an eye, the chopper fired a missile and blew the top floor of my house into splinters. All of us exited the house before we became human kindling. The first floor, deck, and waterless hot tub were the only structures still intact. E.D. shouldered the SAM, and the heat-seeking projectile slammed into the side of the war bird. The wounded craft auto rotated down to the canyon floor, exploding into a fireball that shook the mountain. I could hear secondary explosions from the chopper's ordnance. Now I knew why I hated fireworks. Another wildland fire raced up the canyon. The Forest Service would surely be pissed.

As the chopper crumpled into indistinguishable wreckage, Dragaminov and the rest of his men loaded into the remaining SUVs and made a hasty retreat down the mountain. There were only a few of them left anyway.

How would I explain this to the insurance company and the sheriff? I knew E.D. didn't want to tell anyone about what we were doing, but there were too many bodies lying on my front lawn. Big D owed me big time for this one.

E.D. looked up and shouted, "Is everyone all right? We must leave with the box now!"

I stepped in front of her and explained the situation we were involved in now. "We can't just keep on killing people and burning up the mountain without telling anyone."

E.D. said, "Diamond has enough pull to squash anything local authorities could mount against him. We better get out of here and open the box before he gets his greedy hands on the prize."

Jake, being no fan of law enforcement, agreed.

Outnumbered, I reluctantly agreed to leave this crime scene. E.D. grabbed her pack and the box. Her hands were full, so I took the remaining weapons and threw them in the back of Jake's truck. All three of us got into the front seat, where Jake put the pedal to the metal and drove further into the mountains.

E.D. called Junior on her cell phone and told him what happened. He said that Nakai would be okay but needed to be in the hospital for a few days. I hoped he would make it without complications. We were relieved that we survived breakfast, but I didn't have time to finish my coffee.

Jake drove down the mountain with the precision of a Grand Prix driver. He seemed to smooth out all the curves with a drifting maneuver. A cloud of dust followed the truck with every turn. Fortunately, E.D. had shot down Dragaminov's helicopter, because a blind man could have followed our dust. Jake knew the Forest Service roads like a leisurely drive down Main Street. For the time being, I felt confident that we would be safe from any more danger.

7

Diamond's satellite phone rang with an obnoxious drone. He quickly gulped down caviar on toast points, wiped his mouth, and gruffly answered. The inside of his private jet resembled a mausoleum. The cavernous compartment looked empty with only one passenger. That was the way Diamond liked it. He did not like human contact when he felt stressed out.

His face turned ashen when he heard the bad news from the other end of the line.

Dragaminov informed Diamond that he and his men were foiled again. Strutch's daughter shot down one of his five-million-dollar helicopters with his own missile. "That little pain in the ass is causing me more than heartburn. Get over to Strutch's ranch and wait for that lucky little girl to get there. I need that box. My patience is wearing thin, so do not fail me again."

Dragaminov replied, "Okay, I will not fail you again. What is in that box that so many lives have been lost over?"

"I will tell you when you recover the prize. Don't worry about the mess you left in the mountains. I have a cleaning service that will take care of the bodies. By the way, whose house did you blow up?"

"Some guy named Jerry Johnson. I can't wait to see him face-to-face. He has to pay for killing my comrades."

"Wait a minute, did you say Jerry Johnson? I was in the Nam with a guy named Jerry Johnson and Strutch. It just can't be the same. I can't believe it's really him. What a coincidence! Get a picture of him and I'll see for myself if he is the same guy. Fax it to my plane as soon as you can. And Dragaminov, don't muck this up! I need to make some calls. Get back to me when you have something positive to tell me."

Diamond flashed on the days of yore, when he was young. The only thing he regretted about his war experience was the fact that he couldn't make millions of dollars while playing Marine. He did make a pretty penny in the black market, and screwed his fellow grunts out of most of their money. He devised a scheme to invest most of the company's paychecks while never intending to pay anyone a penny of profit. He just left country when his rotation was up. He cashed in his windfall and, with some money from his family, started Diamond Oil. He built his empire off the blood of his fellow comrades in arms. The money was a good thing, but he relished the fact that he could screw over everyone and anyone who got in his way. The process was the game. He just loved to piss on people.

The whine of the fax machine broke him from his daydream. The pale blue eyes of Jerry Johnson peered at him, like a ghost from the past. He recognized that face even though he hadn't seen it in almost forty years. "I hope old Jerry isn't still mad at me, but he was too idealistic for me. I never understood his hippie ways, all that peace and love nonsense. He never cared for making money. Oh well, I just hope he's seen the light after all these years," Diamond mused aloud.

The plane's steward informed Diamond that the craft would be landing in D.C. in just a few minutes, and asked if he wanted anything before landing. He dismissed the steward with a flick of a finger and shouted, "I want to look at the vice president's beady little eyes and watch him turn over the oil leases." After all, Diamond spent a small fortune greasing the wheels of government.

The huge jet landed on a private runway, which only high-ranking government planes and the ultra-rich used as a hangar. A vintage Rolls-Royce Silver Cloud waited at the foot of the exit doors. Diamond sprang from his plane and hopped in the backseat of his Rolls. "Take me to my house on the Potomac," he snapped.

The weather in D.C. was hot and sticky during summertime. People looked so uncomfortable sweating in the sweltering heat.

Diamond couldn't care less about common folks' misery. A car was stopped at the side of the road with steam billowing from under the hood. A pregnant woman with two little toddlers franticly tried to wave down Diamond's car. The driver signaled to pull over and help the poor woman when Diamond shouted, "Just keep going, she doesn't look like a profit to me!" Reluctantly the driver pulled away while Diamond rolled down his window and shouted, "Have a nice day!"

As the Rolls winded down Billionaire's Row, Diamond only could wonder how much money transferred over the centuries on this street. Presidents, foreign dignitaries, and captains of industry owned property on this prestigious way. Diamond's house was once owned and built by the Marquis de Lafayette after the Revolutionary War. The shah of Iran had also owned the 350-acre estate. Diamond acquired the property in a shady oil deal that made him his first billion. The estate was thrown in as a bonus. Diamond promised to pay the shah twenty million for the property, but fortunately he died and all the paperwork got lost in the shuffle. Iran's government had tried to recover the money ever since. Diamond's team of lawyers buried the payment in litigation. Basically, Diamond got the entire estate for free, and that was exactly how he liked it. The money didn't mean as much as the fact that he screwed someone out of it. That's what gave him the most pleasure.

The powerful automobile glided up hills adjacent to the river with the agility of a cheetah. The opulent English motorcar entered a massive iron gate, with a three-foot solid gold D in the center. It cast a menacing aura throughout the surrounding landscape. A huge granite guard shack stood in front of the fortress gate.

A bulletproof glass window opened as an ex-KGB commando looked straight into the Rolls' window and recognized Diamond. The Russian snapped to attention and pushed a button on a huge console. A large bank of TV monitors scanned the entire property. Another commando viewed the screens with fervor, knowing the boss was on the property. The massive gate struggled at first, shuddered for a moment, then smoothly swung open with an audible creak.

A half-mile winding stone driveway, lined with ten-foot-high boxwoods planted by George Washington for his friend Lafayette, stared at anyone entering the estate. Cameras, motion detectors, and lighting were invisible between the branches of these ancient shrubs. Sliding steel barriers were installed halfway up the drive to prevent intruders from reaching the main house. These and more security devices were controlled from the guardhouse at the front gate.

Diamond could control the entire operation from his cell phone. When they passed a certain point, the paranoid Diamond pressed a code on his phone and the massive steel barriers slammed shut with a loud noise that could be heard for miles. "If anyone wants to get at me, they will have to try a little harder. The shah really knew how to secure a home, and just think—I got this all for free, " Diamond gloated.

The meandering journey took nearly five minutes to navigate. When the car left the boxwood maze, a huge edifice stared the occupants in the face. The sheer magnitude of the main building dwarfed even the White House. Diamond couldn't be upstaged by anyone, not even the United States government. Though his creation looked pleasing to the eye, an eerie coldness loomed over the entire property. There was no love, just lonely stone and steel.

As the land yacht screeched to a halt, servants scurried around the car waiting for orders from their employer. Diamond ignored them and quickly ran through a massive solid mahogany door. A huge gushing oil well was carved into the center. The door, weighing almost a thousand pounds, swung open with just a slight tug. Entering a marble statue-lined, three-story room, Diamond gazed at a massive crystal chandelier suspended from the ceiling. Light from strategically placed skylights refracted more than seven hundred individual crystals, creating blinding rainbows over the entire space. The sensory overload would have been too much for most people, but Diamond reveled in the excess. He gazed into the light show for a few moments and muttered, "I've got to get a hold of the vice president and start pumping my oil."

Diamond dialed his phone, calling Miss Green back in Houston. He barked at her, inquiring if she got in touch with the vice president. She sheepishly said, "I tried quite a few times, but his secretary said that he was in a committee meeting at the senate and could not be disturbed."

"Keep trying and get back to me when you know any news." Diamond hung up the phone and stormed out of the room.

8

The whirl of a five-foot-wide wind turbine fanned the forest from the top of the ridge. Jake had installed that windmill so he didn't have to pay Edison for power. Furthermore, he needed extra electricity to power his clandestine farming operation. Stadium lights and powerful fans ate up enough electricity to fly a red flag to the DEA, never mind the local sheriff. Growing the most potent marijuana in the county took the expertise of a scientist and the nerve of a bomb technician. Jake was a master grower and had the process down to an efficient forty-eight-day cycle. He perfected hydroponics and knew how much light and nutrients made the finished product powerful and tasty.

E.D. noticed a small sign on the gate. It read "Welcome to Rancho Mysterioso, Beware of the Monster."

"Beware of what?"

I told her that it was just Jake's sense of humor running wild. He liked to be a mystery to everyone and anyone who wanted to get close to him. She understood because her own dad acted the same way. We pulled up in front of the house, got out of the truck, and went inside. Jake told us to get comfortable, then excused himself to the barn.

I tagged along and went into his huge barn. There were horse and llama stalls in the front with a secret room underneath the plodding hooves. Jake talked into an intercom and announced his entry into the hidden sanctuary. He hit a hidden lever, and a steel door behind stacked hay bales slid open with a squeak. We climbed down a small flight of stairs and entered a different world. Inside that room under the floor of the barn was a twenty-by-twenty-foot aluminum foil-lined concrete space filled with a sophisticated hydroponics growing operation. Energy-eating stadium lights shined from the ceiling. A complicated ventilation system filtered the air so the exhaust smelled fresh and clean. Rows of marijuana plants stood growing in various stages.

Jake grew only a few dozen plants. He was not greedy. He sold his crop to a high-end clientele that he had known for many years. He helped supply product for medical marijuana dispensaries. Most of the proceeds from the endeavor anonymously went to help people in need. Jake got a kick out of being Santa Claus. He also got Jake Jr. started on the right track and sent him to the prestigious Scripps Institute of Oceanography after he got back from Afghanistan. Jake was uncomfortable around most people. He felt comfortable around me because we shared the scourges of war. I helped him with tasks that he couldn't handle on his own. He had an accountant friend who handled his finances, so the IRS was no problem.

A man and woman manicured the crop as we entered the room. Ernesto and Guadalupe Hernandez were immigrants from Guatemala Jake befriended and took in. He offered them a good life far beyond the repression of their native land. These two took care of the entire property. Jake, in return, gave them a great place to live and security for their family. They had two children in college who were U.S. citizens. They treated the property like their own. Guadalupe wove llama wool and made high-end sweaters that sold for big bucks in Beverly Hills. Ernesto was an artist. He carved beautiful wooden pens and fancy boxes from exotic woods that were the rage all over California. The couple had a workshop in the rear of the barn and made enough money to help their village back home. Life was great for them.

Jake was so secretive with his clandestine operation that no one on the mountain had any idea what he did. Everyone thought that he was just an eccentric Vietnam veteran who raised llamas and just wanted to be left alone. People knew not to bother with him because he had a hair-trigger temper and was ready to mix it up with anyone who got in his way. He once put three guys in the hospital who made fun of him in a bar. He never set foot in that establishment after that unfortunate incident. Besides all his faults, Jake had a big heart, and I was glad to call him my friend.

We left the basement and strolled back to the house. E.D. was on the phone with Junior. Nakai would survive his wounds but would have to stay in the hospital for a couple more days. Junior would be back at Rancho Mysterioso after leaving the vet.

E.D. called her dad at his Malibu ranch, told him of her ordeal with Diamond's henchmen, and mentioned that his old friend had saved her life. Best of all, she had the box and would bring it to the ranch as soon as possible, to finally see what was inside. Strutch did not let anyone know its contents, for fear that Diamond might find out the truth. He also delighted in all the mystery. He told her to wait until the next day to come to Malibu.

Jake secured the secret room, and the four of us entered the house as E.D. hung up the phone. Jake introduced Guadalupe and Ernesto to E.D. She immediately began speaking to them in Spanish. I never stopped being impressed by E.D.'s talents. Wow, this girl could do anything. Guadalupe scurried to the kitchen and began to prepare lunch. She made chile rellenos, black beans, and rice, plus chicken smothered in sweet chocolate mole sauce. Homemade grilled flour tortillas filled the entire house with the exotic smells from her native Guatemala. Ernesto poured glasses of Xabandu, Mayan liquor that had a licorice flavor. That syrupy elixir slithered down my throat and gave me a warm feeling that made me forget our predicament. After we toasted our good fortunes, Ernesto passed around bottles of Bohemia, a dark Mexican beer, and we were ready to eat. I don't care for most Mexican beers, but Bohemia was a different story. It had taste.

Just as we sat down to eat, Junior burst into the room and said, "Smells like Guadalupe's home cooking. I just hope there's enough left for a growing boy like myself. I'm as hungry as a tapeworm!" With that exclamation Junior loaded his plate with all the food it could hold. Guadalupe was pleased that her meal was a success, even though she had reservations about whether Junior actually tasted any of the food because he ate like a man rescued from a desert island. After his third helping he sat back and just smiled.

I really wanted to find out what was left of my house. I reached for my cell phone, but E.D. stopped me in my tracks. She reassured me that everything would be fine. "I'll cover your losses and more, but you can't go back there right now. Diamond will find us and we will never get the box back to my dad." She grabbed a stack of bearer bonds from her pack and said with an air of confidence, "This should more than take care of the cost of rebuilding. Just trust me on this, Jerry." I looked at those angelic eyes and there was nothing I could say at that point, so I just kept quiet.

I took the bonds and asked Jake if he could stash them in a safe place. He said calmly that he had just the place. He took them to what looked like a rock on the side of the mountain. He rolled it over and exposed a hidden compartment on the bottom. He reassured me that an atomic bomb couldn't penetrate the titanium steel walls that lined the fake rock. After he showed me how to open the rock, we went back into the house. Jake turned on the news to see what, if anything, was going on with my blown-up house with the Russian mercenary bodies strewn all over my front yard. To our surprise there was no mention of any exploded house or a crashed helicopter or wildland fire. My mind was blown again! There had to be some mention, but there was none. It looked like things would work out after all.

E.D. jumped in and said, "Diamond has amazing resources at his disposal. I wouldn't be surprised if all the wreckage and carnage was cleaned up by now."

No one has that much power, I thought to myself, but little did I know how much power that maniac actually possessed. The man hadn't changed in over thirty-five years. That Big D: once a prick, always a prick.

Junior asked E.D. if she wanted to go on a horseback ride up to a special place on top of the mountain. She needed to relax for a while before bringing the box to her dad. With a gleam in her eye, E.D. accepted, relishing the opportunity to be alone with Junior. They went out to the barn, where a handsome palomino stallion stood in his stall. When Junior approached, the horse's ears immediately perked with excitement. Sirocco, a full-blooded thoroughbred, loved to run like a hot wind blowing across the desert. He was Junior's horse from the moment of his birth, some fifteen years before.

Boy and animal had an unbreakable bond from the beginning. The two of them had explored the entire San Bernardino mountain range like a couple of nineteenth-century pioneers. But because of the time Junior spent in the Marine Corps and his oceanographic studies, their rides up and down the mountain were few and far between. Today, horse and rider were as one, just like in days gone by. Though they were older, an inextinguishable fire still burned in man and beast.

E.D. noticed the bond immediately while choosing an Appaloosa mare named Daisy. She was a gentle but fast steed. E.D., among other things, knew about horses. She saddled Daisy in an instant and trotted her new friend around the paddock while Junior was petting Sirocco. After a few more minutes of bonding, Junior was ready to head off up the mountain.

They rode through a meadow of fragrant wildflowers on the way to the forest just ahead. Clouds of pollen and the scent of nectar overpowered them, so they had to cover their noses and shade their eyes. Squadrons of honeybees, hummingbirds, and butterflies flew heavily with the intoxicating mixture, in complete ecstasy. Some were lying on the ground unable to move because of the extra weight attached to their tiny bodies. A multitude of sun-drenched colors danced over the meadow, adding to the magic of this special place.

E.D. and Junior galloped through the meadow and slid between two hundred-foot Ponderosa pine trees. In an instant the landscape completely changed. Sunlight filtered through millions of pine needles and created a kaleidoscope of light and shadow on the pine-straw carpet below. Crystalline images of liquid light floated between the branches, making it impossible to keep focused on any one image. As the two riders moved up the trail, the shadows followed their every move. This place was truly magical. For a moment, E.D. forgot about the box or even about Diamond. Love took over her every thought.

Bright sunlight illuminated their path as they exited the forest. The sun reflected off the decomposed granite so brightly that sunglasses were needed to protect sensitive eyes from harmful UV rays. A snow-covered craggy peak of about 2,000 feet stood between them and the top of the world. They were above the tree line, about 9,000 feet above sea level, when Junior suggested they enjoy a snack and water the horses. Sirocco had begun to breathe hard due to the thin air. He needed a break from the grueling climb.

After a short break, Junior broke out a couple of lightweight parkas from his saddlebag and handed one to E.D. "We're going to need these to keep warm on the way to the summit."

Chilly breezes whistled through the riders like icicles. E.D. thanked Junior and immediately stifled the wind with that Gortex insulation. It took but a mere twenty minutes to reach the top of the mountain range. Once on top the two had a 360-degree view of the entire southern California basin. A clear view of the Sierra Mountains to the north, the Mojave Desert to the east, Mexico to the south, and the Pacific Ocean to the west made the trip worthwhile.

As E.D. gazed to the south, reality flashed into her love-soaked brain. Her dad was in trouble somewhere down there, while she was caught up in the complete beauty of this panoramic vista.

She leaned over the saddle and kissed Junior hard on the lips.

"What was that all about?" Junior gasped.

"I just wanted to thank you for showing me this wonderful place."

Junior smiled and said, "You haven't seen anything yet." Sirocco reared and galloped to the other side of the summit, where an enormous blue granite monolith stood like a sentinel, guarding the scene with regal majesty.

They rode up to the front, where the wind instantly stopped blowing and the bone-chilling cold was replaced by soothing warmth. The blue seemed to absorb the sun's heat and spewed prismatic flecks of light over its surrounding realm. A naturally carved bench stood in the center like a throne made for two. As the two equestrians sat in silence overlooking the landscape, waves of love splashed, enveloping their very souls, cementing them together for eternity. Unable to speak, the lovers gazed into each other's eyes and dreamt of what wonders the future might bestow upon them. The future looked endless if everything felt the way it did at that moment. At that moment life was truly good.

Their perch faced due west, where they had a clear view of the shimmering Pacific some seventy-five miles away. Glimpses of massive ships could be seen to the rear of Catalina Island. The entire southern California coastline sparkled with light refractions. The glistening spectacle traveled like runway lights to their lofty perch. E.D. noticed an enormous chasm directly in front of the shelf. It looked to be over 1,000 feet deep. Flecks of mica illuminated the view, and its beauty could be absorbed by all the senses. As E.D. tried to experience the sensory assault, the two lovers melted as one into each other.

Junior looked deeply into her eyes and whispered, "There is a local legend about an ill-fated romance between a young Shoshone brave and the daughter of a local rancher. The rancher found out about their romance and vowed to kill the handsome Indian, rather than contaminate his bloodline. He saw them together and chased them up this very mountain. The two of them scrambled up to this very spot, where they came many times to do what we are doing right now, for this was their rendezvous. With guns blazing, the jealous father, intent on killing the both of them, sprayed the monolith with fire spouting from his Peacemaker. Just as he drew down on them from a point-blank range, the two lovers clutched each other, kissed, and leapt from their nest and disappeared into the light. Since then, this place has been known as the Devil's Cauldron."

"What a story! Do you think this place is where true love blossoms?"

"Only time will tell," and he kissed her deeply.

9

As light dwindled, the two riders descended from the craggy precipice with a newfound appreciation for beauty and the power of love. E.D. asked Junior if he brought all his girlfriends up to that special place. He just winked and kept riding. The events of that afternoon helped ease the tension of the last two days and added resolve for the days ahead. E.D. knew that if she were to save her dad, she needed to use every bit of her skill and cunning. With luck and the help of her newfound friends, she just might succeed. Her total dislike for Diamond made the quest more important.

By the time they rode onto Rancho Mysterioso, night had fallen like a meteor, with the only visible light that of the full moon above the trees. With limited visibility the two steeds instinctively galloped to the barn, where they knew there would be oats and sweet feed ready to repay them for service performed. A bright light shone from an outbuilding, where they could see the shadow of a huge machine. E.D. did a double take when she noticed a helicopter shining in the faded light.

As they rode closer, a windsock billowed in the evening breeze. Jake and Ernesto were working on an actual Vietnam-era Huey gunship. The retired war bird glistened in the bright hangar light and cast an eerie shadow on the landscape. I watched from a lounge chair as the two of them intently affixed the tail rotor. I wanted to help, but alas, I knew my limitations, being mechanically disinclined. I added moral support and brought the hard workers an occasional cold beer from the hangar's well-stocked refrigerator.

Jake was a combat helicopter pilot in the Nam, and he missed the thrill of flying. He bought a surplus chopper a few years ago, and with

Ernesto put it back together piece by piece. Ernesto, a mechanic back in his native land, serviced military aircraft for a former Guatemalan military junta. When they were thrown out of power, Ernesto and Guadalupe were forced to become refugees. Jake rescued them from the death squads, and the rest is what had become a great symbiotic relationship. Eternally grateful, Ernesto and Guadalupe kept Jake from going over to the dark side. They gave him purpose.

When I spotted the kids riding into view, I creaked my tired back from its resting place and helped them with the horses, who were tired, hungry, and wet. They needed attention to reward them for the day's service. Junior and E.D. unsaddled their mounts while I started to wipe them down. Nothing worse than being rode hard and put away wet, like some girls I've gone out with, but that's a different story.

After the horses seemed content, E.D. sprinted into the hangar with an ear-to-ear grin. "Wow, where did you get such a magnificent hunk of flying freedom?"

"We picked her up rusting away in some forgotten junk heap. After we slapped a few coats of paint on her, we thought she might get off the ground again."

E.D.'s eyes grew to the size of saucers, and I could tell she wanted to get behind the controls in the worst way. "When are you finally going to get her off the ground?"

"How about now!" Jake replied.

With a gentle coaxing, Ernesto wheeled the nimble bird from the hangar. I stood there in awe as Jake fired up the jet engine. The massive blades turned slowly at first, but in a few seconds turned to full rotation. I hadn't heard the whelp from Huey rotors in a long, long time. That sound brought back painful memories from a time I would give anything to forget. My mind soared with intrusive thoughts from that never forgotten war. I did not want to go there now, or any other time. I just wanted to curl up into a ball and wait for the sound to stop. I needed to act like nothing bothered me, because I hadn't seen Jake so happy in a long time. He craved the rush to keep his sanity in check. My insecurities would have to be put on hold for the time being.

While Jake fiddled with the instruments, Ernesto made some final adjustments to the engine. With the excitement of a schoolgirl, E.D. immediately jumped into the copilot's seat. It was apparent that she loved flying and wanted to get to the controls of the Huey as soon as possible. It was the bird's maiden voyage, out of respect, she let Jake handle the initial flying.

Jake asked us if we wanted to take a ride. He had to make a delivery on Soggy Dry Lake, in the Mojave Desert just to the north.

E.D. gleamed with excitement, "*Spark this firecracker and let's get airborne!*" Junior passed on the flight because he needed to check on Nakai at the vet. I looked at bullet holes in the fuselage and decided to check up on my house, or what was left of it. I'd had too many bad memories concerning helicopters falling out of the sky. I needed a break from all this excitement.

Ernesto loaded a large duffel and his toolbox into the innards of the Huey and jumped in behind E.D. Jake gave me the thumbs-up and lifted off. With a groan Jake's project lifted off the ground with the grace of a Brahma bull, pitching to and fro, then finally leveled out. In an instant they were gone into the wild blue yonder.

10

Waves of anxiety punched me in the solar plexus as the whirling bird churned its way over the mountain. I hadn't ridden in choppers since the Nam, so didn't think I could handle the flood of memories that I knew would sneak into my brain.

I asked Junior if he could give me a lift to my house on his way to the vet. We jumped into his Cruiser and fled Rancho Mysterioso. The whine of Jake's new toy faded as we crunched our way to the paved road. The mountains after dusk felt like we were traveling through shadows. The moon illuminated our path with a clarity that few people would appreciate. My body felt relaxed in that blanket of stars, but my mind raced and conjured up all kinds of scary scenarios. I hadn't had this much excitement in a long time.

We rounded the corner of my street, and a gaping hole stood where my house once provided me with shelter. Except now, all the debris had vanished from the property. There was no sign of a fire or gun battle. Big D must have had all the debris hauled away. It looked like my property with no house. The only structure standing was my garage. The only reason it survived was the fact that it was away from the main house.

I climbed out of the Cruiser and thanked Junior for the ride, but I needed to see if any of my cars would start. He waited while I opened the barn-style doors and peered inside. There was no electricity, so I asked Junior for a flashlight. I needed to see what, if anything, remained of my vehicles. To my surprise everything seemed to look the same as I had left it two days ago. The beam from the flashlight dimly illuminated the windshield of my 1965 Porsche 356 Cabriolet. When I took off the car cover, there was a layer of dust on the sapphire blue paint. I jumped into the driver's seat and fired up the German engineering masterpiece. The car was a present from a grateful industrialist whose leg I splinted back when I was still a professional firefighter. He had a stable of exotic cars and couldn't drive them all. I guess my karma was extremely favorable that day. Windfalls like that particular one keep following me like a clutch of rabbit's feet. I don't mind them at all.

Stromberg carburetors fed fuel into that spunky rear engine, and she fired up with enough gusto to travel the entire Autobahn. Junior bid me a kindly farewell as I rounded the corner of my street and sped up the canyon. The cool wind comforted me. What hair I still had blew back like the mane of an old lion sprinting after his prey.

Without warning I heard a ten-pound Coulter pine cone hit the top of the driver's side door and ricochet into my arm. Three of the rapier-like woody sepals lacerated my elbow. Blood gushed in a steady stream from the wound. I was lucky. If that coned missile had struck me in the head, I could have been killed. Imagine that, killed by a pine cone. I wrapped my shirt around my arm and headed straight for the hospital. Life didn't feel so good.

Our local hospital was very small, but big enough to service the needs of the tiny mountain community. I pulled into the parking lot and crossed the helipad in front of the ER; the smell of burning flesh filled the air with an acrid odor that brought back memories from unhappier times in my life I really had no need to remember. They must have had surgery and were burning the medical waste. Even though this process was the only way to dispose of biologic hazards, the smell took me back to where that smell of carnage filled the air on a daily basis. I don't think I will ever forget that smell.

As I went through the automatic ER door, an ambulance backed up in front of the door behind me. Members of my old fire department were doing CPR on a pulseless, apneic patient. I stepped aside while they rolled the gurney past me into a waiting room. There was complete chaos, and everyone there worked in a frenzy to bring the patient back to life.

When Mary Smith, an MICN and friend of mine, noticed me, she said, "Glad to see you, Jerry. Give us a hand with the compressions." I saw that ashen near-corpse and showed Mary my bloody elbow. "Okay, you can bag the patient with your good arm. Wrap this Kling around your arm and help."

The blood had almost stopped anyway, so I jumped into the fray with my one good arm. Doctors, nurses, firefighters, and I did compressions, gave oxygen, pushed drugs, and defibrillated the patient in a futile attempt to revive him. Even though I knew our chances were slim, we still had to try.

Doc Costello ordered a chest x-ray to see what was inside the man's chest. "Stop CPR until the radiation passes." The weary team had been at this for over twenty minutes when Doc called the process over. "Let me see the film before I pronounce this unfortunate soul dead." As he looked at the film, laughter erupted. A hemostat had somehow been left under the patient's back, and it looked like it was inside of his chest or he swallowed a six-inch piece of metal. Nurse Supervisor Edna Crab burst into the room and shouted, "There is no laughing during CPR!" She looked like a nun with a ruler instead of a health care provider. With that everyone laughed louder. "This just is not in the steps of grieving." Nurse Crab left the ER in a huff. Humor in the face of disaster tends to take the edge off a bad situation.

As the chaos of the last half hour wound down, Mary told the Doc of my laceration. She removed the Kling and washed the wound out with a solution of Betadine and warm water. There were tiny fragments of pine cone mixed in with the blood. These foreign objects and globs of pine pitch needed to be washed before the wound could be stitched. Mary's gentle touch almost made the pain go away. "We don't want your arm to get infected, do we now?"

Doc then inserted three stitches in my throbbing arm while Mary prepared a sterile dressing to cover the closed wound. "You should be as good as new in a few days, unless pine cones start to rain." I thanked him and went outside to get some fresh air.

Mary followed me to a bench in front of the ER. Her long, gray hair bounced with each step like soothing ocean waves on a sandy beach. I'd known Mary for years and she always liked me, as I did her. She was in a relationship and we never took our friendship to the next level, even though it could have blossomed many times. The opportunity never quite happened.

While I sat with Mary, one of the firefighters noticed a green light flashing under my Porsche. "Hey, Jerry, that light flashes every two seconds, and I hear a faint ping. What is it?"

"I don't know, but let's check it out." The three of us went over to my car and noticed a cigarette package-size box with a green flashing LED with wires attached to the frame. Dragaminov! That Russian scoundrel must have attached the device to my car when we ran to Rancho Mysterioso. It's a good thing my friend noticed the GPS or I would have led Big D's mercenaries right to the box.

Out the corner of my eye, I noticed a familiar black Suburban with the lights off and the engine running, hidden behind a small stand of live oak trees on the far side of the almost empty parking lot. I had to act fast before some innocent person felt the wrath of the Diamond Corporation. I asked Mary to go back into the ER, and I would explain everything later. I just needed her trust for now. She lovingly squeezed my hand and reluctantly moved away from my car.

I looked at my friends Duke and Tom Peterson and said, "I can't explain what's happening, but I need you to distract that Suburban while I leave. As a friend you must trust me and please don't ask any questions. If anyone questions you about this, try not to tell them anything."

"Okay, Jerry, piece a cake. I don't know what you've gotten

yourself into this time, but we've trusted each other for many years. I'll distract them while you do what you have to do. Be careful and I expect you to fill me in."

"Oh, by the way, mum's the word."

I waited for the ambulance to park ahead of the Suburban, blocking them from moving, so I could make my move. The ambulance parked right in front of the Russians. Tom got out and asked the occupants if they needed help. As I watched their conversation, the Porsche leapt from its parking place and headed for a fire road in the rear of the hospital. I sped by the ER door, where Mary worriedly blew me a kiss.

I knew many mountain fire roads, especially the ones around the hospital. I drove out of sight and pulled the magnetic tracking device from the Porsche's frame and sped off down the road just above the dam of an alpine lake. The dam, built in 1886 to hold a stream that flowed through a canyon, created a 200-foot-deep lake of crystal-clear, pure water, so clear that you could see almost to the bottom. An old steam train left behind during construction could still be seen if you knew where to look. This place was truly a breathtaking sight to behold, especially on a starlit night like tonight.

The beauty of this magical place overtook my entire being; then I realized bloodthirsty Russian mercenaries were chasing me. I quickly snapped out of this quasi dream and stuck to a plan that I hadn't quite figured out. Clouds of dust followed me like a blinding brown snowstorm. My pursuers' visibility was next to zero. This fact gave me the plan I knew I would come up with.

There was a dirt bike course where kids practiced motocross next to the dam overlooking the lake. A steep camelback whoop-de-doo, ten feet deep and only eight feet high across, rose above the dam surface. Daredevil kids attempted to fly across the two hills and turned away from the impending doom of falling into the frigid water, or even worse, getting smashed onto the rocks below. A seventeen-year-old motocross rider was killed, and the Forest Service closed the entire area as just too dangerous.

A series of donuts I spun in the loose dirt just before the edge of the dam made seeing nearly impossible. My face was covered in brown dust. I looked like I was dusted in cocoa. When some got in my mouth, it wasn't sweet at all. I threw the tracking device next to the Porsche and exited the car so it would be camouflaged in the dust. If they followed the tracking signal, their Suburban would clear the first hill and smash into the camel's second hump, missing my car.

I heard my pursuers almost on top of me. The larger Suburban cleared both hills and hit the Porsche's bumper. With an unholy screech, both vehicles spilled over the side. A few seconds later, I heard two distinct splashes. My beautiful blue classic and an SUV full of bad guys floated in pure mountain water. So much for my brilliant plan!

I could hear expletives in a foreign language that must have been Russian or maybe Ukrainian. My training wanted me to dive into the lake and save the waterlogged creeps, but the sacrifice of my car was enough. They would survive for the time being, so I whispered "Dowbronots" and reluctantly walked toward the hospital.

Those waterlogged, pissed-off assassins would have some explaining to do when the sheriff found out about the flying cars. The only thing that worried me was I wouldn't be close to my car. Maybe that would be a good thing if people thought I went down with the Porsche. The bad guys would certainly relay this information to Big D, and I would be off his radar for a while. Every dark cloud does have a silver lining.

11

Ireached into my pocket and called Junior to tell him what went down at the lake. He left the vet's office and was on his way to pick me up at the hospital. I told him to come in from the back way so as not to draw any attention to him or to me. "I don't want our zany vacation into the bizarre to become the talk of the mountain. Besides, who would believe us anyway?"

Junior agreed. "Let's go to Rancho Mysterioso and see if they made it back from the desert in one piece without getting killed or busted."

"Before we hit the trail, we need to check for tracking devices." We took a few minutes to check the cruiser for unwanted hitchhikers, found none, and boogied.

Meanwhile, E.D. couldn't contain herself from the sheer exhilaration of treetop flying Jake's new toy. Jake and Ernesto couldn't wipe the grins from their faces. The Mojave Desert gleamed in the moonlight like a jewel under a bright light. E.D. knew her way around anything flyable. Jake had full confidence in her abilities as an aviatrix. He just kicked back and enjoyed the ride. Beaming, he told Ernesto, "We did good, amigo."

"We resurrected her from the dead like Jesus!" exclaimed Ernesto as he blessed himself, kissed his fingers, and offered them to heaven.

"I wouldn't go that far."

As the old war bird leveled off the backside of the mountain, Soggy Dry Lake stood in front of them like a huge bone china plate. The opalescent, circular fifty-five square miles of pure white sand stood in front of the flyers like a mirror image of the moon. The dry lake was once an ancient sea before the climate changed it into the great Mojave Desert. Sharks' teeth and marine fossils could still be found around the fringes of this vast expanse of sand.

Jake talked into his cell phone, and headlights flicked on from an area near the far edge of the lake. The light from the parked vehicle cast an eerie glow over the landscape that reminded E.D. of an old Dracula movie. Jake tapped E.D. on the shoulder and asked, "Will you please land us near those lights?"

"It will be my pleasure, sir."

Jake hated to be called sir, but he was too caught up in the exhilaration of the moment to comment any further.

E.D. feathered the controls with such precision that the landing was as smooth as water flowing from a tap. "Wait here and keep the rotors spinning. I'll only be a minute." Jake grabbed the duffel from under the seat and leaped from the skids like a teenager. The fifty-pound bag looked like it was filled with helium as he darted across the blowing sands. He hugged two people at the waiting car. They were truly happy to see Jake. He handed the duffel to the smaller of the two, while the other person handed Jake a manila envelope. They threw the heavy parcel into the trunk of an Audi A8 and sped off into the night.

Jake jumped back into the waiting bird and exclaimed at the top of his lungs, "Our work here is done! Onward and upward we must fly!" Jake looked like he just saved the world, and maybe in his own convoluted way did just that. The fifty pounds of marijuana were off to a cancer hospice where the magic herb would help dying patients get welcomed relief from the devastating side effects of chemotherapy. Besides cancer patients, returning GWAT (Global War on Terror) vets were experimentally given weed in the treatment of PTSD. That really made Jake happy because he had suffered the scourge of that affliction most of his own life. He'd treated his own PTSD for forty years with the help of the pharmaceutical plant. He had no use for doctors, especially from the VA, and now that they considered this therapy, he was beside himself—in his own way he could help end this waste of humanity.

When E.D. lifted the Huey from the desert floor, she saw happiness in Jake's face. She had to ask him, "What just went down on the dry lake?"

"Oh, it's just a dream of mine finally coming true." She didn't quite understand what he meant, but decided to leave it alone and let Jake revel in his own glory. He was helping a total stranger with an insurmountable task that was unbelievable as well as dangerous. Besides, she was falling in love with his son and wanted Jake to like her.

As they began their ascent, Ernesto noticed the trail of a fast-moving light heading toward them. He gasped and shouted, "Look to your left!" E.D. saw it about the same time and banked the chopper hard to the right. The light passed on their left, just missing them by a fraction of an inch or two. Its burning smells lingered in the cockpit for a long moment.

"What was that?" E.D. gasped.

During the evasive maneuver Jake forgot to fasten his seat belt. He flew across the cockpit, landed on top of E.D., and pushed her hands away from the controls. The aircraft began to pitch and yaw, violently spinning out of control. Ernesto grabbed Jake and ripped his flailing body off E.D. He threw Jake back in his seat. E.D. steadied the crippled bird just before it crashed into the side of the upcoming mountain. With a sigh of relief, the flyers all thanked their lucky stars and waited for the next bad thing to happen.

The flash from the exploded ordnance could be seen all over the valley. Locals would attribute the noise to a military missile gone awry. Mistakes happened all the time in the Mojave. Local residents would probably blow it off as a mistake, but the three occupants of the rattled Huey would know better.

"Diamond's reach must be everywhere," Jake noted aloud.

As the bird crested the mountain peak, loose parts began to fall off the crippled bird. Controlling became more difficult. Rancho Mysterioso came into view when the oil pressure read zero. Black smoke billowed from the engine compartment as the ill-fated crew noticed they were losing altitude. Evasive maneuvering must have shaken loose the oil line, and the engine finally seized. Powerless, the crippled bird started to auto rotate toward terra firma.

E.D. held the controls together with all her strength. They just missed the barn, and the soon-to-be scrap metal hit hard in the pasture behind it. The Huey impacted the soft grass, bounced once, and flipped on its side. The rotors flew off and imbedded into a pine tree. It split in two, smashed into a shed, and reduced it to splinters.

They were dazed, confused, battered and bruised, but alive. Jake stumbled out the permanently crippled bird and kissed the ground. Ernesto ran to Guadalupe. Jake took the unconscious E.D. and extricated her with the brute power of an angry bull and the finesse of a matador. He cradled her in his arms and scurried her away to safety. She awoke in his arms and looked at him and sighed, "My hero, but we must find the secret of the box."

Jake thought to himself, *That box better be worth it!*

12

Diamond paced like a caged pride of hungry lions. He pulled at his transplanted hair until clumps fell to the marble floor. "Who do I have to kill to get the answers I need?" he roared.

As the speed of his maniacal pace increased, his satellite phone rang an obnoxious tone, like fingernails clawing a blackboard. The noise reverberated throughout the massive structure. He liked it that way because he had to control everything at all times. Frothing at the mouth he screamed, "What?" into the handset.

On the other end, Dragaminov, trying to sound professional, asked his boss if the line was secure.

Diamond furiously growled, "This is my own satellite. Why wouldn't it be secure, you Russian twit?"

Dragaminov bit his tongue and replied, "We are at Mr. Strutch's ranch in Malibu. No one is here. We searched the place thoroughly but found nothing except a few animals in the pasture."

"Wait there for that pain-in-the-ass daughter of his, Johnson, and whoever else she has with her and get me the box!" Diamond snarled.

"Mr. Johnson won't be a problem because he and his car are at the bottom of the lake. Two of my comrades took care of him. They went into the lake, but survived."

"Good! When you retrieve the box, bring it to me at once." Happy to think that Johnson was out of the picture, Diamond looked down from his balcony and marveled at his new toy, an electronic wind harp. Tightly strung piano wires were placed in the shape of a horizontal harp. Hundreds of tiny, strategically placed air jets forced air onto the strings, and a powerful computer controlled the airflow to create beautiful music. To achieve a perfect sound, the strings had to be so tight that the slightest vibration would not create feedback. Instead of a soothing classical sound, Diamond had the song "I'm From Texas, Screw You" twanging from the strings. That song spoke to him in a way only his sick mind could appreciate.

After a few minutes of listening to his favorite song, he went humming to his study. Diamond eased into a massive throne-like chair. In fact, it was a throne; the shah's priceless golden jewel-encrusted throne. Diamond had replaced the solid gold Iranian crest with an oil well spewing egg-size diamonds from streams of stylized liquid gold. When he sat in the chair, he felt as immortal as an egomaniacal redneck could feel. All the gold in the world couldn't give him what he most lacked——class.

Just as he started to believe his own delusions, the phone scratched. It was the former vice president. Diamond barked, "It's about time your sorry ass got back to me. Where are my oil leases?"

"We have to talk in person about what is happening with the Alaskan wilderness. When can we get together?" the VP asked.

"What about now? Come on over and don't bring any of those secret service clowns with you. I've got a better idea. I'll send my car to pick you up," Diamond snapped.

"Sounds good. Come around the back of my house and I'll be waiting. Don't tell anyone about this meeting," Haney demanded.

"I may look dumb, but I'm not stupid. By the way, bring my leases."

Diamond called the garage and sent one of his chauffeurs to pick up the former VP. He screamed, "Take the Maybock! I'm making billions so why not use billionaire wheels?" As the $300,000 car purred through the massive gates, Diamond fantasized about all the money he would make from destroying the last unspoiled wilderness left in the good old USA. "I don't like that dick; I just like the cash he'll bring to me."

In about an hour the sleek, ultra-luxury machine pulled up to the gate. Diamond left instructions to let them through and lock the place down tighter than a frog's ass. As they were traveling up the drive, all security measures clicked into high gear. Blast shields from an aircraft carrier blocked the way of any intruder; banks of security camera lights blinked a staccato rhythm; and a pack of attack dogs roamed the grounds ready to rip apart anyone foolhardy enough to join the party. Armed security personnel patrolled the entire perimeter. One would think Diamond a bit over-paranoid, and they would be correct.

Diamond greeted Haney with open arms, like a king greeting one of his courtesans. They shook hands and went up to the throne room to do some business. Diamond looked perplexed when he noticed the former VP was empty-handed. When the two powerful men entered the vast office, Diamond poured two snifters of two-hundred-year-old Napoleon brandy from an antique decanter shaped like a cannon. "This is the real stuff. I paid ten thousand bucks a bottle for this brandy. I bought a whole case. Let them eat cake," Diamond gloated. They enjoyed the smooth, powerful elixir. Both of their heads started to spin.

Haney took a deep breath and commented, "This stuff has a kick to it."

"Just like a Texas mule stomping on a diamondback." Diamond thought to himself that the former VP was the snake, he was the mule, and the mule always wins.

Diamond sat on his throne like the king he thought he was, while the former VP had nowhere to sit but below Diamond's eye level. This made Haney uncomfortable because he was a man used to being above other people. Diamond knew this and made sure the seating stayed that way.

After another Napoleon, Diamond got down to business. "Where are my leases? I don't see any papers on your lying politician ass."

former VP Haney hesitated and in a diminutive voice said, "There's a problem. The new administration and that damned EPA blocked drilling in the Alaskan wilderness. The new congress won't pass the legislation needed to make it happen."

Steam started to spew from Diamond's ears when he screamed at the top of his lungs, "What did you say, you political hack? You never would have gotten elected without my money! Where's the cash I gave you to make this happen, you little piss ant?"

"It went into the campaign coffers."

"Too bad. Pay me back now!"

"I can't, all the money was spent on the election."

"I waited four years to drill and you say no?" Diamond got so mad that he jumped from his throne and hit the former VP over the head with the brandy cannon. Dazed, the now intoxicated ex-public official, with no real power, stumbled to the door with Diamond hot on his heels. The two men pushed and shoved each other like a couple of schoolyard bullies with no weak kids to push around. In a flash, Diamond shoved the now bleeding politician over the rail, and the flailing combatant fell directly onto the wind harp.

Haney's body was sliced to pieces like a hardboiled egg. The harp made an awful sound like a grotesque funeral dirge. Blood splashed over the rotunda. The blue Carrera marble was splattered with his blood. The whole scene looked like a macabre spinning paint wheel from a carnival. The only body part still intact was the VP's bald head, with the omnipresent nasty smirk still on his face that any liberal would love to wipe clean. Diamond gasped, looked at the gore, and sang, "I'm from Texas and I just screwed you!"

Diamond paced in a panic, overlooking the sliced former VP. He got a certain pleasure from killing his former cash cow. His diabolical brain searched for any mistakes he could have made. As far as he knew, no one had any idea he was at his house. The only loose end would be how to get rid of the body. There would be too many questions to answer if the Secret Service investigated the crime scene. It was imperative the carnage be cleaned up and the body disposed of where nobody would find the chunked remains. He shouted to his band of goons to clean up the mess and meet him on his yacht berthed on the Potomac.

"Get my plane ready to fly back to my ranch and erase any footage of the dead sleazy politician from any camera feed around the entire place. Make sure there isn't a drop of DNA from that polecat anywhere. If anyone asks, tell them I went back to the Lone Star State this afternoon."

Diamond opened a secret door behind a bookcase in the library. "That shah really made getting away pretty slick." He pushed a button on a first edition of Silas *Marner*, by George Eliot, a story about a miser who counted his gold every night. Diamond related to the story. The door slid open and followed an underground passage to another secret door in his boathouse on the riverbank.

When he ascended from the secret passage, there was a 250-foot motor yacht berthed on the river. *Black Gold* shined from the transom. It was lit up like a gaudy Las Vegas hotel. Equipped with a swimming pool and helipad, the boat resembled a floating city. A black Bell Ranger helicopter, with a gold D, was perched at the ready on the rear of the behemoth vessel, like a dark angel ready to carry its passengers on a journey straight to hell. Diamond barked, "Dump this diced slab of meat out past the continental shelf! Make sure he sinks to the bottom and never comes up! Call me when the deed is done."

All the Russian thug could say was "Yes sir, Mr. Diamond."

His private jet lifted above the nation's capital, and Diamond gloated that he had killed the former second most powerful man in the country. He was more upset about losing the billions still safely protected underground. "Oh well, at least I'll have the corner on the hydrogen market."

As he jetted across the country, Diamond reevaluated his plan to secure the box. He realized that the box was not as important as where it would lead. "Why not let Strutch's pain-in-the-ass daughter find it for me?" He picked up the satellite phone, told Dragaminov to fall back, let E.D. open the box, and monitor the entire proceeding. "Wire the whole ranch and dedicate a satellite to her every move. Blow the entire place off the map when she leaves. Don't let her know what you're doing and don't underestimate her. She is no ordinary girl"

Diamond was exhausted from the dastardly deeds of the day. He fell asleep and dreamed of billions of dollars floating into his own private banks.

For about an hour Dragaminov and his henchmen wired explosives to some overhanging boulders above Strutch's house. The plan would be to create a landslide and crash the house into the sea. One Russian retreated to higher ground and waited for E.D. to arrive.

13

Junior and I rolled into Rancho Mysterioso; the entire place was a buzz of activity. Everyone scurried around making sure the pile of junk that was once a flying machine did not pose any more of a hazard than it already had been. E.D. and Ernesto stacked the pieces of the fallen aircraft in a huge pile while Jake carted them away to his personal landfill with a front-end loader. He wanted the whole pile out of sight, out of mind. Ernesto wielded an exothermic cutting torch to create manageable pieces.

As Jake lifted the rear seat, E.D. noticed the charred manila envelope. Bits of charred hundred-dollar bills floated into the cool mountain air. Most of the profit from this evening's transaction had been relegated to dust. Jake's only reply was "Easy come, easy go. At least we're still in one piece." E.D. handed what was left to Jake and sighed.

Her melancholy evaporated when she saw Junior. She flung a piece of metal into the bucket and ran to him, beaming. She threw her arms around his massive neck and wrapped her legs around his waist. "I'm so glad to see you're still as handsome as the last time I saw you." She was covered with soot and grime, but Junior didn't care. All he wanted to do was gaze into the love light shining from those beautiful green eyes. The two young lovers forgot the current situation for just a second and enjoyed each other's essence, but E.D. was still on a mission. The spell broke when she realized that the box needed to be opened.

She bellowed, "Let's get the box opened. By the way, how is Nakai?"

"He's a big strong dog and will be up and about in no time. He needs to stay at the vet's for a few more days. Jerry has a tale or two to tell, however."

With that opening staring me in the face, I told the gang about my house, the pine cone, the ER, Dragaminov's thugs, and my Porsche at the bottom of the lake. Jake looked at me with concern, but what the others went through was just as harrowing. We lost quite a lot of possessions that evening, but the mystery of the box still loomed like the end of a rainbow. Everyone silently looked at each other and smiled a halfway grin. *I just love nonverbal communication,* I thought.

I still couldn't believe the sheriff or the Forest Service hadn't sniffed around. We must have led charmed lives or were just biding our time until the whole unbelievable nightmare came crashing down on top of us like a flaming meteor. Maybe there was more to E.D. than met the eye. I was too far into this adventure to quit now. Even though I'd been banged up, I hadn't broken yet. I felt recharged and I couldn't wait to see this mission to fruition. My being a klutz was a hindrance, but I'd give it my all.

E.D. shifted gears on a dime. This red-headed dynamo began barking orders like a Paris Island drill instructor. "Let's get moving. We need to get to Malibu before sunrise. I'd like to get the box opened before Diamond finds my dad. I'm worried that Diamond will get to him before we can secure the contents of the box."

Before E.D. could insist that we get moving, Guadalupe scurried in from the kitchen. Her brown eyes, big as saucers, looked at us with loving wisdom. The diminutive Guatemalan quietly begged us to have some food before we went any further on our quest for the truth. Junior's eyes lit like a Christmas tree. "Yes, let's eat. I'm starving!" I knew that Junior always craved food and acted like he was starving. How could one person eat so much food? We looked at each other and even taskmaster E.D. could not resist a meal created with such love.

As our famished horde entered the house, mouth-watering smells enveloped and dazzled all of our senses. The aroma of freshly baked bread wafted over the entire mountain. The table was set with the finest bone china that Guadalupe made in her pottery studio above the victory garden. Waterford crystal glassware rang out with any whispering breeze that blew by.

Guadalupe outdid herself as she usually did, but this particular meal was extra special. An arugula and anchovy salad with royal palm hearts, roasted red peppers, and artichoke hearts was arranged on our plates like an impressionist painting. A light-golden truffle and saffron vinaigrette was splashed over the colorful concoction. Again, all of our senses overloaded. E.D. looked in amazement, took a healthy bite of the antioxidant delight, and smiled. "Where did you learn how to make this wonderful salad?"

"The Food Channel." Everyone laughed, caught up in the culinary delight, the gastronomic extravaganza, and for a moment forgot about the mountainous task at hand.

Ernesto filled our glasses with a delicate red wine from the vineyards of his native Guatemala. The claret slithered down our throats like the gods lubricated. Next came the main course of lightly panseared panko-encrusted abalone steaks with marinated asparagus spears and spinach almandine. The food was as beautiful as it was tasty. Ernesto popped the cork on another bottle of wine and filled our glasses in a flash. We all enjoyed this banquet with the gusto of a stampeding buffalo herd. Everyone but Junior was stuffed to the gills. He had seconds of everything.

We were ready for a food coma when Guadalupe brought a tray of freshly made maple crème brûlée and a bottle of Canadian ice wine. She took a propane torch from the kitchen and caramelized the sugar coating to a hardened masterpiece. The tastes of the hot crème brûlée and the cold of the ice wine complemented each other like a perfect marriage. All I could think was "Eat, drink, and be merry, for tomorrow we all might not feel very well." Wait a minute. We didn't need any more negative vibes. Life for now was still as good as it got!

When all the food disappeared, E.D. sprang to her feet and tried to motivate us to leave Rancho Mysterioso before the table was cleared. This girl must have lightning in her veins. She rarely stopped. Exhausted, I needed to rest my sixty-something-year-old body before it disintegrated. I suggested we rest for a few hours and leave at the crack of dawn. Junior was already asleep in a chair while the rest of us, excluding E.D. of course, crashed. Reevaluating the situation E.D. caved in and said, "I guess you are right. Get some shut-eye and I'll wake everyone just before the dawn breaks." Even before her exclamation everyone was asleep. Even E.D. fell asleep in Junior's arms. Sleep was good. The only person awake was Guadalupe. The cook was always the last to sleep.

14

As promised, E.D. woke us up before the roosters crowed. Guadalupe brewed coffee in the kitchen. Half asleep, we sat around the table sipping coffee and freshly squeezed orange juice, and we ate Guadalupe's cherry walnut muffins. E.D. went over our plans for the day's activities. She had figured everything down to the last detail. Her plan developed a wrinkle when Jake told her, "Ernesto and I need to stay here to finish getting rid of that pile of junk from the pasture. Give a shout if you need us, and we'll be there like the cavalry, only on the ground." Sadly he couldn't swoop down from the sky. He needed time to digest the loss of his antique whirlybird. The rest of us understood the situation. Jake always had our backs.

We loaded the Cruiser with all the firepower at our disposal. Guadalupe made us a picnic basket filled with goodies. Junior snatched the food and waved Rancho Mysterioso a fond farewell. Jake, Ernesto, and Guadalupe waved back as we slid around the dusty trail in search of truth and bound for glory.

Junior drove his vehicle smoothly and navigated the switchbacks like a Formula One driver. E.D. rode shotgun, checking her iPhone for messages and who knows what else. I just kicked back and listened to the Grateful Dead play my favorite song, "Ripple," which was the song that kept me sane when I came back from Vietnam. Jerry Garcia's melodious tones always put me in a good place.

After a two-hour drive down mountain roads and the Southern California freeway system, we finally saw the Pacific. The morning fog had not yet burned off, but the smell of the ocean felt refreshing. E.D. took out an iPad from her pack while clutching the box, and she punched in some numbers. A steady beep resonated while she intently looked at the screen. I asked inquisitively, "What are you doing?"

"Oh, I'm just checking the area for any sign of Diamond. This is satellite positioning software to keep tabs on the bad guys." Without warning a drone came buzzing by. It silently circled the ridgeline above our position.

"How did you get a drone to help survey the area?"

She just said, "My dad has a lot of unique toys." Again my mind was fully blown.

We climbed up a canyon road to a bluff overlooking Strutch's ranch. From this vantage point we saw pastures, a barn and outbuildings. A huge house was perched on a bluff overlooking the ocean. The fog lifted and various shades of blue twinkled from the cold Pacific water below. A truly breathtaking sight, man and nature melded together beautifully. Again, my mind was blown. I couldn't believe that a close friend of mine I hadn't seen in over forty years lived only seventy-five miles away. *Wow, the aftermath of war strikes again!*

E.D. pointed out a hidden bunker in the hillside. We entered the structure through a hatch disguised as a huge rock. E.D. moved it away with one hand. I felt the boulder and it was hollow fiberglass that looked real. E.D. laughed. "Movie magic. This is Hollywood, you know." Inside was a maze of computers, monitors, and sophisticated communication equipment. Strutch had the whole place wired. A staccato of beeps rang out a disaster warning from a console. E.D. viewed the screen and noticed that Diamond had also bugged the entire compound. She pushed a few buttons and exclaimed, "All done. I disabled the surveillance devices and jammed any satellite transmissions sent to foil our plans. We have to hurry because it takes less than an hour to reprogram a jammed satellite. Junior, will you please stay here and cover our backs? There is a Remington 700 sniper rifle and powerful binoculars in that cabinet. I think you know how to use them. Call us if there is any movement. I can control my dad's other defenses from my iPad. Jerry and I will go down to the house and hopefully open the box." She gave Junior a kiss for luck while we climbed down the hill to the house.

Strutch's house was a giant glass and stainless steel pyramid overlooking the blue Pacific. From the Pacific Coast Highway below, the structure was nearly invisible. While you could see everything below, no one could discern that the pointed structure was a house. Most of the structure was built into the hillside. Chaparral grew around everything, making the house look almost like the rest of the local habitat. It was quiet up here. The only sound was the whispering wind, the crashing waves, and the faint buzz from the drone.

We approached the house, and the labyrinth of tropical plants that grew over our heads looked like an impenetrable jungle. Palm trees with orchids growing from the trunks guided us to the entrance. I guess you can take the man out of the jungle, but the jungle still remains seared in your mind. I would never forget the jungle, but Strutch took the jungle with him, bringing only the beauty without the danger. Even the shadows made you feel safe. I hoped that if and when I met Strutch again, I could commend him for his gardening skills. This place dripped with irony.

E.D. tapped the side of the door, and a steel panel popped open. An eight-by-eight lighted black pad glowed in front of us. A light beam shined from the door at eye level. She slapped her right palm on the illuminated pad, looked into the beam, and with a creak, a massive door slid open. Strutch had palm and retina scanners. This place was locked down like a vault in Fort Knox.

We entered a unique environment only Strutch could create. The walls were covered with a massive array of speakers that echoed perfect sound throughout the entire dwelling. The glass walls pushed the sound to the pinnacle of the structure. Racks of vinyl surrounded the walls. There were thousands of records, a complete music library, alphabetically catalogued by genre. I wanted to dive into the stacks and see how they sounded in this pyramid.

In the center of this unique home, a spiral staircase rose up to a platform where the king's chamber stood. E.D. sprinted to the top, three stairs at a time. I followed at a slower pace, trying to digest what I had just witnessed. When I finally reached the chamber, I had to sit down. My heart felt like it would pop from my chest. When my heart rate felt normal again, I noticed a large twenty-six-inch telescope and an Australian aboriginal didgeridoo. E.D. put on a thick leather glove and pushed a button on the wall. A panel on the west side of this directionally orientated building slid open, allowing the sweet Pacific air to waft over us. Each side of the pyramid faced true north, south, east, and west exactly like the ancient pyramids. As time passed I began to feel energized. Was this all in my mind, or was this an effect of pyramid power? I read books on pyramids in the seventies. The way I felt made me think back to those good old hippie days. "Right on!"

E.D. took the didgeridoo from its rack and blew into the mouthpiece. The drone reverberated through the structure and sounded like a South African soccer game. The tone of this long horn, *vuvuzela*, made the hair on my arms stand at attention. At that moment I felt a strange peace envelope me. Wow, Strutch must have unleashed a mystical power from two ancient cultures. This spiritual experience changed how I looked at the world. I wished Jake were here so he could find peace from all of his demons.

While I was on this spiritual high, a flapping noise broke the spell. A huge peregrine falcon fluttered through the open wall and perched on E.D.'s gloved arm. As the raptor's wings settled down, he looked into my eyes. At that moment I realized that our cause was just. E.D., with the delicate touch of a surgeon, removed a band from the now docile bird of prey's leg. She placed him on a perch and nonchalantly said, "This is Perry, my dad's falcon." My jaw instantly dropped, but nothing could be weirder than the massive weirdness of the last few days.

Perry intently looked at E.D. while she carefully removed a small microchip and smiled. "We can finally open the box now. Maybe some of my questions will be answered." She took the box and placed it on a table in the center of the room; she aligned it to the compass points, where the king's sarcophagus would stand. She placed the chip on the top of the titanium band choking the box. After a few seconds the band began to vibrate. "Stand back," E.D. shouted. I obeyed the warning and watched the vibrating restraint pop free.

What just happened? Was it the power of the pyramid? Was it a parlor trick? Was it modern technology? Maybe it was magic? I had studied the box for the last few days, and was certain that it could not be opened.

E.D. tapped diagonal corners and the lid moved and popped open. She carefully slid the cover off and we both inquisitively looked at the contents. There was a piece of paper and three knives. The knives had a series of grooves carved into the sides. Ancient writing covered both sides of the blades. One had an obsidian blade with an emerald the size of a chicken egg that capped the strange-looking object. The second knife had a bone or ivory blade capped by a yellow topaz and was pointed at the end to look like a bird beak. The third was made of petrified wood with a strange-looking clear turquoise, the familiar pale blue color surrounding the center.

E.D. paid no attention to these curious artifacts and angrily snatched the paper. As she read it, a distinctly confused look showed on her face. "What is this? We risked our lives for a recipe for cherries jubilee?" In disgust she threw the paper on the floor.

I'd never seen her mad. This positive, hard-charging girl had human emotions after all. While she fumed I looked at the paper and it really was a recipe for cherries jubilee. Once I made cherries jubilee with Grand Marnier and when I lit the flaming dessert, the torched alcohol flared and almost burned the house down. Scorch marks reminded me that danger lurked everywhere, especially when you didn't pay attention to the details.

On the bottom of the paper were words printed in a mirror image. I didn't have my glasses, so I asked E.D. to read it. She looked more confused as she squinted. She held the paper up to the glass. "The secret is within you. What in the hell does that mean? Let's get out of here before I freak out." She let Perry fly out the window, closed it, and raced down the stairs.

When I finally reached the floor, I noticed a portrait of an elderly woman hanging above a river rock fireplace. The painting looked very old. The old lady's eyes followed me wherever I went. The old woman was a spitting image of E.D. Trying to calm E.D. I asked, "Who is that lady in the picture?" Imagine me trying to calm down E.D.

She frantically said, "Oh that's my dad's grandmother Eva Di Structione. When they immigrated to America, Di Structione was changed to Struction. I was named after her."

I thought for a moment and a light exploded into my brain. I ran to the record stacks and looked in the M section for Barry McGuire. I took out an album and brought it to E.D. "I think I just solved the mystery. Strutch's favorite song in Vietnam was 'Eve of Destruction' by Barry McGuire. How did he know?"

E.D. or Eva Di Structione made a confession. "I was trying to find you when we met by coincidence. My dad knew you would help. I guess he did not tell me how to find the prize in case Diamond purloined the box. He knew that you, as well as everyone else, do not like Diamond. He hoped that you'd be smart enough to figure out this mystery. I'm sorry, Jerry, that I didn't tell you this before."

"It's all right, kid. This monumental adventure has given me my youth back, and it feels pretty good. Let's see what the record has to tell."

I removed the record from its sleeve and found a hermetically sealed plastic bag with writing on both sides. Our eyes bugged from our skulls when what looked like an ancient Aztec codex stared back at us. It looked authentic, but what did I know about ancient texts? I learned a little about the Aztec culture from an anthropology class

I took at Tumbleweed Tech. There also looked to be writings other than Nahuatl, the written language of the Aztec. There were intricate pictograms surrounding the perimeter of the document. Maybe the box itself had something to do with its secrets. "One of my professors was an expert on Aztec textiles. I bet she could decipher this puzzling document," I said.

E.D. placed the codex back inside the box. It was a perfect fit., "I'm glad to see the codex is back where it belongs," she said. E.D. got some color back in her face and asked, "Can you please see if you can get the codex deciphered? I need to take care of some loose ends. I'll take Junior with me. You can use my dad's car."

"Okay, but I need to play this record first." I blasted "Eve of Destruction" from Strutch's massive sound system.

"You don't believe we're on the eve of destruction" filled the entire space with Barry McGuire's melodious, gravelly, baritone notes. I wondered if this song would be a foreshadowing of our demise, or even better, Diamond rotting in a jail cell. In actuality we had only solved part of the mystery. I still hadn't a clue where the codex would take us next.

We exited the pyramid with renewed gusto. E.D. called Junior and told him that we were coming out. "Will you cover us while we go to the garage?" We traveled out the back and entered a barn that acted as a garage. "There's my dad's car that you can take." She pulled the cover off a shiny new copper-colored Tesla that glistened like twelve and a half million new pennies. This was a 125,000-dollar electric sports car. I started salivating when I realized that I would be driving this land rocket, which would go nearly 130 miles per hour. E.D. flipped me the keys and the box. She warned me to keep it close to the speed limit. I thought to myself it would be hard to comply with her wishes. I jumped into the cockpit with a little trouble. The compact cockpit was a little too small for my long legs, but I settled into the seat like a banana into its peel. I fired that beauty up, and to my surprise, the engine was as quiet as a feather falling to a bale of cotton. Electric cars don't make noise.

As I would learn later, this engineering marvel was different because it had an experimental hydrogen fuel cell that Strutch was working on for Lotus, the English automaker that built the Tesla. This car would travel three hundred miles on a single charge, but would go a lot further on hydrogen. The only byproduct from burning hydrogen is water vapor. No wonder Diamond wanted it all. He wanted to control all forms of energy everywhere.

E.D. jumped into the passenger seat and we drove back to the bunker.

Dragaminov's mercenary ran down the hill with a detonator clutched in his fist. When the Russian thug had a perfect view of the property, he pushed the button that would destroy Strutch's pyramid. Nothing happened. He was perplexed that there was no explosion. Through field glasses he noticed the main detonation wire had come loose from the bomb. He had to reattach it before the pyramid could detach itself and slide into the sea. Anyone unlucky enough to be riding below on the Pacific Coast Highway would be swept away with the rest of the landslide. These creeps didn't care about human lives, except for their own.

As the henchman moved toward the explosives, he had to run into the open. Junior noticed him on one of the monitors. He took aim with the Remington. Just as he had a bead on the culprit, Perry swooped down from the sky. With outstretched talons the raptor dug into the intruder's scalp. Strutch must have trained Perry to be a kind of watch falcon. The Russian screamed bloody murder. With blood running down his face, the bad guy stumbled blindly in excruciating pain. As he ran faster, Perry dug deeper. With blood running down his face, the struggling thug was temporarily blinded. Not paying attention where he was going, the Russian gangster fell over the cliff. While he was in full flight, Perry ripped off his scalp and dropped it at E.D.'s feet. "Good job, Perry!"

The bloody body landed on top of the bed of a semi-truck filled with spinach. It crashed through the netting covering the load and landed softly into someone's future salad. He was lucky he still breathed. If he were Popeye there wouldn't be enough spinach to grow the ex-Soviet a new head of hair. If he ever woke up, he probably shouldn't look into any mirrors for a while.

Meanwhile Junior noticed the detonator lying in a pool of Russian blood. He squeezed off a shot, but missed. After a quick adjustment to his scope, he fired again. This time his aim was true, disintegrating the deadly control unit into a harmless pile of junk. E.D. jumped out of the car and ripped the rest of the wires from the inert explosive and stashed it in the barn. After all, this was Malibu. Maybe this trash could become a fixture in someone's sculpture garden, or adorn the local landfill. *Wow,* I thought, *I must be losing my sense of reality. I need to focus on what needs to be done and not go tangential.*

Junior was relieved that he did not have to shoot anyone today. While dodging another bullet, or should I say bomb, we left the ranch in two clouds of dust. I was on a mission to try to get the codex deciphered, while the two youngsters would do what they needed to do, whatever that would be. As I crested the hill onto the main road, Perry flew right over my head. He tipped a wing and it looked like he smiled. Could birds smile? I may never know the answer, but it was something else to ponder.

15

Diamond felt safe in his ranch stronghold. A landmass the size of Connecticut insulated him from the plebeians, and that was how he liked it. He was not concerned that he had just killed the former vice president of the United States. He had no remorse and felt no guilt about the deed. The only remorse was for the billions of dollars that evaporated when the former VP was sliced and diced. He was not worried about being prosecuted for this heinous crime. As far as he was concerned, the dastardly deed would go unpunished because he was above the law. Money would always win over conscience.

Now that the former VP was history, Diamond could concentrate on the box and the hydrogen facility. At the top of his lungs he snickered and exclaimed, "If I can't drill in Alaska, I might as well go green. Just think what those tree-hugging hippies will do when I become their champion. Right on! Unfortunately, the only green I give a damn about is a pile of good old American greenbacks."

A satellite message from the Black Gold came streaming into Diamond's inscription device. Without trepidation he yanked the paper from the machine and read what he wanted to hear. "The deed is done. The package rests comfortably in three thousand feet of salt water. Waiting further instructions."

Diamond replied, "Head south, cross the Panama Canal, and head for Mexico. I'll tell you where to go later." As he was shredded the document, a news stream appeared on his monitor. "Former Vice President Haney is missing from his Washington home. Secret Service agents have no clues of his location or the circumstances surrounding his disappearance. Foul play is not suspected at this time, although all scenarios remain open. Stay tuned for further developments."

Smiling, Diamond boasted out loud, "I just got away with a snake extermination. I never liked that fork-tongued serpent politician. Good riddance! That will teach you to mess with the Big D. Maybe I'll see you in hell. I just might buy the place at a fire sale and screw the devil in the process. It's just wonderful to be me."

This self-serving egomaniac was becoming more dangerous than ever. The quest for wealth and power remained his only motivation for living. He truly believed that he would never attain happiness until he owned everything, and there would never be enough to satisfy his unrealistic goal. He had no friends, or anyone who even liked him in the least. He didn't care who he screwed over in the process. He believed that throwing money around insulated him from being a decent human being. He believed that being god-like was not out of the question. This delusional thinking would be his undoing, but not now. For now he was on a roll.

Just as he began to gloat over the prospects of owning it all, Dragaminov burst his bubble. "My comrades failed to eradicate Mr. Strutchion's ranch, and we lost contact with the girl and Mr. Johnson."

"What happened?"

"You told me to leave one man to watch the ranch and destroy everything and retrieve the box. One man wasn't enough to accomplish the task. A huge bird ripped his scalp off and he fell off a cliff. He is in a hospital."

"Wait a minute. You told me that Johnson drowned."

"I was wrong. He survived and was with the girl at the ranch."

"Find them and get me the box. If you fail me this time, I will get someone else to do the deed. Get over to Rancho Mysterioso and make that Jake guy tell where the rest of his friends are hiding. I will not accept failure of any kind. Do you hear me?"

"Yes, Mr. Diamond."

Diamond grabbed a clump of transplanted hair and pulled it from its roots. He screamed, "I need to kill something, something big!" He ran out of the house and into his ten-stall garage. He jumped into his fully stocked, ready-for-war Humvee and headed for his private game reserve about twenty miles from the main compound. As he drove his vehicle of military might, froth streamed from his lips. "I need blood on my hands. I don't care what kind. I just need it to flow freely."

An electrically fenced three- thousand-acre private game preser loomed just over the ridge from where Diamond drove. A clou dust followed him like an angry herd of buffalo. He took a fully ed M-16 from a scabbard near the door and emptied a thirt clip into the air. After about ten seconds the banana clip w Cordite and burned powder filled the air with the pung of war. Diamond loved that smell. It made him feel like h -like power over life and death.

As he approached his private killing field, a pra tuck his head from a comfortable burrow. The Humvee's r awakened him from a deep sleep. The cute rodent sniffe and looked around to see what the racket was about. Dia iced his fuzzy little head and threw an M-25 fragmentatic e at the burrow. The concussion blew the defenseless critt nis sanctuary, and the shrapnel ripped his body to pieces. just snickered. The feeling was not as rewarding as fraggir nker filled with innocent peasants. "Prairie dogs or gooks, the il history and I killed them dead. Hooray for me!"

After blowing away the defenseless little creature, Diamond's bloodlust increased. A deranged psychopath, he needed bigger prey. He pressed a button on his dashboard and the chain link gate opened. As the gate rolled open, the electricity was automatically shut down. The fence was reenergized after he drove through the portal. He had all the bases covered when it came to his own safety.

Inside Diamond's private killing field roamed hundreds of animals, some endangered, from all over the world. Diamond was not interested in preserving species. He just wanted to kill them. As he drove the most timid ran for cover. He wasn't interested in them. He needed to kill something dangerous.

He noticed a huge shadow moving through a thicket of trees. The ground shook as a massive body showed itself. To Diamond's surprise the shadow materialized into a black rhino. *What a stroke of luck!* he thought. A dangerous, endangered beast was moving into range of Diamond's field of fire.

He leapt from the driver's seat and opened the hatch to the turret, where a fifty-caliber machine gun stood at the ready. With eyes wide, Diamond placed an ammunition belt into the receiver and slammed the bolt shut. He wasn't the kind of hunter to kill a rhino with a spear. That was for mere mortals. He always made sure the odds were in his favor. He didn't get to be the fourth richest person on the planet by playing fair. He believed that killing things just made him dangerously stronger.

The black armored beast charged at full speed when he noticed the metal beast. Diamond squeezed off one round just to get the animal's attention. The projectile grazed his shoulder. The round had little effect except for making him mad. The agitated animal screamed as he charged. Diamond fired his weapon at its full capacity. As the rounds exploded from the muzzle, he screamed at the top of his lungs an inhuman screech that would curl the toes of any decent person. Diamond surely was far from being decent. He enjoyed his devilish scream. It made him feel powerful.

As the rhino got closer Diamond focused on the blood spurting from deep wounds in the dying beast. There must have been twenty wounds over his body. Blood pumped from the nostrils like a fountain of sorrow. Diamond was bewildered that the beast was still breathing, still charging. When the creature was ten feet from the vehicle, Diamond's fifty jammed. He tried to clear the debris from the breach, but because he had fired the weapon nonstop, it couldn't be accomplished until it cooled. In the futile process Diamond burned the flesh off the palm of his hand.

As he removed his burning hand from the weapon, the rhino struck the Humvee with his last dying breath. His horn pierced the metal skin of Diamond's lofty perch, ripped his pants, and stuck into his leg. The rhino looked directly into Diamond's eyes with contempt as he died. The horn tore the vehicle's skin like a can opener. The Humvee was one of the older models that Diamond got for free thanks to his friends in the DOD. This version of the vehicle was recalled to beef up the body. Many of the older models were inflicted with too many fatal blows from IEDs, small-arms fire, and now a rhinoceros horn.

Diamond extracted the horn from his leg with a jolt. As the point his own blood spurted from the wound on his leg. Unlike the exsanguinated dead rhino stuck to the thin-skinned vehicle, Diamond had the resources to stop the bleeding. He took an envelope filled with powder that instantly coagulated wounds, and spilled the contents onto his laceration. Within a minute the wound closed and Diamond was good to go. War had always been the mother of invention, and in this case it saved the life of a despicably evil man. Technology didn't discriminate.

Diamond had to get out the driver's door to cut the horn from the rhino's ever-stiffening body. As he went to the other side of the now horny vehicle, an ill feeling crept over him like a shroud. The eyes of all of his doomed creatures that he hadn't killed were looking straight through him. They wanted to rip him to shreds. The feeling of doom persisted while he cut the Humvee free. As he cut the last bit of horn free from the fallen animal, it crashed onto the ground with a thud, pinning his foot. He tried to free himself and the air was filled with screaming, snarling, and trumpeting. The animals were pissed.

Diamond dislodged his foot and jumped over the rhino's body. Tires spun as he made his escape. He shook uncontrollably, visibly frightened. He wanted no part of being killed by his own game. The freed horn fell harmlessly to the floor. He took a bite out of the horn and instantly felt better. The fear left him as fast as its onset. He shouted out loud, "This is no aphrodisiac, just me, Harlan Diamond, choosing to exterminate anything I choose. I do feel like a god!"

As the gate closed behind him, lions, tigers, and bears clawed at the fence, trying to get a piece of Diamond. He just pushed the button on the dash and the horde of angry animals retreated, whimpering. Animals were no match for three thousand volts of electricity. With disdain, Diamond turned and flipped off the retreating animals and loudly exclaimed, "You didn't get me this time, but be assured I will get each and every one of you and scorch your once happy home into mineral soil!"

On the way back to his ranch, the Humvee started shaking uncontrollably. The dying rhino had bent the drive shaft, and the entire assembly eventually fell to the ground. This made Diamond angry. He grabbed the horn and an RPG from the dead hulk. He walked up a hill not far from where his once-feared war machine stood. He fired the favorite weapon of the third world. With a swoosh, the RPG hit the gas tank. Once a symbol of American might, the Humvee exploded and was reduced to scrap metal. He called the ranch and told them pick him up in the helicopter. When they asked his location, he just laughed. "Just look for the big ball of fire. You can't miss it. Hurry up. Killing makes me hungry."

As the chopper flew Diamond back to his ranch, he screamed, "Let's go and shoot some wetbacks. I'll give you ten thousand dollars for each one I kill." The pilot ignored his maniac boss's ranting and flew back to the ranch, then immediately quit. Diamond wondered why he couldn't keep employees for very long, but with all his money he could keep a revolving door filled with new people. He bid his former pilot ill will and ordered his chef to cook him some bloody red meat.

16

Driving an automobile like a Tesla elevated my lust for adventure. The quiet machine's suspension droves like it was riding on rails. No way this engineering masterpiece could lose control under normal situations. Driving on the open road in an open car made me feel in tune with the pulse of the universe. The feeling made me almost forget the turmoil of the last few days. The experience was just what I needed to clear my head and focus on our mission. First I needed to scourge on massive quantities of sushi.

I drove north on US 1 to Zuma Beach to one of my favorite sushi bars. Zuma Sushi sits overlooking the blue Pacific. As I pulled into the parking lot, heads turned when the stealthy copper sports car silently slid slowly in front of the restaurant. The lack of internal combustion noise startled them. I had to explain that the car ran on odorless, quiet electricity. Everyone smiled with the realization that a green world was actually a possibility, and not just the pipe dream oil companies wanted us to believe.

Before I went into the restaurant, I gave my former anthropology professor Dr. Ferdan at Tumbleweed Tech a call. She was enthralled with the prospect of deciphering a new Aztec codex; she could meet with me in the morning and looked forward to checking the authenticity of what I had to show her. She was puzzled when I asked her not to tell anyone about our conversation, but I told her I would explain everything in person. As I switched off my phone, an overpowering scent of Japanese cooking enveloped my entire being. My mouth began to water. I had that uncontrollable urge to scourge.

I strolled into the front door of the sushi bar and was struck by the beauty of my surroundings. A simple elegance was enough to set a tranquil mood. Contrasting black and white walls dominated the décor, with the exception of an avalanche of orchids, spilling brilliant color over the whole room. Every color of the spectrum was represented. A golden Buddha silently sat in the corner and scanned out over the ocean. If he were alive, what would he think of today's world? I could only pray that he would think we were on the right track to enlightenment, whatever that meant today.

For some reason I was the only customer and had the entire place to myself. The owner strolled into the back door carrying a freshly caught Hamachi (yellowtail) that he speared in the ocean below his restaurant. The tasty fish dripping with saltwater, the happy chef cleaned and filleted this beauty before my eyes. I inquisitively watched as he masterfully wielded his knife with the skill of a samurai surgeon. I was totally enthralled while the waitress poured me a glass of cold sake that looked like nonfat milk. The sweet elixir slid down my throat with an avalanche of flavor. I was ready to sample the fruits of the sea, where all life came from.

The chef handed me a bowl of sumomono, a seafood salad that opened my palate to a truly unique dining experience. Smiling he said, "You are in for a treat. You can't get any fresher fish than this one that I just plucked from the ocean."

I replied, "In that case you can serve me Omakase." That is where the chef decides what to serve. His eyes sparkled when I gave him permission to guide me through a gastronomic journey of his own design.

The first dish was fresh Hamachi livers. They exploded in my mouth. I never tasted anything that acted like I was one with the sea. The next dish was Uni (sea urchin) with a raw quail egg on top. This strong-tasting creature always reminded me of when life crawled from the sea. I could only imagine what that felt like. The next was Hamachi Kama. This dish was the cooked cheek of the fish. The concentration of fatty oils made this the most flavorful part. Though you must watch for bones, the heavenly taste lingers. After you sample

Hamachi Kama a deep sip of sake and a bite of pickled ginger gets you ready for the next course. Kampai (Bottoms up)!

The next course was a Nato (fermented bean curd) hand roll. This cone of dried seaweed surrounded rice, arrowroot, mint, and the sticky, fermented soybeans. Most people don't like its ammonia flavor.

An interesting fact of its discovery makes for a grand story. During World War II while the Marine Corps laid siege on Okinawa, Japanese soldiers ran out of food. In the rear of a bunker they found cases of fermented soybeans. In better times they would have thrown away the spoiled food. The starving soldiers ate the concoction, and to their surprise found it was delicious. Nato gave them the strength to hold out for a few months longer. The Marines never did capture all the Japanese on the island. Come to find out, Nato, in its present form, contains the most complete protein of any food. To this day Nato is a staple of the Japanese people, often eaten at breakfast.

As a former Marine, I had mixed feelings about the discovery of Nato. On one hand I felt bad that the war in Okinawa lasted longer than it should have, and unnecessarily killed more combatants on both sides. On the other hand I felt grateful for the discovery of the world's most complete protein. Every time I enjoyed Nato, I reflected on the sacrifices made during that conflict. Sometimes small increments of good can outweigh enormous evil. People shouldn't let prejudice cloud progress spawned from depravity. If one can show forgiveness and an open mind, the world may yet prosper into a harmonious place.

After a toast to everyone who fell during war, I continued to eat anything put in front of me. The chef was surprised that I didn't balk at anything he served. I scarfed abalone fermented in its own guts, eel, salmon eggs, and an array of fish piled up on decorative plates.

"Bring it on! I like it all!"

I even ate Ama-Ebi (sweet shrimp with tempura heads). I looked at the eyeballs and tentacles as I stuffed them down my throat.

After I devoured most everything in the restaurant, I felt contented. I almost forgot the crisis at hand. Just as I was remembering my mission, the waitress brought me some green tea crème brûlée. Wow! I ate two of my favorite tastes in one bowl. After dessert, I paid the check and bid Zuma Sushi a fond sayonara.

With a full belly and a feeling of bliss, I checked into an old motel overlooking the sea. I sat on a lounge chair with a panoramic view of the Pacific. Water as blue as the sky from whence it came surrounded my field of vision. The air was clear and void of fog. This was a rare day where you could see Catalina Island as clear as looking at your own face in a mirror. Bottlenose dolphins frolicked in the kelp forests beyond the crashing waves. I felt a peacefulness that only comes when you feel safe and are one with nature. I felt guilty for my part in depleting the ocean for my enjoyment. At that point I realized that as human beings we all have far to go to always do the right thing.

I drifted off to a nap for some well-deserved rest. As my lunch digested I fell into a deep sleep. I really hadn't had complete rest since the ordeal of the past few days began. Hours passed before I awoke from my slumber. The sun was sinking slowly below the horizon. As the bright red ball continued on its journey into night, the sky filled with a colorful array of crimson, gold, and purple. The sky looked like it was on fire. The colors danced to their own tune and clung to the last gasp of light. When the sun finally disappeared, the legendary green flash illuminated the sky. For an instant, everything turned green. Then it was gone. If I blinked I would have missed the unbelievable phenomenon. I always thought the green flash was a myth, but like the events of the last few days, my mind was totally blown again. I guess everyone needed an open mind when it came to the thin line between truth and legend.

After sunset, the colors lingered for a long while, then faded into memory. Stars replaced the fire with twinkling wonderment of another kind. Millions of pinpoints of light peeked down from the heavens and teased us with what might be beyond our tiny reality. A white phosphorescence made the ocean glow, mirroring the radiance of the sky. I needed to find out what made the ocean glow like that. I once knew, but the answer escaped me, like the fading sun I had just witnessed. Maybe it was the phosphorescent plankton. I hoped I'd never lose all the knowledge stored between my ears. Knowledge is only temporary, after all, but important if you intend to live a long, productive life.

After contemplating the mysteries of the universe, I got up from my lounging position and retreated to my room, where I immediately fell asleep. As I drifted into an unconscious, restful slumber, I was immediately taken back to the continuing saga of my own horrors of war. Those thoughts manifested themselves on a moment's notice. I had no control.

When it is impossible to live up to what is right, you better be careful. I had to shelve my feelings from the day's events and get on with the tasks at hand. I needed to carefully adjust the fire Hollywood Steve and I plotted earlier. Potential enemy access routes were covered with predetermined fire coordinates. The entire perimeter would be protected with a ring of fire. This time there would be no unwanted friendly rounds thrust onto our position.

I felt as secure as I could under such circumstances. I remembered where I was and the strange events that just took place. I couldn't shake the memory of Tam. He was a small man with a gentle spirit. With soft, wide eyes he looked deeply into each thought. He spoke with an air of confidence that made you listen. He had a lot to say, but unfortunately, I would never benefit from his worldly wisdom. What were his hopes and dreams? Would he have made a difference if he lived? These questions and more would haunt me forever.

I also couldn't shake the hand in that rice paddy. Was there some hidden cosmic meaning or was I just caught up in the allure of this strangest of places? I prayed Buddha's finger wasn't directed toward me.

The monastery grounds seemed tranquil after being so brutally ravaged. The monks attempted to repair the damage. Smiling, they looked through us as if we were not there. The scene was another contradiction. Peace in the midst of war.

At sunset, light dwindled as magic filled the skies. Red raspberry, butterscotch, and plum arcs swirled a heavenly parfait. This colorful display cast a peaceful glow over the landscape. The air cooled as sweet scents of evening blossoms filled my nostrils. Birds chirped the end of the day. All of these sights, smells, and sounds took my breath away. How could a land of dynamic beauty harbor such unthinkable horror? I needed to savor the entire display because danger once again loomed.

While nature was doing her best to display serenity, a multitude of bells tolled from the monastery. The melodies rang out hypnotic tones that reverberated throughout the valley. As light faded, the sound grew louder and faster. Was this a ritual celebration to the end of the day or a sinister plot to guide our enemy toward us? I could do nothing but wonder and enjoy the beat.

As light disappeared, nature's palette swept from purple to gray, than faded to obsidian. As this transformation took place, millions of stars peeked from the heavens, illuminating the skies with celestial brilliance. Night was crystal clear. Right in the midst of these pinpoints of light stood the Southern Cross. These brightest of stars watched over us like a neon sign, without the "Jesus is Coming."

Shadows filled each object with mystery and fear of the unknown. Night creatures felt safe to enter their realm. We are not equipped to navigate without light. Being out of our element made darkness a scary proposition.

Just as I was getting acclimated to this new environment, the bells went silent. In the distance I noticed a flash and heard the agonizing thud of a mortar tube. This was it, payback. The first rounds missed their mark. Accuracy improved, they dialed in on us like we on them. We returned fire toward the flashes with big barrel-wiggling 175's that temporarily silenced our anguish. They achieved their goal and had us in their sights.

The rest of the night was a cat-and-mouse game, played out by probing our lines to find vulnerability. We repelled each half-hearted assault with the ferocity of 174 years of Marine Corps tradition. They were testing for a much larger assault that would come the next night.

Dawn cracked like a mirror as if it didn't care about the night before, but who would get the seven years' bad luck? Could our superior fighting force, which had the resources of the American military industrial complex, overcome the karmic events of the previous day?

The new day illuminated the land with a renewal that was invigorating, but filled with doubt. What did the North Vietnamese Army have in store for us, and could we overcome their siege? Everyone realized the danger. Preparations for the evening's festivities were carefully planned.

Helicopters with reinforcements and armament buzzed over the monastery grounds in preparation for the forthcoming battle. An 81-mm mortar battery and a 106-mm recoilless rifle added to our protection. The 106 packed beehive rounds held 2,400 flashette darts, and when detonated sent out a wall of titanium that rivaled Pickett's charge at Gettysburg. We now had the firepower on hand to repel most any assault.

Patrols were sent out to see if we had inflicted any damage on the enemy. This was like a scene from **The Last of the Mohicans,** *different century, and different conflict. Though they are different, all wars are just as brutal, leaving the glory for pen and paper.*

I realized I hadn't slept in over twenty-four hours and needed to crash now, or tonight's party would have to go on without me. I immediately began dreaming about paddling a canoe down a river in my native New England, the water swift but pleasing. Patchouli, gardenia, and cannabis scents wafted as smiling, naked hippie girls invited me toward the banks. The Grateful Dead's "Let your love light shine on me," echoed from the tree line. Fireworks exploded red, white, and blue, reflected USA across the water.

I paddled feverishly toward the bank, but the current was too strong to navigate. As I passed, the nubile females sadly threw kisses. When I rounded the next bend, the song changed to "Dark Star." The fireworks were replaced with NVA soldiers shooting RPGs at me from both banks. As the rockets whizzed over my head, a ruler-wielding nun shouted, "Repent," while a bishop reminded me of the Confirmation slap across the face. "After all, as a soldier of Christ, if you have to take a life, do so in His name."

After my brief visit with members of the Holy Roman Apostolic church, the raging torrent became still and I saw Jesus Christ and Buddha walking on water. I checked to see if Buddha had all his fingers. Gliding peacefully above the current, they reassured me that if I lived my life honorably, I would survive this ordeal. Which ordeal—the war or this dream? I wasn't sure.

I was trying to make sense out of this subconscious torture when I heard the roar of a waterfall downstream. My canoe was at the mercy of inertia and gravity as the river dropped into a freefalling abyss. I was in midair with no idea where my creaky craft was headed. Which circle of hell would I enter next?

I could see jaws of jagged rocks below coming up fast, and a familiar voice bellowed, "Are you going to sleep all day? We have a war to fight." I awoke in a sweat, hearing Big D booming like a loudspeaker. With his abrasive manner, our clueless leader had saved me from the ending of my dream. I was thankful, but I still wonder what scared me more: my dream or the reality of my current situation. I could always make sense of that dream with the help of psychoactive substances and various amber fluids, but I needed all my wits intact to survive what was in store for us after nightfall.

After sunset the bells tolled and on cue the assault began. It felt like Uncle HO brought all of his relatives to show their displeasure. They threw everything they could carry at us that night: 122-mm Soviet rockets, mortars, RPGs, crew-served weapons, and small arms were fired at us simultaneously. We returned fire and the battle began.

That night was an exercise in multitasking. I needed to adjust fire from the eighty-one-mm mortar we had at our position as well as artillery. If this wasn't complicated enough, illumination flares needed to be adjusted from a C-130 aircraft flying 3,000 feet above. Each flare was stuffed inside a forty-pound aluminum canister. From that far up they would surely hurt if they landed on flesh and bone.

Even more complicated was the fact that all three activities had to be coordinated on three different radio frequencies. I just parked myself next to the mortar battery and adjusted the fire by shouting. Unbelievably, that worked. I carried the radio back and forth across the perimeter to keep an eye on the entire show. My mind was full of numbers that had to be transferred to words. I was a busy boy.

In all the chaos, I noticed a shadow from an illumination flare's parachute that cast an eerie blue glow on Buddha's statue. It created the illusion that he wanted nothing to do with this mayhem. That sounded good to me because I was becoming weary of this scene, but had to see our mission through. I needed to survive to experience the clarity of a new dawn.

The enemy almost broke through our perimeter. We repelled each repeated surge with superior firepower and the discipline it took to stand fast. The enemy sustained heavy casualties but kept fighting on. They expended all their resources, then left. We successfully overcame a massive enemy force and lived. It was over.

As first light peeked over the horizon, the bells sounded a funeral dirge that saddened me almost to tears. Sorrow was a luxury I did not have the right to enjoy. I was caught in a web of depravity. I felt a sense of pride in helping the company stay intact. There was no escape. Survival replaced any emotional need. Civilized behavior would have to be put on hold if we were ever to make it back to the world. This was war.

As daylight replaced darkness, I could see firsthand the carnage of the night's ferocious interlude. Broken bodies from both sides littered the land as if a family of giants had run through the battlefield, while the living slipped between their toes. I still couldn't believe I'd survived. I was too busy to fire my weapon or even cover myself. Did my friend Tam look out for me from the beyond or was I just blessed with good karma?

I was pondering my cosmic fortunes when I noticed blood streaming from both legs. In my excitement, I failed to notice I was hit with RPG shrapnel. The wound burned a little but I was still breathing. I lifted my trouser leg up to check out the damage. A shard of shiny metal glistened in the morning sunlight, imbedded in my tibia. I tried to pull it loose with my fingers, but it was *stuck. Using my Marine KA-BAR fighting knife, I pried the foreign object from my leg. That was the first and only time I stuck that weapon into human flesh.*

Blood streamed down my leg like a babbling brook. A joint fell out when I took a battle dressing out of my first aid kit. Hmm, this was the perfect time for morning illumination. I fumbled for matches, and Big D appeared. He saw my blood and said, "Looks like you get a Purple Heart."

Looking at all the dead stacked like cordwood I said, "Come on, it's only a scratch," and it was only a scratch before I mutilated myself with that KA-BAR. Years later I would realize the wounds to my mind proved much harder to heal. I received the same medal as those who made the ultimate sacrifice. Where was the justice? Did the North Vietnamese have a Purple Heart? Receiving that medal made a sham of honor, for which I felt ashamed. I became angry and sad at the same time, but shrugged it off as just another strange occurrence of war.

When the guns silenced and the smoke cleared, everyone was happy to be intact. We fumbled about in silence like zombies, still numb from the horror of the last three days. I'd had enough excitement to last me for a few lifetimes. After all, numb was better than dead.

I was relieved to hear we were leaving Buddha's monastery. Those three days changed me forever and forged who I became. I vowed to try to be kind to all people while protecting the planet as I passed the statue. If I were to survive the rest of this war, I would need all the help I could get. That day my youth vanished and was replaced with the United States Marine Corps' semper fi" There would be a lifetime to make sense of what happened and to search for spiritual truth. I said a little prayer for Tam and never looked back. Ooorrah!

That was my summer of '69. Seventeen thousand miles away, in a cow pasture in upstate New York, a quarter million kids were enjoying three days of fun and music. Some say that was a strange trip, but the trip I lived with Lima Company gave strange a new meaning.

I woke up in the familiar sweat that accompanied the unpleasant saga of those dreams. The events of the last few days, though exciting, brought back memories I had packed away many years ago. They bubbled to the surface and gnawed away at the barriers I had masterfully constructed to keep them in the private bunker of my mind.

Enough of this pity party; I had a codex to get deciphered. After taking a long, hot shower, I was ready to take on the next chapter of what might turn out to be the most exciting time in my life, or maybe a brutal end to my life. At this point, all I had were a few friends and my good karma to keep me going down the path to my own enlightenment.

Nightmares made me hungry. I remedied that empty feeling with smoked salmon on a garlic bagel, smothered in cream cheese, lettuce, tomato, Maui onion, and capers. I washed the whole concoction down with a large glass of pomegranate juice and a steaming cup of Guatemalan coffee. I'd become very fond of this brew thanks to Guadalupe. I felt ready to take on my assigned task with renewed vim and vigor.

17

With headlights on, I drove south along the ocean before heading east as the fog miraculously lifted. The sun shined into my windows with a vengeance. I immediately pulled over and dropped the top. I was ready to travel comfortably in this open-air flash of a vehicle.

The trip to Tumbleweed Tech was uneventful. It took me an hour to travel from the coast to the Inland Empire. Because the Tesla rode as quietly as a needle dropping into cotton candy, I could think about the task at hand. Deep in thought I forgot about the speed limit and cruised at over a hundred miles per hour, extremely lucky that the prying eyes of the California Highway Patrol were nowhere to be seen.

I pulled onto the campus, and to my surprise the place had grown exponentially from the time I was a student many years ago. New buildings had sprouted up everywhere. Before locating the anthropology building, I needed to park. There were so many cars and so few parking spaces. As I went through the gate, the guard, a kid, beamed and gushed at the Tesla. "Wow," he gasped, "those things *do* exist. By any chance are you Jerry Johnson?"

Awestruck, I answered, "Yes, I am. How do you know who I am?"

"Dr. Ferdan left word that a Jerry Johnson had an appointment and I was to get you parked safely. I was hoping it was you behind the wheel of that Tesla."

He immediately directed me to VIP parking in front of the new anthropology building. It had an electric charging station. I wasn't sure of the exact location of Dr. Ferdan's office, so the kid offered to take me there personally. This was a ploy to get a ride in the Tesla. I was happy to get his help.

"Hop in and you can show me the way. You can drive if you want." He gladly took me up on my offer and we drove a circuitous route.

As we drove through a maze of parked cars and tried to secure a space, the kid clued me in on the construction. Apparently the San Bernardino campus was the fastest growing in the entire California State University system. When I studied at the place, it was a small, intimate college. The student population had grown fivefold but with what looked like the same number of parking spaces. I was lucky to have an exuberant guide to give me the scoop on what was going on. "I guess I can't call this megalopolis Tumbleweed Tech anymore. There isn't enough open space to grow tumbleweeds. That's progress!"

The kid pulled into a space that read "Anthropology building, permit required." He placed a pass on the dash of the Tesla, plugged into the battery charger, and thanked me for letting him drive. He smiled. "If you need anything else, please let me know. My name is Chip. Remember to return the pass on your way out."

What a nice person, I thought to myself. *I doubt Big D would get the same service.* I took the padded backpack that protected the box and made my way to the brand-new anthropology building. The edifice towered five stories. When I was there we had class in the basement of the library. To get to the front of the building, I had to travel through what was left of an old grove of olive trees that were here well before the university. As my feet crunched the fallen fruit, it reminded me of the sensation you got squashing bugs. Some things never change. They still let this awesome delicacy fall to the ground and stain the shoes of all who passed. When I was here a group of students wanted to harvest the olives. The administration nixed the idea, citing liability. As things change others remain the same. In this litigious society we live in, everyone is a little paranoid.

I entered the building and checked the directory for Dr. Ferdan's office. It was on the third floor. A graduate assistant welcomed me.

He told me that I was expected and to go right in. "Chip from the gate called and gave me the heads-up."

I thanked him and opened the office door. An older woman with long white hair and a wrinkled face, from many years of fieldwork, sat behind an antique oak desk. Though her face showed her age, bright eyes beamed at me like twin lasers cutting through a diamond. She looked at me with an inquisitive gaze and greeted me with a firm handshake. "Hello, Jerry. It's been a long time since you were my student. Things have changed at a blistering pace around here. Sometimes I don't even recognize my own office! What do you have to show me?"

I took the box from its protective pack. When she looked at the box, her jaw dropped. The sun reflected from the yellow surface made her squint. She was speechless for a long moment. After the initial shock, she tried to speak, but no distinguishable words could be heard. This woman, a world-renowned expert on Aztec textiles, looked quizzically at the workmanship of the ancient treasure. The usually composed academic was lost for words. Stammering, she tried to speak. "This artifact, where did you...where did you get it? There are references to at least four ancient civilizations. How did they know about each other? I think this box is gilded in pure gold. If this turns out to be authentic, this would change the way we look at the history of pre-Colombian civilizations. Aztec, Inca, Anasazi, and Pre-Colombian symbols inlayed into one surface with precious stones!"

"If you think the box is amazing, wait until I show you what's inside." I pried the box from her hands and opened the lid. She immediately started shaking when she saw the three knives. She fondled each one like a new baby.

"Aztec and Pre-Colombian technology in one piece. Where did the Aztec get emeralds? Where did they get ivory, this unique turquoise or topaz? What's the meaning of these grooves on the blade? My brain is on overload. If this can be authenticated we will have to rewrite history. I need to sit back and digest what I just saw."

"Wait until you see what else is in the box."

She immediately put on latex gloves and placed the knives into separate airtight containers. Dr. Ferdan carefully lifted the codex from its nesting place and studied the parchment for a long minute. "This looks like the real thing. It looks like amatl, fig bark, with natural pigments used for the text and pictures. I need to go upstairs to the lab to carefully handle the document so it doesn't disintegrate."

"Before you investigate the box's contents any further, I need to tell you the rest of the story. This inquiry needs to be between us until the whole story completely unravels." I immediately told her the whole story, without the sex of course. She looked confused, but agreed for history's sake. "If anyone asks questions, especially Eastern European types, you must deny any knowledge of what I showed you today. Our lives depend on your discretion."

"Mum's the word. Let's go to the lab." She carefully placed the box and its contents into several vacuum containers. She grabbed the codex and we left her office. On our way out she told the grad assistant that she would be gone for the day and to cancel all appointments. She informed him that we would be in the lab and we were not to be disturbed unless it was a life-or-death emergency.

We took the elevator to the top floor, which required a key to exit. "This is my private lab," she boasted. "I don't want anyone messing with my research. It would take a master criminal to break into my domain. I got a federal grant and one from Mexico to conduct research on Aztec textiles. This place needs to be secure."

I thought to myself that it would be child's play for Dragaminov to crack college security. Hopefully it would never come to that; but I knew what the Russian was capable of, and the long arm Big D wielded. Nothing was impossible.

Dr. Ferdan punched a series of numbers into a keypad and the solid steel door silently swung open. She flipped a switch and the whole room was illuminated with ultraviolet light-reducing florescent bulbs.

"Ultraviolet light can destroy the fibers and fade the pigments used in ancient writing," she said.

The learned professional was so excited that she forgot to close the door. I noticed the open door and immediately closed it. I didn't want Dragaminov to just waltz into the room through an open door. I knew I must stop being so paranoid and keep focused on maintaining my good karma.

Dr. Ferdan placed the codex into an enclosed glass workstation that looked like something from a science fiction movie. As she worked under the glass without fear of the damaging effects of airborne pathogens, an array of tools at arm's length were at her disposal. There were a series of magnifying glasses, cameras, and even a microscope for fine work. It looked to me like scientists working with radioactive material. At times I confused movies with reality...

Dr. Ferdan carefully removed the ancient document from the protective covering, and to our surprise the codex turned out to be a number of pages folded like an accordion with writing and colored pictures on both sides. Another document fell from one of the folds. It was different from the others. It appeared to be made of a soft paper and was written in Spanish. To me it looked like a map. My mind was perpetually blown, but this was exponentially more mysterious than anything else that had happened over the last few days.

I asked, "So what do we have here?"

All Dr. Ferdan could say was "I think you may have uncovered the glue that will fill some of the holes in pre-Columbian history books. I need to study this treasure trove of information before I can make any conclusions. I need to photograph the entire document and secure the original. I will need to carbon date both documents: the amatl and the loose velum. Mostly monks in the monasteries of Europe used velum. They meticulously translated the classical Nahuatl to Latin or Spanish. After I photograph everything I will secure the originals in a safe place deep in the university's vast server room, where no one will ever find them. This could be a new Rosetta Stone."

"Don't be too sure about that. Remember what I told you about Diamond. Please be careful."

"I've heard of Harlan Diamond. He's well known in the scientific community as a land rapist," Dr. Ferdan interjected. "If what you tell me is true, I will do everything in my power to stop that egomaniac and help bring him down."

"Good. Please be sure not to tell anyone about our little surprise. Keep me informed. Call me on my cell phone or email me any new developments. Please watch out for anything unusual."

I thanked her for all her help and I left the anthropology building and headed for the Tesla post haste. On my way off campus, Chip stopped me. He thanked me for letting him drive the Tesla. He said, "Some men in a black Suburban with tinted windows and Texas plates were looking at the Tesla. I told security and they escorted them from campus. The Suburban is registered to the Diamond Oil Company. What else can I do for you?"

"I know who they are. Here's my number. If they come back please give me a call."

The kid was more than happy to help after I let him drive history. Then I quietly sprinted off campus with little fanfare. The quiet rocket blasted away from the smog-drenched valley and up to the clear blue mountain skies.

18

As I drove "up the hill" and above the smog, my mind cleared. A cool breeze blasted my neck and filtered into the pleasure centers of my brain. The Tesla straightened the switchback curves as I corkscrewed my way up to the mountain I truly loved. There was always something exhilarating every time I made the journey.

As I rounded the hairpin turn at Panorama Point, I spied my old Westphalia VW bus broken down in a turnout. I pulled off and parked the Tesla away from the road behind the crippled pop-top camper. Visions of good times in that vehicle filled my head with joy. I sold it a couple of years ago to a friend when my back started to give me major problems. It was too difficult to operate the clutch. I always regretted that decision. I should have used it as a planter, but the old girl still had a lot of life left in her.

A young woman struggled to remove the lug nuts from a flat tire. She sweated profusely and couldn't loosen them. She jumped on the tire iron to no avail. Vulgarity spewed from her lips in frustration. She saw me and immediately smiled. Sarah Ann, the daughter of a friend, looked at me with kindness as I offered my help. She ran to me and gave me a big hug, as if knowing everything would be okay.

She explained, "I was on my way home from school when a tire blew out. I was lucky not to lose control and go over the side. Thanks for stopping. My car is in the shop, so I drove the bus today. My mom and dad are going for a road trip up the coast this weekend. I can't let them travel on a bad tire."

Sarah Ann, a former student of mine, attended college in the valley. I inquired, "How's school going?"

She beamingly replied, "Thanks to you I'm on the right track. I'm focused enough to start medical school in the fall. Because of your nurturing guidance, especially the 'mission behavior' you instilled in us, I have the resolve to take my studies all the way."

I didn't know how to respond to such a compliment, so I just smiled and attacked the flat tire. "Mission behavior," at times, held me back. That was a different story entirely.

With all my strength and an audible screech, the frozen nut broke loose. After the first one was freed, the rest came undone easily. I took the spare and placed it on the wheel. I had to bend my bad back like a pretzel, and to my chagrin a sharp pain ran from my back down both legs. I immediately knew that I had to go to Dr. Mac, my chiropractor, for an adjustment.

With my body and the Tesla shielded from the road, three black Suburbans sped past the turnout. They were headed to Rancho Mysterioso to try and retrieve the box.

With the spare secured to the wheel, I bid Sarah Ann a fond farewell. "Say hello to your mom and dad and keep the bus on the road."

"I will, Jerry, thanks again."

As I drove further into the mountains, my back started to spasm with a vengeance. The pain was almost unbearable. All I could do was try to ignore the sharp knife-like waves and persevere. I drove to the rear of Dr. Mac's office, where I thought I could hobble through the door with little effort.

I tried to lift my body from the low-slung Tesla to no avail. I was entombed in an expensive coffin. There was no one around. The pain became excruciatingly real. As I reached for my phone to get extricated from the Tesla, a sheriff's car pulled alongside me. I immediately thought that I would have some explaining to do about my house, my Porsche, or the wildland fire, not to mention various gunfights. My mind raced when I saw a familiar large body step from the patrol car.

Sheriff Dan Alvarado waddled toward my vehicle. This powerful man's portly belly strained at his bulletproof vest. It looked like his buttons would pop. Despite his slovenly appearance he could handle himself in pressure situations. If this corpulent lawman could only cut down on his donut consumption, he might be someone's Adonis. If my back pain would miraculously subside, I could be ready for anything. You know what they say about "if"!

Sheriff Dan peered into the cockpit of the Tesla. He could tell that I was in distress and quipped, "Hey, Jerry, do you want a shoehorn to peel yourself from that fancy skateboard?"

"I'd be grateful if you'd give me a hand into Doc Mac's office."

"Sure thing."

His hand, a meaty paw, resembled a large bunch of bananas. With the grip of a vise, the rotund public servant snatched me from the Tesla like a cotton ball from a wastebasket. As I cleared the seat my back sounded an audible crack. I felt instant relief. He had unknowingly adjusted my back. When he lowered me to the ground, I was miraculously pain free. I didn't need to get adjusted by a professional. I just hoped Dr. Mac didn't look out the window to see this freak medical miracle.

"Thanks, Dan. I've seen you crack bones while breaking up bar fights, but this has to go down in the annals of curing without knowing what actually happened. Wow, you saved me a whole lot of pain!"

He looked at me with a friendly grin and said, "Glad to help and no one went to the hospital. By the way, Jerry, did you know your house is gone? I drove by while checking on a helicopter crash and noticed there's no trace of your place, no debris, not even a standing foundation. We fished your Porsche from the lake. My superiors told me that we were not to get involved. All they said was that orders came from forces with a higher pay grade. I think you need to enlighten me on both instances. Also, where'd you get that Tesla?"

I felt like my mother just caught me with my hand stuck in the cookie jar. Did Big D have that much influence, or was E.D. not telling me the rest of the story? My mind a ball of confusion, I felt like

I was swimming in Jell-O. I took a deep breath and tried to explain something I couldn't fully comprehend.

"Okay, Dan. I can't explain the whole story right now, but I'm helping out an old buddy from Vietnam. When it comes clear to me, you'll be the first to know. There're forces beyond our control that are difficult to explain. I just hope I can get some answers soon. Oh, the Tesla is my buddy's car. He let me borrow it for a while."

"Nice friend! Well, you take care of yourself. If there is any help you need, please don't be afraid to ask."

I felt great, but I needed to get the stitches removed from my arm. This time was as good as any, so I got the stitches removed and was off to see what dangers lurked down the road. As my luck was going, I wouldn't have to wait much longer. I was glad I talked to Sheriff Dan Alvarado. I now fully realized that the forces afoot were way beyond my control. Why were the local law enforcement agencies unable to investigate the very serious crimes? If and when I saw E.D. again, she'd better level with me and tell the whole story. All of these strange happenings did not make any sense.

19

I drove by the lot where my house once stood. The emptiness exuded a ghostly feel to my once comfortable abode. Not being able to see or touch the place I called home for many years made me feel sad. There was nothing I could do about it now, so I just drove into my driveway to reflect on the last few days and try to make sense out of the entire experience.

As I parked in the same spot my house once occupied, a black Suburban blocked my view of the Pinnacle Spires. Dragaminov and three younger mercenaries trained Skorpion automatic rifles at my head and torso. I could see the red laser dots glowing on my body. This did not look like they were playing laser tag. Maybe they were, but the game they were playing did not look like there could be any happy ending for me.

Dragaminov snarled, "Where is the box, Mr. Johnson? We are tired of you people avoiding the inevitable while killing my men. I brought new young troops with me this time. They are fresh from Chechnya. I will let them have some fun with you, because if you don't tell them what I want to hear, you will want to die from the pain they can, and will, inflict."

"Please don't threaten me. It won't work. I don't have anything to tell you, or your Euro-trash goons. Stop wasting my time and get off my property." I couldn't believe I had just mouthed off to four insane Russian psychos with automatic weapons. If they so desired, the deranged bullies could have snuffed me out with the touch of a finger. I usually like to bluff in poker, but this bluff could have ended it all in an instant.

With a calm voice Dragaminov whispered, "We shall see, yes, we shall see. I think I will try one of your American methods to make you talk. Do you know what waterboarding is, Mr. Johnson?"

"Well, I believe this method of torture was invented by Milton Freedman's boys at the University of Chicago when they came up with Shock and Awe. Just ask Khalid Sheikh Mohammed. You heard of him, the mastermind of 9/11?"

"As you Americans say, you are a smart-ass, Mr. Johnson. I bet you will not feel so smart when you are gasping for air as you drown."

"As the famous American Rocky Balboa once grunted, 'Go for it!'" At that point I had nothing to lose, so I might as well go out with a defiant sense of humor. I just hoped I'd survive the miniature deluge about to compromise my airway.

Dragaminov barked orders in Russian to his underlings. They took what looked like a backboard from under the hatch of their Suburban and leaned it against the tailgate. Two of the others unceremoniously grabbed me by the arms and manhandled me upside down on the hard board that reminded me of an exaggerated Trendelenburg position. They tightly synched leather straps with sharp buckles that dug into my flesh every time I moved. The straps were so tight around my legs, I feared my circulation would be compromised. My only hope was that the wet leather would stretch enough to give me relief.

Dragaminov gloated, "Are you comfortable, Mr. Johnson? Would you like a glass of water? Oh wait; there will be enough water to fill your entire body in just a few minutes." He laughed with a hideous shrill. "You can save yourself much pain if you just tell me where the box is right now. We know that you brought it to the university, but we couldn't tell its destination. That pain-in-the-ass kid at the gate made us loses track of our prey, yes, you! No matter, you will be singing like an opera tenor in just a few moments."

Way to go, Chip! Letting him drive the Tesla, a random act of kindness on my part, paid off once again. I am a true believer that if people are nice to one another, only good things can come from even the smallest selfless gestures.

"Hey, Dragaminov, it looks like rain. If you're not careful you could get wet." I could see the blood vessels in his neck bulge with rage. Dragaminov ground a piece of what felt like burlap with impunity over my face. The rough cloth scratched the tip of my nose and smelled like a wet dog. To ignore the discomfort, I started to hyperventilate to get as much oxygen into my lungs before the ceremonial drowning. I could always hold my breath for at least three minutes. Maybe my big lungs would buy me enough time to survive this dire predicament.

Dragaminov stood over me with a liter bottle of fresh mountain spring water. He began to drip the fluid from about three feet away from my face. As the first drops penetrated the burlap, I took a deep breath from my diaphragm. My lung capacity was tested to hold over seven liters of tidal volume. I tried to close my pharynx, but because I was upside down, the liquid death just flowed around my airway. I immediately started to panic. My body started to spasm. The pain was unbearable. It felt like my life was fading away. The only thing that was still intact was my mind. I needed to get control of the situation. I knew that waterboarding was not fatal, if the people who were administrating this method of torture knew what they were doing. Because the bad guys needed information, I was safe from becoming a former living being.

After about twenty seconds of being watered, Dragaminov lifted the cloth from my face. "How does it feel to be a fish without any gills, Mr. Johnson? Are you ready to talk?"

"No way! I feel at peace under water." The art of bluffing was evaporating like I hoped the water in my lungs would. I violently retched and expelled the remaining fluiid from my lungs. Snot mixed with water spewed from my nose and mouth with ferocity. One particularly long one dangled from Dragaminov's nose. The viscous liquid swung like a pendulum. He tried to brush it away, but ended up swallowing the fruit of his torture. His men laughed at the sight of their boss retching, and one of the recruits got the butt of Dragaminov's Skorpion across his face, breaking his jaw.

The other boys tried to give their comrade aid, but Dragaminov turned and shot the new man through the temple, killing him instantly. In Russian he shouted, "Let this be a lesson to the rest of you: Never mock me."

The remaining two snapped to attention. With fear in their eyes, they stood like sheep waiting for the butcher. From that moment they harbored a disdain for their maniacal leader. The three recruits were brothers, unbeknown to Dragaminov. His brutality sowed the seeds of hatred in the remaining brothers. Revenge for their fallen sibling became their silent goal.

The break in the action afforded me time to compose myself. I had to do a better job of preventing the panic from taking over. When the CIA waterboarded someone, they dripped the water for only ten seconds. I was concerned that Dragaminov couldn't tell time. To my surprise the leather straps did stretch. Blood was oozing from where the buckles cut my flesh. I needed to get my head together for the next round of the unwanted shower.

Dragaminov, with eyes ablaze, poured the second dose of water onto the burlap. The water felt cold. The drops seemed to bind together and hold my attention as if they were alive and ravenously hungry. They wanted to eat the life from my now convulsing airway. The only thing I could think of was to visit a place that was more miserable than drowning. The only place had to be with Lima Company. In a trance-like state, I revisited that unforgettable day.

Monsoon's torrential downpours injected themselves into our shivering bodies. It had been raining nonstop for five straight days. It was Christmas Day 1969. The whole company felt and looked like a combination of drowned rats

and prunes. The temperature was a balmy seventy degrees, the coldest I've ever felt. Yes, Vietnam was truly a living, breathing contradiction. Where else on this planet could someone get hypothermia in seventy-degree weather? To keep warm we buried ourselves in red mud. It felt slimy, but we were insulated from the brutal elements.

We were on a fog-soaked mountaintop, spitting distance from Laos. For all I knew we were in Laos. It was the holiday cease-fire, and we were supposed to be receiving our holiday meal delivered by helicopter. One problem; you need to see to fly. The fog was so thick that it felt like you were entrapped in a liquid cocoon. Merry Christmas!

The only positive in this entire situation was the fact that the North Vietnamese Army was too smart to fight in this weather. The Ho Chi Min trail was a river of mud and debris, impassable by any sane being. I just wished our leaders were as smart as our enemy. Besides, even if they wanted to engage us, they just couldn't see. We were safe from attack, but we had to stave off the more pressing attacks from the wet, cold, and hunger. Our situation was bleak at best.

Our only comfort was a waterlogged transistor radio. We all huddled around the tiny speaker, straining to hear rock and roll over the boom of millions of thunderous raindrops. My ears perked when I heard George Harrison's guitar play the opening bars of "Here Comes the Sun." As he sang, "Little darling, it's been a long, cold, lonely winter," a Christmas miracle happened. At the exact moment the quiet Beatle belted out "Here comes the sun," splintered sunlight burned through the heavy sky, evaporating the hanging fog, setting us free from our misery. I never worshiped the sun as I did that fateful day. This unexplained kosmic occurrence, perpetuated by, of all things, a Beatles song, reaffirmed my belief that good karma would protect me from the evils of this unforgiving land. As we ate steak and mashed potatoes, the war went away for just a moment. This had to be the best Christmas present I ever received.

My eyes squinted as I rejoined the living. "Here Comes the Sun" played over and over in my head. That Beatles song saved me one more time. I began to smile until I realized where I was and the situation that confronted me. Confusion replaced my happy state with dread. There was an eerie silence. What just happened? The leather straps stretched enough so I could slip one hand free. It was a piece of cake to loosen the rest. I rolled off the torture table and looked around at the battlefield that was where I once lived. Why was I still alive?

I saw Sheriff Dan Alvarado lying, slumped over a rock. Sunlight bathed his body with a peaceful glow. His car was nowhere to be seen. The Suburban I was tied to was riddled with bullets. Dan Alvarado must have heard gunfire and investigated what turned out to be a hornet's nest. Dragaminov and the two remaining henchmen must have gotten away in the sheriff's car.

I ran over to see if Dan was still alive. As I approached him I noticed blood gushing from his abdomen. He had an ashen pallor and his eyes grew dim. I tried to comfort him as best as I could, but any attempt on my part would prove futile. "Hang in there, buddy. You're going to be okay." Of course I lied.

He wanted to speak, but his words were slow and his breath shallow. He went within himself and spoke. "I know I'm dying, but I have to tell you what happened. I was driving by where your house was and heard gunfire. I noticed you were getting waterboarded. What was that all about? As I got out of my car, the bad guys opened up on me with automatic weapons. I took cover behind a rock and returned fire with my AR-15."

His words were getting slower. I tried to make him stay still as best as I could. I pleaded with him not to speak, but he wasn't hearing it.

"I shot up the front of the Suburban to get them away from you, but they outflanked me. One of them shot me in the stomach through the open space of my bulletproof vest. What a lucky shot. I guess donuts *did* kill me. Before I went down in a heap, I shot the man who killed me. The remaining two took my patrol car. Please, Jerry, find those perpetrators and bring them to justice." After those final words, his eyes rolled to the back of his head, and he was gone. What a waste of a good person. All he was trying to do was help a friend. His last words would haunt me until Big D and Dragaminov were brought to justice. I was just burdened with more resolve to see this terrible situation to fruition.

I looked for my cell phone, but it was nowhere to be seen. The Tesla miraculously was not hit, so I jumped in and headed for Rancho Mysterioso. I needed to warn Jake, and besides, the electric car needed a charge. How were we going to explain the murder of a sheriff? I didn't know how E.D. could defuse this terrible occurrence.

My mind was ablaze with questions about how I survived. I had relied on good karma all my life, but this was the biggest test yet. If it was true, and I believed it was, how long could it last? I would have many more opportunities to find out before this adventure ended. Life was not so good right then, but it could always get better.

My cell phone rang under the seat. I didn't lose it after all. I pulled over to retrieve my phone, and to my surprise it was Dr. Ferdan. With excitement in her voice, she spoke.

"Hello, Jerry. I don't know where you got these codices, but if they are authentic, and I believe they are, this could be the anthropological find of the millennium. We need to talk. When can you meet with me?"

"I need to hook up with some people, and when I do we'll meet you wherever you desire. When I get it together I'll call you back."

"I had to bite my tongue not to tell anyone about what secrets these ancient documents are hiding. Please hurry."

I hung up the phone and proceeded down the fire road to Rancho Mysterioso, keeping an eye out for Dragaminov and the stolen sheriff car. I didn't feel like another shower. The next time he gave me a shower, it could be the full metal jacket kind instead of water.

20

Diamond went ballistic when he got Dragaminov's report from the stolen patrol car. Steam seemed to spew from his ears. He was so mad that he shattered a Ming Dynasty vase with one of his thousand-dollar boots. He kicked the vase so hard, shards of ancient pottery flew across his office and penetrated his furniture. He did not care about destroying the priceless museum piece. The only priceless artifact he cared about was the box. His obsession pushed him over the edge, farther into insanity. How could a man who had so much become so focused on a tangible object? What was his motivation? He possessed all the wealth any one man could ever spend. There was something else driving him to such lengths, including murder, to achieve his diabolical goal.

"Look here, you Bolshevik fool," he scolded Dragaminov. "I'm paying you a fortune to find one small box. What is your problem? No wonder you incompetent boobs lost the cold war. Don't contact me again until you have the box in your borscht-eating paws."

"Very well, Mr. Diamond." Dragaminov was not accustomed to this treatment. A well-respected Communist party member in Russia, he treated people the way Diamond treated him. His patience was wearing thin with this arrogant capitalist. It wouldn't be long before he focused his wrath on Diamond, instead of the box.

The phone rang in Diamond's office. "What is it, Miss Green?"

"The Secret Service is on the line for you, Mr. Diamond. They want to ask you some questions about the disappearance of former vice president Haney."

Diamond's face instantly turned white. "What do I know about him being missing? That fool probably got lost in his own house. Tell them I'm not here. Tell them I'm out of the country."

"Okay, Mr. Diamond, but they seem pretty insistent."

"I don't care how insistent they are. I don't want to talk to them right now." For the first time Diamond felt worried. He thought killing the former vice president was the perfect crime. He racked his brain for mistakes he could have made, but he couldn't think of any.

"Wait a minute, Miss Green. On second thought, I will talk to them."

"Okay, Special Agent Pule is on line one."

"Mr. Diamond, I am Secret Service Special Agent Pule. Our agency is investigating the disappearance of former vice president Haney. We are running down a few leads. May I ask you a few questions?"

"Sure, but I haven't talked to the man in months."

"We know, but this is only routine. Do you own a blue Maybach? A traffic security camera on the day of his disappearance picked up an image of what might be former vice president Haney. The image is fuzzy, so we can't make a positive identification."

"Of course I own that type of vehicle, but as far as I know the former vice president never rode in that car."

"We are checking out every possible lead. Thank you for your time. If I have any more questions, may I contact you again?"

"But of course you can. That man is a very good friend of mine and I'll do anything in my power to get him back safe. Contact me anytime."

"Thank you, Mr. Diamond. I'll be in touch."

Diamond gloated to himself out loud. "That went well. There is nothing like the perfect crime. Wait a minute, I'm from Texas, so screw all of you. Oh, Miss Green, get my plane ready. I need to get out of here for a while. Get someone to clean up my office. I had an accident with an ancient Chinese flower pot."

"Very well, Mr. Diamond."

Diamond got into his private plane and flew off into the wild blue yonder.

21

E.D. and Junior arrived at Rancho Mysterioso. Two men with them looked like pro football linebackers. The sight of them made Jake a little nervous. He wasn't used to having strangers invade his inner sanctum. Junior reassured him that they were friends and not to worry. Junior invited everyone into the house, and Guadalupe served the guests freshly baked brownies and lemonade. They thanked her while making short order of the delicious snacks.

While everyone enjoyed Guadalupe's magic, the stolen sheriff's car entered the property. Ernesto, who was in the barn, noticed the light bar glistening in the sunshine. There was an unwritten rule that when any law entered the grounds, the marijuana crop had to be destroyed. Though they were doing a public service growing medicine, the crop was still illegal to the U.S. government. No one in the house was aware that Dragaminov was driving the stolen sheriff mobile.

Ernesto sprang into action. He unlocked a small door hidden inside the barn, and removed a pin from a lever inside the door. When the lever was pulled, a series of events took place to destroy everything in the grow room. First, the door was automatically bolted from the inside. Next, the expensive stadium lights retracted into the ceiling. A series of burning propane jets popped up from the floor and instantly ignited all the combustible material in the room. The ventilation system evacuated the smoke from the building. The entire process took less than five minutes. The plan was foolproof. When the room cooled, there wasn't even a leaf of evidence.

The plan was devised to prevent federal prosecution. With the ever-changing marijuana laws, it was hard to figure out what to do in this gray area. Jake would rather be safe than sorry. If he had to sacrifice one crop, so be it. It was only a matter of time before the Justice Department had nothing to do with the use of cannabis. For now, the immolation of a few plants was a small price to pay to avoid the hassle of federal prosecution.

A large poster adorned the wall of the grow room, a replica of an anti-marijuana poster from the 1930s. A pot leaf superimposed on an unsavory-looking man dressed in black. The man's face was contorted, with bloodshot eyes, and what looked like a joint hung from his drooling lips. Under the scary figure in capital letters read MURDER, INSANITY, and DEATH. It too went up in smoke. Hopefully, that old tired thinking would go up in smoke with all misconceptions concerning the life-saving plant. What was worse, the murderous greed of Diamond, or what Jake was doing?

Dragaminov and his remaining soldier jumped from their stolen car. They packed the same automatic weapons. E.D. spotted them from the window and sprang into action. She directed her friends to surround the two bad guys. It was four against two. When Dragaminov realized he was outnumbered and outgunned, he and his underling immediately threw their weapons on the ground and, with hands raised to the sky, surrendered.

With vengeful disdain, E.D. looked at the Russians and spoke to them in a loud voice. "How does it feel to be on the other end of a gun? You and your hired thugs won't get a chance to harm anyone here. By the way, Diamond will never get his grubby hands on the box."

A defeated Dragaminov snarled at E.D.'s two friends as they handcuffed him and his young mercenaries behind their backs. Still defiant, Dragaminov spit in E.D.'s face. She wiped the spittle from her cheek and slapped him across the face. With resolve she looked him in the eye and proclaimed, "I guess you like spitting on girls. Not this girl, Comrade Dragaminov." Blood dripped down his chin, as he was unceremoniously thrown in the back of the sheriff's car he had stolen.

E.D. snarled at the defeated Russian as she informed him that he was in the custody of undercover federal agents, and was under arrest for high crimes against the United States of America. She vowed, "We have you now, and it won't be long before your boss, Harlan Diamond, will share a federal prison cell with you. You can make it easy on yourself by implicating your snake of a boss. Rats like you don't have allegiance to anyone, just to money."

Dragaminov stood like a statue and didn't utter a word. His silence, coupled with the lack of eye contact, infuriated E.D. "So be it, comrade. You will rot in prison for what your boss has ordered you to do. Get this filth off of our mountain. See you in court, scumbag."

Dragaminov demanded, with fleeting defiance, "I wish to speak to my lawyer now." E.D. just laughed hysterically.

The two agents—one in the stolen car and the other one in a nondescript vehicle—left Rancho Mysterioso and headed for one of those undisclosed locations you read about in mystery novels.

While driving to the ranch, I saw the stolen sheriff's car. I really didn't feel like tangling with Dragaminov and his wrath any more today. I drove the Tesla into a thicket of manzanita bushes. The coppery color of the woody shrubs camouflaged me from the approaching vehicles. I had a perfect vantage point to watch them pass by. To my surprise, there were two vehicles.

As they passed through my line of vision, I noticed Dragaminov and his young apprentice mercenaries handcuffed in the backseat, followed by the other. I instantly became confused. Did E.D. have help?

Just as the parade neared a switchback, four men, armed with automatic weapons, surrounded the cars. They made the drivers exit their vehicles and freed Dragaminov and his underlings. Dragaminov handcuffed the two agents to the steering wheel of the sheriff's car. He disabled the radios, punctured the tires, and signaled his rescuers. The six men piled into the functioning Suburban and vanished down the mountain.

As I approached the destroyed sheriff's car I asked myself what E.D. was holding back from me. These guys looked like Feds. I freed them with a handcuff key lying in the backseat. They referred to me by my name. "Mr. Johnson, thank you for getting us out of this predicament."

"How do you know who I am?"

"We work with Ms. Struction. It is not our place to divulge any information at this time about who we are, or our mission. She will brief you fully when we return to the ranch."

"Sounds like government double talk to me." With my mouth wide open, the two, whoever they were, squeezed into the Tesla, and the three of us meandered down the dusty trail.

As we passed the "Beware of the Monster" sign at the gate of Rancho Mysterioso, I was just as confused about E.D. and what was going on as I was when I pulled the ignominious woman from that cliff. It was time I got some real answers. What was wrong with the truth, or did everyone in government nonchalantly lie as a matter of principle?

E.D. looked confused when she spotted the Tesla. It did look a bit funny; like a copper octopus, with flailing arms, moving in all directions. She wasn't laughing though. "What happened?"

"It's the same old story. Dragaminov got away. Frankly, I'm sick of all this mystery. I need answers now!"

E.D. spoke with authority. "I'm sorry I wasn't completely truthful with you, Jerry. All I can say now is that I haven't let you in on the whole scenario. Because of the sensitivity of this entire operation, and its secrecy, you might just quit."

As her lips started to let me in on the secret, a snarling ill wind rumbled down from the high peak overlooking Rancho Mysterioso. Its biting ferocity blew an icy force through every living thing in its path. Man and beast shivered from its frozen breath. The temperature instantly dropped into the freezing zone. The sweat on our bodies was flash frozen. I felt like a freshly caught piece of sushi. I just hoped my freshly eaten sushi didn't meet the same fate.

The wind blew with such bluster, the American flag Jake so reverently flew at sunrise and dauntingly took down at sunset was starched straight. It reminded me of the Star-Spangled Banner, but instead of dodging cannon fire, we attempted to get a handle on what was happening.

A black cloud instantly enveloped the ranch. I feverishly looked for the silver lining, but to no avail. Looking up only froze my eyebrows. Without warning this meteorological anomaly slashed open and dumped tiny hailstones over everything. It looked like millions of clear Styrofoam pellets pinging our bodies. It felt like we were in the grip of a frozen, cascading waterfall. That cloud dumped a good three inches in only two minutes. Because the land was pre-frozen, all the plant life gave up to flatness.

Just as quickly as it began, the wind stopped blowing. Everything became eerily silent. Was this how Rancho Mysterioso got its name, or was it just another weird example of the last few days? The landscape looked like Alaska in the winter. We looked at each other's chattering teeth and grinned in awe of what just happened. "Wow!"

The once ominous vessel of frigid doom began to evaporate. Radiant beams of sunlight burst through the thinning cloud. Refracted hail crystals put on a kaleidoscopic light show like none of us had ever witnessed and never would forget. Billions of tiny swirling rainbows danced across everything. The whole landscape was bathed in the colors of the entire spectrum. Red, orange, yellow, green, blue, indigo, and violet danced to the beat of one of nature's beautiful spectacles. The cold created even more color. Soothing lavender glowed over everyone's body, like we were entombed in a veil of resolve, reassuring us that our mission was just.

We laughed and frolicked in a peace reserved only for immortal beings. The sun's healing rays began to restore the earth to its normal state when a single red rose popped up from its frozen grip, defying the cold. Instantly this American Beauty was surrounded by light and looked as if it wore a crown of rainbows. This was by far the most beautiful thing I had ever witnessed.

As the cold disappeared, a giant triple rainbow stretched toward Mexico. After a few minutes of reflection, E.D. looked us all in the eye and stated the obvious. "It looks like the rainbow is telling us where to go. So let's go find out what secrets the codices have to offer."

22

We all left Rancho Mysterioso smiling. Well, just E.D. and I left. Jake stayed behind so he, Ernesto, and Guadalupe could survey the damage from the rainbow storm and the lost crop. Junior and the two mystery feds left on other tasks to prepare for the potential trip south.

When we left, the roads were completely dry. There was no trace of the freak hailstorm, except for all the vehicles stuck in ditches or smashed into the mountainside. It looked like they slid off the mountain simultaneously. Flashing red lights and the scream of emergency vehicle sirens filled the air, while wreckers winched the disabled vehicles from the jaws of the mountain.

Everyone looked too busy to notice our silent copper roadster gliding down the mountain. We breezed on past the mayhem. I felt a little guilty for not stopping to help, but there were more than enough emergency responders on scene to handle the situation. Further down the mountain, I noticed Dragaminov and his henchmen crawling up to the road from their smashed vehicle, which had slid about fifteen feet over the side. They looked angry, dazed, and confused. Hopefully, they wouldn't be bothering us any time soon. These so-called mercenaries looked a little too preoccupied to notice us passing, let alone to try to kill us again. This predicament couldn't happen to a more despicable person. Hopefully Dragaminov's bad karma was finally catching up with him. That was all right by me. I didn't feel like getting waterboarded again.

Tumbleweed Tech was abuzz with activity. Busy students scurried to and fro so as not to be late for class. Chip greeted me with enthusiasm. "Hello, Mr. Johnson. Dr. Ferdan is waiting for you in her office. Thanks again for letting me drive the Tesla. I'll take you to a secure area where nothing will happen to that fine machine."

He led us to a VIP parking area in an underground lot below the anthropology building. We parked in the most secure place on campus. There were only five parking places in this covered private area. Chip led us to the university president's personal parking place. He told us that the president was out of the country and we could park there for up to a week.

Dr. Ferdan greeted us at the door. She looked excited to see me. In her excitement she didn't notice E.D. The usually poised academic scholar bubbled over with enthusiasm. It was as if she were a schoolgirl meeting a rock star. She looked at me in the eye and exclaimed, "I don't know how you came into possession of this box, its contents, and most of all the codices. Come into my office and I'll share what I found out, and maybe we can unravel the mystery."

I shook her hand and introduced E.D. "Dr. Ferdan, this is E.D. Struction. She is the person who gave me the box to have you add credence to its mysteries."

"I am pleased to meet you, E.D. We can talk a little more privately in my office. I have a lot of questions to ask, and I most certainly can shed some light on yours. Please follow me to my office."

We looked at each other while following Dr. Ferdan into the anthropology building. As the door was closing, Chip yelled, "Don't worry, Dr. F., I'll make sure no one disturbs you, or your guests." Dr. Ferdan didn't acknowledge Chip and his offer. I turned and gave him the thumbs-up. If I ever had kids, I hoped they would turn out like Chip, but that's another story entirely.

Dr. Ferdan's office had the feel of a museum library. Sunshine streamed through large windows onto shelf after shelf of books and artifacts of all shapes and sizes. They looked disorganized, but on further inspection there was a method by which everything could easily be retrieved. All of the materials in her office were secretly labeled in a way that only a trained researcher could decipher. This must be how great minds prioritize the voluminous information needed to conduct the monumental tasks required for pure research. I had a strong feeling we were in the right place.

Dr. Ferdan sat at her desk loading a disk into a computer. Her piercing eyes looked through us as an image of the first page of the codex flashed onto a large monitor hanging on the wall.

E.D. gazed at the images with both eyes glued to the Aztec symbols. She had no idea what they said, and didn't have a clue how the pictographs were connected to her dad. With a bit of a stammer, she thanked Dr. Ferdan for deciphering the mystery and excitedly asked, "What does all of this mean?"

Dr. Ferdan gently placed her hand on E.D.'s shoulder. Her reassuring touch made E.D. feel at ease. "Well, dear, in the first place there was so much information, documents, and artifacts that needed to be deciphered. I've been working on the whole package nonstop since Jerry brought this extraordinary box and its contents.

"I guess I will start with the box. It is made of pure gold, with a fired lacquer finish to hide the fact that there is so much gold. The ancients liked working with gold because it was so plentiful and easy to shape with the tools at hand. If the box got into the hands of the Conquistadores, they would have melted it down, cast it into ingots, and shipped them to Spain to help finance the wars that were plaguing Europe at the time. They did not care about art, just the lust for gold. As far as they were concerned, these beautiful objects were works of the devil.

"The box is unlike anything I've ever come across in my almost forty years of studying the Aztec culture. The workmanship is far more intricate than anything that can even be created today. The inlayed symbols fit so precisely that it looks like they are one with the surface of the lid. As for the symbols, I could not believe such an array of different cultures had any contact with each other. This fact befuddled me until I dug deeper. This is where the codices come into play. "

E.D. looked puzzled. Her lips were moving, but not a sound could be heard. She took a deep breath and could only utter an audible "Wow!"

"There are four distinctive documents that were fitted into the box. An ancient wrote the first one on fig bark, as I suspected. The ancients almost exclusively used fig bark because of its pliability and the way it soaks up the natural pigments common to the area. The colors were trapped in the bark in such a way that they retained their brightness, even today. This, coupled with the airtightness of the box, preserved these treasures so they look as fresh as they did when they were first created. The bark was accordion folded into six sheets and written on both sides. Most of the panels were pictograms with some text written in Nahuatl, the Aztec language. The Aztecs almost always drew pictures and rarely wrote in text.

"There also were other written symbols I have never seen before. These may have been written in the languages of the other cultures inlayed into the box. The only trouble is, there is no reference to these strange writings anywhere. What the Spanish didn't destroy was lost over time. That is why these documents may be the glue that binds the entire history of the ancient western hemisphere. These revelations only add to the mystery."

Mystified, I looked at the screen. I couldn't believe what I was seeing and hearing. What did these artifacts have to do with Strutch, and where would we go from here? My mind was ablaze in total confusion. I wanted to follow these mysteries to the end. For the moment though, I forgot about any mystery and paid attention.

"The other side of the document was a translation in Spanish, by a Father Diego Della Vega. He was a priest excommunicated by the church for blasphemy, witchcraft, and conspiring with the devil. It is written that Father Della Vega brought information that contradicted church doctrine to the court of Ferdinand and Isabella. He brought documents that would disprove some of the church's most sacred tenets. This information was so damning to the church that he was thrown into a dungeon, and had a date with the inquisitor. He escaped his torturers and was never heard from again. It is rumored that Father Della Vega went back to the new world. The hierarchy of the church, all the way up to the Holy Sea, had all traces of anything to do with him obliterated from the face of the earth. All documents and his writings were destroyed and his name was never to be spoken again. The pope went so far as to silently cloister all of the clergy associated with Father Della Vega to a monastery high up in the Pyrenees Mountains. The good father and all of his writings were wiped from the minds of all good Catholics. In the church's mind, he never existed.

"Father Della Vega would have been completely forgotten except for the writings of one of his fellow priests, who chronicled the injustice. He wrote this account under the penalty of death. He was compelled to keep his friend's memory alive. The document was found in the ruins of the same monastery that was destroyed by an avalanche in 1631, centuries after Father Della Vega's compadres were long gone. There was no mention of any documents brought from New Spain.

"I only know about this revelation because a graduate school classmate of mine discovered the document while on a dig at the alpine monastery. My classmate, Victorio Estaban, is now the curator of the Museum of Anthropology in Mexico City. We have worked together for many decades on Aztec textile projects. He knows more about ancient Mexican civilizations than anyone alive today. If it is all right with you, E.D., I'd like to consult with him on these matters. He is a man of principle and can be trusted. I still can't believe that this mystery may finally be solved."

E.D. had a contorted, puzzled look on her face. She was under a strict veil of secrecy from her father not to make the box public. If too many people knew about the box, the greater the chance Diamond would find out and foil the whole process. Hesitatingly she told Dr. Ferdan, "If you are positive Dr. Estaban can be trusted, you have my permission to consult with him and no one else. Please convey to him that it is imperative that the contents of the box remain secret. Once the mysteries are solved, the entire world may share in the knowledge I know it will bring."

"Victo, that's what I call him, will not be a problem. Well, anyway, let me tell you what the codex has to offer. I will try to paraphrase Father Della Vega's account."

A glowing red meteorite streaked from the heavens and landed inside a cinder cone rising from the sea, not far from the shoreline. It pulsated and glowed an eerie volley of intermittent colors. Red, yellow, green, and blue lights lit up the inside of the volcano. The surrounding water began to boil from intense heat generated by these objects from space. Boulders crashed together as a maelstrom swirled around its perimeter, like rolling thunder. The sound was so deafening that the people who witnessed this celestial phenomenon were afraid to come anywhere near the water. Even if they were foolhardy enough to try, they would be instantly crushed by the weight of this impenetrable protective barrier.

The boiling water created a thick permanent fog almost to the top around the perimeter of the dormant volcano. It resembled a cake with whipped cream frosting. The interior was filled with the same thick water vapor, which shrouded the colored lights from prying eyes.

The cone formed a perfect circle with four evenly spaced spires at the top. The rim of the fog-drenched cone resembled a crown, floating on a blanket of cotton. The indigenous population called it "The Crown of Knowledge" because of what would be placed inside. Meanwhile, the Spanish called it Corona Diablo, the devil's crown. They believed that this place was so evil that it was the work of Satan himself. Some even speculated that it was the portal to hell. They didn't want anything to do with this contrived evil. The place was so frightening that the Spanish wanted no part in exploring the peak for gold. They left it alone, which was perfect for the locals. Its secrets would be safe.

Sometime later, Quetzalcoatl descended from the heavens in a ball of crimson flame into the cinder cone. The sky was bathed in a flash of golden light as the main god of the Aztec people streaked to the earth. He revealed himself in the form of a giant eagle, perched on a cactus, a rattlesnake in his mouth. Where he landed was called Aztlan, the birthplace of the Aztec empire. Aztlan was situated in a marsh near the ocean, hundreds of miles from Lake Texcoco, where the Aztecs finally settled.

This marshland was full of thick reeds growing in shallow water, which made navigation nearly impossible. Because of its impenetrable nature, not many people had the fortitude or the ambition to penetrate the hostile landscape. The only way the ancients could make it through the reeds was to burn them. Burning was an arduous task, which took too much time and manpower to complete. Besides, there was not much the ancients could use from the marsh, except for the reeds themselves. They fashioned boats and their dwellings from the strong fibers. They just harvested the plants from the edge of the perimeter. The rest were left to grow wild, making it the perfect place to conduct clandestine operations.

Quetzalcoatl taught the people how to efficiently grow crops in the region's fertile soil. He also taught them how to engineer and build massive structures of stone. One such structure was a step pyramid constructed inside the cinder cone where the red meteorite had landed. This site was the perfect place to build a depository to store treasures and knowledge from all pre-Spanish civilizations. It would be the quintessential library, for all to use, only when man was ready to understand the massive powers this complex had to offer. Quetzalcoatl wanted to keep the place a secret. He was afraid that if mankind knew the secrets hidden inside, they would use them to exploit other peoples in the region and around the world.

A lava tube tunnel led from inside the cone to the shoreline. It created a covered river that flowed in and out with the tide. Fresh water flowed into the cone on the outgoing tide and dumped into the sea on the incoming tide. The river formed a small lake, which was continually refreshed with clean water. Rainwater also filtered through the volcanic rock, seeped into the lake, and became some of the purest water on the planet.

Granite blocks were quarried from deposits near the shoreline and floated into the cone on rafts constructed of reeds. As the tide receded, it sucked the vessels into the small freshwater lake inside the cone. The stones were unloaded and fashioned into this massive magnificent structure.

Quetzalcoatl supervised the entire operation. Somehow he used the colored stones from the meteorite to lift and place the granite blocks, sometimes weighing tons, into place. He used the Reed People, as they were then called, to help build and adorn the permanent structure. There was no mention about the building processes involved in the construction in any of these documents. To this day no one knows how these feats were accomplished.

A select group of Reed People was entrusted with the responsibility of maintaining the complex and providing for its security. These privileged few morphed into priests, who eventually developed the Aztec religion. Another group of fierce warriors guarded the sacred place. They became the Yaqui, the only tribe never to be conquered by the Spanish. Quetzalcoatl never educated the people on how to unleash the massive powers of the stones. Legend has it that the powers had something to do with immortality. After the complex was completed, Quetzalcoatl left to help other civilizations, as he did with the Reed People. Over the centuries, other civilizations from all over the Americas brought their treasures and writings to the marsh, where they were displayed and catalogued by the descendants of the Reed People priests. These ancient librarians remained at the cone well after most of the people left for what is now Mexico City, where they built the Aztec empire. As far as this document is concerned, Quetzalcoatl never returned to the marsh.

E.D. was beside herself. "How can this be true? What about immortality? This must be why Diamond is so interested in the site."

I looked befuddled at the two women and added, "Don't forget about the treasure. This scenario is way beyond my comprehension. The whole thing is unbelievable."

Dr. Ferdan agreed with both of us. "There is still more to tell. Just wait to hear the rest. These next revelations will really amaze you. Let me continue with more of Father Della Vega's account. Father Della Vega did escape the inquisitor's wrath and returned to the cinder cone, where he met up with the guardians of the cone."

Father Della Vega did come back to the marsh. He became enamored with the concept of the Crown of Knowledge. The place was like no other. The entire complex was shrouded in fog that could not be penetrated from the outside; and was protected by the impenetrable maelstrom of rolling boulders. There was a feeling of serenity that the good father had never felt before. Underneath the ring of fog, the complex was bathed in golden sunlight that could only be seen from the inside. It was like a two-way mirror. It was perfect for maintaining secrecy.

The many years of being on his knees, in devotion to the Holy Roman Apostolic Church, did not come close to how Father Della Vega felt when he was inside the cone. To him, the place felt like being in the presence of God. As a result, he was excommunicated from the church.

Every cell in his body came alive. All of his senses were heightened. He was able to see more clearly, even in total darkness. He could hear everything, while being able to distinguish subtle nuances in the smallest vibrations. His analytical thought process was so heightened, he was able to know what people were thinking, even before they spoke. He could solve the most complex problems instantaneously. He became stronger than any man alive. He had a bounce in his step and felt like he was floating on air. He felt truly immortal inside of the cone. When he left and traveled outside the cone, the powers dissipated. Understandably, he rarely stepped outside the cone.

The only thing he could not figure out was how the complex got its awesome power. Even though he possessed a higher cognitive consciousness just from being in the cone, he guessed that the red meteorite was the source, but there had to be more to the puzzle. While searching the archives he found the box. Yes, this box. Inside this golden case he discovered what you found, and called them "the knives." They weren't knives at all, but keys. These keys, when fitted in the right lock, would unleash the secrets of the universe.

An array of different types of precious stones was brought to the Crown of Knowledge. The Pre-Colombians brought giant emeralds. The correct stone was fitted to an obsidian shaft. Grooves were cut into the shaft so it would fit into a specific location.

The Aztecs brought the giant yellow topazes. One was fitted to an ivory shaft. The ivory was cut from a wooly mammoth tusk. Yes, a mammoth tusk. These beasts lived as far south as Central America. They were slaughtered to extinction for their meat. A different set of grooves was cut into the ivory, similar but different. Like the other key, the topaz would fit into its own lock.

The Anasazi, from what is now the United States' New Mexico, contributed blue and clear turquoise. One was mounted on a petrified wooden shaft. The stone in the box is rimmed in turquoise, but the center is a priceless, perfect diamond. This stone must be worth millions. It's a good thing I put all of them in a secure place. It may serve a higher purpose than on some shelf in the Smithsonian, or worse, in the clutches of one Harlan Diamond.

Father Della Vega found the locks on top of the cone. He fit all three keys into their appropriate locks, but nothing happened. There was a place for a fourth key, but no key could be found anywhere. He must have assumed that the fourth stone was destroyed, thus missing forever.

Dr. Ferdan added, "I remember seeing a giant blue tourmaline on a metallic shaft in the Museum of Anthropology in Mexico City, where my friend Victo Estaban is curator. The object was found in a sea cave near the Crown of Knowledge, or Corona Diablo. This artifact has been a mystery ever since it was discovered. I wonder if it is the missing key? I am sure Victo would also want to solve this mystery

E.D. hesitated for a moment. She was still hesitant about letting too many people in on what her dad had found. Too many people already knew. "If the cat is let out of the bag, it will only be a matter of time before Diamond finds out." She paused. "Okay, Doctor. Please be discreet."

"Believe me, I want this experience on the up and up. If we are to pursue this quest, the Mexican government should be notified. If we don't eventually notify them, a Mexican jail could be in our future. Victo has the power to bypass some of the red tape. Now that this complication is settled, let me tell you the rest of the story.

"Father Della Vega became disillusioned until he discovered a document that told how to activate the stones. For it to work, the moon had to cover the sun. The light that was left, so-called 'pure light,' would activate the stones, and whoever was in the cone would become immortal.

"This document is in the packet of codices. Yes, a total eclipse of the sun. This revelation is amazing, because there will be a total eclipse of the sun in three weeks. The path of totality will pass over Baja for seven minutes. There is also a crude map that tells us where to look. I'm assuming that what we are looking for is in Baja."

An audible gasp came over the entire room. E.D. chimed in and exclaimed, "I can use the resources available to me to locate any place on earth. If you don't mind, I'll take the map."

Dr. Ferdan looked relieved. She told us that she had no idea where we needed to go. "I'm glad that you can get us there. I made a copy of the map. The original is too delicate to be handled. Please take the copy. The original is in a safe place. Let me continue with the story.

"Father Della Vega warned that if the eclipse lasted too long, there would be dire consequences. He did not elaborate on what they would be, but he alluded to the destruction of the earth. If anyone goes on this journey, I guess they may find out. That must be why the stones were separated.

"The good father took heed of the prophecy and put the codices, his writings, and the keys into the box. He left the tunnel and was in the process of hiding the package on the mainland so no one would have access to this destructive power. As he reached the mainland, an enormous earthquake collapsed the lava tube. Without the convenience of a passageway, there was no way to get to the cinder cone. He wrote about the quake, hid the box, and was never heard from again."

For a moment I thought that this whole story was a cruel joke Father Della Vega made up to mock the church for his excommunication. This story sounded so bizarre that it might be true, or just another legend. My mind zoomed along at warp speed, trying to make sense of the unbelievable story. I could sense that E.D. felt the same as I did. Our curiosity heightened as we looked at each other in awe. Maybe immortality was in our future. Yeah, right!

E.D. thanked Dr. Ferdan for her translation and exclaimed in a strong, confident voice, "I guess there is only one thing to do. We better grab our passports. Will you be coming with us? It could be dangerous."

"Viva la Mexico!"

23

South Texas in summer is not quite paradise. On the contrary, when the sage and bluebonnets stop blooming, all that remains are dry blast-furnace winds, tumbleweeds, and choking dust. The climate is quite suitable for lizards and rattlesnakes, not humans, especially if that person is a mercenary from Russia. Sweat poured from Dragaminov's brow. The salty liquid, mixed with the ever-blowing dust, left a thin paste covering his exposed skin. This non-culinary concoction resembled a chocolate mousse that no one would dare eat. His eyes burned from everything the harsh environment could throw at him. His mood was far from friendly. He desperately needed relief from the elements.

Dragaminov looked up at a nondescript metal building. It looked like any other building in any industrial park, except this single structure was in the middle of nowhere, somewhere on Diamond's expansive ranch lands. An array of huge satellite dishes surrounded the perimeter and peeked at the sky. The collection looked a little like NORAD headquarters, or the front of the ESPN campus in Bristol, Connecticut.

Dragaminov's eyes stung from the sun reflecting off the naked metal, temporarily blinding him. As he reached for the door handle, he gasped. The huge door was locked. His mind was a bit foggy from being so hot. This made him hotter than a swarm of hornets. There wasn't anyone within to buzz him inside either. Instead of screaming, he realized that he had designed the building's security system in such a way that no one would be granted entry without performing the proper sequence, not even himself or Diamond. He gave himself a pat on the back, knowing that this particular building was secure.

It would be disastrous if the wrong people, especially the FCC or the FBI, got a peek of what was inside. He placed his thumb on a pad and jammed a key fob into a slot under his depressed thumb.

With a swoosh the door quietly sprang open, and just like that, the Russian thug felt cool air rescuing his overheated body, temporarily calming his bad attitude. The temperature inside was a cool sixty-eight degrees because of all the sensitive electronic equipment. The building was filled with banks of servers and rows of computers, including several main frames. There was also sophisticated communication equipment linked from the satellite dishes outside to several of Diamond's satellites circling the globe. Definitely no mom-and-pop operation, it was a living, breathing communication center, with more hardware than most countries.

Hundreds of people worked in the complex, including engineers, technicians, scientists, and support personnel. They all lived in luxurious accommodations within the complex. Because most of them were illegal aliens, this was the safest place for them. Dragaminov had tricked these highly skilled people into thinking that this job would lead to United States citizenship. If any of the workers wanted to leave, Dragaminov would just deposit them in one of the many holes in the desert. This was a neat way to keep the complex secure, and expenses down.

Most of the workers didn't have a clue of what was actually going on. All of the clandestine operations were being conducted on the lower level, segregated from the rest of the legitimate endeavors. Most of the people working on the lower level were criminal computer hackers from Eastern Europe. There wasn't a computer these Euro-trash hackers couldn't hack. They had developed a foolproof way to extort huge sums of money from large corporations and individuals. These devious crooks would steal all the computer files and hold them for ransom. If the victims did not pay, all their files would be wiped out, while their assets would be lost somewhere in cyberspace, and eventually end up in the hands of Harlan Diamond. Most of them gladly paid the ransom.

This scam was virtually undetectable because of the satellite network and the hundreds of ground stations Diamond controlled. Most of these stations were in third world countries, places like North Korea, Iran, and Afghanistan. The electronic footprint would be randomly routed and rerouted from satellite to ground station to satellite, many millions of times in just a few seconds. This was a billion-dollar-a-year tax-free license to steal.

On this day, Dragaminov had bigger fish to fry. He was not concerned with the flood of money gushing into Diamond's pockets. He wanted the files from an anthropology professor's computer in California. Yes, his cyber-crook underlings had hacked into the files of one Dr. Ferdan. He burst into their lab with a Cheshire cat grin. In Russian, he inquired, "What news do you have for me today? It better be what I'm looking for."

A lab-coated technician looked at Dragaminov and proudly exclaimed, "We retrieved all the files concerning the box and codices. We also recorded her translation of the documents. You were right about them being valuable. She talks about the written, detailed instructions on how to use the box and its contents to amass a great fortune. There was also some discussion about immorality."

"This is just the information Mr. Diamond is looking for."

"But there is more. According to the author of the Spanish translation, Father Della Vega, there are supposed to be four keys needed to unleash the sequence of events. Miss E.D. Struction is in possession of three of the keys needed to unlock the secrets. A colleague of Dr. Ferdan, one Dr. Victorio Estaban, curator of the Museo de Anthropologia in Mexico City, is in possession of the fourth key. He has a large blue tourmaline mounted on a mysterious metallic shaft.

"This process can only be completed during a total eclipse of the sun. Fortunately for you and Mr. Diamond, there will be a total eclipse in three weeks. If I were you, I'd be making plans for a vacation south of the border."

The technician gave Dragaminov all of the data hacked from Dr. Ferdan. "Here is all of it. What do I get for all my work? Five million dollars would be a fair price for such information."

Dragaminov just laughed and pulled a pistol from his belt, saying, "You get to visit a hole in the desert. I am the king of extortion. Do you think you are clever enough to demand that much just for doing your job?"

Dragaminov grabbed all the documents and recordings. Without even a blink, he put a bullet in the left knee of the greedy technician. He called some members of his security force and told them to deliver the screaming hacker to the infirmary.

"You are lucky I didn't aim higher. If you weren't such a computer whiz, there would definitely be a hole in the desert with your name on it. The next time you try to steal from me, just look down to where your knee once was. Do you now fully understand the consequences if you ever try to steal from me?"

"Yes, Comrade Dragaminov, I do," the technician said as he was dragged away through a trail of his own blood.

Dragaminov walked out of the lab hysterically laughing. "I just saved five million dollars. Immortality sounds pretty good to me. Now maybe I will have the time to spend all of that money. I better call my colleagues in Mexico."

24

Diamond looked down at the wound in his leg. The hole from where the rhino gored his leg looked infected. A nasty, ugly black and beige fluid that smelled like death wept onto his thousand-dollar pants. Blood was also streaming from the same hole. An excruciating pain traveled down the length of his leg, then spread to the rest of his body. His entire body felt like it was on fire. He was in so much pain that he almost passed out. He instantly became diaphoretic. His clothes were soaked in all types of bodily fluids. As he struggled for the phone, he slipped on the marble floor and lost his balance. His massive body fell backward and collapsed on the floor with a loud crash. He screamed, "Miss Green, get my chopper ready. I need to go to the hospital, now! Send in some people to get me to the helipad! I can't make it on my own!"

Miss Green heard the crash and ran into Diamond's office. She saw him lying on the floor, writhing in pain. She knelt beside him and quietly asked, "What's the matter, sir?"

Harlan Diamond barked, "Hurry up, you incompetent fool. Can't you see I'm dying?"

"Very well, Mr. Diamond. Do you want me to call the paramedics?"

"Hell no! My chopper will get me there faster than those public servants can. You should know by now that I expect and deserve the best of everything. I don't want to be down there with the rest of the rabble. Find Dragaminov, and tell him to meet me at the hospital." He barely got the words out before he lost consciousness.

Miss Green, Diamond's secretary for over twenty-five years, was used to her boss's verbal abuse. She was expected to take all the abuse he dished out because he paid her a ridiculously high salary. Because of his tyrannical behavior, the only way Diamond could keep his employees loyal was to throw money at them. He never was, and did not pretend to be, a people person.

Miss Green was getting tired of the many years of verbal abuse. She did not like his dishonesty or his greed. Over the years she had saved up a pretty substantial nest egg from the millions Diamond threw at her. Thusly, money wouldn't be a problem if she were to expose Diamond for his treacherous dishonesty. She was secretly building a dossier on the shadiest of his many shady deals to bring to the Justice Department. She would have done the deed sooner, but she was deathly afraid of Dragaminov and his comrades. Those Russians gave her the creeps.

The helicopter ride to the Harlan Diamond Medical Center took only ten minutes from his headquarters building in Houston. Yes, Diamond owned his own hospital. The building was an ultra-modern edifice, which towered twenty-five stories above the south Texas range. There were floor-to-ceiling tinted windows that looked down at palatial gardens, with fountains and walking paths for patients to stroll freely and forget about their infirmities. All this glitz and glitter was a façade for a more sinister reality. He had fooled the public into thinking that this philanthropic institution was his way of giving back to the community. But in actuality, he made more from the tax breaks than he gave away.

He used the facility to launder billions of dollars from some of his more shady enterprises. This hospital specialized in illegal organ transplants. Most of the organs used were bought on the black market from third world countries. The people in this business couldn't care less for human life. This was the same philosophy Diamond lived by.

He also dabbled in Medicare fraud. His team of unscrupulous accountants cooked the hospital's books and charged the U.S. government hundreds of millions of dollars for services never performed.

Every time the hospital was audited, they passed with flying colors. Diamond just loved creative accounting.

To Diamond, money laundering was not a problem. He also laundered countless billions using banks he owned in Switzerland and the Caribbean. He lived for dishonesty and the lust for wealth. He did not care about the people he harmed, as long as he got his, and most of theirs. In the final analysis, Harlan Diamond, a man not exactly overflowing with human kindness, had to be one of the most despicable people on the planet.

In the helicopter, although unconscious, Diamond's mind drifted toward a time that was impossible to forget. His body was dying, but his mind refused to allow him the peace he needed to reverse this affliction. His mind brought him to a place where horror still lived.

His subconscious mind brought him back to 1969 Vietnam, memories he thought were gone forever. No chance of that ever happening. He was a Marine company commander, operating in the Quason Mountains. It was the middle of summer. The temperature hovered at nearly 130 degrees, with the humidity registering an unbelievable 90 percent. The air was so hot and stagnant that his lungs hurt with every breath.

It was total insanity to be outdoors in that heat, but he marched the exhausted company into the jaws of that meteorological inferno. Those young Marines were loaded down with nearly seventy-five pounds of gear, while he only carried a light pack.

No one in the company could figure out why this insanity was allowed to happen. Come to find out, this insane forced march was perpetuated on a bet between Diamond and another company commander. The other company commander had the good sense to stop and rest in the shade, while Diamond pushed harder to the prize. The bet was only for a bottle of scotch. To him, winning at all costs was the real prize.

As they humped on, the locals watched in amazement. They must have wondered, who are those crazy Marines? As the day wore on, most of the men exhibited symptoms of heat exhaustion. Bright red skin and profuse sweating was the norm. There weren't enough fluids of any kind to quench their insurmountable thirst.

Some people began to deteriorate even further. Their bodies exhibited a dry ashen pallor, coupled with scalding hot skin to the touch. A severe headache usually accompanied the other symptoms. It was heat stroke. When a person gets heat stroke, their body temperature must be cooled immediately. If the body isn't rapidly cooled, death is not far behind. Immersion in an ice bath usually works, but where do you find ice in the middle of the jungle? The corpsman had his hands full treating the victims of this heat stroke epidemic. Some people were in such bad shape they had to be flown out of the bush on an emergency medevac to a field hospital. Flying above the jungle, cool breezes from the medevac chopper ride brought some relief. That chopper ride brought most of the men back to reality.

When a person has heat-related illnesses, their brain begins to fry. They lose the ability to think rationally. Permanent brain damage is a distinct possibility. Some people came up to Diamond, started to speak, and collapsed at his feet. He just ignored them and kept on pushing.

When the company staggered into a small hamlet, things got way out of control. An NVA crew-served machine gun was seen being taken into the jungle. This, coupled with the extreme heat problems, crazed almost everyone. Diamond ordered a squad to chase after the fleeing gun crew. Echoing shots rang out from the jungle. The squad killed a few NVA soldiers, but the machine gun was nowhere to be found. This infuriated Diamond. He so wanted a trophy to show his superiors. This could be the prize that would further his career.

Diamond lost it. He ordered his troops to start shooting everything that moved. Marines who were usually cool under fire started to shoot indiscriminately. The screams of the villagers echoed across the entire valley. Civilian bodies began to pile up all over the dirt streets.

An old woman ran twenty feet in front of the sixty-caliber gun team. They tried to shoot her, but they kept missing. How could they miss at almost point-blank range? *They finally found their mark and shot her in the chest, but she refused to die. She had a sucking chest wound. The corpsman made a one-way valve from the cellophane on a cigarette pack. That Navy corpsman saved her life. She was put in an area where she waited to be moved. The look in her eyes screamed a resounding why. There weren't very many saves that day.*

Diamond's bloodlust kept on growing. He ordered his men to stack all the bodies in the village square. He then ordered everyone in the company to shoot the dead. This added insult to injury. How many times does a person have to die?

The next morning came with an emotional price. The stench of decaying bodies sickened the entire company. Everyone, except Diamond, wanted to leave this cursed place. He wanted more blood. He ordered the squad to go back into the jungle to dig up the bodies that they had killed the day before.

Everyone knew that the NVA buried their dead with their weapons. Diamond used this fact as a ruse for more treachery. The squad dug up the bodies, but didn't find any weapons. They had a surprise for the enemy. The squad placed grenades, with the pins pulled, underneath the dead bodies. As they returned, the whole company heard the ear-piercing blasts from exploding M-25 grenades. Diamond strutted around the village like a cat that just ate a cage full of canaries.

Orders were given to leave these killing fields, but Diamond lusted after the coup de grâce. He and two other Marines, who were just as sick as he was, lined the rest of the villagers against a wall. They unceremoniously shot them all in the head. The last person in line was a young woman holding a baby. They ripped the screaming infant from his mother's arms. The baby's cries reverberated through everyone. The cries of that littlest victim would haunt everyone who was witness to that unthinkable act for the rest of their lives, except for Diamond of course. With a maniacal grin, Diamond, without remorse, blew the poor baby's head completely off. A pink rancid mist hung over the village as its life force left. He then handed the baby's lifeless body back to his mother.

There was a dead silence around that unnamed, cursed village. Many young Marines lost all respect for authority that day. After that dastardly deed was done, Diamond, covered in blood, ordered, "Light this place up! Our work here is done." On his way out of the smoldering village, Diamond told the grief-stricken mother, still holding her lifeless child, "Have a nice day." It's a good thing that poor grieving mother couldn't understand English.

Diamond suddenly woke up from an induced coma. He was disoriented and confused. He smiled as his mind momentarily returned to that demented trip down memory lane. He spoke loudly to himself, "Did I really say 'have a nice day'? Did people use that expression back then? If I didn't actually say that, it makes a more interesting story." Reliving that horrific day only made Diamond smile. If evil people truly do exist, Harlan Diamond would be near the top of the list.

25

I f the first casualty of war is the truth, then the loss of humanity is its costliest. In an instant, I was transported from the naivety of a Ward and June Cleaver existence into the depths of depravity. Some people try to justify the fog of war as duty. That is the most ridiculous lie of all. I can never go back or fill the hole that day burned into my soul.

That was, by far, the worst day of my life. I've tried to rationalize that significant emotional event for over forty years, but to no avail. I haven't been able to shake the guilt of not trying to stop the carnage. In my mind, omission is sometimes just as bad as the act itself. Even though I did not participate, I just stood by and let it happen. I was too numb, caught in that ball of confusion, to even attempt to stop it. A hero should not be measured by what was accomplished on the battle-field, but how he handles the aftermath of war. I just need to forget, take a deep breath, and focus on the future.

On that fateful day, I lost all respect for authority. I needed to let that personality defect go before I really got into a situation I couldn't talk my way out of. Well on my way to settling into senior citizenship, clashing with authority was becoming more difficult, if not impossible. Let's face it. I felt too old to die young. Hopefully, this adventure would help me break the chains which had held me back for so long. It was finally time to let the dark feelings go and bathe in the sunshine. It would be nice to live out the rest of my days with kindness and understanding toward all living things.

26

Diamond's smile was wiped away when he looked down at where his leg once was attached to the rest of the body. Yes, his right leg was gone, from about six inches above where the rhino had gored him. He let out a blood-curdling scream, heard all over the VIP wing of the hospital.

Because Diamond owned the hospital, his suite covered an entire floor of the VIP wing usually reserved for the ultra-rich. Diamond had no problem qualifying himself as a charter member. The opulent adornments did not disguise the medical equipment in the room. A heart monitor, IV tubes, and all the telemetry needed to keep a patient alive in a hospital setting buzzed and beeped. Their nerve-racking noises infuriated Diamond even more.

Doctors and nurses came scurrying into Diamond's suite. They tried to calm his anger, but instead, the megalomaniac went ballistic. "What is going on here? Where is my leg? I only had a cut, and now over half of my leg is missing. I pay all your salaries, and deserve some answers, now! I demand to see the person in charge!"

Dr. Chu, hospital chief of surgery, came scurrying to Diamond's bedside. He tried to calm the crazed Diamond, but to no avail. Still weak from the ordeal, Diamond finally calmed down. He regained a bit of composure, only because he was too tired to cause another scene. "Okay, Doc, tell me what happened, and it better be what I want to hear."

"Very well, Mr. Diamond. My name is Dr. Chu. I am the chief of surgery for this hospital."

"You mean *my* hospital? Why don't you chew on that? Why don't I have an American doctor?"

The diminutive surgeon was not used to such verbal abuse, espe-cially from someone whose life he had just saved. He had been warned about Diamond's demeanor, but was still taken aback by this crude man. Dr. Chu, the consummate professional, thought of the ethics training he had in medical school, bit his tongue, and just stuck to the facts.

"First of all, I am an American. I was born in Massachusetts and I have a medical degree from Harvard. You contracted necrotizing fasciitis, more commonly known as flesh-eating bacteria. The dis-ease is related to streptococcus A, or the bug that causes strep throat. Furthermore, about fifteen to thirty percent of all humans are walk-ing around as carriers of the strep A virus."

"A person contracts flesh-eating bacteria, a very rare illness, from that same strep A, or other bacteria, that enters the body, usually through an open wound. The bacteria can pass from person-to-person contact, but it is unlikely to develop into flesh-eating bacteria without an open wound. Once they enter the body, the bacteria quickly go to work killing the skin, tissue, and fat in their way, leading to organ failure and eventually death.

"In fact, flesh-eating bacteria work so quickly that early treatment is imperative for survival. Treatment usually begins with large doses of antibiotics to fight the infection, removal of the damaged and dy-ing flesh to impede the spread of the bacteria, and treatment of toxic shock symptoms as the body starts to shut down. To treat you, Mr. Diamond, we replaced your blood with fresh, uncontaminated blood. We also had to remove your leg just above the wound. You are very lucky. We got rid of the infection just in the nick of time. You only had a few hours before your organs would have shut down.

"I'm still confused on how this particular strain of bacteria got into that puncture wound on your leg. This strain usually comes from the equatorial regions of the planet. Did you recently take a trip to the tropics?"

"I can help you with your confusion. No, I didn't take a trip to the tropics, but I was gored by a black rhino."

"That would make sense, but where did you meet up with a black rhino in Texas?"

"Texas is a big place, and I own most of it."

Reliving the experience brought chills down his spine. Diamond flashed on the rhino's eyes just before he was skewered. They looked right through his bravado, to expose his vulnerability. The chills quickly passed when he exclaimed, "As he was dying, that horny black beast tried to take his revenge out on me, but as usual, vengeance was mine. I may have lost a leg, but that black devil is still dead."

After the shock of his missing leg passed, Diamond ordered his staff to move into the conference room of the hospital. He was more determined than ever to solve the mystery of the box, and to snuff out one E.D. Struction.

His mind wandered as he started to scream for Dragaminov. He was weak, tired, and running out of people to yell at, so he just closed his eyes and took a nap.

27

Miss Green was busy filling a box with files to be brought to the hospital when Diamond's appointment book flipped open. One page was covered in brilliant red stains that looked like blood. One particular stain reminded her of a fuzzy archery bull's-eye, with an international "no" sign smeared over a specific date. Under the blood was a crude drawing of former VP Haney. She remembered that on that particular date, Diamond was on business in Washington D.C.

She shivered uncontrollably, and her face immediately turned a pale white. She had a strong feeling that there was something sinister about the deliberate way the blood appeared. It looked like the stain was placed there with a gloating vengeance in mind.

She remembered talking to Secret Service Special Agent Pule about former VP Haney's disappearance. This appointment book could be evidence, possibly involving Diamond in his disappearance. If her suspicions had any volition, this could be her way of paying Diamond back for the years of verbal abuse she'd had to endure. At this point she didn't care how much money Diamond threw at her. She just wanted justice to be served. Diamond's fatal flaw, besides being insane, was working with someone who had a conscience. The only thing Miss Green feared was the wrath Dragaminov and his band of mercenaries could inflict. That man gave her the willies.

Miss Green was very organized in everything she did, especially when it concerned her job as office manager for Diamond Oil. She handled all of Diamond's legitimate oil businesses, while the illegal ones were managed from the nondescript metal building by Dragaminov's Russian computer hackers. She had no idea about any of Diamond's extracurricular endeavors.

She managed that office like a military operation, and took pride in how flawless it was run. Everything was in its specific place, and she knew how to retrieve data at a moment's notice. Her leadership was passed down to the secretarial staff in her charge. They handled their duties with the same vim and vigor.

This well-oiled machine was the paragon of efficiency, but the appointment book ate away at her organized mind. She also remembered overhearing Agent Pule ask Diamond about the possibility that his Maybach had been seen on security footage near the former VP's residence on the day of his disappearance.

Because she handled the purchase, she knew there were only a few of these hand-made, expensive automobiles manufactured. Both facts were too damning to be coincidence. After all, loyalty can only go so far when your conscience always tells you to do the right thing. These facts could be much ado about nothing, but she needed to know if her boss was a kidnapper, or maybe worse. She had been that star loyal employee for over twenty-five years, but she could not let this perceived treachery go unnoticed. She just needed to know.

Miss Green immediately called the Secret Service and asked to speak to Agent Pule. Fortunately, he was in the office. He picked up the phone and spoke with a succinct monotone, the way most bureaucrats begin a conversation. "This is Agent Pule. How may I help you?"

"This is Edna Green from Diamond Oil. I think I may have uncovered some information concerning the disappearance of former vice president. Haney" She told the agent about the appointment book and the coincidence of the security footage.

Agent Pule's tone immediately became animated. "These revelations may be what we need to learn what happened to the former VP. Thank you for this information. I will have someone from the Houston office pick up the book immediately."

"Don't you need a warrant to seize private property?"

"Not when it is a matter of national security. The Patriot Act allows us to procure evidence before it can be tampered with or destroyed. I'll send someone right over, and Miss Green, you did the right thing."

Miss Green hung up the phone and agonized over nonchalantly handing private property over to the federal government. She felt trepidation over how the Bill of Rights, especially the Fourth Amendment, could be abused in the name of national security. If they could cavalierly trample over the Fourth Amendment, what would they do to the rest of our sacred rights? This bothered her, but she wrote it off as the price one must pay while searching for the truth. If Diamond committed a crime, he needed to be brought to justice. She rationalized the situation as the changing times we Americans must endure.

Within thirty minutes of speaking to Agent Pule, Miss Green handed Diamond's appointment book over to the Secret Service. As she attempted the transport of the heavy book, a DVD fell to the floor from a secret folder behind the disputed date. The agent picked up the disc. SCREW YOU was written in blood on the face. He immediately showed the disc to a bewildered Miss Green.

"Have you ever seen this disc?"

"No, I have not."

"I better take this also, because it may be important." The agent, wearing latex gloves, gingerly placed the disc into an evidence bag. He carefully labeled each piece of evidence so the chain of custody would not be compromised. If the evidence was not processed by the book, Diamond's attorneys would have a field day getting it deemed inadmissible. Thusly, Diamond would get away with murder.

The agent made Miss Green sign for the collected evidence. He asked her to keep their meeting secret, while the evidence was being processed. She acknowledged the request and stated, "Mr. Diamond is in the hospital. I don't think it will be a problem. He has a lot to think about now. He may die anyway, from his ordeal with that rhinoceros."

The agent looked confused, but stayed on task. "We will be keeping an eye on you, just in case Diamond tries to do any harm to you. In fact, you better take a vacation, somewhere Diamond is not likely to look. You may be a witness in a murder trial."

"That's okay. I will be all right. I don't want Mr. Diamond to get spooked. If he has committed any crimes, justice must be served."

That being said, the agent left the building with a box of evidence under his arm.

28

Splintered sunlight slashed its way through the blanketing mist with scalpel-like precision. Everyone smiled as the sun's warmth burned away the depressing weight of that clinging water vapor. That's the way it was every summer morning around Mission Bay.

A squadron of brown pelicans flew overhead in a perfect chevron, searching for marine life unlucky enough to become breakfast. When these eagle-eyed avian hunters zeroed in on their prey, they broke away and fell from the sky like controlled bolts of lightning, disappearing beneath the blue Pacific. Without warning they emerged with a fish dangling from a pouch under their elongated beaks. What an efficient way to easily search for their sustenance. I always marveled at how these prehistoric flying vacuum cleaners effortlessly went about life. I just wished people could go about their lives as easily as the brown pelican. Maybe that was why they'd survived for so long.

I stood on an anonymous ship's berth overlooking Coronado Island. A medium-sized dark blue ship with "Missing Link San Diego" written on the transom rocked effortlessly to the beat of gently lapping waves. The spires of the Hotel Del Coronado sparkled in the morning sunlight, reminding me of the Emerald City. Coronado was where Frank Baum wrote *The Wizard of Oz* books. A statue of Dorothy and Toto stood in a small park near the ocean. Would our journey take us down the proverbial yellow brick road? Would we be fooled by the man behind the curtain? Only time would tell.

Watercraft of all shapes and sizes, from kite boards to aircraft carriers, dotted the ocean around Mission Bay. Military aircraft took turns flying in and out of the Coronado naval base. Here, Navy SEALs practiced for whatever challenges our country needed them to undertake. America's might was on display all over the area. I felt reasonably safe from the long reach of Harlan Diamond. Wait a minute! When it came down to it, we hadn't been safe anywhere. As a New York City philosopher always said, "Faaget about it."

The dock was bustling with activity. E.D. barked orders to a crew of longshoremen busily scurrying to ready a nondescript ship for a voyage somewhere over the seven seas. E.D.'s luxurious red locks blew in the wind like a matador's cape. Several vehicles were driven and neatly stowed below deck, while a helicopter stood watch from the stern of the tiny ship. Two large satellite dishes proudly pointed toward the heavens. She guided giant cranes, loaded with cargo from a fleet of forklifts stacking pallets. The scene was a lesson in controlled chaos. The entire process resembled a ballet, without tutus or classical music. E.D., as the conductor, knew exactly what to do. The more I was around her, the more I was in awe.

As I walked toward the vessel, Nakai came limping down the gangplank to greet me. His luxurious coat had not yet grown out from the surgery needed to remove the bullet he took for Junior. I was so happy to see that oversized beast alive and recovering. The powerful Malamute's wounds were not fully healed, but he still had the strength to jump up and lick my face. His gargantuan head, so big that it hid my body, almost blocked out the sun.

Junior ran after him. He screamed, "Nakai, you are supposed to take it easy, at least until the stitches come out! Slow down! Who are you slobbering all over?"

"It's only me, Junior. I guess he is happy to see me."

As Nakai released his paws from my chest, Junior noticed who it was behind his dog's girth, good old Jerry Johnson. "Hi, Jerry. Come aboard. The whole gang's here, well, most of us anyway. My dad is still cleaning up Rancho Mysterioso from that kosmic hailstorm. He'll join us in the morning. He knows the whole story, and wouldn't miss the rest of this adventure for anything. Doctors Ferdan and Estaban will link up with us in Mexico."

"That's great. I can't wait to find out what's in store for us inside the Devil's Crown, or should I say the Crown of Knowledge? I like what the ancients called the crown much better. The evil name those superstitious conquistadors conjured up gives me the heebie-jeebies. Let's face it; any place named for the devil gives me bad vibes. Now I need to find E.D. and get my marching orders."

As the last pallet of cargo sank into the ship's hold, E.D. noticed Junior and I talking on the dock. She immediately ran to greet me with open arms. She excitedly exclaimed, "Glad to see you made it to San Diego in one piece. I'll get one of the crew to park the Tesla in that building behind the ship. We need to have a team briefing after all the commotion dies down."

Just like magic, the dock instantly cleared. The only audible sounds were those of waves lapping against the hull of the ship. Nakai's ears perked up just before a glint of refracted sunlight blinded me for an instant. At that moment I sensed that someone was watching us from a hillside above the water. E.D. and Junior felt the same sensation. After further investigation, I could see someone peering at us through powerful binoculars. It had to be one of Dragaminov's stooges. E.D. just blew it off saying, "Diamond has known every move we've made so far. Why would this be any different? We'll keep an eye on that snoop from a camera mounted on that drone silently flying above the ship. We can secretly see what he does next. I'll just send a couple crewmembers up the hill and slow those prying eyes down a bit. Maybe we can, for a change, stay a move ahead of Diamond's wrath."

As I strolled up the gangplank, a bellowing voice triggered distant memories and instantly conjured up faded emotions from the past. "Hey, Jerry! It's me, Strutch!" My jaw dropped as I noticed my old friend limping toward me, with the help of a cane. His left leg sported a walking cast. His face looked like a topographical map, but his eyes were clear. His still powerfully toned chest stuck out with pride, and his pace quickened. "Wow! Is that really you?" As we got closer, he grabbed me by the shoulders and gave me a vise-like bear hug. The force of his powerful grip threw us both into a heap on the gangplank. We rolled down the angled gangplank and came to an abrupt halt on the dock. With my bad back and Strutch's cast, we both realized that neither of us had much balance left. That was completely okay with the both of us, because seeing an old friend was worth any nonfatal fall.

After watching our best Three Stooges' pratfall, Junior and E.D. lifted us to our feet. Even though we hadn't seen each other for over forty years, it felt like we had talked every day. Before I could utter a single syllable, Strutch looked me straight in the eye and inquired, "What's been happening for the last forty years? We need to talk. I'm sorry I didn't let you in on my dilemma sooner, but you must know by now that keeping you in the dark was best to keep you from Big D's treachery. You were the only one I could trust to figure out the riddle in the box. We sang 'Eve of Destruction' so many times that the riddle would be a piece of cake for you, my friend."

"If running from a wildland fire, being shot at, wrecking my Porsche, being waterboarded, and having my house blown to splinters is keeping me from Big D's treachery, I don't know what else could happen. Wait a minute! In the process of saving your daughter and the box, I was forced to kill a human being. That was the first time I fired a weapon since the Nam. Even though I did the deed automatically, without trepidation, I'm still trying to get a grip on that one. I've tried to lead my life without any kind of violence. I haven't eaten red meat since Nam. In some kind of convoluted reasoning, I refuse to kill or eat any mammals because they are so close to humans. I guess that is a tiny gesture of saying I am sorry for what we did over there. "

"But wasn't it exhilarating, you old hippie?"

"Yes it was, but why didn't you contact me before these avalanches of emotions took over my psyche? I must confess, I haven't felt this alive in so many years."

"I made a mistake by not telling you, or my own daughter, the whole story. Big D has his ways to influence people. I don't need his greedy paws all over my discovery. By the way, what do you think of E.D.? Thanks again for saving her life."

"I think you have a remarkable daughter there. That young dynamo has more skills in her little finger than I have in my tired old body. You really have a gem there. If I had kids of my own, I would hope they would be like E.D. Wait a minute! I never wanted kids. Why am I being so sappy?"

"Maybe you are finally growing up."

"Maybe both of us are finally growing up. Hey, speak for yourself. I pride myself on still being a kid inside this battered old body. What's with the cast?"

"I slipped off the cinder cone, like Humpty Dumpty. I fell into the water, where two rolling boulders crushed my leg. It was almost like getting my leg caught in an old-fashioned washing machine wringer, except for the crushed bones. A good Mexican doctor could and did put me back together again. Here I am!"

We just laughed as we helped each other up the steep gangplank.

29

The Missing Link was frenetic with activity. Crewmen were busy readying the ship for the voyage. Captain Bill Bolder scurried over the deck making sure everything was ship-shape. He was a slightly built man with a booming voice. All of his crew performed their tasks with zeal. They all knew who was in charge of sailing *The Missing Link*. Even though Captain Bolder was in charge of the voyage, everyone knew who ran the entire operation. The ultimate leader was none other than E.D. Struction. On this mission E.D. was the queen bee. Her orders were the law. Everyone on board knew she was in charge, including her dad and me.

As Strutch and I entered the communication center below the main deck, E.D., Junior, and the two anonymous fed types I drove to Rancho Mysterioso were busily working at computer keyboards. E.D. was intently watching a huge 150-inch screen fixed to the bulkhead. It displayed high-definition visual drone camera images. They were so precise that she could see the green head of a fly buzzing around the face of that Russian snoop. She moved a joystick to get a better view. Her digital dexterity kept the drone on course. With finite movements, she was able to see everything the intruder was up to.

One of the feds was fine-tuning a satellite dish on top of the ship. The dish was dedicated to hear clear, crisp sounds over a mile away. A high-resolution microphone, mounted on the drone, relayed sound waves to the dish. All extemporaneous noise was filtered away. I was amazed to hear the intruder singing "The Volga Boatman" in Russian. *Isn't technology grand? What will they think of next?*

Perry, the Peregrine falcon, watched intently from a perch next to an open port hole, where he could easily fly in and out of the ship at his pleasure. His sharp eyes stared at me with a laser-like gaze. I felt my follicle-challenged scalp as I remembered what that bird could do to a head of hair. I needed every strand still growing on my head. I hoped he liked me. I noticed that he had a tiny camera mounted just above his sharp left talon. This tool could be invaluable if the observation drone was out of commission with mechanical failure or, even worse, shot down.

E.D. got up from her chair. Confident that the surveillance equipment was working flawlessly, she ordered one of the feds to monitor the Russian's movements. She reiterated, "Let me know if that fool makes any phone calls."

She gathered the non-sailing crew around a large table in the ship's mess to give us our marching orders. She spoke with a confident voice as she informed us of our assignments. "Here is what will go down. My dad and Jerry will travel down the Baja peninsula in a motorhome. You will act as tourists traveling to witness the eclipse. You should blend in with the hundreds of amateur astronomers flocking south. The motorhome will be equipped with all the necessary items needed for your journey.

"You will link up with Doctors Ferdan and Estaban at a resort in the small town of Los Barilles. They will be staying at the hotel. Jake will be flying another helicopter to the Los Barilles hotel's airstrip. After the rendezvous, check into the campground just to the south, in the town of Buena Vista, in view of the Tropic of Cancer monument."

"There will be a detailed plan waiting for you when the motorhome is delivered. There also will be passports and specific directions in the packet. Junior, my crew, and I will sail *The Missing Link* around Cabo San Lucas and anchor near the Crown, close to the mainland. I planned it this way in case Diamond impedes one of our vehicles. I purposely left out some details. If you are confused, don't worry. Everything will make sense when you are on the road. Let's have fun. Maybe we will all become immortal."

"Maybe we all will end up immortally dead."
"We can't, because that is one big oxymoron."
"Maybe we are just plain old morons for attempting such a folly."
We all laughed and went about our assigned tasks.

30

Diamond stared intently at the void where his leg once was attached to the rest of his body. With each glance he became more and more irritated. He took a vase filled with cut flowers and threw them at the hand-carved door of his opulent hospital suite. As the water-filled missile flew, the door opened and a flowery liquid splashed all over Dragaminov's face. Water streamed onto his silk shirt. Blossoms were strewn in a radius across the floor, while one particular yellow daisy hung perfectly from the hired mercenary's ear. The ever-present scowl on his face intensified as he ripped the innocent petaled adornment from his dripping ear and slam-dunked it to the floor. Instead of discarding the unwanted beauty, he found that it was stuck to his shoe.

Diamond let out a belly laugh that could be heard all over the hospital floor. It did not disturb anyone because Diamond was the only patient on the entire floor. Still snickering, he quipped, "I always knew you were a pansy, and by the way, it looks like you wet your pants. You better be here to bring me some good news. As you can see, I'm having a pretty bad day."

Dragaminov, still dripping wet, glared back at his boss and reported, "It looks like we are about to secure the final key from Dr. Estaban. Our operatives in the Mexican Federales assure me that the blue tourmaline will be in our hands within a few days."

"Great news, but we don't really need that particular one. We should let the good doctor deliver it to us on a golden platter. If it's too difficult to obtain the key, we will definitely intercept it when all of us are safely inside the Crown. What about Strutch and his pain of a daughter? Does she still have the other three keys?"

"Well, Mr. Diamond, they are aboard a ship, docked in San Diego, as we speak. I have men monitoring every move they make, but we are not exactly sure of the exact location of the Devil's Crown. They are being tight-lipped about the location. When they set sail we will be monitoring them from every wave and gust of wind."

"Boy, I really like the sound of the Devil's Crown. I think I'll change the name to Diamond's Crown. I want it all, all for myself, especially the immortal part. When you find the location of Diamond's Crown, hijack the ship, and then deliver the keys and the box to me. When you secure the ship, send everything down into the deepest part of Davy Jones' Locker. "

"I intend to do just that. I have a few tricks up my tunic to get the deed done. We have one of our men onboard *The Missing Link*. He will monitor their every move and relay the information to the communication center on your ranch."

"Good hunting, comrade. I have to be fitted for a high-tech wheelchair and new leg in a few minutes. Keep me in the loop on everything."

"Yes sir, it is already happening."

As Dragaminov let himself out, Dr. Chu and a wheelchair engineer entered the room with what looked like a prop from a *Star Wars* movie. The sleek, cold black monster glided over the broken vase as if it was floating on air. While the chair fluidly moved next to Diamond's bed, the lab-coated engineer did not fare as well. With his eyes fixed on the chair's motion, he slipped on the puddle of water from Diamond's outburst. He fell backward, grabbing the armrest. The chair did not budge under the weight of the full-grown man. He lost his grip and landed in the middle of the slippery marble floor in a prone position. He flopped around like a fish that had just jumped from an aquarium.

When he regained his composure, the embarrassed engineer sprang to his feet. Looking Diamond square in the face, he boldly exclaimed, "This was not the demonstration we planned, but as you just witnessed, this chair will never tip over."

Diamond sneered at the sopping wet engineer and snickered. "You just heightened my curiosity about this machine. What else can it do? By the way, thanks for drying the floor with your lab coat."

The embarrassed engineer tried to answer Diamond's question, but was too infuriated to speak. Diamond's abrasive tone had a negative effect on most unsuspecting people. Noticing the tension building, Dr. Chu took the lead. "This is a prototype of the latest technology in wheelchair design. When my colleague, Dr. Grant, dries himself off, he will be happy to explain the particulars of how his amazing invention works."

Dr. Grant, minus his drenched lab coat, explained the capabilities of the chair. "We call this new invention MAV (Modular Anywhere Vehicle). MAV will revolutionize the way handicapped people move around in a safe way. This vehicle will go almost anywhere; under, over, or around almost any obstacle it's pitted against.

"MAV boasts a series of high-tech gyroscopes that prevent this super chair from falling. With the help of powerful magnets, a light-weight titanium-Kevlar frame, and a series of indestructible pneumatic suction cups, MAV can climb stairs, walls, and even travel across a ceiling, without the fear of falling. It took us a bit of practice to trust MAV to move a person upside down. After just a few practice runs, we were confident that traveling upside down was no big deal. If by chance MAV fails, a NASCAR-type roll cage module will automatically deploy, protecting the driver from further injury.

"MAV can also hover above calm water. It will also move on water at about twelve knots. If strong winds or high waves are too powerful to safely utilize the hovering module, an airbag flotation module can be deployed, allowing MAV to slowly propel itself across the water.

"MAV's powerful, newly designed batteries have the ability to recharge while in operation. A hydrogen fuel cell-powered motor, supplies all the electricity needed for an elongated operation. MAV can run at full speed for about three hours, before needing to stop for a charge.

"We have extensively tested MAV in the hospital lab, and are confident that it will be ready for mass production in about two years. One of the only stumbling blocks is the cost. It cost us three million dollars to build this prototype. If we can pare down the cost, MAV will become a savior to the handicapped. Do you have any questions, Mr. Diamond?"

Diamond scratched his head and chuckled, visualizing dollar signs dancing across the ceiling following the indestructible MAV. With a commanding voice, the ruthless billionaire demanded answers to questions that only mattered to him. He didn't care about making the lives of the handicapped better. "I most certainly do. Did you develop this chair in my building? Who authorized this project? Who owns the patents on MAV? Have you developed any military applications? If I sell these gadgets to Uncle Sam, there is no limit to how much money I will make. I smell another fortune for me on the horizon."

Dr. Grant couldn't believe what he just heard. Diamond's lack of compassion made the scientist cringe with doubt. If Diamond had his way, his invention would become just another vehicle for his own greed, without any regard for what it was designed for, making the lives of the infirmed more livable.

The good doctor composed himself and answered Diamond's questions as best as he could. "Well, Mr. Diamond, I am just a scientist and engineer. I'm no expert in financial matters, but I will answer your questions concerning the operation of MAV.

"First of all, this entire project was designed and built in the prosthetics lab. The lab is located in the sub-basement of this building. I was given a grant to develop a new wheelchair-type vehicle from the VA."

"That's great! I didn't have to put a penny of seed money into the project. I just get all the profits."

"As for the patents, my team and I have applied for them with the USPO. We are not concerned with that aspect of the project. We just want to make the world a better place for the handicapped."

Diamond smacked his lips, thinking of how he tried to screw Strutch out of his hydrogen-from-seawater discovery. His attitude spilled over with happiness. To him, money was the only cure for everything wrong with his life. He mused, under his breath, "These bleeding hearts don't really care about profit, but I certainly do. My lawyers will get me the patents. That is a given. I could use a few extra billion."

Dr. Grant hesitated for a long ten seconds before speaking about military applications. Stammering a bit, he looked Diamond in the eye and exclaimed, "As far as military applications, our team developed a laser that can melt anything it is focused on. There are also attached machine guns mounted inside the chair's arms. The hydrogen tanks were adapted to become a flamethrower. All of these applications can be removed for peaceful purposes."

"Don't touch anything on my chair! I like being armed. You never know who will be gunning for me."

"As you wish, Mr. Diamond. I must warn you though; there are still a few bugs to be worked out."

"Don't worry about the small stuff. Let's fire this baby up and see what she can do."

Dr. Chu interrupted, "You are still too weak to get out of bed, let alone test drive a MAV."

"I'll be the judge of that. Help me get out of this depressing bed. I may need to test this contraption's capabilities under extreme conditions. Show me how to fire this puppy up."

Doctors Chu and Grant lifted the lightened Diamond from his bed and placed him into the cockpit of MAV, the super chair. After a few minutes of detailed instruction, Diamond was whizzing his way down the halls of the hospital. He pegged the throttle while racing away from the befuddled engineer. When he came to a locked door, the one-legged egomaniac just took out the lock with the laser. The focused light beam liquefied the case-hardened metal like a white-hot Samurai sword slicing through an ice cube. As the lock melted away, the door swung open with ease. He breezed through the doorway with little effort. Happy to see the obstacle removed, the excited scoundrel fired off a short burst of machine gun fire just for fun. Chunks of wall plaster littered the hallway. MAV breezed through the debris field with little effort. Diamond laughed while ordering Dr. Chu, "Have this mess cleaned up, but leave the bullet holes. They make a fine touch to the ambiance of this hallway."

Hearing gunfire and thinking his boss was in danger, Dragaminov sprinted up the stairs, two steps at a time. Seeing Diamond climbing the same stairway, Dragaminov shouted, "Are you okay, Mr. Diamond?"

"I've never felt better! Check out my new toy. This thing will come in handy when we find the secret to my upcoming immortality."

With overconfidence, Diamond climbed a wall and attempted to drive the MAV across the ceiling. Sporting a cavalier attitude, Diamond ignored all of Dr. Grant's instructions and didn't belt himself into the cockpit. Not ready to defy gravity, Diamond fell to the floor with an audible thud. Laughing, he stared up at the upside-down vehicle stuck to the ceiling. The inverted chair looked as surrealistic as a Salvador Dali painting or an M.C. Escher lithograph. The test was a success, even though Diamond forgot to bounce.

Blood oozed from his flattened nose, but his bruised ego felt more painful. Diamond laughed hysterically as Dr. Chu attempted to stop the blood flowing from his flattened proboscis. He felt weak from his misadventure with gravity. He was more than red faced when he barked, "Get me back to my room! I've had enough excitement for one day. Hey, Grant, take my chair down from my ceiling before it falls on your head!"

Dragaminov and Dr. Chu stuffed the ego-bruised Diamond into a conventional wheelchair and pushed him back to his suite. He was visibly shaken by the experience. Once safely in bed, Diamond immediately fell asleep. He drifted off dreaming of, what else, making money, billions.

Dr. Grant was noticeably worried about the durability of his invention. He did not know how long the suction cups would hold on the upside-down MAV. They never tested how long they would hold in such a precarious position. He noticed that the cups had too much suction and were frozen to the ceiling. He stood on a chair and forcibly attempted to break the suction's grip.

With a great amount of force, he gingerly maneuvered the MAV to a safe, upright position. The fact that the cups froze while in an inverted position, created a safety hazard that needed to be remedied immediately. While prying loose the frozen cups, he had to destroy them to loosen their grip. What if someone was permanently stuck upside down?

Back at the lab, Dr. Grant and a few technicians carefully tested and retested every module of the prototype. They tweaked a few minor glitches, but there was still the lingering question concerning inverted travel. Dr. Grant scratched his head and admitted that his creation was not quite ready to be operational. He was prepared to do whatever it took to make things operate correctly. The only question was what would Diamond think about the delay? The scientist just put that thought out of his mind and kept working.

31

The Missing Link set sail in late afternoon. Captain Bolder was at the helm, diligently scanning the bay for obstacles that could do damage or sink his vessel. There was a lot of traffic on the bay that afternoon. A lightning-class sailboat regatta tacked a little too close to the *Link's* bow. He had to slow down to a dog paddle to let the novice sailors pass without being splattered and sent to the bottom in splintered fiberglass coffins. His steady hand prevented another disaster at sea.

Crewmembers were busy with a final equipment check. E.D. stood on deck supervising the operation. Seamen moved in unison to accomplish their assigned tasks. E.D. was pleased with what she saw. She had worked with most of the crew before, and was confident that they would get everyone safely to the Crown of Knowledge. Unlike Diamond, and the conquistadors, she called the cinder cone by its real name.

As the only woman on board, and the leader, E.D. was more vigilant to the possible dangers ahead. She felt confident that her leadership skills were strong enough to evaporate any gender bias the crew may have harbored. Throughout history, sailors have been superstitious about women being in command. This was not the case with E.D. She had the respect of everyone under her command. With her guidance, this crew would follow her into any dangerous situation she was pitted against.

As *Missing Link* motored under the Coronado Bridge, a pod of dolphins led the way into the open Pacific. When seen through binoculars, the frolicking mammals looked like they were smiling. To the superstitious crew, it was a good omen.

A cool breeze blew in from the west. The moving air, from the cold Pacific, made everyone on deck layer up to stave off the biting cold. They all wore dark blue slickers with the Earth Help logo embroidered on the back that matched the color of the ship. Everything on the ship was color-coordinated. It was E.D.'s good fashion sense that made all the difference.

Captain Bolder proclaimed, "That girl has such an eye for detail as well as being a strong leader. We are in great shape with her in charge."

Cold Pacific waters from Alaska flowed south, while the Atlantic waters flowed north from the warm gulfstream in the Caribbean. Pacific waters are so cold that it is difficult to swim as far south as Mexico. The only nearly warm water splashed onto south-facing beaches. The closer to the equator, the warmer the water became. *The Missing Link* was indeed headed for warmer water.

As *Missing Link* headed west around Point Loma, a low-angled sun reflected an eerie glow from thousands of identical white limestone grave markers. The bluff above the cliffs was the final resting place for sailors and Marines who died in the defense of our country. Most of the graves were the final resting place for those who died in the Pacific during World War II. Their last measure of devotion was displayed on that rolling bluff, ever vigilant, for future generations to remember.

Captain Bolder assembled the crew to pay respect for the fallen. Everyone on board stood by the rail and saluted as the ship passed by the shimmering stones. The ship's bell tolled five times to honor the heroes' memory. Even though there was no one to hear or see the display, the crew all believed that they were communicating grief to the vanquished defenders of freedom.

As the excursion headed west into open water, the horizon was aglow with a display of color only a few have ever witnessed. A blood-red sun, surrounded by layers of colorful hues, showed the way. Friendly clouds held the crimson, magenta, purple, and orange in place. Winds swirled the colorful display, layering the colors into patterns that changed with every puff.

Old sol bobbed its way under the waves, and the rest of the sky became ablaze with tongues of fire licking at the twilight. As daylight transformed into dusk, the fire in the western sky grew brighter. After twilight lost its glow, the fire still burned for the longest time. The celestial display lasted for a good hour before the fire was replaced by millions of points of light peeking from above. This is what the romance of the sea is all about.

While the light show was in its flashing glory, E.D. and Junior held each other tightly. They experienced their blossoming love flowing along with the waves. These two were meant for one another. They glowed from both the love of the sea, and the love for each other growing inside their souls.

As *The Missing Link* sailed into Mexican waters, a meteorite streaked across the sky and splashed between two waves. A momentary flash lit the ocean. While tracking the meteorite's path, E.D. noticed lights from two vessels coming from the east, following the *Link*. She immediately called one of the fed types manning the communication and telemetry equipment. "Can you get a fix on two lights that appear to be following us from well behind the stern?"

He immediately got back to her with discouraging news. "You were spot-on with that observation. It appears that two small vessels are shadowing us, but lying back, just beyond normal radar distance. They are staying about forty miles from our stern. I can't get a fix on who or what is following us."

E.D. thought for a minute and ordered Captain Bolder to "change course to a serpentine pattern. If they keep following us, launch the drone. I'll be down below in a minute. We need to keep tabs on those radar blips. I have a feeling Diamond is very curious about what we're up to."

Before E.D. and Junior could get inside, the drone lazily flew behind the ship and set a direct course to keep an eyeball on the two unwanted intruders. The slow-moving snoop would take about ten minutes to get within spying distance. Until then, E.D. could not determine a course of action appropriate for the situation, whatever it turned out to be.

E.D. sprinted to the communication room, three steps at a time, leaving Junior in her dust. Junior breathed heavily as he finally caught up to her. "What's the hurry? We have plenty of time to waste before we get conformation on what is following us."

E.D. just laughed. "I can't believe that a strapping young lad like you let a girl beat you in a race down into the bowels of this ship. Do you need some oxygen, or an easy chair?" She smiled and gave her new love a peck on the cheek.

E.D. was just playing with Junior. She camouflaged her trepidation by injecting humor into the mix. This momentary distraction put everyone at ease, underscoring the crisis they could possibly have to deal with. E.D., with her overflowing confidence, was the mistress of putting people at ease, even in the face of danger. Her poise and positive attitude reassured everyone that she would always do the right thing. That is what makes a great leader. There was no doubt that she was that great leader.

Everyone's eyes were fixated on the radar screen and the drone's video feed. The lag time between the unknown and confirmation was nerve-racking at best. A plethora of disastrous scenarios clouded rational thought. The crew was on edge, tapping fingers and breathing hard. Only disastrous endings ran through their thought processes.

After waiting a good ten minutes, the drone's infrared camera sent back images of two fast boats speeding along in tandem. They appeared to be cigarette boats; the kind drug smugglers like to operate. They gave E.D. concern, because these speedy vessels would overtake the *Link* in a matter of minutes. Furthermore, the men operating the boats chasing them were wearing official-looking Mexican Customs uniforms. This was odd—*The Missing Link* was in international waters. Mexico had no jurisdiction this far out.

E.D. had a bad feeling about what was going down. She zoomed the camera in tight and noticed light-skinned men with blue eyes speeding over the crashing waves. A shocked look filled E.D.'s face, drained of all color. "The boat driver looks like one of Dragaminov's men. Yes, I'm sure of it! He was one of the stooges with Dragaminov at Rancho Mysterioso!"

As the camera zoomed in, the Russian mercenary waved and smiled. He mouthed a clear "Game over." The video feed suddenly went black. Two inbound missile signatures flashed across the radar screen. E.D. bluntly ordered, "Defensive measures."

Junior jumped up and deployed what looked like a heavy metal band's pyrotechnic light show, high into the air, away from the ship. A magnetic pulse generated from the display, disabled the missile's guidance system, and deflected the warhead's course, then returned them to the two fast boats. A massive fireball lit up the sky, well behind the *Link's* wake.

E.D. boldly shouted, "It looks like they got their heads fatally banged!"

Burning wreckage lit up the night sky. With the drone out of commission, E.D. sent Perry out of the open porthole. The speedy falcon, armed with his trusty talon camera, circled the explosion, sending back images of total destruction.

There was a man treading water some distance away from the wreckage. He looked badly injured. E.D., seeing the survivor struggling to stay afloat, fired up the helicopter with Junior and one of the fed types, then flew directly to the flaming sea in an attempt to rescue one of the men who had tried to blow them out of the water.

With the night sky lit up by burning fuel, seeing the burned, drowning Russian mercenary was no problem. E.D. feathered the chopper to ten feet above the distressed swimmer. The rotor wash separated the burning fuel from the victim. As she got into position, the now foundering, barely floating man lifted his hand with a half-hearted wave and sank below the churning waters of the not-so-blue Pacific.

Junior, seeing the distress on the man's face, dove into the frigid water and grabbed him by the shirt collar. The fire had burned most of the cloth away. What was left of the garment tore away in Junior's hand. He had to dive down about twelve feet to retrieve the sinking body. He swam to the surface with his arm locked inside the armpit of the now dying Russian.

When they reached the surface, the victim was not breathing. Junior automatically started rescue breathing. It was difficult at best to try to revive a near-drowning man in the open ocean, let alone someone with third-degree burns on his face. As Junior attempted to get a good seal, pieces of the victim's burned lip came off in his mouth. Junior almost had his own airway obstructed. Retching, he threw up the semi-cooked flesh. It tasted like death.

Meanwhile, the fed type lowered a rescue basket into the water. Junior lifted the cooked Russian into the mesh basket as best he could. When he finally secured his patient, a giant wave splashed over the both of them. Junior lost his grip and almost went surfing. With his powerful grip holding onto the struts of the basket, he was able to hang on enough to be lifted into the belly of the rotating beast.

When the two wet men were safely in the cockpit, the Russian let out a blood- curdling scream. He was barely alive. He struggled to speak, but had something to say before he went to the great be-yond. With quivering lips he whispered softly, in good English. It was so soft, that Junior could barely hear his dying declaration. "Please avenge my brother. Comrade Dragaminov must pay for killing my brother. Please do this for a dying man. He is evil."

"Try not to speak."

"I must have your word that my brother's death will be avenged.

Please do this for my family in Chechnya. I am sorry we caused you such pain. We didn't know what we were getting into when Dragaminov recruited us. He said we would be fighting for mother Russia. Please help me get justice."

"Yes we will." When he heard Junior's promise, the duped young man held his hand and drifted off. He died with a smile on his face. The three people still alive were physically shaken.

E.D. looked up from the controls with tears streaming down her face. She looked at Junior and said, "We know what we must do. Dragaminov and Diamond will be brought to justice, one way or another. There is no room for such evil on my watch."

The three breathing people and one crispy critter lumbered back to the *Missing Link*. E.D. landed the helicopter on to the deck with flawless precision. When the engine went silent, E.D. ordered Captain Bolder to prepare the Russian's body for a burial at sea. The salty sailor knew just what to do. His crew stitched a white cloth bag around the dead man's body, with the last stitch through the bridge of the deceased's nose. This was a tradition that went back hundreds of years, when sailors were at the mercy of the four winds. The entire crew stood at the rail while Captain Bolder commended his body to the waiting sea. Everyone was in a somber mood.

After the ceremony, Perry flew through the open porthole. The ship's cook gave him a huge chunk of raw filet mignon. Everyone on board let out a spontaneous sigh of relief. E.D. jumped up and exclaimed, "I'm tired! Captain, please sail us south. I need to get some rest. I'm going to bed. Junior, are you coming?"

"Yes ma'am."

32

Secret Service Special Agent Pule did a double take when he saw the disturbing image on his computer monitor. Staring him in the face was an email from the FBI forensics lab. It was the completed report from the blood on Diamond's appointment book. It was the same book Miss Green gave to the federal agents. The blood smeared over the date former vice president Haney was reported missing turned out to be a perfect match. Furthermore, Diamond's fingerprint was on the bloody international "no" sign.

These revelations were only circumstantial at best. There wouldn't be enough evidence to constitute an indictment, but there was enough to make Diamond a strong person of interest. This new evidence, coupled with the Maybach sighting on the traffic camera, was enough to launch an investigation into Diamond's possible involvement.

As Agent Pule read further, he found that the encrypted DVD revealed a totally different story. It clearly depicted Diamond fighting with the former VP and pushing him to his death. These images could be enough to bury Diamond for good. One thing confused Agent Pule about this case. Diamond's lawyers could present a self-defense case. Be that as it may, there would be no defense for an obstruction of justice indictment. Diamond's arrogance and total disregard for the law would seal his fate. Anyone who believes that he is above the law will always contribute to his undoing.

"What kind of person keeps a trophy of murder? He must have known that there is no encryption the long arm of the law cannot decipher. Who is this maniac?"

Special Agent Pule was well aware of who Harlan Diamond was, and his connections to the previous administration. If the government were to pursue these leads any further, they would have to tread light-ly in order to keep Diamond unaware of the investigation. If Diamond were to have any inkling of an investigation, he would hide behind his army of lawyers and vanish from the face of the earth. His well-paid, unscrupulous legal team would stonewall any attempt by government law enforcement agencies to prosecute.

Special Agent Pule notified the Secret Service chief, who in turn notified the director of the FBI, who notified the White House, the National Security Agency, and even the IRS. With all of these agen-cies in the loop, it was just a matter of time before Diamond would get wind of any investigation aimed toward him.

Diamond's intelligence network was much more sophisticated than that of the United States'. Without any constraints, he could circumvent FCC regulations, and he did not care about protecting an individual's rights, afforded by the constitution.

Most intelligence agencies, as a matter of policy, don't communi-cate with one another. They operate as independent fiefdoms, always trying to outdo each other. Diamond always used interagency rivalry to his advantage. This was one of the reasons he had carte blanche to get away with almost anything. This time though, Harlan Diamond's reign of terror could be coming to a screeching halt.

Special Agent Pule, with the help of the Justice Department, pro-ceeded to send the collected evidence to the federal grand jury. The jurors wasted no time in bringing an indictment against Diamond. The DVD clearly allowed proceeding with an indictment a slam-dunk.

The United States of America vs. Harlan R. Diamond read like a bea-con of justice, shinning across the legal-sized paper. The government had tried to implicate Diamond Oil, and one Harlan Diamond, in a myriad of shady deals. Every time they attempted to charge him with a crime, the mercurial tycoon slipped out of any noose put around his neck. This time would be different. Visual evidence of murder was a different story. Even if for some reason he wiggled out of the murder charge, he was very guilty of obstruction of justice. Where was the body?

Special Agent Pule got on the phone and had Miss Green immediately placed into protective custody. She would most assuredly be in grave danger when Diamond found out about her role in his apparent indictment. He also got a call from the Justice Department. A warrant for Diamond's arrest was being handed down from the grand jury as they spoke.

This day was not turning to be a good one for one Harlan Diamond. Maybe his bad karma would finally catch up to him.

33

A shiny new Bounder motorhome pulled into the parking lot of the Mission Bay Marina. The behemoth vehicle looked like a rock star's tour bus. In fact, it was built on a luxury bus chassis. It was so big that a folding ladder was needed to gain entry. The dark blue color exactly matched *The Missing Link*. E.D. had an eye for color co-ordination. A pair of folded satellite dishes made the vehicle look even bigger. Dark tinted windows gave the bus a mysterious appearance.

As the 45-foot luxury giant came to a screeching halt, Chip, the kid from Tumbleweed Tech, bounded from the cockpit. He jumped to the ground, clearing the ladder, causing a cloud of dust. Confused, but pleasantly surprised to see him, I had to deal with the dust in my face. I really liked his enthusiastic attitude, but what was he doing on such a dangerous mission?

As our eyes met, he greeted me with a friendly smile. "Hello, Mr. Johnson. Thanks again for letting me drive the Tesla. I'm so psyched to drive down Baja, to watch a total eclipse of the sun."

As I wiped the dust from my watering eyes, I grumbled, "What are you doing here?"

"Oh, Ms. Struction hired me to drive you and Mr. Struction to Buena Vista, Mexico."

"Did she tell you about the danger? This is not your typical Mexican vacation."

"Things sometimes are not what they appear to be, especially when it involves Ms. Struction. I'm not just a student. I've worked with her on a number of operations. She had me keep an eye on you, without arousing suspicion, so as not to spook you. I may look young, but be assured that I'm experienced. Oh, hi, Mr. Struction."

"Do you know each other?"

Strutch looked at me with a twinkle in his eye. "I guess the cat is out of the bag, or should I say, box. Chip here is a federal agent, assigned to shadow us on our adventure."

"I don't want to know the details."

Chip handed us each an envelope with new altered passports and driver's licenses. My alias was Cal Brady and Strutch's Buck Marlow. We needed new identities to throw off the Mexican government. E.D. couldn't trust any government to be free from Diamond's reach. All he had to do was throw a few bucks to a few corrupt officials and our quest would be over before it even began.

There was another surprise E.D. threw into the mix. We were carrying the box and two of the keys. She split the artifacts between *The Missing Link* and this land yacht; to make sure Diamond would never get his diabolical hands on the entire package. If one of us were compromised, he would get nothing. To me, this plan was a little excessive. E.D. was either very careful or very paranoid. All of this confusion made me more anxious to see this adventure through to fruition. We were all in agreement, so without further ado, Strutch stated the obvious: "What are we waiting for?" Chip took that as an affirmative and headed east.

"Hey, Chip, why are we headed east? I thought Mexico was south."

"Well, Mr. Johnson—or should I say Mr. Brady—Ms. Struction has a reliable contact at the Tacate border crossing. She set it up that way, not to cast suspicion on what was inside the motorhome. In fact, there won't be any record of us crossing into Mexico. As far as the Mexican government is concerned, we do not exist."

"I should have known that E.D. had all the bases covered. I think I better stop second-guessing your daughter, Strutch. She never stops amazing me."

"Good idea, old pal. I've stopped questioning her from the beginning of this fool's errand. We were never close, but when she came back into my life, I let her carry the ball. I'm just here to smell the adventure and enjoy the ride."

"Don't forget about being immortal."

We all laughed, and we left San Diego without looking back. The sun was at its zenith as the three of us chugged over the mountains on our way to the border. To the southwest a dark brown haze hovered over the Mexican city of Tijuana. The air looked like it would swallow anything that passed under its menacing toxic blanket. The further east you looked, the cleaner the air became. No wonder there was so much despair and violence in that inhospitable border town. Anyone breathing that putrid air would always have a miserable day.

I was glad we wouldn't be crossing the border at TJ. Gratefully, we would miss the hot, sweaty, long border wait. Thankfully, we wouldn't witness the constant hawking of trinkets by desperate poor people. I always felt sorry for these nameless souls who must swallow their pride, forced to breathe deadly carbon monoxide day in and day out, while we witnessed their misery in air-conditioned comfort. Why was there so much disparity between two cultures separated only by a line on a map?

There was also the possibility we could get kidnapped or even murdered. Powerful drug cartels ruled that town with violent intimidation. This was the compelling reason for the cultivation of United States homegrown cannabis. Just end the prohibition, and the scourge of the cartels fades away. That was why I admired Jake and his victory garden. There was not a hint of violence in what he did. As our nation becomes more tolerant of this harmless plant, maybe in time, the senseless violence would become just another sad footnote in history. That was maybe asking too much, but it was an honorable goal to strive for. I just hoped I would still be alive to witness that game-changing day.

34

Chip never lost his perpetual smile as he maneuvered the land yacht around the menacing switchbacks, gliding down the back-side of the mountain. Some of the turns were so tight, he had to scrape a few overgrown Scottish broom bushes growing on the side of the road. An audible squeak reverberated throughout the cabin. Yellow flowers flew by the windows, while Strutch and I just focused on the hundred-foot drop over the cliff, just inches from our tires. Our young pilot smoothly breezed around the obstacles. The tricky maneuvers did not faze our young driver at all. E.D. sure knew how to pick a crew that was fearless, as well as proficient in everything they were doing.

The sleepy border town of Tecate was just that. Everyone there knew how to beat the blistering noonday sun. They suspended all activity and took a restful three-hour siesta every afternoon. The streets were void of human inhabitants. The only movement was a few chuckwalla lizards, frolicking in the town square's fountain. For three hours, they had the entire town to call their own, without the fear of a barbecued spit. Oh, to be a chuckwalla at noontime in Tecate. Seeing them gave me a momentary rush of freedom. Happiness must be what all creatures live for. *Wow, I just compared myself to a lizard.* Maybe I was destined for another kind of barbecue spit, with Big D turning the handle.

Crossing the border was a breeze. Chip pulled the motorhome into booth number two. E.D.'s contact greeted us with a smile. With perfect English he said, "Welcome to Mexico. What is your business in our country? Do you have anything to declare? Please show me your passports. You need a passport to go into Mexico now."

Chip looked the border agent in the eye, and with a friendly greeting proclaimed, "We are on our way to witness the eclipse. Here are our passports. Oh, we don't have anything to declare now, but I'm sure we will have plenty of souvenirs on our return trip."

The border agent gave Chip a double wink, stamped our passports, and told us, "There are a lot of gringos traveling to witness the eclipse. I plan to head south myself. It will be a spectacular show." He handed us our passports back and wished us a safe journey.

We left the gate without fanfare and headed due south. I noticed another border agent looking at us with a tepid curiosity, while talking on a cell phone. I wondered if he was calling Big D. It was too late to be paranoid. We were committed to our quest now that we were in a foreign country. It was certainly too late to turn back.

Chip pulled the motorhome into a turnout and jumped to the ground. He took a screwdriver and removed the license plates and replaced them with fresh ones. The new plates read ASTROS, short for astronomers. He got back to the cockpit and told us, "Everything will be all right now. The vanity plates were E.D.'s idea. Don't blame me for that one. Well, anyway, the border agent handed me two sets of papers. One is for the police, if and when we are stopped. The other set is for our return trip. Can't be too careful. By the way, the agent we spoke to gave me a double wink, a signal to let us know that we would have smooth sailing all the way to Buena Vista. I've worked with him before. He is a solid friend of mine."

This cloak-and-dagger stuff made me chuckle. It was as if we were real cold war spies, and not a bunch of bumbling amateurs. Well, anyway, I could only speak for myself. "Hey, Chip. Did you notice that other border agent looking at us while talking on a cell phone?"

"No, I didn't. I better call my friend and see if there is anything to what you saw." Chip made a call on his satellite phone. He talked for about a minute when his perpetual smile was wiped clean from his face. With a serious look he told us, "While I was talking to my friend, a gunshot rang out, and the phone went dead. I hope he didn't get shot."

I was not laughing when I heard the bad news. Chip went into crisis mode. He activated a powerful rearview infrared camera that could focus on moving objects, further than the eye could see. It also could look into a moving vehicle and send images of the occupants to a database that identified the person in a matter of seconds.

Just as Chip activated the defensive optical systems, his phone rang. It was his friend at the border. Apparently, there was a domestic shooting involving a jilted lover and her cheating husband. He had to deal with that mess, having to shut his phone down. He called back to say that we passed just in time to miss all the excitement. In fact, the border would be shut down for hours. If someone was following us, we'd have a minimum of a three-hour head start. Our trip to Mexico was beginning on a positive note.

The Bounder cruised down the Baja Peninsula with a fluid motion. Even though the temperature outside hovered at the 100-degree mark, we were quite comfortable, insulated from the heat in air-conditioned splendor.

Strutch and I kicked back, enjoying a cold Bohemia beer, guacamole, and blue corn tortilla chips. Chip, always focused on his driving, tapped his fingers to Mariachi music playing on the radio. The Bounder had a superb sound system that rivaled a concert hall. It sounded like the musicians were playing among us. We all sang off key to "La Bamba," reverberating in all directions. The ride was so pleasant that the immanent dangers ahead were pushed to the back of our minds.

We drove into the city of Ensenada at the crack of noon. Drunken American college students stumbled out of Husong's Cantina, a popular watering hole, frequented by young gringos. They were exchanging college fight songs, slurring most of the words. It looked like they were having a good time. I remember being drunk at noon, but tried to forget the epic two-day hangovers. I wouldn't wish that agony on anyone. Now that I was older, the thought repulsed me. I guessed those kids would have to learn the hard facts or perish in the process.

All of that revelry made us hungry. Chip pulled into a quaint seaside café, south of the city. The salt air mixed with pungent Mexican cooking filled our nostrils, enhancing our already ravenous appetites.

The rickety family-owned restaurant was barely balancing on a bluff, just above the ocean. A hand-painted wooden sign waved in the breeze. It looked like a parrot in flight. El Papagayo, or Parrot, was totally empty, except for the staff. We had the place to ourselves. That was a good thing, because the building looked like it would disintegrate if any more people occupied the structure.

A cute little girl, about seven years old, greeted us at the door. This pint-sized hostess showed us to a table on a deck, overlooking the crashing waves. She was wearing a zebra-striped pillbox hat, with a hibiscus bloom pinned to the brim. She looked like a miniature Minnie Pearl, only saying "Hola" instead of "Hoowdy." With a wide smile, she handed us menus printed both in Spanish and English. Strutch didn't hold his tight enough. A gust of wind blew the bilingual document into the sea below. Too bad fish couldn't read, or they would possibly have to eat their relatives.

A waiter brought us chips and salsa and glasses of water. Strutch reminded me, "Never drink Mexican water," so instead, we drank beer. We ordered salads with pickled hard-boiled quail eggs, local vegetables, pumpkin flowers, wild mushrooms, nuts, herbs and spices. The salad was dressed with chocolate vinaigrette. Next, I ate raw oysters, crabs, giant prawns, and scallops over ice. Strutch and Chip got fresh fish tacos, beans, and rice. We finished our lunch with fried ice cream. We ordered shots of tequila for the employees. The owner toasted our good fortune and a safe journey. On our way out I gave the little hostess a twenty-dollar tip. Her eyes grew as big as saucers.

That tip would pay for much needed help for her family. She kissed my hand as we left El Papagayo with a good feeling.

As we left the restaurant to check out the ocean below, a 1970s Buick Riviera screeched to a stop. Two burly men, wearing black leather jackets, rudely forced their way past us. They were carrying M-16 rifles and sported side arms under their hot-looking leathers. Chip was fluent in Spanish, so he understood their conversation. Apparently, they were Federales, shaking down the restaurant owner. The leader hit the owner with the butt of his rifle, while the other one cleaned out the cash register and took all of the liquor from the bar.

The cute little hostess cried while they ransacked the place of anything valuable. Her father, with blood dripping from his forehead, tried to console his daughter, but he was hit again. This time he fell to the floor unconscious. The leader, drinking tequila from the bottle, took out a fusee and set the building on fire. They laughed as the restaurant went up in flames, with the little girl still inside.

Chip couldn't handle this brutality. He confronted the drunken bullies with an unceremonious vengeance. Without hesitation, he disarmed them with surgical precision, rendering them helpless, and in pain. With flying fists and feet, the young man incapacitated both of them and left them writhing on the ground. He threw their weapons into the waiting ocean below. Chip cried out, "Good riddance!" He then took all their money and gave it to the bleeding restaurateur. He was grateful, but still afraid. Unbeknownst to any of us, a propane line had been severed in the struggle.

While Chip took care of the now defenseless creeps, I heard screaming from the fully engulfed structure. The little girl was trapped inside the blazing inferno. Without hesitation, I grabbed a nearby blanket and jumped through the flames. I scooped her up, wrapped her in the blanket, and carried her outside to safety. Just as we stepped from the inferno, the rest of the building blew up. The compromised propane tank BLEVE'd (boiling, liquid, expanding, vented, explosion), and blasted into the air like a skyrocket. I could feel the heat scorch my back.

When we were safely away from the searing heat, I noticed that the little girl was not breathing. Even though my hair and eyebrows were singed and smelled like a dentist drilling a cavity, I opened her airway and initiated rescue breathing. After inflating her lungs with fresh air for about a minute, she became responsive. She began to retch and cough up carbon from her heated little lungs.

As she began to breathe on her own, I realized the gravity of the situation. Even though I had decades of experience, and scores of structure fires under my belt, rescuing injured little children and animals always took precedence over my own personal safety. I had reacted without trepidation. All the danger was worth it when I saw her smile. The grateful little girl threw her arms around my neck and sobbed tears of joy. I started to choke up myself, but realized I never cry.

I looked back and noticed that the restaurant was a total loss. The only thing that remained was the now singed sign. The two corrupt Federales were burned beyond recognition. The Riviera was parked too close to the building, and also burned. What a waste of a true classic automobile. We stuffed what was left of their crispy bodies inside the Riviera and pushed the still smoldering wreck into the ocean, where it would meet up with the waterlogged weapons. There was no trace left of what had just transpired.

We put the entire family into the motorhome. The little girl held on to me with a death grip. She wouldn't let go of me for anything. Everyone seemed relieved as Chip drove off. Nobody looked back. If they did, there would be nothing left to see, except for smoke and the lonely parrot flapping in the breeze.

Strutch pulled a wad of money from a bag and gave it to the now homeless family. "I hope this will help get you started on rebuilding a new life."

As we dropped the grateful family off, Chip said, "Don't worry about those bad men. They won't bother you again." We waved good-bye and immediately realized there wouldn't be any guarantees as to their safety. There were always going to be bad men preying on the helpless. At least we had temporarily thwarted two of the worst.

35

The weather in summertime Texas resembled the inside of a pottery kiln. Even though the landscape was not quite hot enough to fire clay, the human body, drained of moisture, could feel like a rack of baked decorative dinnerware. A body exposed to such conditions cools itself with moisture in the form of sweat. As the sweat evaporates, a salty residue leaves behind stained clothes and bad attitudes. Anyone exposed to these elements screams for any cool refuge.

Special Agent Pule, accompanied by a contingent of tactical FBI agents, experienced the heat firsthand. As he exited his vehicle in the Diamond Medical Center parking lot, Special Agent Pule's dark suit and Kevlar vest retained all the moisture the Texas heat could dish out. Most of his clothes were drenched in his own evaporating bodily fluids, which made him feel like he was in a sauna with all his clothes stuck to his flesh. The rest of the agents, in full battle regalia, couldn't beat the heat either.

Special Agent Pule was armed with an arrest warrant for one Harlan Diamond: *The United States of America vs. Harlan Diamond.* There were indictments for first-degree murder, obstruction of justice, income tax evasion, bank fraud, Medicare fraud, and cyber espionage. There would probably be more charges to come at a later date. If Diamond were to be convicted of any of these serious charges, they would most certainly have to throw away the key. There were just too many charges for his army of shyster lawyers to defend.

As the armed agents burst into Diamond's suite, they found a nurse bleeding on Diamond's hospital bed. Diamond was nowhere to be seen. The nurse looked puzzled at Special Agent Pule and his gun-toting backup band. She was bleeding from a wound on her head.

"Who are you people?" the nurse asked.

"I am Secret Service Special Agent Pule. We are here to serve a federal arrest warrant on one Harlan Diamond. Do you know where he is?"

"He and his security detail just left the hospital by helicopter in a hurry. They forced Dr. Chu, the chief of surgery, to go with them, taking a prototype wheelchair and a crash cart with them. They tried to force me to go, but I locked myself in the bathroom. When I thought the coast was clear, Mr. Dragaminov knocked me unconscious with the butt of a pistol. My head is still spinning.

"Mr. Diamond is a very sick man. He needs to be monitored around the clock. I guess that is why they forced Dr. Chu to go with them. Now I understand why they left so quickly. He must be in big trouble to forgo hospital care. What did he do?"

"He killed the former vice president."

"Oh, my!"

Besides the team with Special Agent Pule, more federal agents secured all of Diamond's properties, gathering evidence. The cyber-crimes division of the FBI secured the computers and servers from the nondescript building on Diamond's ranch. INS agents were on hand to check the Russian hackers' legal status. They entered the building without resistance.

Workers inside the building had no love for Diamond and Dragaminov. In fact they told the agents that some of them were being held against their will. If they refused to work, Dragaminov would do harm to their relatives in Russia.

One worker, Yuri Arlingin, hobbling on crutches, gave up all the data and the location of the backup servers and global relays. He was the person Dragaminov had unceremoniously shot in the knee. Comrade Arlingin was happy do this service, not just for revenge, but to cover up the five million dollars he had diverted to his own Swiss bank account. It was the same amount he tried to extort from

Dragaminov for the retrieval of Dr. Ferdan's assessment of the box. For him, payback was sweeter, even if he was still wearing a bullet in his knee. He, as well as most of the workers, told the feds they would be glad to testify in any court of law.

Another large group of agents descended on Diamond's mansion on the Potomac. A full forensics team went over the entire place, looking for evidence. They especially were interested in seizing the wind harp and Maybach. Those two items were trailered to the FBI forensics lab in Washington.

It looked like everyone was ready to give up Diamond. He had lost all loyalty from the people he so brutally trampled over. His ruthless security team had surrendered without a whimper, like the rats they were. There was not enough money to keep them loyal. Diamond's karma was finally catching up to him in a big way.

The U.S. attorney seized most of Diamond's domestic property and assets. For all intents and purposes, Diamond was broke, except for a few billion he had stashed out of the country. If and when he were to be brought to justice, those funds would lie dormant, never to be spent.

Now that Diamond was technically a fugitive from justice and his fortune drastically slashed, he was just an ordinary billionaire on the run, without a country. He had just one play left—to become immortal. The delusional psychopath believed that if he were to live forever, no court would dare convict him of anything worse than jaywalking. After that bump in the road was smoothed, everything would be back to normal. He would go back to doing what he loved best: screwing over everyone he encountered.

36

The Missing Link steamed into the Gulf of California, or Sea of Cortez, depending on whom you asked. A large monolithic rock, resembling a burro drinking the warm waters of the gulf, guarded its entrance. High-rise hotels, glitzy restaurants, and baked sun worshipers from the resort town of Cabo San Lucas stood above both bodies of water.

Pongo boats filled with tourists sloshed their way to get an up close look at the thirsty-looking formation. A natural tunnel, carved between the warm gulf and frigid Pacific, made an interesting portal between the two bodies of water. As the tide went out, warm water would spill into the Pacific. Conversely, when the tide came in, the opposite occurred. Instant temperature change made for a novel way to beat the heat.

This temperature change made the Portuguese man o' war jellyfish overactive. Those blue blobs were not actually jellyfish, but marine cnidarian. The slimy, parachute-looking creatures took out their frustration on unsuspecting swimmers and attacked unsuspecting bathers by wrapping their long dreadlock tentacles around limbs and torsos. They inflicted an unbearable pain from poison glands inside their undulating whips. Multiple stings deposited burning welts over the affected area.

The only sure way to treat the sting was to avoid them altogether. Because the jellyfish were transparent, it was almost impossible to avoid them. The locals said to wash the welts with salt water, rub wet sand over the affected area, and urinate on the wounds. The crew got a big laugh watching sunburned beachgoers urinating all over their burning skin. This bizarre scene could easily have been a Marx

Brothers movie, directed by Federico Fellini. The crew needed a little comic relief after their close encounter with the business end of two incoming warheads.

E.D. was in a particularly upbeat mood as *The Missing Link* sailed into warmer waters. A good night's sleep did wonders for a girl's attitude, especially when a warm body helped with her relaxation. For the same reason, Junior was also in a good mood. E.D. knew that the Crown of Knowledge would be less than a day away.

Dragaminov's spy, posing as an engine mechanic, became worried when he tried to check in, and no one answered. Diamond's worldwide communications network was out of commission, seized by the United States government. Without orders the spy was dead in the water. The confused saboteur made an unordered decision to sink the *Link*.

Before the *Link* set sail, Diamond's stooge stashed explosives in an engine room locker. He decided to sink the boat while the crew was busy watching the zany antics on the beach. As he was moving more explosives, he noticed E.D. walking in front of him toward the stern. He dropped his deadly package and crept up to her and tapped her on the shoulder. She was startled for an instant and let out a yelp. When she turned around, a pistol was aimed against her face. "Do not make a sound, or it will be your last."

E.D. looked down the barrel of the pistol and asked, "What is the meaning of this aggression? Don't take this any further, or you'll definitely have a bad day." She was not used to being threatened, especially by this bozo. As the Russian chuckled, E.D. kicked the gun out of his hand, reminiscent of the Lone Ranger.

She kicked the deadly hunk of metal with such ferocity that the firearm flew harmlessly into the bilge. She drove the palm of her hand into the stunned bad guy's nose, splattering blood over everything in sight. She finished off the under matched seaman with a flurry of blows that put him down for the count. He did not know what hit him, but E.D. definitely knew. Her numerous black belts in a number of disciplines gave her the confidence to quickly vanquish that pipsqueak. She tied him to a steam pipe and went for help removing this human trash.

As her "almost" assailant came to, she laughed. "How will you explain to your comrades that you were taken down by a girl? Wait a minute; you can tell your new roommates in federal prison, tough guy."

E.D. called Captain Bolder and told him what had transpired. She ordered a full search of the ship. When the crew checked the engines, they noticed explosives wired to the propeller shaft, set to blow in just two hours. They disarmed the explosives with great relief. If they had gone off, *The Missing Link* would have become a sinking raft.

E.D. thanked the crew for diligently exposing the possible sabotage and saving the ship from destruction. She gleefully announced, "I guess a rat didn't leave our sinking ship. The ship is not sinking, but he's still a rat. I just hope he likes jail as much as the open sea!"

The mechanic in question was hired as a replacement because the regular crewmember was absent during the final muster. A replacement mechanic was sent over from the seaman's union hall. He had all the necessary credentials. Because of all the chaos, Captain Bolder did not call to confirm the replacement with the union. The man just blended into the ship's routine. After further investigation, the real mechanic was found floating in Mission Bay with a bullet hole in his head, and the union never did send anyone as a replacement.

Captain Bolder felt responsible for the nearly catastrophic mistake. He told E.D., "I messed up big time. There was something strange about that fellow. I noticed the perplexed expression on his face when we had the burial at sea. He was more than confused; he was terrified."

"The imposter must have been terrified that his own people would attempt to fire missiles at a ship he was aboard. He panicked, and prematurely tried to sink the ship before his own people killed him. The more Diamond and Dragaminov interfere with our mission, the more I can't wait for them to be brought to justice. Remind me to throw a big party when they are safely behind bars. Don't feel too bad. We all make misjudgments," said E.D.

"I pray you never do, because it could be permanent for all of us." The two laughed and went about sailing the ship northward, with a course set directly toward destiny.

After about an hour of smooth sailing, E.D. ordered Captain Bolder to pull into a protected cove, where a small river flowed into the gulf. The shoreline was dotted with reeds just beyond a narrow, rocky beach. A dock that couldn't be seen from the main body of water jutted out from the shoreline. A huge glow of reflected light beamed just beyond the reeds and jungle-type vegetation. In a calm voice, E.D. asked Captain Bolder, "Please anchor here while we check something out on shore. We will be back in about a half hour. Our final destination is just around the bend."

E.D. and Junior took the ship's launch and motored to the dock near the beach. Nakai, seeing his master sailing from the ship, jumped over the side and swam to the launch with powerful strokes. Junior, seeing his recovering Malamute swimming alongside of them, pulled the wet dog aboard. Nakai shook the excess water from his luxurious coat, drenching the unsuspecting boaters. "I thought I told you to take it easy while you were healing." Nakai responded by licking the moisture from Junior and E.D.'s faces.

E.D. laughed, petting the giant wet fur ball. "That's okay, big guy. You can come with us. I'm sorry we left you behind."

Warm water and cool breezes made the short voyage a very pleasant experience. After only a few minutes, they were tied to a dock on the shoreline and out of the boat. The two hikers and furry friend followed a path over the rocks and disappeared into the reeds. The cool breezes vanished and were replaced with hot, stagnant air. Sweat poured from the hikers' bodies. Nakai took the heat in stride, running ahead of them, leading the way. Junior immediately took off his shirt to get some relief from the scorching heat. "It is a good thing you insisted we take water. I need hydration," he gasped.

After a long drink, they were out of the canopy and into a large clearing. The cool breezes came back just as fast as they left. E.D. commented, "Was that so bad? Take a look just below that hill. You might want to cover your eyes." Junior complied, donning sunglasses.

Thousands of blinding lights beamed from a south-facing hill. The reflection momentarily blinded the duo, but their vision returned quickly with the help of designer sunglasses. What they saw was a vast network of piping snaked around a solar farm that led into a large building, then into reinforced tanks. They were labeled "liquid hydrogen" on one side of the complex, and "liquid oxygen" on the other. Between the two was a large building covering a mound of pure white salt granules. There were also a number of other buildings scattered around the property.

"What is this place?"

"This is my dad's solar hydrogen oxygen extraction facility, or SHOE for short. He developed a process to separate hydrogen and oxygen from seawater at SHOE. There is an underground brackish river that flows through these marshlands. This is not ordinary water, but heavy water. Deuterium and tritium bind with the oxygen to make up this water. Yes, the same stuff they use in nuclear applications. This water has three times the hydrogen of normal tap water. The salts in the water hold properties that, when heated, separate the pure liquid hydrogen and oxygen. The byproducts are cool, clear water and low sodium salts that can be used in a number of products, including cosmetics, medicines, and even safe food preservatives. A heart attack that never happens."

"Wow, this is unbelievable! How does it work?"

"The solar panels move with the sun. Photovoltaic cells convert sunlight into electricity. The electricity is used to separate the water into its basic elements. The water from this river contains unknown properties that make the separation process happen with less heat. In fact, this process uses far less energy than a high school chemistry electrolysis experiment.

"There are a few bugs that need to be worked out. The solar panels get covered by a desert varnish, which bakes on a coating that renders the cells ineffective to produce optimum electricity output. The other big problem is the water that makes the process so easy makes for a volatile, unstable soup. This concoction makes the cryogenic liquid extremely explosive. There have been a few small explosions already.

"The biggest problem was to keep Diamond from stealing the operation. He initially bankrolled my dad, and argued that the patents and any facility that utilized this process were his. That is why this place is a secret."

"Where are all of the workers?"

"My dad has suspended operations because of the safety concerns, and of course the discovery of the box. After a minor explosion, he traced the course of this river to find the source. During the exploration, he found a cave that was exposed by the shock wave of one of the small explosions. He found the box and codices inside the cave.

"After this discovery he lost all interest in SHOE and devoted all his energies to uncovering the mysteries of the box. He temporarily abandoned this installation. There are only a skeleton crew and a few caretakers left. Someone needs to watch the potential hazards associated with highly explosive materials. They just keep the place from being reclaimed by the jungle. They aren't here now. That is too bad, because I'd like to talk to them. Oh well."

E.D. took Junior to the cave, just a short distance away. She showed him where the box was hidden for over five hundred years.

They were amazed by what they saw. The cave was adorned with intricate drawings, much older than the five-hundred-year-old box, depicting all aspects of ancient life. The reed people must have drawn them.

Nakai's ears perked up and he ran up a small path. E.D. followed him to an opening at the top of the cave. Loose rocks made travel difficult, bordering on treacherous. The two fit people made short work of the dangerous climb, still trailing the fitter canine.

In the sunlight they finally laid eyes on the prize. There it was, the Crown of Knowledge, in its full glory. The spires on the crown could be easily seen, floating above the fog, bubbling over the cinder cone. The menacing rumble of tumbling boulders could be heard from their perch. The rolling, thunderous, igneous spheres were trapped in a maelstrom that would not allow anyone to enter from the outside. The swirling solid moat was the perfect recipe to keep this place a secret.

"That is the reason why no one has, or even wanted to, climb to the top. Anyone foolhardy enough would be ground up, like nuts in a cracker. My dad tried to climb the outside of the cone. He barely escaped with his life. He is wearing a cast for attempting such a suicide mission. I'm glad I didn't inherit his foolhardiness."

Nakai began to eerily howl. His body shook, while he breathed hard. He put his nose toward the crown and smelled an essence permeating from the cone. The big dog felt a friendly presence. His breathing slowed, with what appeared to be a contented look on his face. "This dog must have a sixth sense. This is definitely a good omen. I'm confident everything will turn out just fine," said Junior.

E.D. looked at Junior and enthusiastically proclaimed, "Finally, we made it!" She planted a big kiss on Junior's waiting lips and shouted, "Eureka! Let's get back to the ship. We have a mountain to conquer."

Junior kissed her back. Just as they exited the cave, E.D. got a call on her satellite phone. She spoke for a few minutes and then hung up, smiling. "Hey, Junior, Diamond was just indicted for the murder of former vice president Haney. That creep is a fugitive from justice, a man without a country. Oh happy day! It looks like we won't have to deal with that maniac's interference anymore. He will be too busy avoiding the United States of America's wrath. "

"Don't celebrate just yet. Every time we get too cocky, he shows up, giving us a bad day."

"I guess you're right. I just want to put a positive spin on this adventure." That being said, the two lovers skipped toward *The Missing Link* with ear-to-ear grins. Even Nakai was smiling.

37

The Bounder motored smoothly southward, but the road we were traveling was more than treacherous. Signs that read "Peligro" (danger) were a constant reminder to stay focused on navigating. Waves of heat rose from the blistering pavement and made for a miserable, hot time behind the wheel.

The supposed highway was so narrow that there was barely enough room for semi-trailers to pass, within inches of kissing their extended, elongated side mirrors. Numerous potholes and a gauntlet of debris fields could easily puncture a tire and impede the progress of the most experienced drivers. There was no shoulder to speak of. Wrecks, of all shapes and sizes, littered the roadside with troughs of broken dreams. This particular road was no modern freeway, but what the road to hell would look and feel like. The thoroughfare resembled the road to Baghdad during Desert Storm, without the collection of burned bodies.

Hazards made travel excruciating slow. Frightened gringo tourists were unaccustomed to such dangerous conditions, especially when impatient truckers blindly passed a line of slow-moving vehicles at breakneck speed. Kamikaze road warriors, deprived of sleep and cranked up on speed, unofficially ruled the road. One such fool, after passing a long line of cars, with another truck headed directly for his grill, flattened our side mirror. Chip initiated a defensive maneuver that miraculously kept all six tires planted firmly on the pavement. His superior driving protected us from being added to the collection of grotesque sculptures lining this paved goat path. After the crazed driver passed, the mirror sprang back to its normal position. We weren't driving blind for the moment.

There were shrines dedicated to driving miscalculations from one end of the highway to the other. They were a constant reminder of the misguided glorification of the open road.

Mexico's version of the DOT turned a blind eye when it came to safety. Because of a nonexistent vehicle inspection policy, there were trucks in service that any junkyard in the United States would refuse. These unsafe vehicles, put together with duct tape and prayers, were constantly broken down.

Besides the maniac truckers, we had to maneuver around an obstacle course of disabled vehicles and their fuming mad drivers. At best, this made for a nerve-racking trip we would keep in our memory banks forever. I was relieved that Chip was piloting this land yacht and not me. I might have been caught up in road rage frenzy, and the need for speed could have been a recipe for disaster. I've never been labeled a slow, cautious driver, and I had a resume of accidents to corroborate my personality flaw. I just kicked back and squeezed dents in my padded armrest while Chip merrily cruised to the south.

After an hour of playing extreme dodge traffic, Chip pulled off the highway and parked in a rare turnout. He leapt from the cockpit and surveyed the damage inflicted to our side mirror. That mirror was intact, besides the fact that it could have been lying in a pile of junk, a hundred miles behind us. All Chip could say was "No problem. We have a backup, with a rear-facing camera system if we need one. Isn't modern technology grand?"

While on a respite from the demolition derby, we went outside and stretched our inactive legs. Chip was busy inspecting the Bounder for more damage. He climbed the ladder to the top and adjusted one of the satellite dishes, which controlled the camera system, so he didn't have to rely on old-fashioned mirrors if they were sliced away by another rogue semi.

We were glad to be stopped, even though the raging desert heat was well on its way to bake a soufflé inside our brains. As my skin began to bead up with sweat, my stomach began to flip. A wave of nausea hit me like a tsunami. I immediately began to retch. Sour-tasting, green projectile vomiting made me feel even worse. I couldn't believe how much partially digested food a stomach could hold.

After I hurled my lunch across the desert landscape, the other end started to bubble over. I bolted into the Bounder with a hurdler's stride. I barely made it to the bathroom in time to evacuate the rest of my intestinal contents. Contraction after contraction spilled into the toilet. I felt beyond miserable. What curse was I afflicted with this time? Would this setback prevent me from seeing our mission through to fruition?

After what seemed like an eternity, I joined the living. Chip was busy spraying air freshener throughout the cabin. Strutch had the windows wide open. An exhaust fan blew the nasty aromas into the outside atmosphere.

Sporting a green pallor, I stumbled face-to-face with the reality of the situation. "What just happened to me?"

Strutch laughed. "You just had a bout of Montezuma's Revenge. I told you not to drink the water."

"But I didn't drink any water."

"Oh yes, you did. What did you think chilled your delicious raw seafood platter? Yes, it was ice, frozen water. Now will you listen to me about Mexican water?"

"I can't believe something that appetizing could possibly result in such an adverse reaction like Montezuma's Revenge. I don't even like ice."

Chip came into the room drinking a glass of ice tea. Hearing the ice cubes clanking in the glass made me run back to the bathroom for round two.

38

Diamond's 747 lifted off from a secret airstrip somewhere in a desolate part of his massive Texas ranch. He only used this secret egress when total anonymity was paramount. Under indictment for murder, and technically a fugitive from justice, his whereabouts would most definitely have to remain secret. There was no time to answer these serious charges.

Diamond was arrogant enough to think he was above any law and could beat all the charges levied against him. He didn't have time to be bothered with the laws of ordinary men. He was totally obsessed with his own immortality. These serious charges would become irrelevant, just another bump in the road. For the time being, his lawyers would handle any prosecution-related matters.

The huge aircraft flew below the radar while aiming to the southwest, across a massive expanse of the Great American Desert, on a direct course for Baja. Cacti and greasewood bushes flew past the fuselage like a picket fence. There was no stopping Diamond's plane from escaping the long tentacles of the American justice system.

Just as the southwestern-bound jumbo jet was within minutes of the border, a squadron of F-23 fighters surrounded it with impunity. The war birds flew within fifty feet on all four sides. There was nowhere for the behemoth to escape their wrath. A stern voice on the radio blared an ultimatum to the escaping low-flying aircraft. "Diamond Oil 747, this is the U.S. Air Force squadron leader. Turn around and follow us to a designated runway. We will show you where to land. If you fail to comply, we will be forced to blow you out of the sky. Acknowledge. Over."

Without an escape route, the pilot had no choice but to comply.

"Squadron leader, this is Diamond Oil 747. Roger that. Why are we being diverted? Over."

"Do not ask any more questions; just follow my instructions fully or face the consequences. All four of our aircraft have missile lock on every side of your aircraft. Noncompliance on your part would be a fatal mistake. Out."

"Roger that. Diamond Oil 747, out."

The shadowed 747 flew north, its deadly escort tightly in tow. After about a half hour, a single runway appeared in a small valley, surrounded by jagged peaks. This runway was part of a secret military installation used for research and development of the latest innovations in warfare. This particular installation was not on any map or government guidebook. Most people had no clue of its existence. Giant stealth-cloaking dishes beamed electronic pulses that interfered with radar and communications, thus making the valley virtually invisible. This was the perfect place to take Diamond into custody, far from his legion of lawyers.

Special Agent Pule and twelve federal marshals were waiting patiently by a hangar near the end of the runway. They were there to serve a murder warrant to Diamond before he was safely out of the United States. Because of Diamond's ruthless history, another contingent of federal agents had the perimeter covered with enough firepower, including an Abrams tank, to prevent any violent escape attempts. This extra security seemed a bit like overkill, but the United States government was not taking any chances. They wanted to take Diamond into custody before he set his bloodthirsty pack of lawyers to wrangle him from the jaws of justice.

As the flying armada saw the runway lights flash between the opposing mountain peaks, the lead escort peeled off, giving the 747 a clear shot to touch down. "Tower to Diamond Oil 747, you are cleared for landing. When you land, proceed to last hangar on your left. Shut down all engines, do not move, and prepare to be boarded. Tower out."

"Diamond Oil 747 to tower, beginning final descent. Diamond Oil 747 out."

The 747 dipped below the jagged peaks, and all of the instrumentation failed. Someone had forgotten to disengage the electronic pulses. The giant converted airliner lost all power and didn't have enough airspeed to hit its landing mark. She dropped like a stone skipping across a calm lake. The nose of the plane smashed into three consecutive light towers, shearing the front landing gear completely off. Without front wheels and a nosecone, the crippled bird could not steer, and was at the mercy of the laws of physics.

Skidding across the runway at nearly 150 miles an hour, without power, the jet's wings crumpled away from the body, spilling jet fuel in their wake. The rest of the plane began to cartwheel sideways and hit a fuel storage tank-farm head-on. The ruptured tanks ripped open like a can opener piercing aluminum. A deluge of flammable liquid drowned the crippled bird, creating a tsunami that crested over the entire base. Everything was covered in a shallow sea of vaporizing fuel and choked by a flammable mist.

Because the flammable jet fuel was too rich to initially burn, the spill stayed liquid. An injured occupant jumped from the plane and screamed, "Mr. Diamond," and was overcome by the noxious vapor cloud. His dying words echoed across the canyon, easily heard by many witnesses. There was no sign of Diamond.

The vapor cloud thinned, and a sparking wire ignited the spill. The vaporized liquid flashed with the ferocity of an atomic bomb. The brisance was so powerful that the explosion could be seen and heard for fifty miles.

When the gasses were burned away, the liquid burst into flames. Billowing black smoke, interspersed with orange resignation flames, blocked all visibility. The fire was so intense, and vast, that it burned for days. The canyon walls kept the heat trapped inside their boundaries, kept everything cooking like an out-of-control oven. Everything on the base was totally destroyed. In fact, there was no evidence of the 747. The former luxury liner of the skies was instantly reduced to a puddle of molten metal. There was no physical evidence left for fire investigators to process. It was days before the conflagration cooled enough to search for the ignition point.

As flames licked the entire base, Special Agent Pule and his small army took refuge in an underground ammunition bunker complex. They ran down a long corridor, until they reached a heavy steel door. Without trepidation, four of the biggest agents unceremoniously forced the door from its hinges. Flashlights illuminated the dark, musty room. What they saw made them quiver with fear. Looking directly at tons of explosives, the reluctant visitors did an about-face, quickly exiting without looking back. There was an empty transport sitting in the passageway, which ran along the rows of magazines for over a mile. By the time they reached the end of the hall, they could hear and feel the exploding ammunition, one magazine at a time. They were tired, but lucky to still be alive.

Just as their eyes adjusted to sunlight, they witnessed the total destruction of this well-guarded secret. Everything was reduced to rubble. Few people would know what happened here, or even care. Why would they care about a place that did not exist? Only in America!

Special Agent Pule was sadly elated. He was sad that lives and property were lost. He couldn't believe that Diamond could cause such mayhem, even in death. He was elated that *The United States of America vs. Harlan Diamond* was finally over. "Good riddance!"

39

The Bounder deliberately plodded its way across the bumpy highway. Ruts, potholes, and a constant washboard vibration made for a slow, uncomfortable ride. Chip tried to smooth out the road as best as he could, but this converted goat path made any hope of an enjoyable ride wishful thinking.

While we made slow, calculated progress, I began to feel better from my bout with Montezuma's Revenge. All of the toxins had exited my body from both ends. Hunger and thirst replaced the spasmodic pain. Bottled water and fresh fruit were my ticket back to the living.

Strutch noticed I felt better and couldn't help toying with my misfortune. "Hey, Jerry, I mean Cal, would you like some raw seafood, chilled with local ice?"

"No way! How would you like to be inconvenienced with the sights, sounds, and smells of another bout with my favorite Aztec leader's revenge?"

"Touché." We all laughed hysterically while the Bounder slowly made progress, navigating the unpredictable desert highway.

Chip answered the satellite phone with a friendly hello. E.D. called to tell us about Diamond's 747 crashing. She couldn't give any details, but she did tell Chip that there were no survivors. That crash made me feel much better, but I was so looking for Big D to rot in jail. The only trepidation was the fact that Big D still owed me that cash from the Nam. We toasted to Diamond's demise with shots of tequila. Strutch put it into perspective when he said, "Oh, happy day! It couldn't happen to a more deserving scoundrel. Let's get cracking. We have a box to deliver."

After another hour of pinball-esque travel, the road miraculously smoothed. Chip took advantage of this welcome stroke of luck, maintaining a faster cruising speed. Eighty miles per hour on a firm, newly paved highway made driving a breeze. We were, so to speak, walking in tall cotton, or in reality, riding without the constant brain rattling. Just as the road quieted, I fell asleep. I hadn't had any meaningful rest since that insidious bug took over my body.

The rhythm of constant smoothness knocked me out with a vengeance. It began to feel like this was a vacation and not a whirlwind adventure. Wait a minute! What had been happening for the last week but a whirlwind adventure? I really needed some rest.

After a four-hour restful nap, a bright orange light shined through a west-facing window, nearly blinding me. When my eyes could focus again, I noticed the sun was setting between the humps of a mountain saddle. Layers of yellow and orange swirling clouds, resembling colored cotton balls, spilled from the heavens. Chip also noticed them and pulled the Bounder into a convenient turnout.

All three adventurers zoomed from our cocoon, amazed at the light show on the horizon. As the sun squeezed between two peaks, the colors became more vivid and animated. The entire desert was bathed in an aura of changing colored light. Dust particles infused with color drifted over the landscape. Another huge grove of tall cacti, which resembled six-fingered hands outlined in orange and yellow, appeared to be waving. As the giant hands waved, ribbons of light hurtled past, covering us in the same brilliant glow. We had just witnessed the duality between beauty and the reality of an unforgiving wasteland.

As the sun disappeared, most of the colorful light show reluctantly faded. A single shining sliver light beamed toward our viewpoint. Everything else was muted in shadow. It was like someone had shined a colored spotlight in our direction. Even though darkness was rapidly approaching, we continued to clearly see a lighted pathway to the mountains.

Just as things couldn't get any stranger, a figure, bathed in naked light, moved deliberately toward our vantage point. We couldn't distinguish much detail because of the fading light. Was this an apparition or something real? When the figure got closer to us, it was evident that it was, indeed, real.

What we saw was an old man scurrying from the wasteland. A halo of subdued light surrounded his head like an angel in a Renaissance painting. His long, wool, hooded serape and worn huarache sandals made him look like someone out of central casting in a 1940s Pancho Villa movie. A large wooden cross hung heavily around his neck like the clock around Flavor Flav's. I was pretty sure this person was not into rap music.

He swiftly glided toward us, carrying an elongated wooden staff that clicked with each step. His weather-beaten face resembled leather saddlebags after a heavy rain. His well-defined facial features exuded an air of trustworthiness. His clear gray-green eyes looked through me, as if he was checking me out from the inside. I needed to hear what he had to say.

When we were face-to-face, this interesting-looking man spoke in perfect English. "My name is Diego Della Vega, Señor Johnson."

"Who? No way! You can't be over five hundred years old. How do you know my name?" Meeting this dude was definitely the strangest part of our odyssey yet. Strutch and I looked at each other in awe while we carefully listened to what he had to say.

"This is all correct, Señor Johnson, and you too, Señor Struction. Obviously, I am not who you think I am, though I am aware of Father Diego Della Vega. In fact, this was his cross, which hangs from my neck. You must put all of your trust in what I have to say, and do exactly what I tell you to do. As we get closer to the Crown of Knowledge, the mystery will become crystal clear. Now, may I please have a look at the box?"

I had to touch his face to see if he was the real deal or an illusion.

As my fingers came in contact with his leathery cheek, a soothing calm enveloped my mind and body. Just from being next to me, Strutch felt exactly as I did. We both knew that this was real and not some cheap, New Age swami's snake oil demonstration. For the rest of this incredible journey, we only had to follow, while having our minds constantly blown.

Strutch and I spoke at the same time. "Please, come on in. We will be proud to show you the box." There was no need to question this unique individual about anything.

Chip had the door open already, and we climbed into the Bounder. From the compartment hiding the box, a soothing hum reverberated throughout the cabin. Old Della Vega's ears perked as the hum grew louder. Even though the box was carefully hidden, our visitor moved directly toward the prize. Our eyes were glued to what would transpire next.

Della Vega reverently fondled the box, as if he was in the presence of the Holy Grail. With a wave of his steady hand, the lid flipped open, exposing the keys. They alertly stood at attention, pointing downward, exposing their bejeweled tops. The gems began to glow, spewing ribbons of color throughout the confines of the Bounder. The light felt more kosmic than any liquid light show projected behind the band at a Grateful Dead concert. The light reinforced a single specific clarity. Our cause had to be just.

Della Vega placed the keys back into the box. He did not hide the box, but gingerly placed it near an open window, where it could soak in the remaining fading light rays. Looking at us with the resolve of a general planning for the throes of battle, Della Vega began to speak. "Now that you have witnessed the power of the box, I must prepare you to enter the Crown."

Without warning, moonlight illuminated a narrow, dusty road, showing us the way. Even though the three of us had no clue where we were going, Chip obediently followed the old man's direction as if he was driving down his own street. Groves of those giant six-fingered cacti pointed the way. Like a psychic GPS, the thorny digits pointed toward the appropriate turns.

Light and shadow played tricks on our senses as Chip navigated further from the highway. Even if we wanted to, there was no place to turn around. We were willingly committed to this side trip. We could see what looked like ghostly figures from the codices, escorting us to our unknown destination. They looked like they were happy to see us and were glad to show us the way. I dismissed the visions to hallucination, or the residual effects of Montezuma's Revenge. Even though I tried to keep an open mind, those visions looked real. Where were they escorting us?

After an hour of spewing plumes of dust, we reached a clearing, butted against the face of a monolithic crag. Our ethereal escorts instantly faded into the landscape. We were in the middle of a Mexican nowhere, following a caricature into the unknown. Many unthinkable dangers could be lurking behind every rock, but we did not care. An overwhelming sense of adventure lured us further into the unknown. Chip stayed behind, guarding the Bounder because, in his mind, this was our trip.

Pale moonlight exposed a narrow trail winding up the mountainside. Della Vega motioned us to follow him onward and upward. He set a blistering, sure-footed pace up that narrow lizard path. My wide shoes overlapped the trail, slipping with each step. Strutch, still sporting a walking cast, had a tougher time navigating. He almost vanished into the abyss a couple of times.

After climbing about fifty feet above the desert floor, an escarpment flattened our climb. This place reminded me of a Tarzan movie. I waited patiently for the ape man to come swinging through the trees, even though this was a desert with no trees or vines to swing from. Wow!

A circle of moonlit stones outlined a dome-like hut. Branches and animal skins covered the exterior. Wisps of smoke puffed from cracks between the coverings. A small flap of deerskin acted as a door. Men, dressed in white, carried red-hot stones through the narrow door. Four other men stood guard, one at each cardinal compass point. With outstretched arms, they stood gazing at the heavens. Rhythmic drumbeats reverberated from the rocks above. Hypnotic rhythms echoed a soothing beat across the vast expanses of the desert. My heart rate slowed until it matched the drum's cadence.

I wondered, *Where are we? Who are these people? What are we doing here?*

Hearing my silent thoughts, Della Vega answered, "You are in a sacred place, where Yaqui warriors purified themselves before battle. The men you see are direct descendants of the warriors who guarded the Crown of Knowledge. Generations of warriors have been guarding the Crown since the beginning. They willingly protect its secrets, if need be to the death. No warrior has entered the inner sanctum without being purified. This is why you are here, to be purified."

"Wait a minute! I was only a participant in war, not a warrior. All I did was try to keep the company and myself alive while being kind to the indigenous people."

"You are exactly who we were looking for. Being kind does not preclude someone from being a warrior. You shall see just what I mean. Please go into this sweat lodge with an open mind."

We got on all fours and crawled through a tiny opening. There was a circle of small boulders, large enough to sit on. In the center, red-hot rocks heated the entire space. There were others sitting around the fire. All eyes were fixed on the glowing embers, and the people chanted to the beating drums. I couldn't understand what they were saying. The rhythmic vibrations made me feel at ease. We sat down and soaked in the warmth, instantly becoming drenched in our own sweat. I took off my shirt to let the perspiration flow into tiny streams, unimpeded by restrictive clothing. Soothing heat filled my entire being with a calm that opened my mind up to accept what would come next.

Della Vega poured cool water over the glowing coals. Steamy water vapor filled the preheated space with a fine mist. We had difficulty seeing the mystery man through the thickening cloud. Della Vega softly whispered, "You need to have an open mind with what comes next. Concentrate on how you felt when your war was over. Try to recapture your innocence."

Della Vega sprinkled a handful of leaves onto the glowing coals. When heated, the space smelled like Juicy Fruit gum. The sweet, comforting aroma made me think of the carefree days of youth. While forgetting about the complexity of modern life, a wide smile filled my warm face with simple joy. We tend to make life too complex with luxury problems, while we forget what really matters. I guess separating the two is what makes us better human beings.

40

I couldn't stop thinking about Della Vega's challenge as my body completely relaxed. I tried to concentrate on the time I returned from war. At first, I didn't understand why, but the further I relaxed, the more I allowed myself to remember. It only took a few seconds to drift back to that forgotten time.

My body left the war when I boarded that freedom bird in Da Nang, but my mind remained glued to the jungle canopy. I vowed that all the horrible memories would dissolve when I left country, but that proved impossible. To Country Joe's "Feel Like I'm Fixin' to Die Rag," a Continental Airlines DC-10 lifted us from one living hell to another: an unfamiliar USA.

The perception of our native land had changed with such ferocity. It became alien to me. I just couldn't get a handle on my emotions. I was out of harm's way but still scared. Something was missing. There was no way this experience could possibly affect me because of my upbringing and moral grounding. Then everything changed. In my mind I could never leave the bush. The American dream and hope in the future seemed like a distant memory. I could not shake the emotional baggage I collected during combat. Shame and guilt replaced youthful exuberance. I needed to forget the horror. This burden weighed heavily on my psyche, and never left.

All I could do was temporarily mask the pain. In 1970 there were a multitude of costumes to fit any mask. There was the lack of respect for authority of any kind that justified outlaw behavior. Laws made by the same institutions that started this conflict meant absolutely nothing. This was a recipe for confrontation with anyone who had power. Oftentimes such confrontations ended with disastrous consequences, including emergency rooms or incarceration. After surviving the Nam there was nothing to lose.

There was a burning desire to revive the adrenaline rush of combat. The mask of daredevil behavior and the lust for sexual conquest, coupled with the constant drone of loud, loud music, recaptured the warrior feeling. Nothing was too dangerous or irreverent. Cheating death over and over again felt so, so good.

Spirituality was just another joke. How could anyone who participated in such unspeakable acts have the audacity for spirituality? I lost faith in any god who could condone such depravity. Blasphemy gave me another irreverent mask.

This emotional confusion had only one cure: psychedelic substances and the allure of amber fluids. Alcohol, marijuana, and LSD became the temporary savior that was the most far-out mask of all. Expanding the mind with foreign substances was supposed to sort out the confusion while arranging it into the proper perspective, eventually leading to spiritual healing. Drugs and reading books were the answer to enlightenment. That hippie dream sounded wonderful, but forgot to mention hangovers.

There was no room for honest, meaningful labor. The Christian work ethic did not go along with full-time escapism. I tried to fit into the workforce, but the mundane routine just brought back the horrors. When you spend all of your time trying to kill yourself with thrills, there is no time for societal endeavors. Besides, I was too tired to work every day anyway. Remember, there is no such thing as too much fun.

All of these physical and emotional stresses placed an enormous burden on my health. Injuries healed quickly, but physical healing could not ease the emotional pain. After the body felt normal, the mind ached even more. How long could I keep this pace up? I needed relief and the peace everyone deserves. I did not want to die.

The only comfort was looking at reality deep within the mirror. I could gaze directly into the glass and feel the depths of my soul. Looking through pale blue eyes at the future seemed futile. The pain of guilt ruled my future. My future was bleak at best. I needed to release myself from the shame that prohibited me from enjoying life to its fullest.

As I looked deeply I could only picture her eyes. Those eyes pierced through me like a dagger every time I tried to sleep. They were the eyes of an old mama-san who was in the wrong place and definitely the wrong time. That wrinkled, defenseless crone was the unfortunate recipient of a grenade I threw into the bunker where she was hiding. We were ordered to blow up all bunkers, to ferret out any enemy taking refuge. I pulled the pin and rolled the frag into the hole just as an old lady poked her head around the corner of that underground maze. She looked so innocently at me with piercing eyes, which felt the anguish of that misunderstood land. She knew her fate.

There was nothing I could do to save her. The die was cast, and in those few seconds before detonation, I saw in her face the hopelessness of the situation. She was crying out for relief, but all I could do was watch her die. Those eyes looked down on me with a constant barrage of shame. I had uselessly killed another human being. The act was not only condoned, but also praised. When I walked away, that innocent but deadly mistake drifted into the fog of war. It pushed me to the edge of insanity.

Those eyes would become a constant reminder of the downside of my Vietnam experience. The mirror would be the vehicle to conjure up emotions. From that reflection it was clear what needed to be done. On a rainy summer night I got into my MGB and drove alone, south to the seat of government, Washington D.C. No one had any idea where I was headed, nor did I tell anyone of my sojourn for many years. It was something I just had to do on my own. Not too many people could understand anyway.

With a six-pack of beer and a Purple Heart on the seat beside me, I drove like the wind. The top was down while it rained. Still I drove, as if I were on one final mission. The stinging rain dripped down my long hair, allowing it to stay in place. Raindrops and a soothing wind on my face cleansed away all doubt and placed a clear resolve on what needed to be done.

I drove into the storm oblivious of my surroundings. Connecticut, New York, the entire New Jersey Turnpike, Delaware, and Maryland breezed by in an instant. In the blink of an eye I stood in front of 1600 Pennsylvania Avenue. The six-pack was gone but I was clear-headed and focused.

The White House stood stoically guarding the leader of this great nation, Richard M. Nixon. His power was unrivaled throughout the free world.

He could pull the plug on Vietnam anytime, and the country would legally reelect him in a landslide; but he and the rest of the shortsighted politicians were stuck in that "stay the course" mentality. All he had to do was ask the 63,000 dead if the war was worth keeping the Vietnamese people from embracing communism.

If he asked me I would certainly explain the situation in detail. Since that was not likely to happen, I decided to show my displeasure for the fiasco in my own private way. I took my Purple Heart and flung it in the air. That symbol of gallantry felt heavy in my hand. It sailed over the fence like a tiny unguided missile, landing with George Washington looking in my direction.

Security lights reflected his image encased in that ounce of pure gold. Instant relief flooded my entire being. I felt joy that I hadn't in a long, long time. At that moment I came home. While looking at my medal on the lawn, a giant weight lifted from my being. I could see Tam and the old lady in the bunker smile, as if everything was all right now. It felt so, so good.

There was no way I could cherish an award that I received from the president of the United States, so I gave it back. I did not want or deserve the same commendation bestowed upon all those young men who gave everything. I threw it over that fence for everyone on both sides who were affected by the scourges of combat. I threw it over the fence for my fellow Marines who sacrificed so much, but were repaid with guilt and shame for surviving. We must still live with the horror. Maybe now I could travel down life's highway with the knowledge that with this small gesture, I tried to make it right.

As the first rays of sunlight peeked over the Potomac, I knew it was time to leave the war behind. I was not alone. People started going about their daily routines to grease the wheels of government. I had accomplished my mission and needed to go home. I'd have a six-hour drive to sort out what had taken place on that rainy night. I gave my Purple Heart one final glance and hopped into my car. The medal looked at peace.

I drove near the National Mall, and the Washington monument stood high above the rest of the history on that hallowed ground. It reminded me of that other obelisk in the middle of a rice paddy, the one with Buddha's finger inside. Let's hope it lasts as long and no one ever tries to destroy our freedom.

Della Vega whispered to me as I came out of that trance, "You don't have to be ashamed anymore. Let your sorrow fly over life's fence, and live each day as a quest for truth and beauty. You've beaten up yourself long enough. Now you are ready to enter the Crown of Knowledge."

My eyes opened on a new day. The steam was gone, and so was Della Vega. I felt a heavy weight lifted from my psyche; I was ready to live the rest of my life in that quest for truth and beauty. I wanted to thank Della Vega for allowing me to re-experience how I first successfully coped with the horrors of war. Della Vega reminded me of what I always knew but, after decades of hiding the emotional baggage, conveniently forgot. Was he real, or was he what I desperately needed to carry on?

Strutch, stretching his arms above his head, looked like he was saluting the sun. We looked at each other and uttered a collective "Wow!" There was no need to speak, because we had both experienced a lesson in redemption. A powerful force, triggered by the smell of Juicy Fruit gum, reaffirmed what we always knew about ourselves. There was nothing we could do to change the past. All that mattered was how we traveled into the future. With clear minds and a purpose, we were more than ready to carry on.

We crawled from the sweat lodge and took a long, hard look at the sunrise. Cooing mourning doves welcomed us to the refreshing crispness of a new dawn. It felt wonderful. We smiled as our feet glided down the rocky trail. With a newfound confidence, we knew that the Crown of Knowledge was only a day away. Oorrah!

I could smell fresh coffee wafting from the Bounder's kitchen. Chip had blueberry pancakes, avocado omelets, and fresh squeezed orange juice waiting. We thanked him for his kindness, and with the zeal of a school of piranha, the three of us proceeded to inhale the delicious culinary delight. After breakfast was just a memory, we left the magic and made tracks for an appointment with destiny. The six-fingered cacti waved a fond farewell as the Bounder sped south.

41

E.D. felt a renewed vitality as she supervised equipment being unloaded from the *Link's* holds. She was relieved that this nightmarish adventure was almost a footnote in history. With her confident eye for detail, the gear was meticulously arranged on the beach, readily available for use. The tiny beach looked like a military supply depot, filled with everything needed to assault the Crown. The *Link* would still function as a command post, while the beach was the staging point. The Bounder would act as an electronic triangulation beacon for what would hopefully become the biggest archeological find known to modern man.

E.D. was still in a guarded state of relief. Diamond's plane crash seemed too good to be true. Even though there were no survivors, she was not totally convinced of his demise. She prayed that the mercurial scoundrel was vaporized on that ill-fated plane. If he was, chalk one up for the good guys. If not, she would still keep one eye open, just in case he somehow resurrected himself from the burning wreckage. She was secure with the fact that Diamond was no phoenix. With a big smile on her face she said, "He has to be dead. For the time being, I might as well forget about Harlan Diamond."

The beach was abuzz with activity. Landing craft were inflated, engines fired up. Junior surveyed and tested the climbing gear. The ship's crew scurried about hauling equipment to wherever E.D. desired. They resembled colony ants on a mission. After about an hour of intense labor, everything on the beach was in place for the assault.

The fed types were busy orientating the electronic surveillance dishes to the cinder cone and the surrounding waters. For the sensitive electronics to work properly, a relay was placed on the peak overlooking the Crown. Another dish was aimed toward the sky, ready to document the upcoming eclipse. This hardware was designed to track the sun and moon as they converged into one.

E.D., Junior, and Nakai lifted off in the ship's helicopter to get a bird's eye view of the Crown of Knowledge. They took the key with them to see if it had the advertised power. Nakai became agitated as they cleared the beach. He pawed at the window and barked at the rocks below. Junior became concerned about what danger he may have seen. "What's wrong, boy? Who's out there?"

Alerted by Nakai's warning, E.D. took a closer look at the surrounding hillside. Firing up the chopper's thermal imaging camera, she noticed a number of heat signatures coming from the rocks below. She could clearly see eyes intently gazing up at them. "It looks like we're not alone. I just hope they are friendly."

E.D. radioed the ship, concerned about who was spying on them. The fed types were still busy calibrating the equipment. In fact, it wouldn't be online for another hour. Because the *Link* did not have the luxury of their blown-up drone, E.D. suggested they try going old school, with a twist. "Why don't you release Perry and his trusty talon camera?"

"Good idea, boss. That's why you get the big bucks."

Loud laughter was heard over the radio. Junior scratched his head in awe. "This is the first time I've heard those nerds laugh. In fact, I've never seen them crack a smile."

"Give them a break. Everyone can't be Mr. Personality like you, my dear." She pinched him on the cheek, then kissed him deeply on the mouth. They both had a good laugh while monitoring Perry's spying.

The speedy avian jet sent back images of men hidden from sight behind rocks and bushes. They appeared to be locals, just curious about what was transpiring with all of the equipment on the beach. As a precaution, E.D. advised the ship to "keep an eye on the inquisitive. After all, we are waging war, so to speak, on their homeland."

After E.D. determined the threat was minimal, she flew straight for the prize. The Gulf of Cortez looked to be peaceful. Large, puffy, shape-shifting clouds danced lazily under the hot summer sun. Vaporous sculptures created an array of ever-changing images, conjured from their imaginations. They could have watched this celestial spectacle all day, but were on a mission.

As man, woman, and beast hovered near the Crown, the maelstrom swirled around the cone as foretold by the codices. With an earth-shattering snarl, tumbling boulders made the gulf appear to boil. This scary vortex churned in a clockwise rotation, making a water landing difficult, if not impossible. Any ship sailing in a direct path would be repelled back into calmer waters. If a watercraft ever broke free from the swirling torrent, growling boulders would crush that vessel into pulp; or even worse, slam it into the face of the cone, trapping it there for eternity. Who in their right mind would consider such a foolhardy venture? No wonder the Spanish called this place the Devil's Crown.

A constant lingering mist hung over the entire formation, surrounded by a thick frosting of fog. These formidable obstacles protected the Crown with an illusion of invisibility. Because of these barriers, it was impossible to see the Crown with the naked eye. This inhospitable weather phenomenon created the perfect camouflage. The only things visible were the four spires penetrating the fog, which gave the Crown the illusion of floating on top of the fog. They really made the cinder cone look like two separate entities. Whoever named this formation was spot-on. With the keys in place, the Crown would truly be restored to its intended majesty.

After witnessing the sheer power of the Crown's natural defenses, E.D. became concerned about their upcoming assault. She would have to devise more than one strategy to effectively get inside. Her mind struggled with which course would be the safest. She needed to see the inside before any strategy could be considered.

The chopper rose above the vaporous phenomenon with ease, like a daring young man on a flying trapeze. Unlike in the circus, the helicopter became suspended in flight. There was no change in direction. It was stuck in midair, with no place to go. A strange force held the unresponsive bird above the rocky formation. E.D. tried everything to break the force's grip. She pegged the engine's throttle almost to its breaking point. It looked like they would hover in that spot for eternity, or run out of gas.

Nakai sensed the predicament and grabbed the jeweled key in his powerful jaws, lifting it to the window. A melodic buzz instantly filled the cockpit. Brilliant golden hues illuminated the interior of the flying machine. In an instant, every thought became crystal clear. Life would not be the same for those involved in this incredible journey.

Without warning, the fog melted away. The force that held the chopper trapped weakened, then finally dissipated. E.D. did not touch the controls. The engine powered itself down. A stronger force gently lowered the chopper into the depths of the cone, like falling into an airbag. The 300-foot gentle free-fall felt like an autumn leaf leisurely floating to the ground. An infectious calm filled the interior. E.D. looked directly into Junior's eyes and proclaimed, "We've finally arrived. I can't wait to bring the rest of the gang into this magical environment." There was no need for further verbal communication. Nakai wagged his tail in agreement, Junior just smiled. His grin told it all.

Despite the choking fog covering, a thriving ecosystem flourished inside the cone. Somehow sunlight filtered through, creating the perfect environment for all types of tropical flora to thrive. Orchids of every color grew from palm tree trunks throughout the cone. Ferns and other exotic plants clung to golden walls. Smells from the blossoms filled the space with an intoxicating sweetness, which filled every breath with happiness.

Beyond the chopper's skids stood a step pyramid, reminiscent of the Aztec structures around Mexico City. Unlike those cold, vacant stone relics from the past, this one teemed with life. Its steps rose to the pinnacle with a warm golden hue. In fact, the entire space sported the same colorful tones. The steps were adorned with enormous vases, filled with a variety of unknown plants and seeds, creating more aromas, which filled the travelers with more mystery.

A red pulsating beacon shined from the top of the structure. Each flash was synced to the intruders' beating hearts. The light shined from the same location where Aztec priests ripped beating hearts from unfortunate victims unlucky enough to be sacrificed to their bloodthirsty gods. Unlike those violent altars, no blood spilled from this pyramid, only the red light of love and understanding.

The enlightened travelers soaked up the wonders of the cone for about an hour, when E.D. decided it was time to get back to the beach. They did not get out of the chopper, because it was not right to disturb anything until the rest of the group could discover the wonders of this magical place together.

E.D. fired up the engines, vowing to return with the rest. With newly restored power, the crew rose free from the interior. The fog then returned with a vengeance, protecting the cone from unwanted trespassing, patiently waiting their return. It was obvious that one of the keys was needed to enter the cone from above.

The flight back was filled with the sounds of silence. E.D. and Junior knew what needed to be done. After witnessing a small taste of the cone's majesty, a full scientific exploration was in order, but without disrespecting its powers. When they landed on the *Link's* deck, E.D. said, "We have to step lightly, as not to irreverently disturb the sanctity of that mysterious paradise."

"I agree totally!"

42

The Bounder chugged up a final steep grade when the weary travelers reached our destination. From the top we could see a monument marking the Tropic of Cancer, the 25th parallel. A stone angel overlooked the sea. She reminded the travelers that this leg of our journey was about to end.

Chip pulled into the parking lot of Los Barriles Resort. The resort boasted the best game fishing in Baja. A fleet of boats dotted the harbor, ready to take anxious anglers to hunt for blue marlin, sailfish, and dorado. The warm waters were teaming with potential trophies. People paid thousands of dollars for a crack at decorating their walls with one of those monsters.

A private airstrip provided wealthy fishermen the opportunity to fly their planes yards away from fishing nirvana. Flying was a lot easier than negotiating Baja's suspect roadways. I noticed a helicopter parked near one of the hangars. Two men and a woman were getting into a six-passenger, open-air vehicle sporting a striped pink-and-white fringed top. A hotel employee drove them and their luggage to the lobby. Jake, Dr. Ferdan, and another man, presumably Dr. Estaban, walked into the hotel without noticing the Bounder. We followed them into the lobby, anticipating our rendezvous.

The hotel lobby was crowded with tired, sunburned fishermen and drunken tourists. Inside the open lobby, a group of young people crowded around a lion cub chained to a palm tree. One smashed girl placed her necklace around the cub's neck, while another put sunglasses and a straw hat on his head. They laughed while cell phone cameras snapped pictures. The poor thing looked annoyed, but reveled in all the attention. Apparently wealthy young Mexicans kept lions as a status symbol. I can guarantee you, those girls would not dare pull the same stunt when the cub grew longer teeth. Oh well, to be young again, when painful mistakes are part of growing up.

Jake noticed me looking at the sideshow. His meat hook of a hand squeezed my shoulder, buckling my knees. "Do you have to inflict pain on me every time we meet?" I complained.

"Sorry, old buddy. I guess I still don't know my own strength. Ha ha! Well, anyway, what's happening, you old hippie devil dog?"

He always did that to me. I should have been used to his Vulcan death grip by now. Jake was not used to being around people, so I couldn't be mad at his uncouth behavior for long. Under that rough exterior beat a heart of gold. "I'm still in one piece, besides the pain in my shoulder, and twelve hundred miles of bad road. How was your flight?"

"E.D. fixed me up with a new Bell Ranger helicopter. I flew across the border with no problem. That girl must have some kind of pull. Everything was handled, right down to our stamped passports."

"Nothing amazes me about Ms. E.D. Struction. For over a week now, I've been awed by her confident demeanor. I trust anything she says or does. I will follow her anywhere, even though I may die trying. You are the one who has to worry, because she might become a member of your family soon."

"I know. I can see that spark between them. It must be love."

"You better be prepared for the patter of little feet running around Rancho Mysterioso."

"That sounds pretty good to me. Just call me granddad. The two of them will make me proud to be part of the family. Wait a minute, aren't you getting a little ahead of yourself?"

"You're absolutely right. Let's go get something to eat. All this talk about babies makes me hungry."

Doctors Ferdan and Estaban were at the front desk checking into the hotel. Dr. Ferdan noticed me and introduced Dr. Estaban. In kind,

I introduced Strutch. After the introductions and a few pleasantries, I told the new arrivals we'd join them for dinner in an hour. "I'll call you where and when to meet." They acknowledged the request and followed the bellman to their respective rooms.

Jake, Strutch, and I walked to the campground, just a short distance down the beach. While we met Jake and the good doctors, Chip had moved the Bounder into a slip overlooking the Gulf of California, in all its glory. The crystal blue waters, contrasted by pale purple mountains, looked more like a painting that any museum would proudly display. The pristine beauty took my breath away. Della Vega had suggested I search for truth and beauty. I guess this view was the perfect place to start. Flocks of seabirds chirped melodic tones, carried on warm breezes. Their singing invited us to share this magical land with all its inhabitants. I immediately fell in love with its overwhelming beauty.

Chip was busy unfolding the two satellite dishes that lay flat on the roof of the Bounder. The circular aluminum antennas needed to be aligned to their proper position, to triangulate with the *Link* and Crown. He gingerly pointed the powerful antennas into the clear blue sky, finitely adjusting their beams to the *Link* across the sea.

Pink Floyd's "Dark Side of the Moon" streamed from the Bounder's sound system. Ever-changing natural sounds complemented the intense guitar riffs. My mind and body soared with higher vibrations. How perfect was that? Experiencing this phenomenon kosmically linked us to the future. During the eclipse, we would be witness to the dark side of the moon. Drinking in so much beauty felt like victory in its purist form.

When Chip finished testing the electronic equipment, we walked back to the hotel for dinner. The restaurant was packed with a myriad of customers. Wealthy sportsmen, dressed in the finest fashions, looked annoyed at young millenniums whooping it up. They were dancing to loud hip-hop music while pounding shots at an adjacent bar. A thunderous bass beat nearly cracked crystal stemware precariously balanced on white linen tablecloths. A classical guitarist couldn't compete with the frantic frivolity in the adjacent bar. After just one song, he gave up and quit playing.

Management tried to turn down the racket, but was unsuccessful. When the maître d' pulled the plug, a riot nearly broke out. He was serenaded with a chorus of boos and four-letter words. He coaxed the revelers to move their party to the beach bar with a few rounds of free drinks. One drunken girl shouted, "Free is for me," and they all staggered off to the beach.

We finally could hear ourselves think when the herd of revelers disappeared into the din. We listened to louder music in the days of our youth. Bands like The Who, Jimi Hendrix, and Blue Cheer cranked up the volume so loud, my entire body visibly vibrated with every chord change. Exploding artillery shells and fire engine sirens didn't help stabilize my auditory function. No wonder I answered most questions with a resounding "What?" I could only hope those kids didn't replicate my generation's total disregard of ear protection. This was just wishful thinking. They must learn the hard truth for themselves. Ah, growing up.

The restaurant was quiet once again. The interruption didn't faze the musician in the least. His performance continued without missing a single note. Classical guitar melodies flowed through the dining room like a gentle breeze, whispering to our taste buds. His soaring fingering and rhythmic chord changes somehow made our food taste better.

After the grueling journey, grilled fresh blue marlin and local vegetables hit the spot. Tender asparagus, squash, chilies, and wild mushrooms—cooked in a delicate wine sauce—assaulted our hunger with a vengeance. Each ingredient complemented the rest with a culinary synergy that filled our stomachs while satisfying the spirit. The meal concluded with a dessert of vanilla bean crème brûlée, and coffee mixed with cinnamon.

Dr. Estaban toasted our good fortune with snifters of Grand Marnier. "Welcome to our country. History may be rewritten tomorrow. Do not take this new information lightly! The rest of the world may not be ready for what is inside The Crown of Knowledge. Good hunting, my friends."

Thick orange brandy slid down my throat with a sobering reality. *What if the codices are real? I may not have taken this quest seriously enough. I better keep an open mind, and not get sucked further into the mystery.*

My mind continued to bounce from one scenario to the next, like a kosmic pinball machine. What if the codices were written as a cruel joke, perpetrated by an Aztec mystic playing with his conquerors? What if the church was truly petrified of the Crown's association with the devil, discouraging any exploration? What if the original Father Della Vega wrote them to get revenge on the church that wronged him? What if the cone was a portal to hell? What if the codices were spot-on? This would be the scariest scenario of all. I couldn't wrap my mind around hell, but immortality sounded intriguing.

Strutch found the box, which told of a legend spawned from a dream. We acted on the dream and created a full-blown mission into uncharted waters. Would these waters sail us to the fountain of youth, or flush us into the abyss?

After dinner we said good night. The two doctors went to their rooms for a good night's sleep. I doubted that they could sleep a wink, because tomorrow would be the end of the journey, one way or another. I sensed there was more than academic research between them. Strutch felt the same way, saying, "Those two must have been more than classmates. Did you see how they looked at each other? What could be more romantic than being together for eternity?" We had a good laugh and disappeared from the hotel.

The rest of us walked back to the campground. Chip ran back to tweak the electronics before bed. We old dudes leisurely took up the rear, digesting our food. After about five minutes of slowly walking, I sensed someone spying on us from the bushes. Strutch and Jake went ahead, while I pretended to remove a rock from my shoe.

Sitting on a bench alongside the path, I could plainly see rustling leaves. When Jake and Strutch were out of sight, Della Vega appeared from behind the leaves. He was dressed as a tourist, wearing a flow-ered shirt, linen slacks, a floppy hat, and expensive sandals. He also sported a handlebar mustache. Seeing him startled me. "What are you doing here, dressed like Salvador Dali? How did you get here? Besides, it's too hot to be wearing long pants."

"Hello to you, señor. It doesn't matter how I got here. I needed to blend in with the tourists, not to arouse suspicion. I'm just keeping an eye on you and your friends. You will need my help getting into the Crown. I know an easy way to get inside. Furthermore, I like long pants. Why do you always wear shorts?"

"Because I hate those bifurcated leg prisons. I'm retired and don't have to dress for anyone but myself. I like the wind blowing on my bare legs."

"I am not here to debate fashion. I suggest you get to the Crown as soon as possible. Now would be the perfect time. There is much to do before the moon covers the sun. Don't fret over how I can quickly move from place to place. I will link up with your people when you arrive."

"That sounds good to me. I've stopped trying to make sense out of anything you do or say. Oh yeah, thank you for the sweat lodge ex-perience. I know now that I don't have to be ashamed about anything that happened in the fog of war. Maybe I can spend the rest of my days without negative feelings about my Vietnam experience. Only time will tell. Oh, by the way, what was in those leaves that smelled like Juicy Fruit gum?"

"For now, don't worry about that. Just get across the gulf as soon as you can. All of your questions will be answered inside the Crown of Knowledge."

I turned my head for just a second when a refreshing, cool breeze blew across my face. It made me feel clear-headed. I turned to face the gentrified Della Vega, but he was gone, just as mysteriously as he had appeared. I was more anxious than ever to finally arrive at our final destination. I tried to make sense out of what just happened, but like everything on this journey, confusion clouded rational thinking.

I reached the campground after a short stroll. The entire place was abuzz with activity. It seemed like everyone was looking skyward at the stars. Telescopes and powerful binoculars pointed toward the heavens. Hundreds of astronomy buffs and academics were concentrated in this small space. They were all here for one reason, to witness a total eclipse of the sun, the most spectacular event visible from planet Earth. This was the perfect place to anonymously hide in plain sight. We were just a bunch of astronomy geeks trying to make sense of the cosmos.

Groups of people wandered around the campground comparing notes on the different magnification devices. The Bounder had five people from an astronomy club in Cleveland viewing the sophisticated telescope mounted on the roof. E.D. had the electron telescope installed on the Bounder's roof to legitimize the ruse of anonymity.

Chip felt like a rock star demonstrating equipment most astronomers only read about. No one there had a clue about the Bounder's real mission. They were viewing the Teapot constellation on a monitor, mounted outside the Bounder. E.D. incorporated another layer of secrecy to make the Bounder's real mission inaccessible to prying eyes. Besides, these people only cared about the images on the monitor, while dreaming of someday traveling to the remote corners of space.

Weaving my way between the curious astronomers, I climbed into the Bounder almost unnoticed. The door slammed shut with a crashing sound, making Jake and Strutch jump. They were checking out the stars from another monitor inside the cabin when they heard the slamming door. After the initial startle, they came at me with clenched fists. "Hold on, boys. I'm a friendly. Sorry I pushed your PTSD buttons, but we must go to the Crown right away. Della Vega showed up on our walk back and advised me to get there as soon as possible."

Strutch scratched his head and asked, "What did you say? We just saw Della Vega on top of that mountain yesterday evening. How did he get here so fast?"

"I can't figure that one out. This trip has been filled with unfathomable mysteries none of us could possibly explain. We came this far not to question Della Vega's motives. He imparted wisdom that changed my way of thinking about how I deal with shame, Shame that has eaten me up for more than forty years. One night in that sweat lodge helped me more than a decade of therapy. I put all my trust in that man, even though I'm not too sure if he is real or not. So I think we should get cracking and fly across the sea, now. Besides, you were the one who found the box and initiated this chain of events; we've gone too far in to stop. I should be mad at you for the sneaky way I was brought into the mix."

"You're right. I'm sorry for not telling you the whole story. I was afraid of Big D's treachery to put you in more danger. I am eternally grateful for your help. I guess we are friends for life, depending on how tomorrow shakes out. Let's go for it!"

Jake's ears perked, hearing fragments of our conversation. "Did I miss something? Who is Della Vega? What about tomorrow?"

"Our plans just changed. We need to fly across the sea tonight. Will there be a problem flying at night?

"Not in the least. I can fly forever in this clear sky. Remember, this is Mexico. There is no FAA here to tell us if we can fly or not. I'll get down to the chopper and make sure she is fueled and ready for some over-water night flying. I love night flying. Who is Della Vega?"

"Don't worry about Della Vega for now. I'll introduce him later."

"Okey dokey, artichokey. Catch you on the flight line. Semper fi, do or die!"

Strutch and I snapped to attention and yelled, "Semper fi to you too." My eyes began to well with happiness, knowing we had each other's backs. I just hoped Jake's words, especially the "die" part, were just his way of telling us not to dwell on the real danger of this situation. After all, like we used to say in the Nam, "It don't mean nothin'!"

Chip came into the Bounder smiling. "You guys should check out the star party outside. Those people know about space."

"I wish we had the time. We are flying across the water to link up with the others. Call the good doctors and tell them to meet us at the chopper. You will be our eyes and ears. Call E.D. and tell her to be ready for our arrival," I said.

"Will do. I hope the Crown of Knowledge is worth the hassle. Stay safe!"

43

C hip called the hotel to tell Doctors Ferdan and Estaban that they were to meet Strutch, Jake, and Jerry at the helicopter. He first called Dr. Ferdan. "There's been a change in plans. Could you please be ready to cross the sea tonight?"

"What's the rush?" asked Dr. Ferdan.

"Please take everything you need for the exploration. Jerry, I mean Cal, will brief you in the air. Could you please tell Dr. Estaban?"

Chip could hear a voice in the background that sounded like Estaban. "What is the problem, darling?"

"We need to prepare to leave for the cone now. Go to your room and pack what you need. I'll meet you at the concierge desk."

Chip heard what sounded like a kiss. He realized there was more to the good doctor's relationship than research. A warm feeling came over him when he realized doctoral romance was flowering under the Mexican moon. With a half grin he said, "I guess I don't need to call Dr. Estaban."

"That's right, Chip, and it feels good."

Like a lioness protecting her cubs, E.D. was feverishly pacing around the *Link's* communications room when the satellite phone rang. The monotonous tones temporarily snapped her out of the anxiety plaguing her thoughts. She charged across the room like a bull running in the crowded streets of Pamplona, Spain. Instead of goring foolhardy runners dressed in white clothing and red scarves, frightened technicians dove away from their charging leader. Regaining her composure, E.D. took a deep breath and uttered, "This is *The Missing Link*."

"This is Chip, Ms. Struction. We made it to the campground in one piece."

"That's good. Tell my dad I'll see him tomorrow."

"Wait. They are flying to your location as we speak."

"What? There must be something wrong to risk a night flight."

"Don't worry. The chopper will contact the *Link* when they are close. Be ready for their landing. Their ETA will be approximately forty-five minutes after takeoff. "

"Sounds good. We will be waiting to hear from them. Call me back if things change. We'll talk later."

E.D. was perplexed as she tried to make sense of the Bounder's transmission. Junior and Nakai strolled into the ship's communication deck and noticed a puzzled look on E.D.'s face. Junior put his arm around her shoulder and gave her a comforting kiss on the cheek, while Nakai snuggled against her legs. "What's wrong? You look like the weight of the world just dropped on your shoulders."

"Your dad and the rest of the gang are flying to our location now. There must be a good reason for attempting a night flight."

"Look outside and notice the clear skies and billions of stars illuminating their path. This is a perfect night for flying, and my dad can fly in most conditions. Now that Diamond and his goons are out of the picture, they must have wanted to get a head start on tomorrow's festivities."

"You're right. I'm glad I have you around to keep me focused. We make a good team." She gazed into his eyes and said, "Thanks. I needed that," and kissed him deeply on the mouth. Nakai just shook his head and fell asleep at their feet.

Junior almost forgot why he was looking for E.D. in the first place. "Some of the crew and I just got back from checking out different ways to get inside the cone. We tried to get through the maelstrom in an inflatable boat, but the strong current kept repelling us back into the sea. That moat of boulders almost crushed our tiny vessel, like paper through a shredder. The engine had just enough power to escape disaster. Furthermore, the face of the cone was slick with a slimy film that dripped green algae over everything. We might as well forget about climbing up the side of the cone. I guess it's back to the drawing board."

E.D. stood silent for a moment scratching her head. Her eyes lit up, and a big grin filled her face. "I've got the answer to this dilemma. Why don't we string a reverse zip line from the ship to the crest of the cone? *The Link* carries enough cable to traverse the distance. I could fly one end to the top and bolt the cable and a pulley system into the rock. The ship's winch could pull passengers up on a boson's chair. To return, just slide down the cable back to the ship. Easy!"

"You are a genius! I don't know how I can keep up with you for the rest of my life."

"Are you proposing, Junior? Keep that thought; we have work to do." She took off like a shot to give orders to the crew to construct her idea.

E.D. designed a plan to stabilize a zip line to the Crown's peak. The other end would not be a problem, because the ship's winch could easily handle the weight. She advised the ship's engineer of her idea. "Can you fabricate a strong matrix and mechanical advantage pulley system that would hold approximately two tons?"

"Sure I can. All the materials are readily available on board. I might need to cannibalize some pieces from the ship, but I won't compromise the ship's superstructure. The entire project should be finished by dawn. The assembly needs to be strong because of the weight it must hold. How will you attach the structure to the Crown's lip?"

"We have a bolt gun capable of shooting large-diameter bolts into solid rock."

"I better make enough holes for the bolts."

"Sounds great. I'll pick up the finished product at the crack of dawn. Thanks again."

44

Jake busily circled the Bell Ranger, conducting a preflight inspection, as the academics unloaded boxes of gear from the hotel's vehicle. They carefully placed cameras and sensitive recording devices into the waiting chopper. The doctors carried laptop computers and dressed like they were on safari with Ramar of the Jungle. Matching khaki vests, Panama hats, hiking boots, and wool knee socks made them look like they were ready for big game hunting.

Strutch and I looked at each other and chuckled. We were dressed in ratty T-shirts, well-worn shorts, and Birkenstocks, like a couple of middle-aged Woodstock refugees, forty-something years removed. "Maybe we should have them pose for a picture with the hotel's lion cub. Now that would be a hoot."

"Cut them some slack. We must look just as silly to them."

"I guess you're right. I am definitely not the fashion police, even though they still look like walking stereotypes."

"Tolerance, my friend. Remember, we fought for personal freedom. Let them have their fun, even though Halloween is months away."

We buckled in and blasted off into the starry, starry night. Billions of celestial bodies twinkled above the lightless bay, with a mirror image of reflected starlight bouncing up to meet our wandering eyes. Comets, asteroids, and meteors zoomed across a static sky, bringing movement to its palette. No earthly light would dare defuse their pointed brilliance. A sliver of the waning moon refused to compete with comforting starlight reflecting off the accommodating water. The sea and sky became one as we sliced our way through the din, on a direct route to destiny. Jake sported a Cheshire cat grin as the

Ranger seemed to fly itself. No one uttered a sound; this illuminating beauty infused our very beings with blissful contentment. There was no need to speak.

A solar eclipse requires a new moon in perigee, or the closest distance to Earth. Conversely, the sun needs to be in apogee, the farthest yearly distance from Earth. If all three bodies line up perfectly, the moon's shadow nearly covers the sun, except for the outer edge, or corona, of pure light. This recipe makes for nature's most spectacular light show.

Ancient people feared the sun would disappear forever, bringing the end of days. They believed that their people had angered the sun god. They did not understand the physics of this unique phenomenon. With the advent of astronomy, the ancients were able to predict where and when an eclipse would occur. Pure enjoyment replaced gloom and doom, without the fear of global annihilation. This was a perfect example of science trumping superstition.

Everyone on board thoroughly enjoyed the spectacle. The stars spoke to our wonderment. Those voices in the sky made me yearn for what mysteries we may find inside the Crown of Knowledge.

Jake noticed shining lights about ten nautical miles away. He radioed the *Link*. "*Missing Link*, this is Ranger 1, requesting landing instructions, over."

E.D. replied, "Ranger, this is *Missing Link*, you are cleared for landing on the beach behind the dock. Strobe lights will mark the exact location. I can't wait to see all of you. We have a lot to discuss, over."

"Roger that. Ranger out."

Junior and one of the fed types anchored strobe lights to the beach. The pulsating beams made landing a walk in the park. Jake flashed on the times he had to fly hot into a landing zone with bullets whizzing by. This LZ looked like a kiddies' amusement park ride, with friendlies to wish them well and not hell-bent on killing them.

Jake maneuvered the Ranger into the wind, above the ridgeline.

He was accustomed to land this way, to get a panoramic view of the topography surrounding the LZ. When he was confident that the LZ posed no imminent danger, the war-experienced pilot gingerly touched down, like falling onto a feather bed. No one on board could complain about the landing. While we were turning, I noticed a large vessel anchored in a cove about twenty miles from our location. In my exhilaration, I just blew it off. After all, we were home free and had an appointment with destiny.

E.D. and Junior met the Ranger while the engines powered down and the rotors stopped spinning. The two of them welcomed us with open arms. E.D.'s flaming red hair appeared to burn in the pulsating strobe flashes. Her confident poise and contagious smile projected a regal air, almost god-like. As usual, I was in awe of this unique person.

With hugs all around, I started to hum "Kumbaya." I felt like all the danger and hassles were behind us and totally worthwhile.

The scene was aglow with activity. Crewmembers unloaded gear from the now idle Ranger, while others were busily constructing the anchors for E.D.'s zip line. Junior helped a hobbling Strutch to a table near where the *Link* was moored. In obvious pain, he dragged his broken leg behind. Sweat poured from his furrowed brow. There was no way he would dare complain.

Some people might think stoic behavior is ridiculous. I, on the other hand, completely understood. As Marines, we were trained to put pain aside, suck it up, and complete the mission. Mission behavior worked well in combat, but not in civilian life. People easily construed the frenzy of completing the mission with not having an attention to detail. This minor personality flaw held me back from succeeding in the modern world. Hopefully with age, the mission wouldn't consume everything in life. I was still impatiently waiting.

A solitary figure approached the *Link* from the shadows. I couldn't believe my tired eyes. Della Vega stood before me, smiling, still dressed as a wealthy tourist. My jaw dropped to my chest, and I was unable to speak. After a few seconds of silence, I stammered, "Wait, wait, wait a minute. I can't believe this is happening! How did you almost beat us here? Where is your brother?"

"Nice to see you too, Mr. Johnson. Don't worry about how I got here so fast. My job is to guide you into the Crown. When you are inside, everything will become crystal clear. Don't try to rationalize what is happening; just experience the process."

"I'm sorry, Señor Della Vega, for not greeting you with respect. I just got my mind blown for the umpteenth time this week."

"That's okay. I tend to have that effect on most people. I need to speak with Señorita Struction. Please don't ask me how I know of her."

"When talking to you, I will never outwardly question anything. I've got the picture."

"You're a fast learner, Mr. Johnson."

"Just call me Jerry. I have a problem with being called Mister."

"Very well. Now take me to Señorita Struction, I mean E.D."

"I won't ask. I guess you know everything."

Señor Della Vega sprinted onto the *Link* like he was a crewmember. I barely kept up with the old man's blistering pace. E.D., Strutch, and Junior were standing on deck admiring the Crown's majesty.

Strutch noticed Della Vega first. He couldn't believe his eyes. The shabby man who had guided them into the kiva looked like a different person, but there was no disguising those penetrating eyes. "Is that you, Señor Della Vega? You look different cleaned up."

"I need to alter my appearance from time to time, Mr. Struction, sir."

"Just call me Strutch."

"Why do all you Vietnam vets refuse to be addressed with well-deserved respect?"

"That is a good question. Fighting that unnecessary war, while taking orders from incompetent leaders, made us lose all respect for authority. It would be hypocritical of us to be addressed the same way as those we loathed."

"You don't have to feel that way anymore. This is a new century, where people show respect by addressing vets as 'sir.'"

"I've heard all this before. I'm sorry, but I can't get a handle on false patriotism. This is how I feel about respect. Respect must be earned, not thrown around like mindless text messages."

"Now I understand. Hopefully you can dissolve these destructive feelings inside the Crown."

I finally reached the deck, 30 seconds behind Della Vega. Sweat poured from every pore, and my heart felt like it would burst free from my chest. "Hey, Della Vega, what's the rush?"

"Sorry about my burst of speed. I needed to burn some excess energy. I must speak to Señorita Struction. It is a matter of great importance."

"Your wish is our command. "May I introduce Ms. E.D. Struction, leader of this expedition? E.D., this is Señor Diego Della Vega."

"Who?"

"Don't worry about who I am. I've already had dealings with your dad and Jerry. First of all, I am here to guide your party into the interior of the Crown of Knowledge. Second, you can stop building that zip line. Even though your matrix has structural integrity, it can never be strong enough to withstand the Crown's power. And lastly, there is an opulent-looking motor yacht, the *Black Gold*, anchored a few miles to the south."

E.D.'s face turned white as a ghost. She jumped to her feet and screamed, "Diamond! But he got barbecued in his plane! We need to find out who is on board. Excuse me, I must organize a recon of that ship."

"That will not be necessary. I've taken the needed precautions to neutralize any threat. We need to go to the Crown now."

E.D. was reluctant to place all her trust in this mysterious stranger. "Why should I follow someone who just materialized from the shadows?"

With fatherly warmth, Strutch placed his hand on her shoulder. Looking into her eyes he said, "You can trust this man with your life. Jerry and I were able to put our past into the proper perspective from dealing with this wise man. Don't worry, he knows what he's talking about."

She tenderly kissed her dad on the cheek. Smiling, she exclaimed, "Take it away, Señor Della Vega. Your wish is my command." E.D. immediately swallowed her pride and relinquished her command. To me, this was the sign of a true leader.

"Thank you for your confidence. There are a few things that I must go over before we enter the Crown. First, there is no need for weapons. They will not work inside. Secondly, we need your inflatable boats and climbing gear. Thirdly, photographs and recording devices may not work. Take them if you must, but don't be disappointed if they become high-priced anchors. Most importantly, please bring the keys and the box. Without them this whole trip would become an exercise in futility. Are there any questions?"

Dr. Ferdan, looking at Dr. Estaban, asked, "How will we be able to document this historic moment if we can't record our findings?"

"Good question. I know you academics rely on empirical data for scholarly works. I've heard the expression 'publish or perish' before. This is definitely not your routine expedition. I can't tell you how to conduct research, but electronic equipment may not work inside the Crown.," the old man replied.

"I've got the picture, but I will bring this iPad and pocket recorder just in case there is a chance they do work."

Without speaking, everyone looked at each other in awe. E.D. finally spoke. "It's almost dawn. We have a Crown to conquer; first, I need to keep an eye on that ship. "

E.D. winked at Della Vega and set the expedition in motion. She ordered the crew to get three Achilles inflatable boats ready for a short cruise on the Sea of Cortez. The fed types manned the control center on the *Link*. They were already looking at satellite images of the *Black Gold*. E.D. instructed them to keep her advised of any movement. "If you try to contact me, the transmission may not go through. If so, take the necessary precautions we spoke about."

"Very well. Good hunting."

Junior stowed the climbing gear into the lead boat. Della Vega, E.D., Junior, and Nakai hopped into the lead boat, with Junior at the helm. Strutch and I were in the middle boat, while Jake and the academics took up the rear.

Perry flew ahead to scout for danger, armed with his trusty talon camera. E.D. ignored Della Vega's warning. She had to have eyes on the surrounding area, to be in total control of any situation that could put the expedition in harm's way.

45

Della Vega led the small armada into a plain of reeds just beyond the shoreline. Men dressed in white, armed with automatic weapons, lined their route in small wooden boats. They resembled the men who stood guard at the sweat lodge. Looking directly at Della Vega, I asked, "Who are these people? They look familiar."

"Very good observation, my friend. These men are Yaqui warriors, entrusted to keep the Crown safe from unwanted guests. They are direct descendants of the originals, some five hundred years ago. No one has ever breached the Crown's security. They boast a perfect record. Furthermore, a small force monitors the *Black Gold* as we speak. We have the situation well in hand."

As our flotilla made its way through the reeds, all traces of our being there vanished. After we flattened a path through the razor-sharp foliage, those resilient stalks sprang back to their original position, an endless plain of nondescript, impenetrable grass. Who in their right mind would dare penetrate this gauntlet of pain? Perfect!

Navigation was a tedious, hot ordeal. The ten-foot-tall flora retained heat like a sweatbox. Each time someone accidently brushed the reeds, small slices of skin oozed tears of blood. My arms were cut to ribbons. Blood mixed with sweat, the cuts stung like hundreds of mosquito bites. Oh yeah, there were swarms of real mosquitos buzzing around everyone. A strange cacophony of slaps reverberated from all of us. All I could think about was the insect repellant we were issued in the Nam. That poison looked like Crystal Lite and burned like battery acid. If it were mixed with blood, I could only imagine the pain that unholy brew would inflict. That thought made me endure the situation at hand. No matter how dire a situation feels, there are always worse ones lurking around every corner.

After about twenty minutes of struggling through the reeds, we stopped at a small beach below a monolith rising above the plain. Della Vega pointed to a small opening beyond a narrow ledge, some twenty feet above the ground. "We need to get out of these boats and climb up to that opening."

E.D. jumped from the Achilles. She grabbed the coil of rope and some anchors, and climbed freehand to the prize. She navigated the climb with the agility of a cheetah and the focus of a bomb technician. Once on top she shot anchors into solid rock with a bolt gun. Confident they would hold, she rigged a mechanical advantage haul system, which would raise everyone with little effort. Strutch looked concerned his little girl might place herself in harm's way. "Don't worry, old friend. I am a witness to her climbing ability. She blew a cap rock from a gold mine vent shaft, with a wildland fire licking at her heels. She saved the day then, and I'm confident she will do it again."

Junior manned the haul line and lifted all of us to the ledge above. The good doctors needed extra attention navigating the climb. Dr. Ferdan clutched the rope with a death grip. The elderly scholar froze with fear and refused to move. E.D. repelled down to meet her with a reassuring tone. 'Don't worry; you are as safe as climbing up stairs. Look at me and I'll guide you step by step. Just keep looking at me and take one step at a time, and don't look down." E.D. held her arm and guided the frightened anthropologist to safety.

When they were safely on the ledge, Dr. Ferdan threw her arms around E.D.'s neck, whispering, "Thank you for saving my life. I've always been afraid of heights, but your reassuring voice guided me to safety. Thank you again."

"I'm glad to be of service."

After the rest of the expedition was safely settled on that lofty perch, Junior and one of the Yaqui warriors winched the rest of the gear up to the rest of the party. Della Vega and two other warriors stacked the gear near an outcropping. Junior scurried up the rope and thanked his helper, who remained on the ground, guarding their boats. E.D. stowed the ropes back into her pack of tricks.

From our vantage point, a panoramic vista stood before us like a photo spread in a *National Geographic* magazine. Miles of reeds undulated on gentle breezes, while the bay glistened in the breaking dawn. Beauty flourished over this magical land. Dr. Ferdan snapped a few pictures with her iPad. "I hope they come out."

I scoured the ledge for an opening, but there was nothing but solid rock. Della Vega noticed my confusion. "Check this out." He grabbed a small bulge in the rock and turned it counterclockwise. The heavy slab of granite pivoted like a lazy Susan, creating an opening large enough for all of us and our gear to easily slip inside. After we were safely inside, Della Vega gently secured the slab back into its locked position.

Smiling, he turned to me and whispered, "Ye of little faith. To open any door, all you need is the right key. The same holds true with why you always dwell on the horrors of your past. The reason you struggle is because impenetrable barriers block the right path. It is impossible to break down these barriers by ramming your head into them. All you receive for your efforts is a headache, while the suffering never goes away. You've always had the key to unlock the barriers. There is nothing you can do to undo the past. This key has always been in your heart. The key is in the way you live life, with kindness and compassion for all living things. Life must continue, with or without what can't be undone."

A massive, dark cavern waited for us inside the pivoting stone door. An eerie feeling hung over everyone except Della Vega. "Don't be frightened. Stay where you are while I light a torch."

Realizing our dilemma, E.D. took several LED headlamps from

her pack and handed each one of us bright lights that illuminated what turned out to be a treasure trove of ancient art. Giant murals of daily life before the Spanish conquest were drawn on spaces larger than an IMAX movie screen. There were paintings from every ancient civilization within the western hemisphere. Even though these priceless works were a bit dingy from centuries of torchlight soot, the colors jumped out at us.

Artifacts from each civilization were neatly placed below each pictogram. Tools, weapons, clothing, religious relics, and art gave the ancients substance. A good deal of gold and precious stones sparkled at the curious.

I noticed a fishhook cast from solid gold. Dr. Estaban added, "Gold was the material of choice, because of its availability, softness, and pliability. This glittering metal could be fashioned into many things needed for daily life. The Spanish plundered thousands of tons of this treasure. They took beautiful gilded art and melted it into bars, and sailed the precious cargo to Spain, where it was recast into religious articles and used to finance wars in Europe.

"The main cathedral in Mexico City was built on top of an Aztec pyramid. The Spanish believed that holiest of places was built by the devil and must be purified. They added insult to injury by building their cathedral with tons of their most precious artifacts. The sacristy and altar were adorned with plundered solid gold. Taking away the vanquished indigenous population's identity wasn't enough for the bearded men from across the sea. They enslaved the locals and forcefed them Christianity. Not the proudest moment in our history."

Tapestries woven from thousands of hummingbird feathers also hung from the walls. The light from our headlamps reflected changing colors. Hummingbird feathers are naturally devoid of color. Light from different angles reflected back changing color patterns, creating moving pictures. These particular tapestries were painstakingly sewn in such a way that the colors had meaning. This technique had to be the precursor to the modern motion picture, hundreds of years before Edison. It must have taken hundreds of hours to create this masterpiece.

The good doctors were beside themselves. The two of them acted like they had discovered the secrets of the universe, and maybe they had. Dr. Ferdan took picture after picture of what the walls said, while Dr. Estaban chronicled everything on a small digital recorder. "Look at the walls, Victo," said Dr. Ferdan. "I can't wait to catalogue everything. This museum, and it is complete, has to be a bigger find than King Tut's tomb."

"You are most correct, my dear. We must save these national treasures for the people of Latin America and all mankind. Our research could easily change recorded history with the secrets within these walls."

We could not believe what we were witnessing. Everyone was busy checking out the vastness of the cavern. Della Vega became a little miffed with the pokey anthropologists. "Can we please keep up the pace? There will be plenty of time for academic pursuits. We have a distance to travel."

Dr. Ferdan noticed Della Vega's concern. "I'm sorry, Señor Della Vega, but you must understand that, as anthropologists, we are on a perpetual quest for knowledge. From now on, my eyes will focus forward."

"Very well. Thank you for being so understanding."

We left the gallery and entered a long, descending corridor with stairs chiseled into solid granite. As we walked deeper into the mountain, the temperature significantly dropped. After being so hot, it was a relief to cool off. The pleasant temperatures made travel a breeze. Strutch especially welcomed the cool air. His cast was beginning to weigh him down. He did not complain, even though he was in excruciating pain. Junior noticed his distress and offered to help carry his pack. "I usually don't like to be helped, but this time I really can use some. Thank you for being so kind." Junior just winked, while gladly carrying double.

E.D. looked at her love and whispered, "My dad must really be hurting. He must like my new boyfriend." She smiled and tenderly pinched his cheek.

After a good hour of steady walking under the bay, our path abruptly ended. Another impenetrable slab of granite stood directly in our path.

46

From the hills above, dozens of eyes intently peered down at the anchored *Black Gold*. They patiently watched for anything out of the ordinary, especially movement toward the Crown. A platoon-sized contingent of heavily armed Yaqui warriors and one of the feds hid behind rock outcroppings sprinkled with small trees, communicating with *The Missing Link*. The other relayed triangulated pertinent information gleaned from circling satellites, and from the Bounder across the bay.

The Missing Link's sound surveillance equipment couldn't penetrate the landmass between them and the *Black Gold*, but the Bounder had a direct line of sight. Chip coordinated the surveillance in air-conditioned comfort. The young agent could eavesdrop on anything said aboard the *Black Gold*.

At first, there was normal shipboard chatter, mostly in Russian. After about an hour two voice signatures sent shivers up and down Chip's spine. The Bounder was equipped with voice recognition software, where certain individual voiceprints were programed into the system. This latest technology was 100 percent accurate. Dragaminov and Diamond were both on board!

Chip immediately tried to contact E.D. with the depressing news. She could not answer, because miles of solid rock and a hundred feet of bay blocked any chance for viable voice communication. They were at the mercy of their own wits.

When communication with E.D. became an exercise in futility, Chip called the *Link* on his satellite phone. He apprized one of the fed types of the situation. "Bummer, dude, it looks like Diamond and Dragaminov did not go down with his 747. I will keep an ear open for any conversation that might help."

The fed aboard *The Missing Link* immediately contacted his partner and apprised him on this latest revelation. "The situation just took a turn for the worse. Diamond and Dragaminov did not vaporize. They are alive onboard the *Black Gold*. Keep Chip and me informed of any movement. Now would be a good time to disable the *Black Gold*."

"Roger that. Have Chip call me if he hears anything."

The fed type and two Yaqui warriors, armed with an underwater exothermic cutting torch, swam to the stern of the *Black Gold*. With the focus of a juggler riding a unicycle across Niagara Falls on a tight-rope, the three men went about cutting the propeller shaft. The torch cut through the case-hardened steel with little resistance. Sparks and molten metal flew in a haphazard radius, momentarily blinding all three saboteurs.

Just as the prop was nearly cut away, the powerful engines fired up. The out-of-round propeller wedged itself into the housing, jamming the entire mechanism. As the engines revved, torque finished amputating the shaft. Shrapnel from the spinning disabled propulsion mechanism cut completely through the chest of one of the Yaqui warriors; the wound so complete, he exsanguinated in less than a minute.

The bay turned a dark crimson, attracting a school of hammerhead sharks. Those perfect eating machines showed no mercy. Still alive, two swimmers frantically tried to flee the wrath of a feeding frenzy. They swam toward the shore, but were too slow to escape the inevitable. The doomed fed type tried to barbecue the onslaught with the penetrating heat from his cutting torch. He stabbed the weapon into an advancing predator's eye, then into another. The two blinded denizens of the deep thrashed like they were penetrated by a flaming whaler's harpoon. This desperate act distracted the rest of the school for only a moment.

The remaining sharks attacked with a vengeance, ripping apart the two unlucky humans. The only trace of their life force was a stain left over from the bloodbath, their screams muted by the churning sea. The three men were reduced to a meal by an unsympathetic foe just trying to survive. From the shark's simple perspective, they were just food. They fed without feeling guilty about anything. While the shark only cared about survival, horrors like a feeding frenzy come with guilt associated with being human. After just a few minutes, life was back to normal.

Seeing the blood-slick on the bay, three warriors franticly paddled a boat toward their friends to see what, if anything, they could do to help. Exposing themselves from the safety of the rocks turned out to be a fool's errand. Crewmembers from the *Black Gold* noticed the intruders and fired a quad 50-caliber machine gun, mounted on the deck. A wall of steel cut the rescuers into unrecognizable chunks of flesh and bone. A steady stream of tracers punctured the early morning sky. This made the sharks happy, because the bite-size morsels made for a pleasurable dessert.

After seeing six of their compatriots murdered and eaten, the remaining warriors opened up on the *Black Gold* with all the firepower at their disposal. Automatic weapons, handheld rockets, and mortar rounds returned the favor. A full-fledged naval battle ensued. The two adversaries exchanged volley after volley of lethal destruction.

Unlike their ancestors, who only had spears and arrows to repel Spanish galleon cannon, these modern warriors held the tactical advantage. Without a propeller, the *Black Gold* was reduced to a sinking morgue. Unable to flee the onslaught, the once powerful luxury yacht was now a barely floating target. After about an hour the crippled floating palace became an uncontrollable inferno. This once proud symbol of excess was on the verge of disappearing.

Without warning, a helicopter lifted off the deck, escaping the crippled yacht's inevitable demise. It was a miracle the bird made it off without so much as a scratch, disappearing into the sunlight.

At about the same time, the ship's launch bolted away from the fray. Dr. Chu, the head of surgery at Diamond's hospital, and Dr.

Grant, the MAV inventor, along with three non-combative crew-members barely escaped the sinking coffin. Within minutes, the once-proud *Black Gold* was reduced to a minor footnote in naval history, a permanent resident of Davy Jones' Locker.

The barely seaworthy launch had sustained extensive damage from the battle. A large hole in the bow started taking on massive amounts of water. The five survivors valiantly tried to bail the onslaught, but their efforts became an exercise in futility. Without mercy, the launch sunk from underneath them. They didn't have to abandon ship, because their vessel abandoned them. They were grateful to escape the carnage, but were left helplessly bobbing in the cruel sea.

Two sailors suffered from burns to their hands and smoke inhalation. They had a hard time staying afloat. Dr. Chu tried to administer first aid, but he was a surgeon. Without an operating room full of staff, he was unable to render much help. The three unscathed survivors tried to give the injured comfort.

After struggling for a time, the most injured slipped away, joining his shipmates. Dr. Chu took off the dead sailor's life preserver, allowing him to reverently sink into the abyss. The remaining survivors floated aimlessly, at the mercy of that unforgiving sea.

Just as a veil of hopelessness began to set in, two ships steamed toward the exhausted swimmers. The two Coast Guard ships flew different flags. A Mexican ship escorted an American vessel on a joint operation between the two neighboring countries.

The two ships split off into different directions. The Mexicans made a beeline toward the still burning *Black Gold*, but when they arrived at the fire scene, the only trace of the *Black Gold* was a burning oil slick. All the evidence had sunk to the bottom of the sea.

Without physical evidence, they looked for witnesses on shore, but no one was there. Bloodstains and spent shell casings littered the ground. The smell of cordite and burning fuel filled the air, but no one to tell the tale.

While the frustrated Mexicans were still scratching their heads, the American ship plucked the waterlogged swimmers from the shark buffet. The four grateful survivors thanked their rescuers. Dr. Chu, worried about the injured seaman, asked, "By any chance, do you have a hyperbaric chamber on board? This badly burned sailor sure could use the benefits of infused oxygen."

The ship's captain hesitantly smiled. "This vessel has a chamber on board. We use it to decompress divers, but there is no doctor to supervise the treatment for a burn patient."

Dr. Chu happily answered, "I am a doctor. This man requires immediate attention. Please show me the way to the sickbay."

The ship's crew carefully transported the burned sailor below to sickbay, where Dr. Chu and the ship's medical corpsman carefully debrided the burned dead flesh, dressed the affected area, and placed the man into the waiting chamber. Dr. Chu advised, "Please monitor the patient and advise me if his condition changes. I need to wash the burn off of my body and take a nap. Wake me up in four hours."

As Dr. Chu left sickbay, a stranger introduced himself. "I am Special Agent Pule. We've been looking for you and Dr. Grant, ever since Harlan Diamond kidnapped you from his hospital. We thought all of you died when his plane crashed. Can you confirm that Diamond was aboard the *Black Gold*?"

"I certainly can, but he and Dragaminov cowardly left the yacht while it was under siege. Those scumbags left everyone else on board to die, while they made their escape. We were lucky to escape that doomed inferno alive. Why do you ask?"

"That sounds like something Diamond is capable of doing. Well anyway, the Mexican government agreed to accompany this ship, myself, and a Navy SEAL team to serve an arrest warrant for murder and kidnapping."

"Dr. Grant and I will gladly to testify against those despicable scoundrels. Excuse me, but I've been swimming for an eternity, and have a patient inside the ship's hyperbaric chamber. I feel like the walking dead. We can talk when I wake up."

"Very well. The corpsman for the Seal Team has experience with burn victims. He has gone to sickbay as we speak to monitor your patient."

"That's great. Now maybe I can finally get some sleep."

Dr. Grant stumbled into the room and added, "I made improvements to the MAV while we were prisoners aboard the *Black Gold*. It's more powerful and faster than the prototype at the hospital. I was also coerced into beefing up the armament systems. They are more powerful and lethal; but not to worry, I programed a few surprises in its operation. Diamond just might be fatally surprised when he needs them the most."

"Good!"

47

There we were, staring at another dead end. This time, a massive slab of shimmering blue granite blocked our path. Iridescent azure and gold flecks jumped from the stone, kaleidoscopically projecting a host of patterns across our field of vision. They intensified with each movement of our headlamps, creating sensory overload. The blinding light made my head feel like it was ready to explode. Was it possible to witness too much beauty?

A smiling Della Vega asked Dr. Esteban for the tourmaline key he was carrying. When the museum curator took the key from his pack, the granite's reflection faded, replaced by an even more intense purple light. The entire space was lit with a thick three- dimensional light, all movement suspended. We were frozen in its brilliance. Unable to move, I watched Della Vega carefully thrust the key into a crack inside the stone. Without warning, the stone dissolved. In actuality, the stone was an optical illusion; a force field, designed to discourage entry into the cone. Without the correct key placed in the precise area, entry would be impossible.

The key fell harmlessly into Della Vega's waiting hand. When he carefully placed it into his pocket, an amazing spectacle unfolded in front of our bewildered eyes. A tunnel of soothing purple light stood before us, like a beacon. Della Vega motioned to follow him into the light. When fully immersed in the purple, I felt a calming sensation, unlike anything I'd ever experienced. The top of my head suddenly sprouted a full head of hair. I felt tendrils where there was only bare skin before. My back straightened, without pain. I felt whole, with energy to spare.

Strutch ran up to me minus his cast. "Check this out. The purple light melted my cast, instantly healing the shattered leg I thought I might lose for good! Purple is supposed to be the healing color, but this experience takes it to a new level. Man, are we in heaven?"

"If I believed in heaven, this place would definitely qualify."

Jake stood next to us with a different attitude on life. "Wow, I don't feel the least bit angry. Life doesn't suck! I can't wait to interact with people again. I need to apologize to everyone. I don't care if they forgive me or not."

We all looked at each other with a renewed sense of purpose. Our eyes were open to a new way of looking at life. It was almost as if the chains of the past had vaporized, along with the baggage that had strangled us to the point of social suffocation.

The rest of our party felt at ease. Doctors Ferdan and Estaban, minus the wrinkled faces, looked like they did when their search for knowledge was new and exciting. E.D. and Junior held each other a bit tighter.

Nakai's ears perked up. The faithful Malamute jumped up and down, spinning around, testing his recently repaired hip. He felt like a pup. Even hair the vet shaved before operating on the bullet wound grew back, restoring his luxurious coat.

Perry flapped his wings vigorously. The falcon's acute vision more powerful, it proudly rode on Nakai's strong back, vigilantly scanning the area for danger.

E.D. mused, "What is this place? It looks like we just journeyed through a healing tunnel".

Della Vega looked at us and winked. "Do you get it now?" He pointed the key into the sky, closing the force field behind us. "We are here. Welcome to the Crown of Knowledge."

48

A black helicopter riddled with bullet holes limped across the calm waters of the gulf. Acrid black smoke billowed from a nearly seized engine, choking the passengers with noxious fumes. Obstructed visibility prevented the pilot from seeing clearly. He kicked out the windshield, blowing toxic smoke away from his face. This last-ditch maneuver blasted fresh air throughout the cockpit. The added drag slowed the wounded bird almost to a stop.

After a valiant effort to stay airborne, the engine finally seized. The once proud aeronautical marvel slammed into the reeds like an anvil dropped from a hayloft. The hard fall buried what was left of the fuselage deep into the muck. Tall reeds camouflaged the rest from detection.

The damaged spinning main rotor decapitated the pilot, his headless body permanently belted to the airframe. Fuel gushing from a compromised tank flowed freely into the marsh. Lighter than water, the escaping hydrocarbon floated a thin sheen evenly over everything. The highly combustible mixture became a prime candidate for disaster, and the air was so heavy with vapors, a tiny spark had the potential to vaporize everything in its deadly path.

Two people wiggled themselves from the wreckage. Dragaminov and Diamond looked at each other like they had just cancelled an appointment with the Grim Reaper. Diamond's one good leg couldn't support his weight, and he unceremoniously flopped in the fuel-tainted water, spasmodically retching the noxious fluid from his open mouth. Still weak from the bout with flesh-eating bacteria, he could barely stay afloat.

Dragaminov exited next, dragging two MAVs from the grip of

the potential coffin. The Russian criminal bled a steady stream from a small laceration on his scalp. Blood mixed with floating fuel created macabre crimson Rorschach inkblots on the water. Too bad there was no time to interpret their meaning. To slow the blood flow, he wrapped a filthy piece of cloth around his head, and after a minute, the bleeding slowed to a trickle. They were barely alive, but defiantly ignoring the inevitable. Not to worry, they would become immortal soon.

Eerie screeches resonated from the trapped copilot. His legs were pinned between the seat and firewall. "Please help me out of this coffin!" His screams for help fell on deaf ears.

Diamond muttered, "Do you hear anything?"

"No, comrade, I only hear an insect chirping."

"Let's get away from this bomb." Diamond slid into the MAV. Ignoring the cries of his fellow mercenary, Dragaminov jumped on the other. They floated away from the crash site, and Diamond lit the fuel spill. They watched the chopper burn to the water line, while the screams quietly disappeared.

The two psychopaths smiled, and Diamond quipped, "That just lowered my payroll. I need all the money I still have." The only sounds heard were of belly laughs, moving away from the heat.

The two MAVs glided away from the inferno like a Frisbee slicing through a vacuum. Dr. Grant's latest modifications allowed his inventions to hover above water with more stability at speed. The hydrogen-powered vehicles could travel at twice the speed of the original prototype.

Cool sea breezes cleared the cobwebs from their diabolical brains. Diamond decided they would need a way to get out of the Crown. "I think we need another helicopter. Why don't you steal, I mean *appropriate*, Struction's chopper. While you're at it, take care of that ship and hydrogen plant. That plant belongs to me, even though it is not in my name. Make sure *The Missing Link* is missing forever."

"Very well. I have an idea how to accomplish both tasks at the same time."

"Good. I'll hover to the Crown while you procure our ride. When the deed is done, meet me for our date with immortality."

The two floated away in different directions. Diamond set a direct course to the Crown, while Dragaminov followed the shoreline. Calm waters made for a speedy excursion to their destinations. Diamond would reach the Crown before Dragaminov could commit a host of felonies.

Diamond arrived at the prize in less than an hour. To his surprise, waters were calm around the Crown. Unbeknownst to him, the maelstrom and tumbling boulders had ceased to be a problem. He wouldn't get smashed into the side of the cone today.

The MAV attached powerful suction cups to the slippery, nearly ninety-degree slope, and methodically maneuvered its way up the outside of the cone. This painstaking process took quite a bit of time. As one set of cups detached, another set attached, making for a bumpy ride. While slowly plodding upward, Diamond sat perpendicular to the slope.

To maintain balance, he needed to look up to the sky. Not having a total view made for a scary ride. Each time there was a suction change, the vehicle slipped a little, giving the occupant the sensation of falling.

After twenty minutes of constant torture, Diamond was a basket case of nerves. Once he looked down, seeing the water below made him hurl his stomach contents into the sea. Fish jumped from the water, snapping up chunks of vomit floating on the bay below. He never knew, or cared, if his expelled stomach contents gave them indigestion.

Diamond felt physically spent when he finally reached the summit. His missing leg screamed with phantom pain. He really needed to rest his battered body. Before nodding off, the nearly dead criminal noticed the fog had dissipated from the top of the cone, exposing a golden light. What he saw next made him rest more comfortably.

"Look at all that gold! I need to figure a way to make it all mine." He fell asleep with a smile on his face.

49

As we passed through the open portal, I instantly felt like the smartest person on the planet. The entire history of the Americas somehow had become securely locked into my brain. I now possessed the ability to share this information with total recall. There was no need for books or computers, because I had it all in my personal RAM. My mind raced with the possibilities this gift could bestow on the rest of the world. Strange as it seemed, I had a strong feeling we were in the presence of a higher consciousness.

The rest of our ragtag expedition, especially the anthropologists, looked like sharks enjoying a school of anchovies. Dr. Ferdan shouted out loud, "My knees are shaking! We finally have access to the complete validated history of the western hemisphere, with all the gaps filled. What do you make of these revelations, Victo?"

"We now have the tools to rewrite history. I can see years of painstaking work ahead of us. Between the museum and this place, there is enough work to last a lifetime. Are you ready to make a lifelong commitment?"

"You bet I'm ready," said Dr. Ferdan. Gazing into each other's eyes, the two renewed lovers sealed their pact with a long, passionate kiss.

While everyone was self-absorbed in their newly found intelligence, we forgot to notice the surroundings. The Crown of Knowledge stood before us in all its glory. The cone dripped with a thick coating of gold. So much gold that if put on the open market, the world's economy would instantly crumble.

Precious stones of all shapes and sizes littered the perimeter. Yellow topaz, emeralds, turquoise-covered diamonds, and tourmaline—like those mounted on the keys— sparkled with each subtle movement of the sun. It took awhile for my eyes to adjust to the bright, twinkling gems.

Multiple species of tropical plants flourished in this environment. Thousands of fragrant flowers, most of which were unknown to me before that day, thrived on huge slabs of shiny obsidian. The black volcanic glass made the perfect contrast to the palette of color. Palm and fruit trees also circled the perimeter. Multicolored butterflies and hummingbirds flitted between the blossoms, spreading pollen, insuring the survival of future generations. It was impossible to feel stress.

Herbs and medicinal plants grew in neatly terraced rows. Large vases, filled with seeds, stood in front of each species. Ancient grains, like amaranth, maize, quinoa, and tiff, thrived in this environment. The conquistadors had nearly obliterated amaranth, because this healthy grain was used in Aztec religious ceremonies. They believed this plant was grown by the devil. Amaranth had more protein than any other plant source. Fortunately amaranth was making a comeback. I ate ancient grains in my breakfast cereal. Organized religion had done it again. Justifying their brutal actions in the name of God, the conquerors could better control their newfound slave labor force.

Jake noticed marijuana growing in one of the rows. The unmistakable odor pleasantly wafted in his direction. "Hey, Jerry, check out these gigantic buds!" He happily sprinted to the vase, scooped a handful of seeds, and gently placed them in his pocket. Those particular little footballs were three times the normal size of anything he'd ever seen.

There were pot plants cross-bred with hops. They grew in a vine close to the ground. This could be a new way to think about beer. Jake filled his other pocket with seeds. "It looks like I discovered a new hobby for when I get back to Rancho Mysterioso."

A lagoon stood in the front of a golden Aztec step pyramid. Crystal-clear waters reflected golden hues over the entire space. A number of small reed boats peacefully bobbed to the pulse of subtle changes in the moving water.

A smiling Della Vega, dressed in his ancient priest robes, stood on the first golden step. "Let me be the first to welcome all of you to Azatlan, the birthplace of the Aztec civilization. First of all, I am Father Diego Della Vega. Before you question me, Mr. Johnson, I did not tell you everything that night in the desert. If you remember, I never said I wasn't the original. My father was also Father Diego Della Vega. I may be excommunicated from the Holy Roman Apostolic Church, but I never lie. There is a difference between telling a lie and not telling the whole truth. If I said I was over five hundred years old, you may not have continued on this journey."

"I realized your true identity as soon as we entered the Crown," I replied. "At the time, my mind was too busy being blown to make the connection. I still can't wrap my head around this heavy-duty revelation. I'm sure the answer lurks somewhere inside my information-swollen brain. After all, this is the Crown of Knowledge."

Della Vega blushed, forgetting the obvious. "I'm glad I don't need to deflect questions concerning my age, now that you know my true identity."

"The jury is still out on that one. I'm awestruck over the concept of this magical environment, let alone your age. The codices alluded to immortality. I dismissed them as another mysterious tale and nothing more. I'm in no hurry to jump to conclusions about what I think I perceive as truth. I'm positive that the answers will come to me in a cerebral bolt of lightning," I said.

Della Vega smiled, motioning to follow him up the golden steps. A soothing red light that looked like a squinting eye pulsated from where the main altar once stood. Human sacrifice could have been performed on that spot. Every time I looked directly into the crimson eye, a feeling of serenity filled my senses with pure joy. The feeling was so intense, my body felt like it was floating up the steep pyramid steps. My mind refused to acknowledge bloodletting sacrifice of any kind, taking place within this peaceful structure. I noticed the box— yes, that box—precisely situated where beating hearts were ripped from bewildered bodies.

Della Vega led me up the stairs to a hallway carved into the stone, where a series of chambers lined the walls. The ancient ex-priest motioned to follow him into the first. Once inside, I couldn't believe my eyes. I was in the midst of an Aztec street scene.

I visually witnessed everything stored inside my information-packed brain. All the sights, sounds, tastes and smells felt real. I could smell food cooking. My mouth burned from an interaction with hot chilies.

People, dressed in period costumes, strolled by, oblivious to my presence. One such group headed toward my position on a collision course. There was no way I could avoid them. To my surprise, these real-looking Aztecs invisibly passed through my body without missing a step. I was in the midst of some kind of virtual reality experience, a theater of the mind. How cool was witnessing visual validation? Teaching as we know it could mean an end to the smart board and overhead projector. With this newly discovered technology, developed before the world invented the concept, mankind could learn from our historical mistakes.

This journey was one mind-blowing experience after another, but this latest revelation exponentially changed everything. I could not figure out if this place was spawned from mysticism or science. More questions arose every time the previous question was answered. I left that room with a newfound appreciation for life's mysteries.

Della Vega wore a quizzical look on his deeply furrowed brow. "What do you think of our classroom?"

"There must be a catch. This place seems too perfect."

"There is! For someone to take advantage of this unique information, they must be pure of heart. They must use this information to better mankind, and not for personal gain. From what I perceive, you and your companions qualify."

We left the room I had dubbed the Aztec Cultural Experience, and we traveled down the hall to the next. The rest of the expedition flitted in and out of the various rooms with the same enthused wonderment. The thirst for knowledge propelled all of us to drink and savor every drop.

We entered the Inca Cultural Experience next. The room looked identical to the others, except for a different cast of characters. This time I witnessed the Festival of Illopa, the Inca god of lightning, near Taquile Island, off the shores of Lake Titicaca. People who lined the lake's shore witnessed the spectacle in awe. The king, covered in gold dust, stood inside a boat, where everybody could gaze at his body shimmering in the blinding, reflected sunlight. The Inca believed gold was the excrement of the sun, reassuring his subjects the king was indeed a god. After the sun faded, the king dove into the lake, washing the gold from his body. This act symbolized the king was both god and man.

Goose flesh covered my body with excitement. I couldn't believe the effect this powerful ceremony had on the bystanders. They jumped into the lake screaming, while hypnotic drums heightened the frenzied atmosphere. Everyone swam to the king, paying homage to the majesty of his station in life. After this show of power, no one would dare question the king's divine right, because his power came directly from the sun itself.

The Inca people loved their king, in life as well as in death. After the creator-god ruler's death, his mummified body was paraded through the streets. The same type of procession is held today, during the Fiesta of Saint Santiago. A statue of Saint Santiago is carried along the same route as that of the ancient dead king's. These powerful beliefs were transferred from the ancients to that of the church. To achieve the same effect, the church just changed the cast of characters.

Both groups used this tact to reassure the people that there had to be life after death.

I left the Inca Experience with an understanding about how different groups manipulated faith to achieve an end. This was why new ideas were similarly dissimilar; or as circumstances changed, the idea remained the same.

Della Vega led me further into the bowels of the pyramid. We passed rooms dedicated to every civilization that ever lived in the western hemisphere. I decided to enter the Anasazi Experience because I had visited the Chaco Canyon ruins in New Mexico. The Anasazi were shrouded in mystery. How could a thriving, advanced civilization just vanish? Some anthropologists speculate a prolonged drought forced the once powerful people to abandon their cities and disappear into the vast southwestern desert. I was curious to learn what really happened.

Della Vega gently tugged at my shirt, motioning me to follow him down the hall. "I need to show you a special room that may change how you feel about yourself. After the eclipse, there will be plenty of time for solving nagging mysteries."

"Okay, lead the way."

Della Vega led me up a narrow staircase, which led to a small circular opening. "I need to ask a few questions before entry. I know you are ashamed of certain events that happened during combat. Which ones haunt you the most?"

"Wow! I feel like I've just been blindsided. There must be a good reason for me to surface these memories I tried to bury for decades. I've trusted your guidance up until now, so there is no reason for me to question your motives. Firstly, I am very ashamed that Tam, the ARVN interpreter, died saving my life. The unknown saddens me even more. How many innocent people died at my hand from unneeded indiscriminate fire missions, raining destruction down upon an unsuspecting population, without ever witnessing the results? Not knowing cemented the anguish in place. I may never know what really went down."

"Please enter this room. You may or may not like what you learn, but it will be the truth. I'll be waiting outside until you have your fill of the truth."

I barely squeezed through the pint-sized opening. A strange force pulled me into the center of that pitch-black room. Gentle, soothing breezes circled my entire being and replaced my fear with a comforting calm that felt like I had inhaled the sacred truths of the universe. What were the sacred truths of the universe, anyway?

Without warning, a pale blue hue gradually lit the room, allowing me to get a glimpse of a transparent shadow lurking in the corner. As the shadow moved closer, I recognized the ARVN interpreter Tam. His inviting smile filled me with a confusing joy. Dumbfounded, my teeth chattered like an old teletype machine, while tears gently streamed down my cheeks. My body refused to cry all these years. The salty fluid that had felt like a burden was beginning to wash away my perceived sins.

"Are you real? After you threw me into that hole, I felt your last breath jam into my soul, unselfishly giving yourself up to save my life. Why did I live, while you willingly committed the ultimate sacrifice? For forty-some odd years, I've been reliving that fateful moment over and over. I feel guilty for how that scenario went down. I feel ashamed that you died while I lived."

"It's good to see you," said Tam. "Don't feel guilty about an act over which you had no control. The fact of the matter was that you were closer to the hole. There was just enough room for one of us to fit into that earthy sanctuary. I made a split-second decision to save one of us, rather than both of us dying. You don't need to beat yourself up over that fleeting moment in time. I don't feel the least bit angry. The fog of war can distort the truth with agonizing doubt. Let it go, Jerry. Only you can free yourself from its debilitating grip. You've suffered enough."

Tears flowed onto my shirt, cooling my skin from the evapora-tion, and a heavy burden began to dissolve from my psyche. I reached for my friend to give him a thanking hug. He disappeared, and my arms held the mama san I fragged in that bunker. Her sunken black eyes peered directly into mine. "I survived that blast by hiding behind a large wooden beam," she said. "I lived a full life, and died of old age a number of years later. There is no need to beat yourself up over something that never happened." She gently caressed my teary cheek, and disappeared into the blackness.

I sat alone in the dark, attempting to make sense out of confront-ing my perceived demons. After a moment with my thoughts, Della Vega pulled me from my contemplation. "What just happened?" I asked him.

"You finally witnessed the truth. Sometimes the truth can be a bitter pill to swallow, worse than those giant orange malaria pills you were forced to take in the Nam. How does it feel finally knowing what really happened?"

"I don't know what to feel. Actually, it felt cathartic to shed a few tears. It was like solving one mystery with another mystery. I feel like my mind played with my sensitivity for all those years. I need more time to process what just went down. There is no way I could be ashamed of something I never witnessed. Thank you for exposing me to an alternative perception. Thank you for understanding."

"I'm glad I could help. Sometimes the simple truth is the best. We need to gather the rest of your people. We have an eclipse to prepare for."

50

Dragaminov stashed his MAV in the reeds adjacent to the hydrogen and oxygen tanks above *The Missing Link*. His head wound began to bleed through the greasy rag, burning his lacerated scalp. Tiny sanguine droplets followed him into the control building. The pain from a mixture of gasoline and his compromised flesh throbbed with the intensity of a jackhammer. He almost passed out.

Once inside, the crafty criminal disabled the safety mechanism that prevented the cryogenic fluid from being released into the environment. He opened a few discharge valves, releasing liquid oxygen and hydrogen into their respective containment ponds. After the deadly mixture rose to just below the brim, he restricted the flow, leaving the open valves flowing at a trickle. If and when the two vapors mixed to the right flammable range, the slightest ignition source would rain destruction in its path, more powerful than an atomic bomb. Maniacal revenge and the promise of immortality drove the psychopathic criminal to take such a suicidal risk. He had no clue of the consequences from his irresponsible actions.

Dragaminov couldn't care less about vaporizing *The Missing Link*, or the aftermath of the ensuing environmental catastrophe. All he cared about was the destruction of *The Missing Link* and its crew. His twisted treachery had the potential of turning this beautiful, pristine landscape into a toxic wasteland, devoid of all life.

The trickling liquid froze as the drips became vaporous. Dragaminov tried to open the valves to maintain a constant flow, but a small amount of the discharged hydrogen splashed his hand and face, freezing the exposed flesh solid. A few drops splashed into his right eye, instantly blinding him. Frozen flesh sloughed off his hand and face like a dripping candle, rendering them hideously useless. The disfigured Russian ran from the control room...directly into the main vapor cloud, where more flesh fell away from his compromised body. His lungs burned, making breathing a painful ordeal. The once powerful psychopath was dying.

Painful screams could be heard aboard *The Missing Link*. They sounded like a wounded animal caught in a trap. Captain Bolder, looking through binoculars, saw a man staggering aimlessly from the control building, disappearing into the foggy mist. He clearly saw Dragaminov stumbling into the vapor cloud. After a few seconds the screams quieted. The only sound was the hiss of escaping gasses.

An errant gust of wind momentarily exposed Dragaminov's frozen, statue-like corpse. His motionless body resembled the disturbing Donatello sculpture, "The Penitent Magdalene." The 1455 statue depicted an old Mary Magdalene after spending forty years wandering through the desert, doing penance for her wicked ways. Her grotesque features and sunken eyes vacantly stared into space, pleading for forgiveness. Unlike Magdalene, Dragaminov would never beg for forgiveness. No one would mourn his passing, only wishing it happened sooner. He was one maniacal psychopath who would never again inflict unnecessary pain on the innocent.

E.D. warned Captain Bolder of the potential dangers involving her dad's cryogenic holding tanks. He heeded her warning, and sent a party of seamen to investigate, to see if anyone had survived the toxic cloud. The remaining fed type focused a powerful thermal imaging camera, penetrating into the spill. Worried, he advised Captain Bolder of the absence of a heat signature. "I don't see any sign of life, but the area around the containment ponds is extremely hazardous. We need to recall the rescue party and get out of here immediately!"

Captain Bolder quickly recalled the rescue party. He advised the two Coast Guard ships to weigh anchor and leave their mooring before all three ships got caught in the deadly cloud. With the rescue party safely aboard the *Link*, all three ships left the contaminated area. When the ships were safely away, the cloud slowly dissipated. Dragaminov had failed to disable the redundant safety system. The liquid miraculously stopped flowing, but the area between the tanks and the beach was still extremely hazardous. The ground surrounding the tanks was permeated with a flammable mixture of hydrogen and oxygen, and it would take days for the liquid to vaporize into the atmosphere.

All three ships anchored three miles from the shore, where they diligently monitored the spill's progress. The local winds changed direction and blew away from the shoreline, where only the reeds would be vulnerable to contamination. Captain Bolder knew the prevailing winds could change direction at any time, leaving the vessels vulnerable to the dangerous wrath of a hydrogen explosion, and moved farther away. Vigilant of the impending danger, the mariners would sit tight until E.D. was able to communicate.

51

Della Vega assembled our group on top of the pyramid, with a bird's-eye view of the now intensely glowing golden box. A pulsating crimson eye penetrated our consciousness with a matrix of light, connecting everyone to the box. After a few seconds our eyes adjusted to the brightness, allowing us to experience everything more clearly than ever before. An intense calm spread over us like an electric blanket, soothing any fears left over from our painful pasts.

Jake shouted, "Is this what heaven feels like?"

Della Vega laughed. "The concept of an afterlife was invented by the men in charge as a way of controlling the rest of the population. There has never been any empirical evidence to substantiate the existence of heaven, so they invented faith, and the rules needed to follow the right path to the Promised Land. Over time, these rules continually changed to suit the whims of the powerful.

Furthermore, church dogma dictates that man is born in sin and must suffer forever for that original sin. The only way to speak to god, people must go through them. I still have trouble with the Church's grasp on humanity "

Della Vega punctuated, "I've had centuries to ponder these questions, and I still believe I was unjustly cast out of the church for my so called sins. After all the harm the church inflicted on me, I still believe in a merciful God".

E.D. spoke up. "I guess this means that you can't marry Junior and me."

Dr. Ferdan joined in by asking, "What about marrying Victo and me?"

Della Vega smiled and scratched his chin. "You know that I can't perform any sacraments on behalf of the Catholic Church. I was convicted of heresy, blasphemy, and consorting with the devil. Your marriages can never be blessed by the church."

E.D. added, "We don't care. You are by far the holiest person we've ever known. It would be an honor for you to give us your blessing, sanctified or not. We have to make it legal by the State of California anyway. I don't think they will certify a marriage by a 500-year-old ex-priest. It just feels like the right thing to do."

Blushing, the ancient priest exclaimed, "I haven't married anyone in such a long time. I've even forgotten the words to the ceremony. Besides, no one here could understand a ritual that is half a millennium old."

"That's okay. We can wing it. In this case, the result is always more important than the process, anyway. Remember where we are, inside the Crown of Knowledge. Everyone already knows the words to the ceremony. We don't even have to utter one word. How cool would that be, to participate in a silent wedding?"

"In that case, it would be my pleasure to give you my blessing."

Jake, Strutch, and I fashioned garlands from the abundant supply of exotic flowers. We placed the fragrant blossoms, resembling crowns, around the two couple's heads. *Imagine that, four small crowns resting inside the larger Crown of Knowledge. I don't pretend to be a sage, but if I hang around here much longer, who knows, I just might discover the meaning of life. Wow!* I thought.

Della Vega, dressed in his finest colorful vestments, brought capes fashioned from thousands of hummingbird feathers, like the tapestries we saw in the cave-museum. He fastened the sparkling heavy garments around the shoulders of the soon-to-be newlyweds, and the four lovers embraced, intensely gazing into each other's eyes. E.D. and Dr. Ferdan looked like goddesses, radiating beauty with every breath. E.D.'s red hair appeared to be shooting sparks that bounced off the golden walls. A pulsating visible aura bathed them within a cocoon of ever-changing color, and an overwhelming feeling of pure joy enveloped everything.

After their gaze was broken, Della Vega handed the newlyweds four ancient gold rings fitted with a red gem, reminiscent of the eye above the box. They placed the rings on each other's fingers. They fit perfectly, as if a jeweler had just sized them.

Della Vega held the four hands and pronounced, "In the sight of God, I pronounce you together forever. You may now seal your love with a kiss." The just-married couples wasted little time pressing their lips together. When their flesh became one, the rings began to sparkle. The rest of us took note of this kosmic phenomenon and looked at each other as if these golden bands were commonplace inside the Crown of Knowledge. We were beyond the point of having our minds blown, so we just went with the flow.

Della Vega explained. "The stones sparkle every time they speak to each other in a loving manner; conversely they remain dark when they speak in anger. Now we must prepare for the eclipse. First contact begins in less than an hour."

Della Vega took the four jeweled keys from the coziness of the box and handed one each to E.D., Dr. Ferdan, Strutch, and me. We were told to place them into slots on the rim of the cone, on the four cardinal compass points. E.D. and Junior took the turquoise-diamond to the north wall. Doctors Ferdan and Estaban took the tourmaline to the south wall. Jake and Strutch took the emerald to the east wall. The two new fathers-in-law could revel in their new family situation. I took the topaz to the west wall, while Della Vega stayed atop the pyramid with the box. The glowing red eye watched over everything.

Each key guided us to the appropriate wall, where staircases showed the way to the pinnacle. Once on top, the keys were fitted into slots carved into the solid rock. When all four keys were in place, ribbons of colored light radiated away from the Crown.

After a few seconds, the lights spun in a counterclockwise

direction, braiding together like a horizontal maypole. Strange as it may seem, these particular lights did not travel in a straight line; they swirled around the other lights, maintaining their color. As the colors bent around each other, an infinite number of subtle hues appeared. In fact, every possible color could be seen. There were so many different combinations, the color disappeared, creating a transparent mirror of filtered light.

The patchwork of color fanned away from the rim in an outward cone. This strange phenomenon allowed everyone inside the Crown to see the entire sky, clearer than the most powerful telescope. Brilliant, filtered sunlight could be seen without squinting. I couldn't believe what we were witnessing. What were we in store for during the main event, the total eclipse of the sun?

After the keys were thoroughly tested, all seven of us joined Della Vega at the base of the pyramid. An air of excitement filled every molecule inside the Crown. A higher vibration, like a harmonious chant, lifting our spirits to lofty heights, never before experienced. I've never felt so aware of my being as I did at that moment. The wow factor needed to be adjusted to a new level. Let the games begin!

52

Ribbons of brilliant-colored light woke an exhausted Diamond from a much-needed rest. He still felt groggy from the helicopter crash and the assault up the Crown's outer wall. His entire body screamed with pain. The once powerful billionaire was on the verge of dying from his misguided ego. Now an international fugitive, Harlan Diamond had nothing to lose. Maniacal logic hung on the belief that immortality would reverse his temporary streak of bad luck. To him, these problems were just another bump in the road of life. Unbridled greed and the quest for power drove him to the brink of extinction. In fact, he still believed he could have it all.

A gaunt, diaphoretic Diamond barely had the energy to maneuver the MAV's subtle controls. With labored breathing and racing pulse, he faded in and out of consciousness. A strange force guided the MAV down the slippery, steep, gold-laden wall. Remarkably, the suction cups easily slid over the slick wall, making for a smooth ride that its occupant couldn't enjoy because he was out cold.

The MAV slowed to a screeching halt when the innovated super chair reached the Crown's floor. Diamond suddenly awoke with a blast of newfound energy surging throughout his broken body. His discomfort miraculously evaporated, along with the pain. He hadn't felt this good since before he was skewered by that angry rhinoceros. He took a moment to look at all the riches just lying on the floor and walls throughout the Crown. Looking at all the gold and precious stones made him salivate.

"Immortality feels divine! I must be a god! I can't wait to own it all! I'll need eternity to spend my newly found fortune!" Yes, Diamond was so smug and full of himself, he believed he could dismantle this sacred site and use the spoils for his personal gain.

Without warning, the MAV fired up and made a beeline toward the pyramid. Diamond tried to slow the runaway chair, but it surged forward, as if an outside force took over the controls. Once at the landing, the mechanical wonder climbed the golden stairs with the ease of a mountain goat.

E.D. saw the MAV with Diamond riding in the chair. She couldn't believe what she was seeing. The hair on the back of her neck stood straight up as her face turned the color of her ruby mane. "What are you doing here? You died when your plane crashed!"

"As you can see, I'm more than alive, I'm immortal! If you're a good little girl, I might give you a job washing my cars. Then again, you've been such a pain, I think I'll just put you out of your misery." The ungrateful megalomaniac pivoted the MAV's machine guns toward E.D.'s torso. Without a second thought, he blew her a kiss and unremorsefully squeezed the triggers, but the guns would not fire. He sat there speechless, looking down at the malfunctioning weapons with disdain.

E.D. reacted to this aggression with some of her own. Without hesitation, she jumped up and lunged toward the moving chair.

Della Vega grabbed her by the collar, preventing her from ripping Diamond from his ride, or worse. "There is no need for any type of vengeful violence here. This place is a refuge from the evils of the outside world, where malice of any kind must not be tolerated. Besides, no one ever dies inside the Crown of Knowledge."

"I'm sorry, Father. That man has uncaringly brutalized so many people, as well as plundering the environment for profit. He needs to pay for his crimes."

"Do not worry, my child. Trust me, he will get his. We need to get ready for the eclipse."

As Della Vega and E.D. philosophized about man's inhumanity to man, Diamond climbed the remaining stairs to the hallway, where the Experience rooms stood. He regained control of the MAV and maneuvered the chair into the room where Jerry had participated in the Aztec Experience. It was empty, as were the other rooms. He was unworthy to participate in the experience.

At the end of the hall stood the staircase Jerry had climbed to reach the Truth Room. Diamond felt uncomfortable looking at the small opening above the staircase. He tugged the joystick to the reverse position. To his surprise, the MAV climbed the stairs instead, as if it still had a mind of its own. He tried to get out of the chair, but the seat belt tightened, making it impossible for him to move. This was one of Dr. Grant's improvements while he was prisoner aboard the *Black Gold*. Diamond had no choice but to literally sit tight, without enjoying the ride.

A small circular opening in the solid rock stood between Diamond and a place he wanted no part of. Diamond peered into the opening and gazed at a cold blackness, devoid of light or color. He immediately felt a surge of pure terror quivering through his restrained body. There was no way this man who always needed to be in charge wanted anything to do with that void.

Without warning the opening enlarged like an eye's iris, allowing the MAV just enough space for entry. Once inside, the opening slammed shut, with a screech that reverberated through Diamond's shattered nervous system. He was a virtual prisoner, without any clue to his circumstance. He had no choice but to silently wait for the karmic hammer to drop.

Alone inside silent blackness, Diamond felt a strange force clawing at his compromised being. Real and thorough fear completely occupied his thoughts, and he began thinking of the people he had wronged. These stinging revelations made him even more uncomfortable. Before being trapped inside those walls, he had reveled in getting one over on everyone unfortunate enough to come in contact with his wrath.

After a few minutes, his fear evaporated. He boldly shouted, "I am who I am, and I will never feel the slightest compassion for anyone foolhardy enough to challenge me or get in my way! Besides, I'm so rich, nobody has enough power to ever challenge me! Now that I'm immortal, watch out, world! In time, I will eventually control it all!" Feeling exalted, Diamond started thinking of how he would amass enough wealth to own it all, but he could never be happy with just enough.

Diamond's exercise in himself was short-lived. A bright spotlight shone in the corner, projecting grotesque shadows throughout that confined space. A familiar voice rang out from the light. It was the former VP, speaking directly at his captive audience.

The shadow materialized into the man Diamond had sliced up with the wind harp. He resembled a jigsaw puzzle whose pieces didn't quite fit. The former VP ran toward him wielding the bloody wind harp. "Hey, Diamond! How would you like being sliced into eighty-eight pieces? I can tell you from experience, it hurts. I'm not from Texas; now it's your turn to get screwed."

Showing no quarter, former VP Haney thrust the shadowy wind harp into Diamond's body over and over again. The smell from his body parts being ripped apart made Diamond nauseous. He projectile-vomited over everything, making the smell even more unpleasant.

"Wait just a minute Haney! I killed you fair and square! Besides, you are not real. Is that all you got? Bring it on!"

"If you insist. Check out the pain, and tell me if it feels real."

Real? It sure was. Each slicing wire sent excruciating pain responses to every cell throughout Diamond's body. It felt as if the pain completely took over. He had inflicted so much pain on others that it was second nature. He got off on the act, but being the recipient gave him a reason to reevaluate his priorities. Diamond started to realize what suffering was all about.

"You made your point! Please make the pain stop!"

"I can't believe my ears. The almighty and powerful Harlan

Diamond used the magic word, 'please.' I've never heard that word spoken from your lips. Now that's progress."

"Please may be the magic word for most people. I'm not most people. I prefer NOW as my magic word. Let's see how a salvo of machine gun fire feels, NOW!" Without a nanosecond of compassion, Diamond blindly emptied both guns into the darkness. The only visible light came from the gun's muzzle flashes, but he was shooting at shadows. How do you kill something that's already dead, or not even real? Shards of gold flew away from the walls like bees escaping a burning hive. Pure gold littered the floor a foot deep. Diamond felt a little less stressed with all that gold lying at his feet.

A voice called out from the darkness. "You missed."

"How stupid do you think I am? I wasn't trying to hit what I couldn't see. I fired to ease some pent-up frustration, and do a little mining."

The room fell quiet after all the fireworks. Burnt powder and cordite filled the room with an acrid smell, reminiscent of combat. The only audible sound was Diamond's heart thumping in his chest. Perpetual darkness put him back into the same funk he had momentarily lost. He was a prisoner, literally sitting on an unspendable fortune. Desperation hit him like a mule kicking in his stall. Unfortunately, Diamond's was built from solid granite. He would need the kick from a thermonuclear explosion to free him from his secure entombment.

Another bright light glowed from the opposite corner. A solitary figure whose face continually peeled away like the layers of an onion materialized through the smoke. Diamond squinted to recognize the statue-like figure. As the smoke cleared, a smile replaced his painful frown. Dragaminov silently stood in the corner motionless. Diamond had a compatriot to free him from his restraints. He laughed out loud. "I'm glad to see you, comrade! We need to figure out how to procure all this gold."

Dragaminov didn't answer. His body appeared to be frozen.

Without warning, what was left of the Russian's shell shattered into thousands of tiny pieces, like an axe smashing out a car's window. As the cryogenic fragments evaporated, Dragaminov was reduced to a bad memory.

A dire reality jammed into Diamond's now broken confidence. He had no one to protect his back. Alone and wounded, all he could do was scream. His blood-curdling wailing reverberated throughout the Truth Room. He now knew the business end of suffering first-hand. "Is this how the people I wronged suffered?"

After a momentary lapse of reasoning, Diamond reverted back to his old demented self. He kept telling himself that none of this was real, just parlor tricks aided by smoke and mirrors, even though he could smell the smoke and see reflections of people he wronged jumping from the golden walls.

A parade of victims surrounded the MAV, reminding him of the decades he rode roughshod over the innocent. Each one looked him straight in the eye, showing their disdain for this monster, and as they passed by, each victim prodded him with bony fingers, chopsticks, even pitchforks. Each painful jab reminded him of the circumstances of their demise. Thousands of people reminded him how he had snuffed out their lives in the name of greed and the almighty bottom line.

Just as the throng thinned, he heard a sound he recognized. The rhino he had killed charged his good leg. Smoke blew from the beast's nostrils while he set his sights on fresh meat. The rotund creature speared Diamond's good leg just for fun. He charged again and again, T-boning the MAV with a vengeance. With each strike, the pain amplified to a crescendo. Then, just as it began, the pain abruptly stopped. The pain had been so intense, Diamond had drifted in and out of consciousness. He was happy to get some relief, even though he knew this wouldn't be the end.

After only a few painless moments, the sound of thundering

hooves broke the silence. The rhino set his sights on Diamond's now not-so-good leg; the one that looked and felt like an elevator door dragged it up twenty-seven floors. This time the beast held a rider. Diamond couldn't recognize the passenger; whoever or whatever rode on top was just a blur.

An instant before impact, the rhino came to an abrupt stop, catapulting the tiny rider into Diamond's chest. The innocent, diminutive body wrapped its tiny arms around Diamond's craning neck in a death grip. Terrified, he looked down at a headless baby—the same one he had handed to its grieving mother, minus its head; the head Diamond had disconnected just for sport.

Diamond freaked. The putrid smells of combat wafted from the hole where the poor little infant's head once was. Bodily fluids splashed over everything, transporting them back to the little hamlet where Diamond's depravity hit an all-time low. He witnessed the disgusting act over and over again.

By this time, Diamond was ready to end it all. He grabbed a knife from a pouch hidden in the MAV's arm and thrust the razor-sharp blade toward his heart. Just before it made contact, a hand grabbed the knife, dropping it harmlessly to the floor.

Diamond looked at the person who had prevented him from taking the coward's way out. To his surprise, the baby's mother looked at Diamond and boldly said, "What goes around comes around. Have a nice day!" The depraved joke wasn't funny anymore.

Diamond tried to pry the headless infant's death grip from around his neck, to no avail. He desperately activated the hydrogen flamethrowers to rid him of the horror. The only thing that happened was the gold surrounding the MAV liquefied, then hardened. Diamond was restrained in a gilded prison, with nowhere to spend the booty.

With the dead infant still clutching his neck, Diamond screamed louder than a howler monkey caught in a leg trap. His pathetic cries for help could be heard throughout the Crown. He was immortal, with an eternity of horror consuming every waking moment.

Those hauntingly desperate cries were all too familiar to Jake, Strutch, and me. They were the same agonizing cries for help we heard in the jungle some forty years ago. We never left anyone behind then, and we weren't about to do so now. We had to save Diamond, even though he had an appointment with the death serum administered by the Grim Reaper.

Junior looked at us and said, "I'll go with you three jarheads to cover your backs. Besides, this is a perfect time to bond with you, Dad, and my new father-in-law."

E.D. just shrugged her shoulders, but was glad her new husband had the same resolve. "I really don't approve of anyone trying to help that despicable stain. You boys be careful. Don't stay too long. Did you forget about the eclipse?"

It was probably amusing to see three old warrior-hippies hobbling up the pyramid stairs, obviously on a fool's errand. It was even funnier to see Junior waiting patiently, while the old-timers slowly navigated the steep stairs. How were we supposed to rescue someone who deserved to be in the predicament he bestowed on himself?

As we reached the iris, Diamond's cries grew hauntingly louder. There was no way we could breach the solid granite barrier. Junior tried to move the massive door, with every muscle bulging from his chiseled physique. This lesson in futility lasted only a few minutes before it was deemed useless.

Finally realizing there was nothing we could do for him, we retreated to where the rest assembled. I admitted, "We had to give it a shot, even though it was half-hearted. Maybe Big D needs to be locked up for eternity with the demons he greedily manifested. It's definitely instant karma time."

E.D. looked miffed. "How could you old fools want to save that diabolical rat from where he belongs? Where is the logic behind your misguided folly?"

"We just reacted. After all these years, *semper fi* still has meaning."

Junior bellowed a resounding, "OORRAH! I finally get what that unbreakable bond means. Thank you for allowing me to experience it firsthand."

Della Vega chuckled. "Did you guys have a good time fighting windmills? Don't worry. Diamond still needs to experience more terror without inflicting any of his own. The Crown of Knowledge has its ways to get even. He needs to marinate in that kosmic stew for a while longer. Besides, we don't need his negative energy jamming up the eclipse. Speaking of the eclipse, it's just about that time."

53

The rugged mountains to the west began to gently vibrate, grabbing my spirit in anticipation, as if they were alive and hungry. This was the moment to deploy the light mirror. On cue, the keys spun their magic—weaving colored lights together while reflecting pristine images of wonder for everyone to fully enjoy, except Diamond of course. Besides, he was too involved in his own misery to enjoy this spectacle of spectacles.

A high-pitched squeak rode shotgun alongside the soothing vibrations. The sound intensified to a level we humans could not hear. Nakai's ears stood straight up, intently listening to sounds only he could disseminate. This massive dog whistle calmed the powerful beast to a state of sheer bliss. He rolled over on his back, with his legs pointed to the sky. To him, the sound felt like his belly was being rubbed by hundreds of tiny fingers.

Perry also could hear the music played by the moon's shadow. The speedy falcon joined Nakai in staring into space. Junior noticed the two perceptive creatures enjoying the pleasure this celestial event generously bestowed upon them. "Check out those two. They look like I feel." We all chuckled, waiting for what would happen next.

The vibrations grew in intensity as the moon's shadow rhythmically danced across the water on a direct course to devour the noonday sun. A violet hue hung over the moving shadow, adding a hint of mystery to what it had in store for us.

Confused night birds abruptly awoke from their daytime slumber. With their biological clocks askew, they had no feeling for the exact time of day or night. They noisily took flight, feverishly circling under the blue star of twilight. Cooling temperatures, fueled by gentle breezes, allowed seabirds to frolic on the foaming waves in comfort. The twenty-degree temperature drop gave the usually scalding Baja relief, as pleasant as a Hawaiian sunset.

The faster the lunar shadow charged toward the waiting sun, the clearer the sky became. When the moon finally reached the sun's corona, everything changed. At first contact, the new moon stood between Earth and sun in perfect alignment, or syzygy.

The sky was so clear, eight planets were visible with the naked eye. Mercury, Venus, and Earth of course, Mars, Jupiter with its largest moon Titan, Saturn, and Uranus shined brightly into our consciousness. The Milky Way lit a brilliant swath of pure white pinpoints of light across the depths of our sightline. A faint Andromeda, the closest galaxy to our own, gave birth to the light we were witnessing, billions and billions of years ago. I realized firsthand how small and unimportant we humans were compared to the big picture we call the universe. Our constant fighting and inflated petty problems made me feel like a speck of dust, unworthy of mentioning.

At second contact, shadowy dots appeared on everything inside the Crown, including us. We looked like walking Dalmatians whose spots were continually changing. These images, or Baily's beads, were reflections of the moon's peaks and valleys, bleeding through the thickening lunar shadow. The phenomenon lasted until the moon completely covered the sun's inner disc, or totality.

During totality, the only visible light shined from the sun's corona. We were inside the Crown of Knowledge, or corona, witnessing this glorious phenomenon involving the solar corona. If our adventure was anything, kosmic topped that list. The only thing close to how I felt would have to be an orgasm. Totality would turn into a seven-minute-plus orgasm. No wonder I felt spent.

Totality multiplied the wow factor many times over. We were clustered in the center of the Crown's floor. Everyone inside the Crown stood frozen, with our eyes and mouths wide open, transfixed on the noonday sky in anticipation of what would happen next, and it did just that.

An instant before the eclipse entered third contact, the corona projected the Diamond Ring, by far the most spectacular sight I've ever witnessed. In one voice, everyone shouted, "Oh my God, the Diamond Ring!" My whole body felt a spiritual presence I could not begin to explain. No wonder the ancients took this phenomenon as a vision of God.

For me, the jury was still out on the existence of God. If God does exist, the spirit has to be merciful not vengeful. I needed to process what just happened to make a definitive leap back to faith. Forty years of being angry with God for allowing that ugly war still had a tight grip on my soul. However, this spiritual experience may have had nothing to do with the God I was brought up to fear. It had more to do with the interaction between Father Sky and Mother Earth. The Native American worldview made more sense than a sentence of burning in hell ever did. These heavy philosophical quandaries needed to be sorted out at a later date, when I had the time to ponder them objectively.

The newlyweds, took the Diamond Ring as a sign their marriage would last the test of time. They held each other so tightly, the Jaws of Life couldn't pry them apart. Their own rings sparkled, while the red eye above the box glittered to the same cadence. They stared at each other and the box with an unbreakable gaze. It was like the box sanctioned their love.

Together, Jake, Strutch, and I took a long, deep breath. The three of us communicated without speaking. We knew what the others were thinking. A single tear slid down each of our cheeks, validating the gravity of the situation. It was like the battle had abruptly ended for us. After witnessing the light show, nothing could keep us from keeping on. Smiling, we embraced each other with a powerful group hug. I couldn't believe Jake, Mr. Hard Ass, was participating.

We hugged so tightly, it felt like a vise was squeezing sense into our still-confused bodies. These emotions were real.

In all the excitement, Della Vega was nowhere to be found. It was like he blended into the universal flow of the Crown's majesty. I was looking forward to hearing his take on what we had just experienced. A strange feeling overpowered me with the realization that I may never see him again.

Just as hope was fleeting, Della Vega stood in front of the box, basking in the brilliance of the glowing red eye. The ancient holy man spread his arms to the side; with palms up, pointing skyward. With a subtle flick of the wrists, he gestured a parting wave. The light suddenly brightened, and in an instant, he disappeared into its glow.

Without warning, the light mirror changed its orientation, from a horizontal plain to an ascending cylindrical cone. A tiny opening on top pointed to a bright pinpoint of light none of us had noticed.

The Crown's walls unmercifully rumbled with the force of a six on the Richter scale. The angry tremor slammed us to the floor. Objects violently crashed over everything. Gold and jewels ripped from the walls, zinging gilded missiles throughout every inch of the Crown. Miraculously, none of them even grazed our exposed bodies. Fear took over from the joy we experienced only moments ago.

The glowing eye above the box frantically circled the Crown. Its light separated, resembling biblical tongues of fire. They momentarily paused over all of our heads. This reassuring act blew the top of my mind completely off. What just happened? Parlor trick or not, the tongues of fire were a nice theatrical touch, but there still was too much symbolism to fully process. The only thing I felt sure of was that this brief strange trip still had a ways to go.

The lingual red lights joined together as one, slowly circling the newly formed vortex. As the blood-red eye rose, the circles spun tighter, speeding up, allowing the eye to linger. When the eye reached the opening, the vortex glowed a translucent red. After a second or two, the friendly red eye changed to a pale yellow, then to an explosive white flash. Without fanfare, the explosion shot upward into the heavens, where it disappeared without a trace. The only reference of where the red eye traveled was the pinpoint, framed by the vortex. I never forgot its location.

With the loss of Della Vega, emptiness covered the Crown in a deepening shroud of mystery. When his work with us was complete, did he travel into the cosmos or just disappear into the shadows? I wished I knew his whole story. Some people might say he was the embodiment of God. For me, this ancient holy man was simply a catalyst for positive change. He exposed us to a different way of looking at life, without the emotional, heavy burden of shame that held us back. His empathic sensibilities and unique sense of justice made him one of a kind. I truly believed I'd become a better person for knowing Father Diego Della Vega.

54

The localized earthquake opened a gaping split in the center of the extinct volcano. An acrid, sulfur-smelling steam belched from its breach. The tremor unleashed a series of events needed to awaken the beast. This was a real fire-and-brimstone event.

Red-hot diamonds spewed from the compromised crater, splashing into the liquid oxygen containment pond Dragaminov had filled from the larger cryogenic storage tank. The first few hot stones dissolved into nothing. To completely destroy a diamond, a superheated stone must be dunked into liquid oxygen. The concentrated oxidizer dissolves the precious carbon-based matter into an expensive memory.

The next volley didn't fare as well. This time the flaming gems landed in the hydrogen containment pond. Those superheated stones didn't harmlessly dissolve, but catastrophically ignited the vaporizing hydrogen. When the burning hydrogen mixed with oxygen, both containment ponds flashed. The heat from the first ignition breached both tanks. The ensuing explosion violently rocked the Crown. As the temperature rose, both main tanks split open. Because the deadly mixture was too rich to burn, the mixed cryogens smoldered. A great deal of liquid soaked into the ground. It was just a matter of time before the volatile mixture reached the proper flammable range to fully ignite.

E.D. jumped up and screamed, "We better get out of this coffin before the entire cone vaporizes! Let's get into the reed boats and paddle ourselves to safety!" We meticulously worked our way to the lagoon, while navigating a gauntlet of debris.

Nakai led the way, while Perry flew out the top of the Crown. The doctors had a particularly difficult go of it. The old academics slowly plodded along, with help from Junior and E.D. Dr. Ferdan had a hard time breathing in the thickening toxic smoke.

Junior built an impromptu stretcher from two fallen palm trees and ropes E.D. carried. He tied the lead onto Nakai's collar. The muscular canine bolted toward the lagoon as if he were the lead dog in Alaska's Iditarod dog sled race. The pads on his feet began to heat up, which made him run even harder. He reached the water before the rest of us, hurling himself into one of the boats, with Dr. Ferdan in tow.

The rest of us struggled to reach our destination, enduring rising temperatures and thickening smoke. Our shoes began to smoke, and it became more difficult to breathe. After what felt like an eternity, we finally saw our way out of this quickly degrading situation.

The lagoon's once pristine azure water turned into a foul-smelling, clouded brown toxic soup. With the grace of a drunken, stampeding elephant herd and little fanfare, we flopped into the boats. After we paddled to the opposite end of the lagoon, a strong wind blew clean air over our ragged flotilla. We rejoiced with deep breaths of pure, clear air, while retching gooey black gunk from our compromised airways. It felt wonderful to breathe clean air again. We humans take the simple automatic act of breathing for granted, until it stops. Forget about luxury items when you're minutes away from the urn.

I heard someone screaming from inside the pyramid. It sounded like Diamond. "I guess he got his wish. Immortality didn't work out for him."

E.D. chimed in, "It couldn't happen to a more despicable scoundrel. All his money and power won't get him out of this predicament. There is still justice in the world." We all laughed hysterically, wishing him the worst.

A swift current carried us through a pitch-black lava tube, naturally carved into solid rock. We were definitely not in the Magic Kingdom, and our escape route was no *Pirates of the Caribbean* boat ride. For all I knew, we could have been floating down the river Styx, into the jaws of Hades. Darkness can play tricks on an overactive mind. After all we'd gone through, anything could happen.

After about fifteen minutes of speedily racing down that raging torrent, our reed boats shot out of an opening between two rocks, about a mile away from the Crown. We tumbled ten feet into the gulf. Our woven lifeboats broke apart upon impact, and shattered reeds floated aimlessly in the calm waters of the waiting sea .

E.D. took it upon herself to build a life raft out of the debris. We sat comfortably while we waited for something else to happen. It always does.

Perry flew by our pathetic raft and perched himself on Nakai's back. The camera and GPS were still attached to his leg. E.D. spoke into the mike. "Hey, Chip. If you copy this message, we would appreciate a ride back to civilization, and bring margaritas."

55

The area surrounding the hydrogen plant was thick with a gaseous fog, begging for ignition. All it took was the sun shining through a discarded beer bottle. A pinpoint of focused light heated the fog just enough to unleash the wrath of the two mismatched elements.

A tiny puff of smoke rose into the fog, setting in motion what would turn out to be a major cataclysmic event. Within seconds, both tanks exploded, launching their skins high into the atmosphere. The brisance was seen fifty miles away. The hydrogen still above ground exploded with the power of a hydrogen bomb. In actuality this event was a hydrogen bomb, without the radiation.

The Crown of Knowledge took the full force of the blast wave, listing it to the west, reminiscent of the Leaning Tower of Pisa. The oxygen and hydrogen that soaked into the ground rumbled, tearing massive chasms into the rock.

This secondary explosion sheared off the shoreline ledge, plummeting it into deeper water. As the severed landmass displaced the water below, a tsunami rose from its depth. The rogue wave slammed the Crown with enough force to send the volcano crashing into the bottom of the bay, a thousand feet below the land.

Unfortunately for him, Diamond experienced an E-ticket ride into the abyss, where immortality just got interesting. The Crown's justice was swift, but fair. Diamond was left to his self-made horror, far away from human contact, insulated by a thousand feet of his own personal cruel sea. He was left alone to scream as loud as he dared, without disturbing anyone for eternity, except for perhaps a wandering whale.

We leisurely floated on calm waters, waiting for *The Missing Link* to pluck us from danger. E.D. worried that Chip didn't copy her plea for help. Just sitting in the hot Baja sun made us anxious to be rescued. We sat there numbly, trying to digest what happened on our excursion inside the Crown of Knowledge. No one spoke because of dry mouth. We were thirsty. Dehydration was beginning to cause a problem. If we weren't rescued soon, it would become a really big problem.

I turned around just in time to witness the catastrophe playing out on the shore. A blinding flash, followed by a mushroom cloud, almost welded my eyeballs to my skull. The blast wave pushed our tiny raft further toward the opposite shore. Drops of blood oozed from our compromised auditory systems. All I could say was "What!"

Next came the deafening sound of the landmass plunging into the gulf, spawning a tsunami. The massive wall of water took out the Crown in just a few seconds. We gasped at the reality that everything inside the magnificent structure was lost forever.

Without visible evidence, our journey would be dismissed as just another *National Enquirer* cover story. For the time being, the loss of the Crown could be a good thing. The world wasn't ready for the truth all at once. It would drastically change how we looked at religion and what may be out there, beyond planet Earth. People needed to be fed the information one piece at a time, or who knew what consequences would be in store for humankind? Five thousand years of faith-based history would need to be reevaluated, with objectivity in mind. I still couldn't wrap my mind around everything we had witnessed. How would the rest of the world believe us without tangible evidence?

A chilly wind blew in advance of the big wave. Our tiny raft changed direction and was sucked straight into its barrel. E.D. screamed, "Paddle as hard as you can into the wave!" There was no time for discussion, just action. We furiously paddled directly into the teeth of the monster. Looking at certain death, we rose straight up into the clutches of the curl and were flung into the air.

Miraculously, that liquid harbinger of death passed us by without even a scratch. We looked at E.D. in awe. "How did you know we would be saved from being crushed into greasy toothpicks?" I asked.

"I didn't know for sure. I saw a show on tsunamis that showed a fishing boat saved by climbing up a wave under full power. I took a wild guess, and it worked. Just don't ask me how."

"We hardly used the same amount of power as a diesel engine."

"Let's just chalk this one up to another mystery of the Crown of Knowledge. We could write a book on all the mysteries we witnessed within its walls."

"Maybe we should, but it would definitely be stacked in the fiction section." We tried to laugh, but were too tired to even smile. All we could do was to fall out and take a nap.

After a period of time, who knows how long, the sound of a diesel engine woke me from a deep sleep. I was dreaming about that fishing boat taking on the tsunami, but this was no dream. *The Missing Link* blew her horn, throwing us overboard. Chip stood on the bow with a pitcher of margaritas. "Is anyone thirsty?"

We unanimously shouted, "Boy, are you a sight for sore eyes".

We scurried up the gangplank, grateful to be alive and rescued. After a long sip, we were ready to join the living.

"Did you guys have a fruitful adventure?"

We just laughed, while finishing our second glass.

Nakai's ears stood straight up. He sniffed the air and dove into the water. Junior looked concerned. Why would his trusty pet jump back in the water the rest of us never wanted to go near again? "What's wrong, boy?"

The perceptive canine pushed a shiny object toward the gang-plank. He nudged the item onto the lower stair. "What do you have there, boy?" We all looked at each other and gasped. I couldn't believe my eyes. Our adventure ended just as it began. There it sat, the box, in all its kosmic glory.

The End

Epilogue

Gentle mountain breezes majestically blew over Rancho Mysterioso, soothing the spirits of our happy throng, seated around a long table, under the shade of a grape arbor. Jake welcomed everyone who shared this special occasion. "Thank you all for celebrating the marriage of my son and his beautiful bride."

Junior and E.D. beamed as they acknowledged his heartfelt greeting. Everyone hoisted a glass to toast the newlyweds. For obvious reasons, the two newlyweds were married for the second time in California. They thought it best not to mention that a five-hundred-year-old priest had already married them, in a silent ceremony inside an extinct volcano. We all knew which ceremony had more meaning.

Doctors Ferdan and Estaban sent their congratulations from Mexico. The two anthropologists were busy cataloging the momentous glut of artifacts discovered in the cave museum. Their work could take years to complete. They were also married again inside the cave.

Like the rest of us, the two prudently forgot to mention the existence of the Crown of Knowledge. With the Crown safely hidden under the Sea of Cortez, its secrets were safe for the time being. It was decided to search for substantive empirical evidence hidden in the museum, before springing these revelations on the rest of an unsuspecting world. They had to tread lightly if they were to take on organized religion.

Strutch was in the process of rebuilding the SHOE facility. Major automakers embraced the technology with open arms. Strutch was on the verge of providing the world with abundant, renewable, green energy. With the advent of this breakthrough process, the earth could help heal itself of unwanted carbon dioxide.

Jake used the seeds he found to create a new industry. He grew the hybrid marijuana-hop seeds, and opened a brewery that produced a libation with healing properties that all but eliminated certain diseases—with the bonus of providing the best buzz the world has ever known.

Everyone who was involved in our expedition into the Crown of Knowledge met with good fortune, except for Diamond of course. He was too busy screaming in pain to enjoy his eternity of terror.

Wedding gifts of various shapes and sizes were displayed on a table near the back door. Guadalupe weaved two identical, beautiful llama wool sweaters. The Crown of Knowledge adorned their back. I contributed the five-pound gold nugget that I found in the abandoned gold mine, with "E.D. AND JUNIOR, REMEMBER THE CONE" inscribed on the top. Like they would ever forget the cone. The expensive gift was my way of thanking E.D. for her resourcefulness escaping the jaws of that near fatal mine disaster.

Guadalupe served a feast fit for a king and queen. Foods from all over the world were placed in front of the ravenous guests. Everyone gorged on delicacies Guadalupe had created from viewing the Food Channel. I couldn't believe that she made sushi! She winked at me when my favorite food was placed in front of me. At that point life was definitely good.

Just as we were ready for dessert, Chip drove up laughing in his new Tesla that Strutch gave him. "Am I late? I met an old man hiking on the road up here. He gave me this wedding gift and asked me to deliver it to you. I asked him if he wanted a ride, but he said he would see us later. I got a strange feeling I'd seen him before, but I couldn't place him. The encounter was bizarre, but the old-timer had a strange feeling of calm about him, so I took the gift without question."

The red stones on E.D. and Junior's wedding rings began to sparkle, just as Guadalupe brought out the dessert. They opened the gift, and everyone gasped! It was another box, different from the original.

A shot of reality jolted throughout our bodies and minds. *Oh no, not again!*

A single spark shot from the box onto the dessert and lit the confection with an orange flame. Guadalupe almost dropped the flaming cherries jubilee.

Cherries Jubilee

1 pound black cherries
1 tablespoon sugar
1 tablespoon cornstarch
¼ cup warmed Grand Marnier
Cherry Garcia ice cream

1. Pit the cherries and reserve the juice.
2. Mix the sugar with the cornstarch and one cup of the cherry juice, a little at a time.
3. Cook for three minutes, stirring constantly.
4. Add the cherries and pour the Grand Marnier over the top.
5. Ignite the Grand Marnier and ladle the sauce over the cherries.
6. Serve over the Cherry Garcia ice cream.
7. Be careful not to burn the house down.

CPSIA information can be obtained
at www.ICGtesting.com
Printed in the USA
FFOW02n1131130618
47135828-49706FF

9 781478 750611